KING DANIEL

THE LOST AND FOUNDS: BOOK 6

EDMOND MANNING

Author: Edmond Manning
Editor: Theo Fenraven
Cover Artist: L.C. Chase
Typesetting/Formatting: Beaten Track Publishing
http://www.pickwickink.com
pickwickinkpublishing@gmail.com: General Inquiries

ISBN#: 978-0-9978608-6-3

KING DANIEL

THE LOST AND FOUNDS: BOOK 6

EDMOND MANNING

TRIGGER WARNINGS

If you're the kind of person who wants trigger warnings, read this page. If not, move along—serious spoilers ahead. I respect the need for trigger warnings. I've learned I have no stomach for graphic descriptions of kids being hurt or killed. Those things could happen in a book about a war, or a book about sick kids in a hospital, and I'd read both of those without trigger warnings. But in those situations, you know and accept what you're getting into. I have a friend who says, "Literature fucks you up," and I agree. But sometimes we choose how much.

This story deals with a man who was severely abused as a child. Daniel was permanently damaged by his abuser. His rage at what was done to him is central to the book. The abuser also shot and killed Daniel's childhood dog. Daniel occasionally reflects on the abuse, his childhood hiding spots, how he eventually freed himself from this nightmare existence, and the challenges he faces accepting his history. This book does not contain chapters or even long paragraphs of graphic descriptions about it. There are NO scenes in which Daniel repeatedly remembers more and more gory detail, but it is mentioned in sentences. It shaped him.

I did not enjoy writing about abuse. It made me sick. But Daniel's story deserves to be told. I think his kingship deserves to be witnessed. He's a powerful survivor. My goal was to honor Daniel, and through him, other survivors. If you were abused, and you're still considering reading this book, well, you're amazing. Survivors of child abuse amaze me. You did it. You're here. You deserve honor as much as Daniel. Those children who did not survive deserve honor and love as well. Let their names be spoken. If you want to give me feedback on how the abuse was handled in this book, email me. I will listen to you.

DEDICATION

To every reader who followed Vin's journey.
He was never alone as long as he had you.

The events of this novel take place in 2013.

ONE

I T SOUNDS LIKE an urban legend.

One of those ludicrous ghost stories related while we huddle around online campfires. We park our butts before glowing laptops and lean closer, a link sparking curiosity, tethering one person to another to another to another, until somehow we're reading a fifty-two-year-old Arkansas woman's blog, chronicling her vegetable garden and villainous mother-in-law. The sixteen-year-old girl in Seattle who reviews Netflix, the music hipster in Mississippi who began blogging after Hurricane Katrina. Twelve-step blogs, cake-decorating blogs, adoption blogs, application-to-graduate-school blogs, and then the weird shit blogs: awful first dates, terrible roommates, and disastrous family gatherings. Everyone has a story to tell, even if the tale isn't ours. "You won't believe last night! My neighbors screamed for hours and then the cops...."

These are our campfires.

As the night grows longer, the tales grow softer, deeper in their nature. We crowd each other, legs bumping awkwardly as strangers question how to live, what kind of destiny to shape for their unfolding lives. This is how we find each other, those of us who live in limbo, through blogs, electronic wings fluttering, vibrations that whisper, "Am I alone in this? Are you out there, too?" I have no doubt, when future technology permits a harmless fire blowing out a serial port, we'll roast marshmallows.

That helps put my last three days in perspective. It's just a campfire tale—a ghost story too. Chasing links, I found a blogger, his most recent post demanding, REMEMBER THE KING. Like every good campfire tale, his began, "I swear this is totally true. This really happened. Not to me, but to a friend of a friend." First time I read that, I snorted.

In a dozen paragraphs, the blogger summarized how one October weekend in San Francisco, an investment banker named Perry came to believe himself "a king." Because more than a decade had passed, the blogger felt he could at last reveal highlights, if none of the specifics, regarding his pal's King Weekend.

King Weekend was capitalized, like Space Camp or a trademarked Disney cruise. When I googled it, I discovered millions of hits, which means nobody had officially claimed it, branded it. More proof none of this was real. Everything is branded these days. An art gallery party brought Perry in contact with a vacationing tourist, who offered to change Perry's life. He challenged Perry to submit for one weekend. Do everything that was demanded. In return, the tourist would help Perry remember his *true kingship*, whatever the hell that meant. For reasons not explained, Perry agreed.

I admit it hooked me.

I'm not inclined to follow blogs about UFOs or Bigfoot sightings. I'm captivated by the insanity in how we treat each other, urban legends of human behavior. I follow one blog devoted to passive-aggressive handwritten notes, two evil coworker blogs, and eight or nine sites where gay men kiss and eagerly tell of their raunchiest, most disastrous adventures. I admit I like reading bizarre humiliations in others' lives; they make my own failings feel more manageable. But this one was the opposite of my preferred end of the spectrum. Perry got kinged.

The weekend included a sewer cleaner king with a magic flute, a stolen duck, and a smashed birthday cake. I didn't buy it. Sneaking around Alcatraz after hours? Abandoned on Mount Tamalpais? If you want people to believe your lies, you have to make them believable. Yet the blogger swore the erotic and verbal ravishment was all true, leaving Perry devastated by grief and somehow stronger, more alive. He claimed that after his King Weekend, Perry loved with "all his love."

The blog didn't elaborate on that phrase.

"Once there was a tribe of men, a tribe populated entirely of kings. Odd, you may think, and wonder how anything got done in such a society with everyone making rules. But these were not those kinds of kings." Perry didn't memorize the words, the blogger said. The story lives inside him.

Right.

Soon after his King Weekend, Perry vacationed in Australia, where he played his cello naked in the outback. A local rancher heard funereal music echoing off an outcropping of rocks and figured Death had come for him early, to end his lonely days. He emptied his pockets on the kitchen table, left a note for a brother in Sydney, and took his trombone into the desert to play one final duet. Instead of finding Death, the lonely rancher found a naked cellist and fell in love. Perry fell back. Perry and the sheep rancher have been together thirteen years, according to the blogger.

Bullshit. Called it then, and I'm calling it now. I can't even find confirming proof online. Yet here I am, rereading it for the seventh time. Eighth time? I need answers. I need to know if this is true. I wouldn't have even visited a second time if I hadn't been so surprised by one of the comments, posted a day after the original blog publication.

I also spent a weekend with Vin Vanbly. I remember who I was always meant to be. Have I found my brothers at last?—King Mai the Curious.

I read it over and over. Obviously, it was left by the blogger himself using a fake email address, something to lend credibility to this crazy tale. Nothing more than a good campfire story, and everyone loves letting the smoke get in their eyes—it just smells woodsy. And Vin Vanbly? Fake-sounding name, like a never-quite-made-it action hero. Fake, fake, fake.

When I returned less than twenty-four hours later, the comment from King Mai had been deleted. Every other comment remained, including one promising LIVE RUSSIAN GIRLS. It didn't make sense. More comments were added and none of them deleted. Is it possible King Mai's message was real? I don't know. I can't believe it was.

I toyed with the idea of leaving a smart-ass comment. I almost did, but my king name popped into mind. King Schadenfreude. I like misfortune. Not death or dismemberment, but disgraces and failures. It makes me feel better about myself. I want to think good things about people, I just don't. I decided not to comment.

If I am truly honest with myself, I didn't return to check for more comments or the King Mai mystery. My real question dawned slowly, while folding laundry and later while fixing the kitchen sink. I thought it was just an interesting detail. Many kings left their sparkling kingdom, living anonymously in the world of man. I could not remember if the story explained their fate. The nagging became a question, which became a wondering. I keep revisiting this campfire, looking for an answer in the smoke.

Even though I do not believe in this King Weekend crap, I find myself making a decision to breach the anonymous internet for confirmation. While trying to dissuade myself from this course of action, I simultaneously refine exact wording for my lie. Using one of my fake Yahoo accounts, I type an email directly to the blogger.

Hi,

This is going to sound peculiar. I think I know the Human Ghost. Vin Vanbly, right? He took me on a King Weekend, too.

King Michael

I know it's stupid to care, but this campfire piqued my curiosity. Plus it's not like I'm using my real name. Tempting to add "the Tugboat," or "the Peach Lover," like the silly names I read, but best to remain vague until I tease out more information.

I shouldn't waste my time on this. But why not? I've got nothing better to do, just internet surfing. Jacking off. I don't go out much, only to grab food from restaurants that don't deliver. No job. No obligations. I don't contribute much to the real world, and I might worry about that, but the real world doesn't seem to notice.

I don't know when it happened exactly, but I've abandoned the idea of finding a boyfriend or friends. I've got sixty-four Facebook friends I've never met. Late at night I blog and ask the questions, "Am I alone in this? Are you out there, too?"

Let's find out.

I click Send.

Less than two hours have passed when I am notified of a new message. The blogger. Why is my heart pounding? He explains Perry is delighted to meet one of Vin's kings. *Just to confirm, Perry asked me to ask you to describe how Found Kings sometimes honor each other.*

Well, crap.

There might be thousands of secret codes, words like, "vanilla pudding blow torch," or a handshake. A curtsy with "Your Majesty..." feels, well, too *Game of Thrones*. I don't know why I'm guessing at this. Who cares? They probably want money. This is probably a scam. I must remain wary. But in case this fucked-up fairy tale is not entirely fucked, I will use a simple bluff in hopes of prolonging our conversation. I want to ask my question about Lost Kings.

With respect. That's what Vin taught me. Treat each other with honor.

Will this work? Dunno. Who cares? It's just for fun.

I click Send.

They didn't reply yesterday. Did the bluff fail?

Two full days. They know I lied.

Three days have passed. Obviously, they aren't going to reply. That's spooky. "Once there was a tribe, populated entirely of kings...."

No.

There are no kings.

Sure, there are some good men around. I guess. But you can't appoint yourself a king and believe it, let that knowledge guide you to do things you would never do, live in a way you had only dared to dream but required some missing light, something golden shining through you. That's not possible.

But who is Vin Vanbly?

And what happens to a Lost King if he doesn't get found?

Does he just stay lost?

Two

I REGRET I DIDN'T try to trick the blogger into revealing Perry's last name. The blogger won't answer another email, not from that address. I may be blocked. I could try again from another account, but I doubt they will respond. I tried to deceive them, and they stopped me at the castle gates. This is crazy. I should let it go, forget it. Once again, electronic campfires have kept me awake much too late. Kings, however, are on my mind. I wonder if the Human Ghost still roams Alcatraz. No. Nobody spends twenty years secretly camping on Alcatraz. It would be reported in the papers or bragged about online.

Of course I search for Vincent Vanbly, which leads nowhere. He's a google zero hitter, an internet ghost. The only related hits are a few paid-for links to the Department of Motor Vehicles. Google only sees V-I-N as Vehicle Identification Number. I pay a few bucks for one of those former classmate searches, casting a wide net resulting in nothing.

He doesn't exist. I knew it.

Fake.

Over the next week, more comments are added, saying things like, "Cool fuckin' story." Someone typed, "I owned a duck oncce. LOL. they smelld bad!!!! P.U.!!!!!!!!" Nothing relevant. No more kings checking in. This is where my interest should die, but I can't let go.

According to the blog, Perry moved to Australia. I google a number of Australian cities, combining relevant words, like "Perry" and "ranch." I find nothing. Lots of ranching in Western Australia, and Perth is the biggest city out there, so I search for "Perry" combined with "Perth." Fifty thousand results. Well, fuck. Why are so many Perth men named Perry?

Click and read.

Click and read.

Click and read.

The first two dozen links reveal nothing. This is not a smart way to search the internet.

Click and read.

What's Perry's last fucking name?

I stare at the words, but nothing emerges. I need a clue. Something more to google. Wikipedia research on surrealist painters reveals nothing; there are ten million of them. No sons named Perry. The blog says Perry's father was never famous. The dropped birthday cake displayed Perry's full name as an anagram but the anagram isn't in the blog.

The cello!

I search again, combining three words: Perry, cello, Perth.

The seventh link sounds promising, describing Perry Mangin, a hobby-cellist. He's not orchestra level, just a local eccentric whose occasional performances are packed to capacity. Devotees queue up early to hear the sorrow in his hymns, his joyful inventions, the tension he creates in each throaty note. Smaller musical venues, I gather, but a welcome treat for citizens of Perth. His sister, Cecilia, often accompanies him on the piano.

One review, three years old, describes Perry and Cecilia giggling through a jazzy improv, using sibling rivalry to one-up each other. When their riff concluded, both fell over, laughing. The audience roared into a thundering ovation. This startled Perry's pet ducks, who often join him on stage. They chased each other, quacking and flapping. The reviewer deplored the lack of professionalism in modern musicians, reminding his readers these two were *Americans*. Another link leads to a Perth magazine that interviews local musicians. When questioned about his faithful following, this strange musician replied, "I play with all my love."

I found King Perry.

Now that I know who I'm looking for, it's easy to find more links.

He's a financial advisor, completely internet-based. He advises non-profit groups and favors those who fund cancer-related research. In 2008, he was named Philanthropist of the Year by one of these charity clients, and he must have earned them a bundle, because they flew him to Boston for an award ceremony. According to the jovial tone of their online newsletter, they promised if he would play the cello, they wouldn't require an acceptance speech. The newsletter struck a more somber tone when describing his composition, *The Lost Ones*, during which audience members wept openly.

What the fuck happens to Lost Kings?

On his niece's Instagram, I find Perry and his Aussie lover sitting on the same horse. The Aussie is much younger than I imagined. His unruly blond hair and surprised expression makes it look as if he awoke seconds ago, astonished to find himself upright in a saddle. He looks friendly. Surprised and friendly. Behind him sits Perry Mangin. Perry looks so... normal. He's definitely handsome, but he's not celebrity handsome. He's just some hot guy in his forties, wearing a cowboy hat. A guy with stupid love on his face, playing *Brokeback Mountain* but with a different ending.

I stare into the eyes of King Perry the Forgiver.

Instead of feeling better, I feel worse.

I don't want to be a Lost King.

It's not hard to find Perry's email address; he teaches advanced economics for a local university. According to their website, the waiting lists for his next two classes are full. I lied to Perry, burned that bridge. What could I possibly write to him?

I'm sad, sad because I lied, because that's who I am sometimes. I don't think of myself as a liar. It's just the internet. Fake emails. Anonymous comments. It doesn't bring out anyone's best. I sometimes argue for the sake of arguing, not even believing my own words. I just need to participate in the world, to not feel invisible. This isn't who I want to be. In this frame of mind, I compose an email.

King Perry,

Forgive me. I'm the guy who pretended to be "King Michael." I lied to your blogger friend because I didn't want to admit how much your story meant to me. I was afraid you wouldn't answer if I was just me. I lied because that's the way the internet works sometimes. You lie to get what you want. I don't know how to have faith in Bolinas. I'm truly sorry. I ask your forgiveness.

I found you searching for your first name combined with cello and Perth. Nothing too creepy. I am desperate to know if your story is true. Did you have sex in Alcatraz? Were you abandoned with a duckling? If you don't respond to this email, I promise I will never bother you again. I give you my absolute promise. I'm not a stalker.

I'm writing because what I really want to know is this: what happens to Lost Kings? Ironically, I must beg you, please don't lie to me. I'm thirty-six, and I'm too young to give up on the world, but I can't see much reason to stick around. I don't want to be a Lost King anymore. I'm tired. I want to come home.

Daniel (my real name)

I use my primary email account, the real me. I include my blog address. Before clicking Send, I hesitate. If I do this, he could read about me—my views on the world, favorite music, links, my whole online life. Nothing too revealing, though. I'm well protected from my former life. Still, sharing my blog with Perry is my best answer to the question "What would you risk?" It's not much, but it's all I have to offer.

Rereading my words, I'm embarrassed. If I click Send, I look like a begging idiot. I'm admitting I believe. It's as ridiculous as bear-walking in public, something I could never do.

Fuck that. I'll bear walk.
I click Send.

Three agonizing days later, his reply appears.

Daniel,

In this email I reveal a private part of my life. I ask you not to betray any part of my trust, not six months from now, not in ten years or twenty. This trust is how I show you that you are forgiven. But do not contact me again.

Vin kinged men who were early internet adopters, guys he met through AOL and CompuServe. But he also kinged men he met on his travels, men like me. By the time I connected with the others, they had already begun to refer to our tribe as The VV, a tribute to the man who found us, a man whose initials happen to look like a crown.

We know of men Vin kinged in Italy, Japan, Canada, and several in England. Vin's kings live in more than a dozen cities around the United States. We are not convinced we have found all our brothers. Vin never issued a roster, as he felt it was disrespectful. We honor his decision but want to make sure any man he kinged can find us if he chooses.

This is challenging, because The VV prefers to keep a low profile. Years ago, one among us, a king we call DC, suggested we occasionally dangle bait on the internet. Any of the men Vin kinged might recognize the mythology of The Lost and Founds, camping in odd places, breaking into public buildings. Using DC's approach, several men stepped forth. They had been discretely searching for us. DC knows what he's doing. This year, it was my turn to share. Next month my story will be purged from the blog. The VV desire low visibility.

We even heard from men who declined the invitation. A few begged us to put them in contact with Vin, but we will not. Since 2005, Vin no longer kings men. His website is down. The one gift we can give Vin in his current state is to protect him from the outside world. Make no attempt to find Vin Vanbly. We will stop you.

Daniel, you asked me what happens to Lost Kings. I do not know. But there is a king who can answer your question.

Find him.

Perry

THREE

A S A KID, I thought I could escape my life, becoming an astronaut or a cowboy, or *both*—work on a horse ranch between adventures to Mars. I never imagined I'd be wealthy and unemployed. I'm sure it sounds great to people, the American dream achieved. I hate it. No one told me money is isolating, that my challenges in making friends would be compounded by wealth, and I would often mistrust anyone who even *talked* about money, afraid they would somehow uncover my secret. And how can you not talk about money with a friend?

I live in a comfortable two-bedroom apartment in an older brick building. Second floor. I love the built-in hutch. I could have paid cash for a big house, but I thought I might make more friends in an apartment. A lifetime spent watching NBC sitcoms influenced me, I guess. It hasn't worked out that way. Maybe I live in the wrong time slot.

I remember when I first moved in, whenever I'd hear keys jingling in the hall, I'd leave, offering my neighbor a cheery hello. I thought maybe we might strike up a conversation, which might lead to some laughs and the mutual suggestion we should order a pizza sometime. I didn't care if they were gay or straight, single or married. But hallway conversations never happened. I don't have good social skills. After each nonencounter, I would go downstairs to the lobby and check my mailbox, which I knew was empty. But hey, that took a good twenty minutes.

I don't know what to do with my life.

There are only so many books you can read, so many movies you can watch. I tried online gaming, and I stuck with World of Warcraft for a few months, but online friendships made me hunger for real ones. I constantly debate getting a job, if only to meet people through work. But with my political science degree, I'm not sure what I'm qualified to do. I hate the idea of dragging myself to work every day.

I'm not a religious guy. I don't want to shave my head and join a cult. I want to do something that matters, so my life on the planet is not this big waste. I want something I can't quite taste. What do I do to meet my real life, the one where I vacation in Mexico, snorkeling with my boyfriend, my true love, and when we come home, we're still in love? I fantasize our voicemail is maxed out with fun messages.

Pathetic.

I guess this pity party is my way of admitting I am a Lost King. At thirty-six, I'm still obsessed with kid fantasies. I'll never be an astronaut or cowboy. Now I want to be a king?

I'm an idiot.

For hours, I've stared at Perry Mangin's photos. He's more handsome than I originally gave him credit for—ocean-blue eyes, perfect smile. Digging through archives, I found a photo of him shirtless. I'm tired of A-gays and their perfect fucking lives. These urban legends never happen to ordinary people, their noses too big or their beauty not revealed through a good eyebrow tweezing. Men who shop at stores like JCPenney or Walmart. Perry was a stud before he met Vin, and after a weekend of frolicking in San Francisco, he became a stud king.

Perry's email gave me hope, but hope is fleeting. I thought clues in his email would help me find another king. Google shows 63,000,000 links for the "VV" or "The VV." Wikipedia has thirty-nine possible definitions for this abbreviation, including Volvo, varicose veins, and a WWE wrestler named Val Venis. Googling "VV kings" reduces search results to only 1,000,000. The first link is to a Myspace page, where the opening quote is "the blood of kings and queens run through my veins." The background for his page is an enormous marijuana leaf. Obviously he's not Vin Vanbly.

Is he?

Fuck. I don't know.

Perry warned me not to contact him again. I'm supposed to find the next king on my own. Why give me "The VV" as a clue if there are no leads? How the hell?

Wait.

I know another king. King Mai the Curious. He left the deleted comment. I google him, and after about fifty useless links, I strike a solid lead. A woman who bought an art history book on eBay came in contact with "King Mai." She blogged about it six years ago.

Get this, not only was the book I purchased in flawless condition, but he sent an equally expensive companion book! This second book is worth $200! He just included it! For free! I emailed and asked him if it was a mistake, and he said, 'No, it's a gift from King Mai the Curious.' How fantastic is that?!

If I ignore her over-punctuation, I'm excited. It's him. I email her, compliment her blog, and explain I wish to contact King Mai. Would she be willing to either share his contact information or tell him someone seeks audience? I have learned my lesson about lying to people online, people whom I may want to meet.

Right above my name, I type, *Please. This is very important to me.*

I click Send.

If she never responds, I will have to accept it. I already know I'm not going to get anywhere through trickery. I tried that. The Found Kings don't work like that. Why do I care how "Found Kings work?" I'm a fucking idiot. I shouldn't stare at my inbox. She won't respond this quickly anyway.

Nevertheless, I click Send/Receive.
Send/Receive.
Send/Receive.
Quit it. She's not going to reply—
Send/Receive.

That's it. I'm sending a second email. Four days is enough time for her to reply. How do I phrase this one? Pleading?

No. Be patient.

Ooopsie, sorry for the delay! I was on vacation!

During their brief correspondence, King Mai directed her to several art history websites he thought may be of interest. They shared interests in organic gardening and the poet Rumi. She explained she never received a reason for his generosity; he deflected her questions. She looked through her email address book and found he had been expunged; their meager exchange was several operating systems ago and she is a ruthless housekeeper. However, she recalled his package arrived from a Chicago suburb.

Sorry and good luck!!

After reading her last sentence, I compose a gracious thank you, because it seems that's what a king would do, and I am trying to, well, become one. There's no point in lying to myself anymore.

Gardening. Chicago. Rumi.

Where are you, King Mai?

Oh.

Perhaps I've been approaching this wrong. Instead of looking for existing links, I could put something out there. That might work. It suddenly strikes me how ridiculous this is, searching for one specific guy without knowing his real name. Or where he lives. Or what he does. All I know is he's a fairy tale king.

This might seem odder if I hadn't already slain a dragon in the World of Warcraft with a twelve-year-old warrior girl, a frost mage from Dubai, and a shy goblin, possibly from Wales. We live in strange times. So I will hunt down a curious man whose full name I do not know. Maybe I will have to slay an internet dragon along the way. Where do I find a king? I need that bar where Luke Skywalker and Obi-Wan meet Han Solo. An anything goes kind of place. A website?

Yes. Duh.

There is a place where anything can be bought and sold, traded and rented, where everything is lost and found, most of all relationships. Dates, fuck buddies, escorts. It's all on Craigslist. Online scams abound, and a few years ago, a Craigslist killer. Minus the alien band, it's pretty much the Star Wars bar.

There's no guarantee King Mai will see a Craigslist ad. Why would he? But if the letters *VV* are truly a code, maybe someone sees it who knows someone, who knows someone. It's a long shot, but an ad might work as a beacon. In fact, the few times I tried to meet a guy through Craigslist, I received replies from Oregon, Florida, and everywhere, because people do nationwide searches. I'm a huge turn-on to some fetishists, which immediately turns me off to them. I had hoped to find a man into *me*, not my legs. While I have never experienced success on Craigslist, I understand its reach.

Now. What do I write?

Message for The VV

King Mai, I request an audience. Most curiously, an LK.

This works.

This is probably the twelfth variation, but I like this one. Short. Coded. Gotta factor in the Craigslist haters. If they don't like my post, they'll flag it. Don't give them much to react to. This will work. I could try—no. I'm overthinking my overthinking. Do it. Pull the trigger and click the Post button.

I click Post.

Done.

I feel nervous excitement, like a kid who broadcasts by shortwave radio for the first time, whispering, "Anybody listening?" Does anybody still do that shortwave radio thing? I already know I will spend the next three hours staring at my inbox, with my old friend, the Send/Receive button. Waiting. Sending and receiving.

I may be an idiot, but at least I feel excitement. Feeling something positive is good. I will post twice a day, morning and evening during peak visibility hours. Stay under the flaggers' radar. Four alternate email addresses. Be smart, Daniel. Subtle.

Where are you King Mai?
Are you listening?

Three days into it, and my strategy seems successful in not drawing out haters. That's good. But where's King Mai? I received only junk—a few encouraging possibilities but mostly crap. With each new email, my heart skips before the inevitable disappointment. I received one promising, *It's me, King Mai.* That one thrilled me until I realized it was someone just like me, fucking with an internet stranger to see what kind of response they get. I guess I deserved that. I've now gotten a half-dozen pretending to be King Mai. I typed a reply to the most convincing, wordsmithing carefully until I noticed the email address was <u>cumdumpster12@gmail.com.</u>

Thanks, asshole, for raising my hopes.

The ad gets flagged. I hold my breath. Six days, no flagging. This is only the first. As King Schadenfreude, I know how this works. Once Craigslist regulars decide to hate your ad, it's flagged every time it appears.

Evening post stayed. I think my best strategy is to quit posting for two full days, so my ad doesn't seem quite so methodical. Flaggers hate regular posters. Can I wait two days?

Patience is not one of my virtues.

Two days is a long time.

Uh-oh.

One response screams *WHAT THE FUCK IS YOUR PROBLEM?* The body of the email isn't much kinder. *Quit posting your goddamn stupid post!* The headline on the next reply reads *Dear Dickhead.* This is not good. I waited three full days but this ad didn't last fifteen minutes before being flagged to death. The ad lasted two full weeks. I guess the kings never saw it. It was a longshot anyway. I'll have to think of another way.

I skipped last night's ad, hoping to throw them off my track, but they circle like vultures this morning, dive-bombing until my ad is yanked in less than five minutes. Two more junk replies, one from someone asking, *Who do you think is going to respond?*

I hate those the most. I hate the earnest questions.

I haven't come up with another idea that's better. I guess I keep doing this?

Damn. I thought posting under a different category would mislead them, but nope. The ad I posted ten minutes ago is already gone.

Okay, new plan. I think it's time to give up on Craigslist. I've now got a Plan B. As if a confirmation, another angry email appears in my inbox.

DEAR ASSHOLE

I flagged your pathetic ass four years ago in Seattle, and I flag you again, motherfucker. I will be around to block your VV idiocy the next time, too. Stupid, fake posts!

I stare at the words, reading and rereading again.

I didn't post four years ago. A shiver races through me and I shake it off. This—I am not the only seeker. Was it another Found King, like Mai, wondering how to find his brothers? Or someone who'd caught a whiff of this urban legend, like me?

I feel as though I have glanced down at the soft earth between my legs and discovered footprints. I walk where others have tread. Who else is looking? How many people know? Words from the blogger's post float through my brain. *Odd, you may think, but these weren't those kinds of kings....*

No. I'm inventing conspiracies. This is too fucking weird. But my Craigslist campaign lasted three weeks. If these *VV* guys are out there, they must know I'm looking. Wouldn't Perry have told them? Why didn't King Mai the Curious reply?

Wait.

Wait a minute. What if he did?

No.

They were all fakes. None were real. Unless perhaps, *perhaps*, one of them was the real deal, and I didn't catch it. What if one of the emails I'd deemed wacko actually came from King Mai? My heart beats faster, and I already know he sent me a clue. I didn't see it because I expected a reply from kingmai@obviously.com. He sent something. *Something is here.*

I must collect all the worthless replies, retrieving them from the Deleted folder. Right now. Every time I drag one, I feel anxious, as if I'm moving expensive glassware. I may want to compare the send dates and times if I find no clues in the text. This feels crazy. I'm being crazy. I don't care. I have nothing to do anyway.

I'll print them all. Microwave that leftover pizza, and then print every one.

I sit at my dining room table, creating categories, seeking patterns. I examine email addresses and search for puzzles hidden in the body of text. How many have similar messages? Exact same words? It's beyond strange, this thing I'm doing, comparing phony Craigslist responses. I hate rereading the ones asking, *Why are you doing this?* Many replies employ the word *curious*, but I can't see a connection. The best fake response was written by cumdumpster12. Am I being too judgmental? No, he doesn't feel right. I even look twice at the woman who wanted me to breastfeed. If there's a clue there, I can't decipher it.

Hang on.

I recognize this email address—I saw it in another stack a moment ago. Right there. Got it. The first email reads, *Why are you doing this? I won't judge you....* Same crap as the others. My hands shake as I rifle through the miscellaneous stack. Same email address. The second one reads, *Hey, bubba, tell me five things about you nobody knows.* I remember this. When this second email arrived, I barely scanned it because of the first one. Is this second email demonstrating curiosity? Were they throwing me off track?

Sent from Jimbo5amgday@hotmail.com.

Holy shit.

It contains the letters *gday* or g'day, if you are from Australia, where Perry lives. Yeah, this is a goddamn clue. Why not? I create new email addresses for one-time use. The *5am* is significant, too. The blog post said Found Kings greet the dawn. It's a thing. They wear colorful king shirts, something beautiful that helps them remember, and they raise their heads to the sun. I don't know what this accomplishes, but I guess it's special for them.

Since reading the blog about Perry, twice I rose early to watch the sunrise. I thought it might inspire me. Once I watched from my building's roof. Sunrise was pretty. Yellow. Orange. Chilly for April. Did I feel like a king? No. I tried to think uplifting thoughts about life and believe good things about other people, but mostly I worried. If that roof door swung closed, nobody would have any clue I was trapped up there. I couldn't scurry down a fire escape without getting myself killed.

A week later, I took an Uber to a city park, a more beautiful environment, to try again. I sat on a bench until the sun rose. Reds, oranges. Blue sky, eventually. I felt serene enough to contemplate how this happens daily, but kingly? No. On the return trip, my Uber driver took one look at me and exclaimed, "Jesus, what happened?" Serenity lost. The adventure made me sad, another reminder I am a truly a Lost King.

The references to *g'day* and *5am* are not accidental. The "Jimbo" remains a mystery, probably there to bury the lead: *I talked to Perry. He vouched for you. If you're the kind of guy who notices details, say hello.*

Am I crazy to think this? Why the first email asking *why are you doing this*? To sow doubt? To rankle me? I almost missed the real communication because he was fucking with me! Was he fucking with me?

Hmm. He wants to know five things about me.

Crap.

I already shared my blog with the Forgiver King. I have no doubt Perry forwarded it, which means Mai wants five things nobody knows, and I can't use anything I blogged. How much do I share? On my blog, I control everything. Nothing specific about my upbringing. I don't even blog about public access or disability issues. Nothing either parent could use to find me. I've worked hard to vanish my existence.

Oh, hey. That's one of my five details—I don't like to talk about myself. What else? What is Mai looking for? As I consider details nobody knows, it's hard to avoid the elephant lurching around on canes. King Perry's story flashes into mind— surrender. Perhaps to get found, I must reveal my true self. Now that the word *surrender* dances through my brain, five details emerge immediately. Individually, they don't reveal much, so that's good.

1. I don't like to talk about myself.
2. I am wealthy, result of a large lawsuit settlement. Few people know this. I live simply.
3. I would love to sing and dance in a musical, but I never will.

4. Both my parents are alive, but I haven't spoken to them since I was a teenager.

5. I invented an amazing recipe—gnocchi pasta with bacon and caramelized onions—a special dish I make for myself regularly but never for anyone else. The first person I will cook this recipe for is my husband, if I ever find one.

Number five makes me nervous, as it betrays a biggish secret. I am afraid a lifelong relationship will never happen for me. In fact I'm sure of it. I've only been in love once, and I think I romanticized Eric more than loved him. I shouldn't share—no. Don't chicken out.

I click Send.

Then it hits me.

Anger.

Those *fuckers*.

I can't believe I allowed myself to play mind games with these shadowy internet guys. I've spent years deliberately not sharing any personal information. What possessed me to be so reckless? I confessed to a stranger I'm saving a pasta dish for an imaginary future lover. What kind of pathetic loser does that?

Only two hours have passed, and here's his reply.

Pretty good, bubba. But what's the big one, the one you don't want to reveal? Don't fuck around, Mary, not this close to the finish line. Name it.

No signature.

Mary?

I opened my fucking heart, and this asshole replies without a polite word and has the nerve to fucking demand "the big one?"

Fuck. That.

I'm done.

Fuck this. Fuck them.

As I stagger around the apartment, banging pots, cleaning up from last night's roast, my angst and anger leapfrog each other. The big one. Please. Remembering his tone—calling me *bubba*—pisses me off, and I let the weightlifting bar clatter hard onto its supports. Fuck you, *Mary*. What an asshole. The apartment feels small, just me and that goddamn email, so I'll head out. Go downtown. I hate walking Columbus's crowded sidewalks, but I can't stay here.

Go be part of humanity.

Maybe being angry with sidewalk strangers will distract me.

Reading my book in the Barnes & Noble's cafe, I feel conspicuous. I'm so used to doing everything online or in my apartment. Are people staring? It's my imagination. I recall why I spend so much time alone. I don't like people. I don't like being in public.

I could take an extended vacation to get away, exclusive and people-free, but where? Aruba? I guess it's where rich people go. I can't get around on sand. Travel means airplanes, airports, and unfamiliar terrain, all of which I desperately try to avoid. I don't know where to go. I don't know what to do with myself. I could buy something online to make me feel, well, anything. Buy what? The longer I stare at my open book, the more I keep seeing nothing in front of me.

Nothing.

I'm tired of a futureless future. I'm tired of being alone. I'm also tired of holding back and not talking about this shit. I mean, yeah, I talk to Margaret. I care for her, but you can't count your therapist as your friend. I have zero friends. No wonder I'm a Lost King.

On Perry's King Weekend, the Human Ghost told him the lack of forgiveness is what kept the Lost Kings lost. Perry forgave me. Maybe I need to forgive Mai for the tone of his email and demanding *the big one*. Maybe I need more curiosity.

I'm going home.

When I get to my computer, my reply is snarky. Vulnerability or submission, whatever this is, does not come easily.

Okay, King Mai, here's the big one. *Growing up, my father beat the crap out of me so regularly, so viciously, he considered it a second job. He was a surgeon, so he was skilled in hiding the damage. Burn marks, cuts. Broken bones were for special occasions. He had a fascination with Norman Rockwell and that mythical all-American family. His pride and joy was a 1970's family station wagon with original wood paneling. When I was sixteen, he used it to run over my legs. Twice. Surgeries could only fix so much. For the past eighteen years, I have strapped canes to my arms to drag myself around. In the street, people pity me and look away, sorry for my pathetic stumbling. Children point at me. Their parents scold them not to stare. Is that good enough for the big one? Did I pass?*

I sneer as I click Send.

I storm around my living room, imagining furious conversation. Is your curiosity satisfied, mighty asshole king? You think you won something because I caved? Well, congratulations. You should know I am strong. I don't take pity well. Remarkably unwell, in fact. If any condescending tone, any—*I'm so sorry*—bullshit appears in your reply, I will quit this lame-ass quest for an answer, and this time, I'm not kidding.

VV *assholes*!

You fucking assholes.

I bet Mai is plucked and pretty, a party boy having great sex with all the buffed elite of Gaydom. Laughing, fucking, champagne brunches, and big city circuit parties. I bet Mai never gets depressed, thinking about how he can never be an astronaut or cowboy, or equally impossible for me, walk into a gay bar and men don't avert their eyes.

I buzz around my place, enraged over the lack of reply. When it comes, if it comes, if there's one fucking drop of pity, I will... I don't know. Fuck those assholes.

When the reply finally appears, I find there is literally nothing for me to analyze or criticize. Just a phone number, area code 815, which I discover online is rural Illinois, not a Chicago suburb.

I dial the number.

"Hello, Mr. Lost King," says a light voice. "This is a temporary cell phone number and voicemail, which I will discard after our phone appointment. I suggest we talk on Thursday at 2:00 p.m. Clear three hours on your calendar. If this day and time don't work, leave a message and suggest another. I'll update voicemail with a confirmation. Call at the appointed time. Oh, and have a great day."

I feel nervous leaving a message. Why do I feel nervous?

"Thursday at 2:00 is fine." *Don't let him hear your voice shake.* "Talk to you then."

I hang up.

I'm nervous. That's stupid. He can't do anything to me.

Am I sure about that?

But seriously, why the high drama? That's the first thing I'm going to ask.

"Oh, yeah. Sorry," Mai says, "I know it's unusual, the secrecy. You meet guys over the internet much? Some real whack jobs out there."

"I guess."

As Mai chats about challenges in online dating, it's... normal. He's a guy on the phone. His voice isn't sinister and foreboding. It's like when you call your Visa card company and get that friendly representative who isn't monotone, and you think, *Hey, a real person.*

"By the way, I'm Mai Kearns. What's your name?"

"I'm surprised you don't already know." I'm sure I sound sharper than I intended. He didn't explain the secrecy. He sidestepped it. They owe me answers.

Mai says, "Of course I know your name, bubba. I just wanted to hear how you'd introduce yourself."

"I see."

Fucking mind games.

"We know who you are, Daniel. I'm new to The VV, so they explained how this works. Every couple of years, someone stumbles upon The Lost and Founds mythology and start investigating to discover if the story is real. The kings call it 'questing.' Isn't that funny?"

"Is it real?"

"Which brings us to our next topic. You have to choose. I asked you to tell me five things—"

"Six, actually."

What's wrong with me? This is exactly what I wanted—to find the next king. I'm should feel gratitude, but I don't. I'm pissed. I'm always feeling the wrong thing.

Mai says, "You're right. Six. Now it's your turn. Ask me six questions about my life, The VV, anything. Ask why The VV make themselves difficult to find. Ask how many men Vin kinged. Or ask how many kings live near Columbus, Ohio."

I'm glad he can't see my shock. I've taken pains to hide. The lawsuit money protects me from being found by reporters or anyone I may have known from that life, and most importantly, him. My apartment is leased under the name of an imaginary roommate. But Mai knows where I live. How?

"Ask what happened to Vin in 2005. Ask me the same thing you did Perry, 'What happens to Lost Kings?' Honestly, the answer won't mean much without hearing the story of my King Weekend. It would be like in *The Hitchhiker's Guide to the Galaxy*, where the ultimate answer of life is forty-two. If you don't ask the right questions, you won't get satisfying answers. Your call, Daniel. Six life and VV questions to quench your immediate curiosity, or all six questions get rolled into one, and I tell the story of my King Weekend, which will further your quest. But when I finish, no more questions. Not one. Understood?"

"Why make me choose?"

"I take it you're going with Option A and using one of your six questions?"

"No. Gimme a second."

To learn anything useful, I need to hear King Mai's story. I'm not disappointed, not exactly. This was what I wanted. But there was a price, and I had hoped to coast along for free. Fine. He got me.

"Please." I try to hide my resentment. "Tell me about your weekend with Vin."

"You got it. Do you remember the beginning of the farm crisis, early 1990s? Maybe you were too young. Many of us farmers were lost."

FOUR

I CAN'T BELIEVE HIS story. I can't.

The King of Curiosity spun his tale for hours, describing every thought and feeling, how the fury inside him was transformed. That part terrified me. Anger is my most regular visitor. I couldn't let go of it. I need it. It defines me.

I don't understand what happened to him. I mean, sure, I understood, yet a thrill streaks through me, a stubborn warning, "Does Not Compute." Vin Vanbly orchestrated all these events and bought Mai a farm? Manipulated former high school classmates into revealing sad stories, and now they're Mai's family? That's not possible.

Mai says, "Before we parted, Vin offered me three options, stories about his life before he was twenty-one. I had to choose one. It's not my place to repeat his story to you. I can say this. After a full weekend discussing curiosity, he revealed my kingship in an entirely new perspective. I bawled my fucking eyes out."

He is quiet.

My heart pounds.

Finally, he speaks. "Somehow, after Vin's terrible childhood tale, we fucked around one more time. Sure, it was a little twisted, but that's Vin. We were so in love all weekend, and this story made me love him more." After a pause, he chuckles, a short guffaw that could work itself into a real laugh but doesn't. "Vin had a great cock. I coulda sucked that beauty for hours. Well, assuming scarecrows weren't attacking me. While we whipped out our dicks, Vin told me one last story about King Jimbo and A Curious Army."

He won't tell me Vin's childhood story, but he's got no problem describing the graphic sex. I blush to remember—I got hard a few times during this afternoon's tale. Did he describe those details to titillate me? No, that's crazy. Maybe. I don't know. I feel lightheaded; our entire conversation makes me dizzy, and my mouth is dry. I try to focus on his voice. Mai's cadence is easy, relaxed. He betrays no reluctance or distance, spilling his tale as if we were best buds. He cried twice, once when describing his heart when he witnessed the Butterfly Tree. I teared up, too, because of the sheer rawness he managed to communicate—his overwhelm at generous love. I understood, or rather, I *would* understand the surprise of being loved, if someone actually loved me. I hate how self-pitying that sounds, but fuck it. Nobody even knows I'm alive.

Mai says, "I kissed him goodbye. A minute later, I come bouncing out of the cornfield, totally scaring the shit out of Randy and Jen, and also my mom. They all jump back, which made me laugh, because they had been screaming at me to *get out here* and when I jumped out, they were surprised. My mom had a knife, and I was like, 'What the hell are you doing?' She said she was slicing bread when Randy and Jen arrived, but one glance at Randy, and I knew she was lying. I started laughing. I mean, laughing hard. My mom was going to attack Vin with a bread knife. Total craziness, man."

I smile.

Mai laughs more before he can speak.

He says, "In her defense, Saturday morning, twenty-five high schoolers showed at dawn, announcing they needed to assemble a Butterfly Tree in her yard, during which time she discovers the internet stranger on a weekend date with her son is a world-class liar. She keeps it cool, expecting to meet Vin and talk about these lies. Instead, he and I run corn. Then we escape in his pickup truck. Later the same day, Mrs. Fee phones, alerting mom that "her son and his life coach" ran through her cornfield. Mom's up all night Saturday waiting for news, but nothing. Then Randy and Jen appear Sunday noon, freaking her out with vague references to 'things that happened last night.' She knew I wasn't dead. She had seen me a few minutes earlier walking around the farm with Vin, but Randy wouldn't say any more than *Vin was dangerous*. She had just watched me disappear into a cornfield with him. Poor Mom. For the next few years, whenever anything mildly exciting happened on the farm, I'd yell, 'Grab the bread knife.' She'd get mad, but I'd laugh my ass off."

His laugh is contagious. I can't help myself.

Mai says, "I kept my promise. For thirteen years, I never researched The VV or sought men Vin kinged. I had to quit AOL so I wouldn't be tempted. Only a year ago, I began searching for the others."

Hang on—thirteen years after 1996 would be 2010. Three years ago. Why did he wait until 2012?

"Funny thing, I didn't know they'd be so goddamn hard to find. Back in 1995 and 1996, there was an AOL chat room dedicated to the King Weekends. Guys would log in, typing, 'You wouldn't believe what I went through.' When I could find no internet trace, I realized they must have chosen to deliberately go underground. Instinctively, I got more cautious, too. Right then, I figured it could take a while.

"You and I found the same blog, but I didn't find it by accident. With a buddy good at programming, I had designed customized search algorithms for uncovering references to The Lost and Founds. Despite seeing Perry's king name and reading about weird camping, I was still skeptical. Once I saw the words 'the Human Ghost,' my heart finally accepted I had found them. I immediately thought of the story Vin told me before we parted."

Mai stops speaking and I hold my breath.

He says, "I think his whole life, Vin Vanbly has been a human ghost. Hell, half the weekend we spent together, I never saw him, just heard his voice. To this day, I run the corn in late August, hoping to hear the Human Ghost dancing in the row next to mine whispering stories in the rustling ears. I know that's twisted, but I find the idea comforting."

I am speechless.

There is a long silence. Long.

Mai says, "Uh... the end."

I can't speak.

"You still there?"

"Yes." My voice is gravel.

What story did Vin tell Mai? The VV secrecy—what are they doing? What about the Sunday party Vin promised—did Mai invite the bubbas? Of course he did, if any of this story is true. But how could a garage mechanic pay off a farm mortgage and get people in town to agree to this crazy fucking shit? What did Mai tell his parents? How did they react? Did Mai Kearns ever fall in love again? Who was in those AOL chat rooms? *What happens to Lost Kings?*

I can't ask any questions!

Mai fucked me good. If I ask anything, say something snarky, argue or try to trick him into revealing more, he will tell the other Found Kings not to assist my quest, because I don't play by the rules. A dozen or more questions rush through my mind. Is Randy still married to his wife? I can't ask, not anything. I can't breathe. This curiosity will kill me.

In his unique, lilting tone, Mai Kearns asks, "Anything you'd like to say?"

More race through my mind, each one pushing and shoving to get to the front. *I can't ask anything.* I just got punched in the jaw with bubba love.

"Yo, Daniel. Say something."

Thank him.

"Thank you." The strength in my words surprises me. I will accept my unanswered questions. I will stay curious. "Thank you, King Mai, for the gift of curiosity."

He laughs.

I laugh, too. Kind of cool, as I consider this. Deeply unsatisfying, true, but I will grow my curiosity in the world. I can do this. I will get curious. But damn, how can I not ask any questions?

Mai says, "You did good. I wasn't confident you'd resist."

My eyes well with tears. I stay silent, pondering him, pondering me, our strange phone conversation. I don't know what to think of any of this. I can't think. My skin is tingling. My brain is tingling.

"As a reward," he says, "you get one question. Call this a king's blessing before parting. Think carefully. Choose wisely."

I wipe my eyes. Focus up! One question!

Do I ask *what happens to Lost Kings*? Is that what I truly want to know? Do I ask him how to find Vin? He won't answer that. Or is boldness and risk-taking rewarded? Perry said The VV protects Vin "in his current condition," so maybe they won't answer anything directly. What current condition? Is he in a coma? I can't think. I don't know what to ask.

Mai says, "Hey, man, take your time. Hurry up, though, because I promised to make pancakes for dinner, and Mom likes to eat by six. I gotta hustle."

Three dozen relevant questions flit through my brain, but one already feels right. "Who is—wait! Don't answer. I'm going to rephrase." Carefully, like wielding a knife, I carve out the intentional words. "What is the next step on my quest?"

He chuckles. "Good question, bubba. I thought you might ask me for Vin's home phone number, which you gotta know, I was ready to answer truthfully without giving the real digits."

I passed the test. I knew they were testing me. But holy shit, *they're testing me*.

He says, "As far as next steps, you won't meet any more kings over the internet."

I don't know why this stuns me, but it does. All afternoon I experienced shock after shock. What's one more?

"Daniel, mind if I mix flour and eggs and stuff while we finish? I have a few dishes to prepare. Mom's on a schedule."

"Yeah, sure."

This king makes pancakes for his mom. He's not one of the A-gays, like Perry. He's still a small-town farmer. I hear whisking. Maybe his life didn't change. Maybe I made a bigger deal of this king thing than it warrants. Perry was probably the exception. But all afternoon it sure seemed life-changing for Mai. I heard it in his voice.

Mai says, "No more internet or Craigslist. We're the ones who flagged you. We'll stop your future postings, too, any city. Starting now, we flag your first post."

"Oh." I suck in a deep breath. "Who will?"

"The VV. We will shut you down, bubba."

Fuck this. Anger gives me words. "Back to cloak and dagger?"

"Yup. But nothing creepy or illegal. No one's going to break into your home or chase you into a car wreck. Found Kings don't work like that."

I'm fucking pissed. "*Thanks*, I guess. How does this work, exactly?"

"Ah, any number of men in The VV could provide you a very satisfying answer. After all, Vin started when he was twenty-two. That's a whole lot of king energy."

How many?

He chuckles. "If you're still curious, we'll open doors. Pay attention. Look for signs. Put some skin in the game. Thanks to your email, we know you're wealthy, so nobody's going to FedEx you plane tickets. Do your homework and pack your bags."

Travel? I can't travel.

"Oh my god," Mai says with excitement. "I used a sports metaphor! That skin in the game thing? How butch am I, Mary?" He laughs.

I know it's a question, but I have to say something. "Just to confirm. The VV won't drain my bank accounts, right?"

"Right. If you're not interested anymore, drop it. Have a good life." Mai's voice moves away from the phone receiver. "Hey. Would you grab that? Thanks."

Who's there? A lover? Is his mom in the kitchen? Everything feels important right now, remembering details. I take deep breaths and examine my right hand. Still feels tingly.

"Hang on, Daniel. Gotta mix something quick."

A whirring comes to life, something mechanical. Blender?

So many delicate questions tease me. He touches every phrase or word so lightly, makes it… I don't know. I can't define this tantalizing sensation crawling over my skin. All afternoon, these wonders, soft revelations, strange little prizes unwrapped but still obscured. What does it mean, what does it all mean? The hallucinations he described when the corn flew by—everything felt intentional. I think he's been pouring king energy into me for hours. Am I nuts? This is ridiculous. So why does this feel so sparkly inside my chest?

He says, "Sorry, I had to mix in a protein powder, and you can't just stir the stuff in. We eat breakfast foods for dinner now. My mom has Alzheimer's, and these days, mealtime is always breakfast. She doesn't remember she loves eggs, so I have to sneak protein into her pancakes."

I shake my head.

"The protein power isn't as bad as you'd think," he says as if he sees me. "With fresh fruit, you don't notice the taste. Not much. She likes blueberries best."

"Oh."

Mai says, "A minute ago, I explained how I didn't start searching for The VV until 2012. I thought answers might ruin my curiosity, which I had come to cherish. Especially after what happened to him in 2005."

What happened in 2005?

"That morning I posted my comment on the blog, they emailed me to confirm. Perry called an hour later. First words out of his mouth were 'It's really you.' Over the years, men had compared stories and decided the King of Curiosity was real. Their policy is to not actively search for other Found Kings. But they knew I was out there. Somewhere."

Why is my heart pounding?

"Same day, eight hours later, I hear car doors slam. I leave my barn, expecting to see Jamie or Randy. Instead, I discover three men in sparkling shirts. We stare at each other. It was… intense. Three hours later, two more kings showed. Next day, six more kings flew in. DC told everyone about me. Those first two weeks were insane. I never dreamed it would be like this."

"Like what?"

I couldn't stop myself.

"Like...." Mai's voice tightens. He clears his throat. "Like discovering me was the best thing that ever happened to them. They were waiting for me. They're all amazing. Perry is like, wow. We've Skyped half a dozen times already, and we're planning my first trip to Perth. I gotta hear his cello in person. You've researched him, right? I had never even heard of the Bolinas Project, but twelve European cities adopted his financial model to help the homeless. That's only one of his projects. Not just Perry. You wouldn't believe what these guys are doing. They're influencing things."

Tears stream down my face. I don't know if I'm happy for him or jealous.

"Anyway," Mai says, laughing.

I hear telltale wet-mucus noises, a snort, his voice muffled.

"If you want validation my story is real, google me when we get off the phone. Kearns with a *K*. I think you're smart enough to know not to contact me again. Your audience was for today only, and now it's over."

"Wait! You didn't answer my question."

"I sure did, bubba. Hope you were listening."

"I'm not—"

With a soft click, he is gone.

Dazzled and exhausted, I stare at the phone. My brain hurts. Should I call back? No. He's done with me, that's obvious. I don't—I don't know what he said, the clue. I'm exhausted. I should rest.

Rest? I can't fucking rest.

It's not hard to find online information about Mai Kearns. Not hard at all, in fact, if you're regularly featured in magazine articles and a dozen farming blogs. His farm's website has twenty-seven separate pages. Last year, at their LGBTQ Prom, all six male chaperones wore matching tuxedos and John Deere caps. In photos, they are grinning, arms around each other's shoulders. Only one looks Asian. He's ordinary but handsome. Short black hair, gray temples. Gray is always sexy. Actually, I was wrong. He's not ordinary. Kearns is hot.

In another picture, Randy Phinter places a crown on the prom king's head. When Mai described Randy chasing Vin into the corn, Mai said it was odd to see Randy running full-speed. He said Randy was big. This picture of Randy shows a total stud, broad shoulders and a tight build. Even in a tuxedo, he looks strong. All those years playing corn tag paid off, I guess.

Photo of a sixteen-year-old before a small, attentive audience. Caption says she's arguing a crop rotation strategy based on water table fluctuations.

Visitors to the farm's website are encouraged to apply for a three-month, six-month, or year-long internship on any of six farms, depending on interest: farming, chemistry, project management, nutrition, organics, hydroponics. An accounting internship, if you don't mind also working in barns for two hours every day. Everyone works the land. There's even an internship for "farm minstrel," whatever the fuck that is. At the bottom of Mai's application is a single sentence in nine-point font, so tiny a person may not even notice. *All curious are welcome.*

I switch gears to read a Chicago news magazine's feature from last year. A spotlight, not even the focus of the article, describes how Mai cares for his mother, promenading her daily through a half-acre of gardens, picking flowers and introducing her to interns, usually the exact same students every day. While she may not remember, every day is rich with new friends, vegetables, and evening strolls. A photo, taken from behind, shows her learning on him. He points at a tree alive with monarchs, orange and black fluttering everywhere. The image sears into memory.

The main article describes how in 1997, Mai and the bubbas wondered what might happen if you linked six farms economically, leaving full control to the original families who owned them. They called their gambit "the six pack," and it succeeded. Another six pack—all graduates of DeKalb's 4H program—established itself in nearby Rockford. The bubbas mentor the Rockford Six Pack and two others, one in Iowa and another in Wisconsin. Small-town farmers have a fighting chance again, if you trust your best friends to work the land with you.

Scholarships.

Internships.

Their home-grown curriculum crosses eight disciplines. Mai couldn't become a college professor because even five miles away, Northern Illinois University was too far. Instead, he turned his farm into a fucking university. He leads an army of farmers, reimagining America's breadbasket. They're *influencing* things.

I lunge for the nearest paper—the back of an envelope—and scribble anything I recall from the last ten minutes. Did he emphasize the number of visiting kings the first day? Perry and Mai have Skyped six times already. Is six a clue? This isn't big enough. I rummage in a drawer until I find a clean sheet of paper and write hurried notes. Mai answered my question, he must have. He told me to google his farm. That was his suggestion. Did he post a clue on his website? Later. I'll study it later.

I jot impressions on Mai's tone, word choice, and any particular emphasis I recollect. Names mentioned on his King Weekend. He deliberately told me Vin used real names in The Lost and Founds. How does Jimbo the Bruiser fit this puzzle? I saw Randy's middle name is James. Is Randy Jimbo? I scribble theories.

When this intensity spells itself, I am surprised to discover three full pages and one electric bill envelope covered in ink, my frenzy yielding nothing but mad ramblings. What do I know? What are the facts? Maybe these are not facts. Vin lied to Mai all weekend. Would Kearns lie while giving me clues if it helped me grow my heart?

Assume nothing.

Review everything.

I lay the papers side by side, riddles before me, taunting. Who is the next king? In the margins, I draw four ears of corn. Didn't seven kings visit him the first day?

First three, then four more? Five? I don't remember! Everything swirls, words spinning, clues sparking like maybe they did for Mai when he raced through a midnight cornfield, wearing only a green-glowing jockstrap, a ghost at his side.

Breathe, I tell myself. *Breathe.*

Here's one fact I do know—they know I am questing. Involuntarily, I jerk my head back, staring straight up. Through the ceiling, through the roof, I imagine blue sky, maybe a few cloud wisps, and a circling brown speck swoops lower, a hawk named Kalista, maintaining a watchful eye.

I think I just joined an army.

FIVE

I HATE NEW YORK.

The city scares me, the sheer weight of it. I've never slept in a place where I worried about the strength of the earth to keep everything in place. How can the ground sustain so much pressure? Skyscraper after skyscraper, each scraping its neighbor. Bulky cement everywhere, colossal theaters, and public buildings impressive enough to make Washington, DC, wince with jealousy. Millions upon millions, eating and rushing and pushing this city lower, the billion katrillion footsteps tromping and stomping through a city sprawling and overweight for two hundred years.

I hate it here.

Margaret was surprised as hell when I announced my New York visit. She thinks I'm on an extreme adventure, a misguided attempt to connect with people. I didn't dissuade her of the notion, which is bullshit. I lied to her, but how would I explain this? *Margaret, based on a photo of a farmer pointing at a tree, I'm looking for a man in New York whose name I don't know. I think he likes butterflies.* She'd have me committed. I should be committed.

The weight of the city isn't even my top worry.

Cars, cars, cars, cars.

Uncountable thousands of them race past every day. A thousand after a thousand after a thousand. What kind of idiot, crippled by a car, goes to the place where they're densest and fastest? Impossible not to flinch every few seconds. Every time I hear screeching brakes, I remember those milliseconds when every sensation merged into a raw unbearable scream, something nameless. I will spend every second of my life remembering that sound, my bones splintering. I died under that weight. The life I could have lived *died* that day. A life with legs that worked. Through New York, I relive it every fucking hour. Even inside this shithole restaurant, hearing the screaming, unending traffic, I cringe. I can't get away from it, not even in bed at night. The only place I don't hear cars is the subway, a different kind of terror.

Three weeks and four days living in this nightmare city with nothing to show for it. The never-ending horror of people and steel and cars and people and steel and cars and cars and cars and cement and people... I can't fucking breathe. I try not to be traumatized, but I am on the fucking edge. I howled in terror when I heard that car accident last week, and it was down the block. I fucking shrieked at the top of my lungs. People laughed at me. I fucking hate it here.

Calm down. Quit trembling. I'm fine. I'm sitting here, sipping cold coffee, in no danger. Think good things. Calm things. This coffee is disgusting.

Street food. Street food is fun. I like that. Flags rippling in the wind. My suite is beautiful. Subway riders who go out of their way to make me feel okay, like it's no inconvenience I occupy two spots where others could stand. My first week, an older black lady asked me to peel her orange. She didn't give one flying fuck about my legs. She recited her life story until the train squealed into her stop. She took her orange and joined the departing frenzy. No thank you, no goodbye. She didn't see a cripple. Hell, she didn't even see me as a person, just a convenient orange peeler. You know your life is pathetic when you treasure an anonymous subway interaction.

Sympathetic people crumple their faces, communicating, *I understand.* I'd like to yell, *you fucking don't.* I want New Yorkers to accommodate me on the sidewalks and in subways, but I don't want them to make eye contact, or if they do, I want them to look bored and frustrated, like they glare at everyone else. I'm insane. Do I want people to see me, acknowledge me? Or do I want to be invisible? Vin Vanbly would understand my dilemma. If he truly is the Human Ghost, he would understand.

I feel strange gratitude to New Yorkers who bark, "Move it." They hate my inconvenience, but their hostility feels honest. Although there wasn't much solace in that muscle queen barking, "Watch your fucking canes." That's happened *twice* since I got here. Both huge muscle guys. I would have told the second guy to fuck off, if I hadn't been busy drooling. I've never experienced such a high concentration of gay men actively ignoring or hate-cruising me. Not exclusively gays, though I'm more susceptible to their scorn. Self-righteous pricks. Fuck you, New York. Fuck you.

I should go back to Columbus.

Today's wild guess will amount to nothing, as did yesterday's, and the day before that, and the day before that. Every lead has been a dead end. They open in fifteen minutes, so I may as well check out Monarch Consulting. I'll ask a few questions, my standard ones. See if anything is revealed. Then back to the Belleclaire. Then what? I'm running out of ideas.

Where is the Butterfly King?

This coffee sucks. Sitting here for an hour, my skin feels damp with grease. This is a greasy spoon restaurant, and it literally smells like grease. Everyone packed into booths. Watching them jabbing, stabbing, slicing, grinding, and chewing with fury, you'd think they hated forcing eggs into their pie hole. Restaurants are always noisy, but in this dump, conversation is a deafening competition, everyone focused on victory. The fucking nightmare crap I've overheard in this city. Breakups, breakdowns, every mean-spirited snark imaginable. You'd think eavesdropping here would be King Schadenfreude's dream, but I want to go home.

Adrenaline kept me hunting for butterflies longer than I expected. I thought it might take a week, tops. Every night I lie awake, listening to the goddamn honking, thinking, *one more day, just one.*

I can't leave.

I've replayed the scene a thousand times, wringing hope from the meager encounter, my first hour, checking into the hotel, my chatty bellboy giving me an overly-enthusiastic tour of my top-floor suite. I hadn't noticed him much, not even his name, only the thick Jamaican accent, the clacking of his braid beads whenever he jerked his head. I remember wondering if he was deliberately working me for a bigger tip. But after I handed him forty bucks, he tucked it sharply into my shirt pocket, saying, "Keep it, mon. Expensive city."

During my split-second astonishment, deference slipped away from his smile. He seemed older than I had originally assumed. Without a word, he took my hand. He raised it, and I was powerless to stop him. The pale pink of his lips touched inside my palm, under the thumb. The king's kiss, exactly as Mai Kearns described it.

With no trace of his Jamaican accent, he said, "Enjoy New York."

He turned and strode across the penthouse. He no longer popped and jerked, he sauntered with lanky confidence. He peeled off his wig. When I called after him, he did not answer me. He closed the door with a soft click. The front desk confirmed no bellboy had been sent to my room. The kings knew when I'd arrived and where I was staying. They'd gotten someone into the hotel—into my room— within the first hour.

Kearns said the Butterfly King was a New York businessman. Years ago, he interrupted muggings in Harlem, he and his army of butterflies. I do not want to go door-to-door in Harlem. That's insane, but I'm out of options. *Hi there, stranger. I'm from Columbus. Do you know the Butterfly King?*

I wish to fucking hell I had taken notes during my hours with Kearns, because I know Mai mentioned his name. What if they'd thought I was taking notes? Was I supposed to? They should have told me to take notes. Would I have done it? No, probably not. I didn't realize curiosity would bloom into obsession. Why are they making me work this hard? They know I'm here.

Seven butterfly dry cleaners, nine stationery stores, and seventeen florists with butterflies in their logo. I did surveillance on all of them and saw nothing king-related. I ate four meals at The Butterfly in SoHo. Great steak, no clues. Ten bakeries, four garden shows, and sat through a shitty horror musical called *Butterfly, Pinned.* Sat on a stone bench for six hours in The Met's butterfly exhibit, until the docent finally asked me to leave. While she stuttered her request, I understood from her mortification, she'd probably already given me a few hours leeway. Cripple privilege.

Butterfly Garage in Queens. Little League team in the Bronx called the Butterfly Boys, a team name ripe for daily wedgies. I bet those kids get the crap beat out of them. A trio of drag queens perform on Christopher Street, calling themselves "M Butterfly's Bitches." Nothing.

Where are you guys?

I should leave New York. Go home.

Home to what? Nobody needs me. No job, no friends, no groups where someone would say, "Why isn't Daniel here this month?"

I'm worried about how much time I spend alone. I want to live. Maybe that's why I hate New York. It's a constant reminder that in a city of millions upon millions, forever fucking, yelling, chewing, grinding, sinking into the earth, I'm alone. In a city of a million angry people, I am probably the angriest one here, and I still can't connect. What I wrote to Perry sounded vaguely suicidal. I'm not. I should never have written that.

"You a private eye?"

Sour-faced Debbie stands with one hand on her hip, carrying empty coffee mugs in her other hand, a caricature of waitresses everywhere.

"No."

She indicates the building across the street with her jaw. "Why you bugging?"

Uneven caramel streaks make her hair colorist seem guilty of smearing melted caramel bars down the side of her head. Looks terrible. And that nametag is a lie. No way is she a Debbie.

"You been here way too long."

"Fine. Charge me for another coffee."

"Oh, we way beyond coffee. You renting this table. Fifty bucks. Right now. Fifty bucks for fifteen more minutes."

She's right. I overstayed, which is stealing her tips. I don't want to come across like a total pushover, so I take my time.

I hand her the money. "I'd like more coffee, Debbie."

"Fifty bucks don't get you coffee. And my name ain't Debbie."

I hate this city.

Every street corner is an event. I've only got a few more seconds to strategize how to cross, causing the least amount of inconvenience to the two hundred people crossing against me. Gotta move as fast as they do, because death-by-cab is real. I'll head to the right. Those older people in front of me will create a natural slowdown. I'll walk in their wake. If not there, I'll go left—

Sunlight blinds me. Damn it, right into my fucking eyes. This is no time to be blind. Gotta go! Gotta go! Fucking hell—I can't see a goddamn thing. Look down. Focus on down.

We surge.

Shit. I can't see where my canes hit the ground—just an afterimage of the thing that blinded me, a purple rectangle. Heart rate spikes. Don't panic. I can't afford to stumble. I'll slip on garbage and fall, sprawled in the street.

"Watch it, asshole."

No point to apologizing, they're already gone.

I can't see! *Don't panic.* Canes hitting the ground, and I can't see where. Okay, okay. Calm down. Vision returning.

"Watch it, cripple."

"Jesus, watch it."

Fuck you, New York. Fuck you very much.

Okay, this is better. My vision is definitely better now. Temporary blindness is a mere inconvenience to most people, but it could kill me.

Another reason to hate New York—garbage. Last week I almost landed on a used diaper, middle of an intersection. Cigarette butts and soiled gyro wrappers everywhere.

Made it.

I can rest for a second. What the fuck happened? What blinded me? I have to be more careful when I look around. Candy wrapper stuck to the bottom of the right cane. I hate this garbage city. Eric told me, "You spend your whole life looking down."

I glance up.

The parking lot in front of me is packed, attendants racing like rats, moving cars. Jesus, people are honking their cars in a parking lot. Why? Nobody can move! Next to it, the building with Monarch Consulting is the same gray concrete as its neighbors throughout Midtown—same size windows, a flimsy-looking fire escape clutching the side, dropping right into the parking lot.

The first floor is commercial, like most buildings in Midtown. Fashion Hosiery, tourist crap store next to it. I may not wear panty hose, but I am pretty sure this isn't the place to go for fashion.

Okay. Building directory, right on the exterior. Good. There it is, Monarch Consulting, sixth floor. If they work normal business hours, someone should be around now. I'll ask my questions, and when this fails, I'll—do what? I've exhausted all the possibilities I could imagine. Is it time to accept door-to-door in Harlem? Gotta be a smarter way. Up and down every brownstone's stairs, ringing buzzers? No way.

There's the thing that blinded me, an engraved gold plaque, weirdly positioned above and to the right of the revolving doors. I guess the sun hit it. Too high to easily read, bigger than an index card, but not by much. Why place it all the way up there? The words are all capped—

TURN AROUND AND SAY HELLO TO THE VV.

Holy fucking shit.
I can't stop reading the words. *Turn around and say hello!*
Holy fucking shit.
I cannot turn gracefully, but I manage.
Nothing.
Nobody.
What did I expect? A man wearing orange wings? Just ordinary people, a woman arguing with a drunk girl passed out on a bench. Business people, striding hard, pushing the sidewalk deeper and deeper into the earth. Woman on her phone, kids loudly—there. Right there. A video camera attached to the awning's steel frame, filming right where I'm standing.
This is it. I found him.
I'm surprised I know how to say hello. I lean back against the building, shifting weight on my left arm, freeing my right hand. Ignore the constant stream through the building's revolving door. Ignore the Fashion Hosiery shoppers. I kiss the underside of my palm and spread my arm widely. The king's kiss. My life is changed in this moment. *I found him.*
"Hello, Butterfly King. I'd sure like to meet you." My voice trembles. "I'll stay for a while, in case you come downstairs now."
A few people notice me in conversation with an awning, but they don't care. They're not even curious. I'm having an insane life moment, and nobody cares. I'm just ordinary, New York crazy. I want to laugh, but I am content to grin big and wait. Maybe someone will come down to meet me. I'll wait.
I found the Butterfly King.
In a city of millions, I found him.

Nobody's coming.
Maybe they review the tapes once a week. Or maybe once a day, but I'm guessing it's not monitored by a live person, because I've been standing here an hour. Took three fucking weeks, day and night, dragging my ass from borough to borough, but none of that matters, because the joy, the fucking *elation*—and the thing is, I've examined that damn plaque enough times in the last hour to know a few things.

It's weathered. They didn't put that plaque out specifically for me. It's for anyone seeking The VV tribe. How many people know about them? How many of their secrets are hidden right out in the open? My brain won't stop spinning.

I won't go upstairs. I'm done debating that. These guys like their little rules. Instructions are to say hello. Did that. Twenty more minutes and then getting a cab.

I fucking found them.

The Belleclaire Hotel feels like July, despite the slight chill of this crisp May day. The hotel's summer flags *fwap* against the exuberant breeze. I am exuberant! They are victory banners today. Sunlight warms the brick, making me appreciate my home away from home. The streets are still packed with people arguing on the sidewalk, throwing their garbage down in this car-obsessed city. I hate it here, but right now? I love New York. The Belleclaire looks better at night, bricks lit and glowing blood-orange, hiding years of grime. Right now, the grime is invisible because this is my castle, and I am the court jester. I haven't felt excitement like this in—in never. In fucking *never*. Will they call? Did I do it right? Yes. I did it right. Besides, they sent the bellhop.

I found them.

Even struggling to get out of the cab can't upset me, not much. Okay, some. Cane is stuck. Jesus, quit honking. Wait, not directed at us. Cabbie takes my money with gratitude. I tip well, I know that.

Look down. No garbage ahead.

Roger's on door, no big surprise. Always shows big deference for the crippled guest, but even he can't dampen my spirits. Not with green castle flags celebrating me.

"Good morning, sir."

He refuses to call me Daniel. I hate his toady bow, reminding me even a bellman has more power than I do when it comes to opening a fucking door, the most basic thing in life.

"The floors should be dry, sir."

"Thanks."

"Car tonight? I know you like to go out at night."

"I don't know. I'll call down."

"Yes, sir. I'll be happy to accommodate you, sir."

They probably all think I'm out with prostitutes. I wonder if they talk about the crippled rich guy in the suite. They must. A three-week guest in the expensive, top suite can't be normal. Or maybe it is in New York. Worth every expensive penny. Thank god, I can finally leave New York.

I bark out a laugh. Soon, I can leave!

Nothing on the floors to trip me. Roger said *all dry* and he was right. I have to be nicer to him my last days here. I can do that. After my first few nights here, I noticed the number of WET FLOOR signs doubled whenever they scrubbed the lobby. I resent special treatment, but they're trying. I need to feel more gratitude. I do like this place, intersection of big money and quirky taste, sprawling rugs, fake moose heads jutting from the purple walls, unique enough to impress hipsters. Despite my happiness, I do not want attention, which means looking bored. But it's hard to stop grinning.

"Mr. Connors?"

I recognize that front desk voice. I like Jeanette. "Yes?"

Jeanette does not fuss. Others exhaust me, working hard to prove my shitty legs do not repulse them. *Having a good Tuesday? Need more towels? Have you visited the Met?* I know they're trying to treat me normally, but surely they see how they don't make the same effort with other guests. I respect her for not trying. Does she see a crippled guy or just a guy? I think just a guy. Today she is queen of Castle Belleclaire. Thank you, Queen Jeanette, for allowing me to feel normal.

Jeanette says, "You received a floral delivery. I'll send them to your room in ten minutes, if that works."

"Great. Thank you."

The Butterfly King sent flowers. How nice of him.

I fucking found him.

This grinning bellhop, I recognize. Though familiar, I haven't seen enough of him to learn his name. He's wearing the official uniform, gold tassels on his shoulders, but he's not carrying anything.

"I was told you had flowers."

He says, "Please open your door. I think the best place is the desk. I'll move the chair."

He bumps against one of my canes and bursts into apologies.

"You're fine. Don't worry about it."

"I'm so sorry!"

"I was standing too close to the door."

I can't even anticipate the pleasure of this bouquet because now I have to repeatedly validate him. God, what is that smell?

I cough.

He says, "I'll be more careful in the future, Mr. Connors."

To my surprise, a pair of locked hands enter the room, carrying a giant bucket. What the hell?

Holy shit.

It's massive. I've only seen arrangements like this watching the Kentucky Derby. It's overpowering.

The guy carrying it coughs. Okay. It's not just me.

His guiding buddy says, "Over to the right more."

Holy shit—this is absurd. I don't care—I love it. I worked my ass off for three weeks and this—this ridiculous explosion of floral feels like they're acknowledging my effort. *Well done*, the flowers cry out. *Well done!* Once the guys succeed in landing the bucket, they make sure the whole thing is centered, safe from falling over. They stall, giving me time to invite them to stay while I read the card. Sorry, gentlemen, this is private.

"Thank you again. That must have been very heavy."

"It's cool. We have a cart in the hall. Need anything else, sir?"

"No, thank you. Thank you."

I'm excited to tip today.

Lingering a moment longer, they finally close the door.

So many roses, I can't estimate their number. Pale lilies narrow to flaming fuchsia throats. Gerber daisies or something. Wait, Gerber is the baby food. Lilacs, spikes, things like hollyhocks. Nice detailing etched into the steel bucket. This is not cheap. Not at all.

I should have tipped more. My hands shake. I extract the white card, fingertips running over the textured, white front. I am conscious of my breath. Open it.

TONIGHT. MONARCH CONSULTING. OUT FRONT. 11:45 P.M.—BK

Here we go.

Tonight I meet the Butterfly King.

SIX

WHY DID I arrive so early? A dare? *Come get me.* Same invitation I'm telegraphing to nearby criminals. I should feel afraid. I'm overconfident, but it feels so damn good to be excited about something. Anything. I'm sitting in the dark, on a New York bench across the street from Monarch Consulting, smiling.

Is this street safe? This morning it was chaos, people and cabs, everything swerving, but now, empty. No Debbie-not-Debbie. No forks scraping plates, yelling-eating. Also, no late-night cabs, which is not a good sign. The only drama is overflowing garbage, chewed burgers, soggy lettuce, Styrofoam cups, and assorted shit that could upend me in the middle of an intersection. Over there is Hell's Kitchen, gritty dark buildings. Been there a few times, hunting the elusive butterfly.

Streets are still shiny from the rain earlier, like they worked up a sweat and can't cool down. Homeless guy hasn't moved from his cardboard since I arrived. Curled up sleeping. I wish caramel-streaked Debbie-not-Debbie would appear with shitty coffee.

Despite my giddiness, I still see the city for what it is. New York puddles are completely unromantic, balled-up wrappers and cigarettes floating, tiny barges chugging through gray milk. The scent of rotten eggs wafts to me, and I know it's not eggs making that odor but something worse. Today's eight hundred thousand tromping feet left their stink. I should feel relief at the absence of cars and people, a break from the crushing weight. I don't. I am so anxious I could scream.

Look around. Calm down.

To be fair, the city can appear majestic, skyscrapers a testament to humanity's achievements, etcetera. Lights are pretty. I get it. It's just hard to be impressed when I'm focused on cracked asphalt and street milk. That floating butt makes me nauseous, making tiny ripples. Well, quit staring, idiot.

You spend your whole life looking down.

I sneered at Eric. *I'd love to look up.* I'd knocked over my canes for emphasis. When I met Eric's sorrowful gaze, I understood. He didn't mean physically. I hated him. Hated him for dating me. Hated him for not giving me more chances. Mostly, I hated him for being right. Yeah, I look down. Given my history, how can I not?

I demanded he answer me, if my history had happened to him, might it possibly impact his optimism? His up-with-people attitude? He agreed that it would. But that changed nothing. He didn't dump me because of my legs. He dumped me because of my negativity.

Goddamn it, look away from the cigarette. Watching it sink won't help. The lower floors are dark. The fashion hosiery shop is long closed. They were smart enough to abandon this block long before midnight. Even the shitty souvenir shop is closed. A bodega at the far end of the block is open.

I hear scraping from the fire escape. A bucket is pushed out, seventh floor maybe, and followed by a woman, crawling. She uses the railing to pull herself upright. Her cigarette smoke weaves an uneven halo. I didn't realize women still used hair rollers. A 1950s housecoat, the very definition of hausfrau. That fire escape sees a lot of action. Half an hour ago, I witnessed a lovers' quarrel. They emerged, argued, made up, and crawled inside. I guess fighting out there counts as *private* in this city. On a higher floor, a secret smoker emerged, stole puffs. A few minutes later, another secret smoker. Both of them waved their hands to dissolve the proof before crawling inside.

As expected, she dumps her bucket straight over, splattering one of the few remaining cars in the lot below. Disgusting. An extra wet splash—yup, there it is. She poured out her sponge. She stares after it, swears, then leaves. It's not possible to crawl inside from the fire escape with grace. Everyone looks awkward. They look like I feel every time I get out of a car.

Two black men appear near the bodega, goofing, shoulder shoving, too far away for me to hear any conversation, only giddy play. Inside jokes, easy friendship. They irk me, and I know it's jealousy. Must be great to have a friend like that.

It's 11:40. Okay. Shit. *It's time.*

This is it. Get up. Go.

I've been waiting weeks for this moment, but now I want more time to think. What's going to happen? What will he be like? What if I say the wrong thing? What do I expect from him—to give my life purpose? What could he possibly say to dazzle me? Do I want to be dazzled? Do I play it cool?

Calm down.

Stand.

I slide my arms into the metal armbands. Center my weight. No turning back. It's time, *it's fucking time.* I wish I had been able to sleep this afternoon. I'm razor-sharp tired. Leery. Itching. I'm too dull for this meeting.

The black men cross in front of the revolving doors.

No traffic. I'm going to cross right here. I feel an illicit thrill, doing this ordinary thing I've watched a thousand New Yorkers do—cross the street outside a crosswalk. In daylight hours, I wouldn't stand a chance. This isn't supposed to be my life, apologizing constantly for taking up space, strategizing crosswalks. I should be able to stride through Midtown. I should be looking up.

As soon as I reach halfway, sure enough, headlights hit me. No fucking car for five minutes, but now, yes. Taxi. Ignore it. Keep going.

The cabbie rolls down his window. "Need a ride?"

"No, thanks."

"You sure?"

"Yeah. Just go."

He pulls to the curb. He gets out. Why do I have to justify my every decision to a person who can walk? "Look, I don't want a fucking ride."

He glances but doesn't answer. He leans against his trunk, lighting a cigarette. Oh.

The two black guys jostle each other against the parking lot's chain-link fence, creating that recognizable metallic clatter. The hausfrau appears in her yellow bathrobe through a lobby door at the side. Robe open, the tie dragging. Thick slurred makeup. Korean? Maybe.

Navigating around me, Hausfrau says, "Asshole."

I wonder how being called an asshole fifty times a day damages you. I guess I'll find out.

It's exactly time. I'm here. Where are you, Butterfly King?

Hausfrau demands the black men get out of her way, and then she demands they unlock the chain-linked fence. She wants her sponge.

There. Standing at the far end, in front of the bodega.

When did he arrive? Tall, maybe six feet. Leather kilt. Black boots. Shimmery orange dress shirt, glowing. His king shirt. *It's him!* Darker-skinned, not coal black, not light-skinned, and despite our distance, his eyes capture mine. Even this far apart, I feel the weight of his gaze. Why is everything so heavy in this city? We're all sinking into the earth.

He flicks his head, the tiniest tic. *Come to me.*

My stomach lurches. I wish I had slept.

The chatter behind me swells. Even the Butterfly King breaks eye contact to check it out. The two black guys out-talk Hausfrau, requesting cigarette money. She keeps repeating, "Only sponge! Only sponge!"

Fuck. Guys, don't ruin this. I'm meeting—The Butterfly King signals a stronger *come,* but he doesn't wait. He disappears around the corner. What the fuck? I'm hustling the best I goddamn can. The voices get louder behind me. She calls them both *assholes.* This is not good.

Hurry forward.

The Butterfly King returns, backing into my view. Why? What's happening? He spins to face me and strides purposefully, thick legs moving with intention. Nubbins for his hair, maybe the beginning of dreads, and his shirt ripples in apricot waves. It flaps open, a black tank top covers his belly. Muscular as his enormous shoulders are, he's got a gut.

Behind me, she yells. I jerk my head. The homeless guy stands, unsure. This can't be good. Behind the Butterfly King, a small crowd of black men emerge, eight or nine, everyone carrying baseball bats—holy shit, holy shit, *holy shit*. What the fuck is this? I've got to get out of here. The bodega grocer emerges on his front stoop, arms crossed in disapproval. As they pass, they grab oranges from his bin.

"Hey," he yells. "Put back. Pay or put back."

They ignore him. A few toss oranges into the air.

"Put back!"

The Butterfly King draws closer. I see gray in his hair, bristles against his head. "Turn."

There is a throaty menace to his command.

He says, "Hurry up, Legs. There's another building entrance through the parking lot."

Panic rises. I can't get away. He knows that!

He passes me. "Secret entrance through the white SUV parked in the last spot. Open the back. Go in."

Go into what, a car? A trunk? I don't understand. The baseball bats are dragged along the sidewalk. I turn to follow him. The men with Hausfrau laugh, and she screams. I never saw the cabbie get into his cab, but I hear how the engine refuses to turn. They're six feet away, the men and Hausfrau, arguing before the padlocked gate.

The Butterfly King says, "Get through the gate."

"The people!"

He says, "Combination is 7-16-32. Hurry."

I can't catch my breath.

I hear catcalls and whistling behind us, much closer. Hausfrau screams and runs into the street. They chase! They're going to hurt her. *I've got to get out of here!* If something happens, I die. I will die on my back against a chain-link fence in New York City because I can't fucking run. He turns to face the approaching crowd.

Shit!

He says, "Open the lock. 7-16-32."

I grab the padlock, but my hands are shaking. My fingers won't work.

I hear the cab door open, and a sharp voice demands, "Get out."

I fumble, I fumble. 7-16-32!

Behind me, a man says, "You're taking our men."

The Butterfly King says, "No. Not intentionally."

"Maybe not intentional, but you are."

7-16-32! 7-16-32!

He says, "If they want out of gang life, we help. Men work off their crimes through community service. Nobody wants trouble. Butterfly Men want peace."

I have to focus on the combination, breathing, getting my fingers to twist the tumbler.

"Hear that?" the leader says, louder. "He just want peace. *Peace* what he want."

Men grumble their disbelief. From the corner of my eye, I see an orange fly into the air. I can't make my fingers stop shaking. I hear the smack when it lands in an open palm.

"I'm here alone," the Butterfly King says. "I am no threat. Let us be men of peace."

Hausfrau screams, "Assholes!"

"We notice you alone, gee," the man says. "We *know* you all alone."

Damn it, I missed the sixteen. Start over. Calm down, start over.

"We have a truce," the Butterfly King says. "All are agreed."

"Yeah," the leader says, "but yo' team got greedy."

"No, not greedy. Butterfly Men do not recruit. That is not our way."

7-16-32! 7-16-32! 7-16-32!

I got two of the three numbers, breathing, breathing, one more try.

She squeals, maybe in pain. My father made me scream. He relished my screams, his eyes lit—don't remember that now! *Focus.*

The bodega owner yells from down the street. "Ma? Ma? Let my mother go."

We're going to die.

The final number clicks, and my tug pulls the lock open. I want to slump to the ground, my relief is so profound. I have to free the chains, but I can't. I'll lose my balance. The cab driver complains loudly, repeating he wants no part of this.

"We have a problem, Mr. Butterfly," the leader says.

I lean against the fence, jerking the chain until it obeys gravity's demand, heavy links slithering to the hard pavement. We have to go. I push one side wide open. We have to go. Now.

"Yes," says the Butterfly King. "We have a problem."

I hear a gasp above me. The two lovers have returned to the fire escape. *Get the fuck inside!*

"Cousin, *no*," she cries. "Leave him alone."

I glance behind me. The leader is chubby, which surprises me.

He yells to her. "Go inside, Maria. Butterfly King, you know how we solve problems."

The men grunt menacing chuckles. I glance up to see a spinning orange and watch it land in the palm of the man who tossed it.

I don't want to die!

The Korean grocer runs toward us.

I have to go through the fence, but I can't. They're hurting Hausfrau. I can hit one man with a cane as I fall. One chance to do some damage. Then they'll start kicking me.

Louder, the leader says, "I said, you know how we solve problems."

Oh God, oh God, oh God.

The Butterfly King says, "We dance it out."

"Got that right," the leader says with a snarl.

The woman on the fire escape screams, a blood-curdling shriek, slashing open the night.

I'm going to die!

I duck because gunfire—do I throw myself to the ground? I hear the loud cracking again, powerful, but it's not—that isn't gunfire. I know the sound of gunfire.

Nobody's screaming.

Did he say *dance*?

Oranges rise and fall, tossed higher, two bats swung hard into each other. That's the cracking sound, like gunfire. Men back away, moving into the shiny, black street.

The fire escape woman screams again. "Not dancing."

I glance up to see her collapse in her lover's arms.

One of the posse tosses an extra bat to the cab driver, who snatches it from the air, jumping into position and swinging hard, connecting with his neighbor's bat. The orange tossers stand between bat men. The homeless man pulls out an orange, falling into the second row. Fat oranges leap into the black night, spinning against the New York skyline, landing easily in men's open palms.

What the fuck?

The two black men wrestling with Hausfrau lift her, supporting her forearms, causing her to curl and flip around them. She lands behind them, pulling them into her, spinning them out. They unfurl, twirling, facing her again in attack position. She rushes them, leaping, and they catch her, lifting her, her arms stretching upward like a bird in flight.

My heart pounds.

Oranges jump skyward at various heights, like a fountain spraying water, then tumbling back to the hands that tossed them. Bats smash. I steady myself, wincing at each smashing sound, still clutching chain-link, facing this madness, the grocer flipping toward two black men, who are flipping toward the grocer. *Shit, they will collide*—but no! He flips between them. This is choreographed. All of it. A pulse throbs through ever-growing numbers. Black men emerge from shadows to take their spots. They belong. This is their story, too. The pulse. What does that mean? *What story?* I don't understand my own fucking thoughts. I can barely breathe.

There's a pattern. The pulse...it's a pattern. I step away from the fence. They toss the pulse between them with cracking bats, a drumroll, the noise soaring and falling as if it were an orange, each man tense, poised, ready to crack! Crack! *Crack!* The power sparks whenever bats collide, a commitment to power. What do those words mean? Orange tossers spin around while their fruit spins above.

A screech from the fire escape shocks me, and I jerk my head to see the woman twirl in her lover's arms. A dozen people—different floors—twist over the railings like gymnasts, orange glowing cigarettes revealing their movement. That can't be safe! I want to scream, but my brain still fights for understanding—they snap into position, jerking their arms straight toward the gunfire bats.

The pulse gains speed, sprinting, stealing my breath, thirty men assembled, baseball bats cracking everywhere. Forty men? Where did they all come from? The pulse is too strong, too much energy. It's alive, the pattern now too complex for me to follow. I witness half-veiled repetitions, the light—*what the fuck does that mean*—pushing harder, faster, bursting from their rawness, screeching, a direct current, pounding electricity directly at the Butterfly King, the crackling pulse electrifying him. It all leads right to him.

He spins—shoving me hard, open palms. I am lifted off my feet, up and backward, my god, *I'm falling*—and the fire escape woman shrieks, "*I love you!*"

Falling—

Air is forced out—

Caught!

I gasp, "Pow."

I stare into sky, skyscraper light squares, fighting terror. What happened? A throne made of arms caught me. Holds me safe. He shoved me off my feet, but he was six feet away. How was that possible?

I finally look to the street, every man on one knee, head bowed, panting. Hausfrau and her attackers. The bodega owner. Homeless man. Orange tossers, balancing their fruit on their knees.

They kneel.

I wipe tears away, but they keep coming. I told Mai Kearns I'd love to sing and dance onstage, but I never could.

I was just in a New York musical.

I was the star.

SEVEN

I'M TERRIFIED BY how I feel, how cared for. Loved! I don't understand. I'm angry! What—what the fuck did they do to me? I have to rein this in. Wipe my face. Confusion feels like joy, and it scares the fuck out of me, a wildfire burning away darkness to store the impossible—*I was in a musical*. I was *central* to—how dare they? They—what's a word stronger than terrified? I thought I would die. How fucking *dare* they?

The Butterfly King says, "Notes tomorrow night."

With effort, he rises. The chubby-faced gang leader offers him a hand, which he accepts. "Orange tossers, late on your third cue. Discuss it. Work it out. Good scream, Leslie. Nice work, people."

The fire escape woman blows him a kiss. Twenty people, crawling and dancing around that fire escape moments ago, disappear through windows, none of them moving with grace.

What the fuck just happened to me?

Baseball bat men rise, pulling each other upright, sometimes offering a bat to be grabbed by the kneeling man. Unkneeling. I don't think that's a word.

It's over.

I'm... I'm what?

The throne of arms remain steady, their collective strength holding me upright until I am ready to accept my weight. I should stand. I feel them encourage me as I lean forward. Elation screeches through me but seconds ago, I thought I would die. Now, everyone's leaving. No speaking. Not a word.

The Butterfly King says, "Sit rep at 7:30 a.m. Big shipment of daffodils on Pier 4 at Branson's. Get what you can. Pansies?"

"We're on it." The man who replies is a bat man, but which one? Men who emerged from night shadows stroll back into them, bats on their shoulder. The last inning played. He shoved me so hard, my feet left the ground. I fell *up*, then back. That couldn't have happened but I lived it. I rose from the earth.

"Take Keenan tomorrow." The Butterfly King doesn't need to yell. "And two more men to carry boxed flowers. Wrap it up, people. Traffic opens in five."

He strides with fluidity I witnessed minutes ago, a man using his legs purposefully. He brushes past. "Let's go, Legs. We only have until sunrise. My story deserves every minute of that time."

The orange fabric bunches over his ridiculous biceps, fat cantaloupes. I imagine succulent juice dripping down his muscular back. Why am I thinking that? How did they punch joy into me? I relive the feeling of falling *up*.

"Legs." Hausfrau—sans rollers—is in his late twenties. Thick makeup, melting. "Hang in there. Worth it."

The Butterfly King says, "Silence."

Hausfrau laughs as he backs away. "I can't keep quiet, Butterfly K. You know me."

"Silence."

"I'll work on that."

"Silence."

I follow the Butterfly King through the chain-link gate, dazed, wanting to demand answers, barely able to stand. Did I understand correctly? He shut down a New York street? What about the pulse? The pattern, too complex for me to follow. What the fuck was that? He's walking too fast.

Slow down!

Before he reaches the SUV, the lights flash. The hatch rises, and the back lowers, which—cars can't do that. He stoops and disappears almost immediately, walking down. That's impossible.

I wobble, re-terrified. It's over. It's *over*. Why am I still panicked? Or is this joy? They knelt before me, all of them, as if I were special. Every feeling fights for dominance. A realization—it's painful to think myself special, that hurts most. He had no right to devastate me. My arms quake with anger.

Sound of dragging metal makes me turn. One of the men who attacked Hausfrau yanks the chain through the fence, securing it behind us. Above me, windows shut. A dancer enjoys his post-performance cigarette, the tiny orange glow seems significant beyond reason. That flicker, soon extinguished on a New York fire escape but so important at this second. How does anything small and fragile survive this overweight city?

I want answers. I want them now.

No backseat, no car frame, just narrow stairs, leading into the building's basement, like he promised. The stairs are too narrow for me to navigate. I sit on the top step and throw down my canes. Under the green light spraying the landing, they look like instruments on a surgery table dedicated to alien autopsies. I scoot down each stair, like a fucking child. Why humiliate me like this, making me crawl on my ass? This guy is unbelievable.

Made it.

No railing, so I'll have to flip on my stomach and push one arm into the—I can do this. Almost standing. Done. Okay, just messy. I'll rest a minute, wipe my hands on my jeans. We couldn't go in the front fucking door?

I emerge into a wide hallway with giant wooden pallets, shrink-wrapped contents. I inhale damp mustiness, that basement smell common to everywhere. Not like the garage, every tool polished and gleaming. The perfect operating theater. This feels different. He stands at the far end, illuminated under a red EXIT, transforming his skin purplish-burgundy. He looks like a god from ancient times.

"Move it, Legs." His voice is confident, measured. Sharp without effort.

Asshole!

What kind of maniac terrorizes a cripple visiting his city? I also imagine him on bended knee, this powerful leader. My heart loves him. I starred in a musical tonight, a dream realized. Something impossible happened tonight. What was that pulse? How could I recognize it?

I move cautiously, ready for someone to jump out from behind a pallet. Anything could happen, any trick, any *gotcha*. Maybe the real trick is I'm following a stranger into a Midtown basement. When I reach him, he pushes Up. The elevator whirs. I need him to explain what the dance meant—the pulse, how he lifted me from six feet away—but I'm—I don't know how to react, grateful and furious as fucking hell.

"Quite the show your friends put on a minute ago. I thought I might actually die. Don't you think that's a particularly shitty thing to do to someone who can't escape? Terrifying someone like that?"

He looks puzzled.

The gloom in shadows has a texture I cannot name. The air is thicker. I should be more afraid right now, feeling his power crackling off his skin. I stare openly. I've earned that right. The Butterfly King's power is barbed wire, shimmering and dangerous, illuminating his purple glow. Is this real? Is he real? Am I waiting to board an alien ship or standing next to an elevator with olive-drab doors, half a word knife-scratched into—*cocksuc*. What is that internal knowing, understanding the exact second when your elevator arrives? I feel it. A split second later, the elevator *bings*, echoing forty times louder into the dirty corners with peeling paint. Once inside, he commands so much physical space, I wonder if I will fit next to him. I am conscious of my movement, insect-like and scrabbling, nothing like him. I'm a sand crab next to a swan. I do not like how he makes me feel.

He pushes a button and we ascend.

He says, "Leftover adrenaline converts into sensory awareness. You are susceptible to colors, sounds, sensations. Observe."

In slow motion, his index finger feather-brushes flesh under my right ear down my jawline, flooding me with images, a lake, sawdust sprinkled into corners—dad said was necessary for Norman Rockwell authenticity—giving a report in high school, crying after the third surgery, Eric's tenderness. Running to Frank. I gasp.

Whoa.

I feel the after burn along my skin, like the scratch of striking a match. He barely touched me, but I feel its warmth. How—what made all those images appear?

A cheery bing announces our arrival, the eighth floor. I'm dizzy. I'm not ready for whatever happens next. My jaw still tingles, his touch—the delicacy, so unlike his voice, a sword. The elevator door opens.

An oversized chaise lounge—lipstick red—absorbs all color and light, the rich fabric imprinted with a subtle curlicue design that curls into soft maroon. A school of rainbow prisms, thrown from a nearby chandelier, darts to a polished onyx floor.

He walks away.

Once sure of my footing, I follow. Despite its appearance, the floor isn't slippery. This loft is cavernous, and at the far end, a black fireplace matches the floor, polished to gleaming. Patterned rugs hang on exposed brick, medieval banners almost, boasting luxurious power. Stark windows stand naked and strong, allowing New York's skyline inside, just as naked and strong. The skyline is mirrored against the polished black floor, a shocking illusion. I feel this floor is the true New York and outside a clever trompe-l'œil. This space tricks my eyes. Or is this what he talked about, the sensory stuff? A dozen chandeliers—more than a dozen—spin prisms through reflected New York, rainbow koi swimming this midnight pond.

His kilt drops to the floor. "I prefer to be naked. Make yourself as comfortable as suits you."

Each ass cheek jiggles as he walks the skyline. He turns the corner. I didn't realize there was a corner. When I catch up, he's in an adjoining room, smaller than the main room, too large to be considered an alcove. Kitchenette, bedroom area back there, a few couches and conversation. The space is dominated by a long table, mirroring the floor's black polish. Floor-to-ceiling windows are filled with hundreds of glass circles. Stained glass. I can't quite discern the pattern, but there is one. It scratches at the periphery, familiar.

"Are those beer bottles?"

He says, "Yes."

All the glass is black, but only because it's night. I distinguish greens, some orangish hue, browns, dimly lit by five chandeliers. What is with all the chandeliers?

He says, "The window was designed and crafted by men who self-identify as alcoholics. Some men sober for decades, some for six months. This art is their commitment to themselves, to their people. Whoever their people might be. Men from all religious backgrounds including those who worship science and those who have no faith. This wall of light is their commitment to life itself."

Everything feels like a hard gut punch. Do not start crying. The throne of arms, the way they caught me, they were ready. How could they anticipate me being flying up before back? He's wearing glasses now, wire-frames, and studying a piece of paper. I'm only weepy because I'm so damn tired.

"Legs, I need you to do something. Take a chair. You'll use my laptop."

I lurch to obey before stopping, mid-step.

"I know we haven't been formally introduced, but I'm not a fan of your nickname. I'd appreciate *Daniel*."

He seems surprised, then nods to the chair.

It takes me longer to sit than most people, and I have plenty of time to eye his cock, almost at eye-level. Is it a big one? Seems fat. You can never tell with a soft dick. I'm a grower, myself. I love his gut, his muscled shoulders and round biceps, all of him beefy and hot as fuck. A smattering of short black and gray curls on his chest.

He hands me the paper. "Log into that bank's website and access the account listed."

"Why?"

"Do it, please." He turns away. "Tea? Water?"

"Water."

The kitchenette is three feet away. As he busies himself, I google the bank's real website to confirm it matches the one he supplied. Surprisingly, it does. A big global bank. He makes tea in silence, like we are an old married couple, no need for words. The login works, and I stare at an account balance which must be wrong, so pure and round are all those zeros. I count them a second time. Eleven million dollars.

Why does this shock me? I'm richer than this. I've had the lawsuit money all my adult life. But I didn't earn it. I hate the money. Real wealth, the roundness of these zeros, unnerves me.

"Do not explore the account. There is information there which is none of your business. Do you see the balance?"

Asshole!

"If this is none of my business, why the fuck would you make me log in? I'm sick of these games. I wish you people would talk to me. Tell me what's happening."

"Do you see the balance?"

"How did you shove me from five feet away?"

"Do you see the balance?"

"Yes. I see the fucking balance. Eleven million goddamn dollars. Could you maybe answer one or two fucking questions? I saw the pulse. I felt it until it got too complex."

"Make an online transfer. Transfer any amount up to $3 million. Pick a number. Transfer it to my personal account, also listed below. My login information so you can validate the transfer."

"No."

"Do it, Legs. Please."

"No. I'm tired of doing what you people want with no explanation. How do I know this is legal, or if you're scamming me—"

Oh god. Of course this is a scam. Of course it is. I look for video cameras and check if the webcam is on, but I don't think so. Could I be monitored from a cam in the beer-bottle window? Maybe. *This is all a scam.* No—I was in a musical. You don't do that, make that effort, when you're scamming someone. They loved me. They showed me love.

"Do it, Legs," he says with the same patience he told the Korean man, *silence.*

"Not until we discuss what happened out there. And you use my fucking name."

He says, "Turn over the second piece of paper. The one face-down on your right."

I glare in silence, but it's already obvious who will win this stare down. He's not even looking this way and he's winning the stare down. I have to obey. I snatch it loudly to communicate my displeasure. The document promises the transfer is legal. I am identified by name, excused from any accidental wrongdoing, and the document is notarized.

"Your copy. Everything is legal. We can verify through outside sources if you like. Email yourself an electronic copy."

"That doesn't mean this isn't a trick."

He's older, maybe fifties? Sixties? I can't tell. Love handles. If he's in his sixties, his ass looks better, rounder, than mine ever did. I fight my instinct to lust. I love eating ass, limited experience that I've had. His is amazing.

"Finish up, Legs. You get two minutes to email yourself, verify from outside sources. Then, we move to the fire."

I reread the disclaimer, verifying its legitimacy as much as I can. I guess I'll do this. This feels like an insane thing I'm doing, a money transfer between accounts unknown to me. But it's not even my bank, so I am risking nothing. I think. I would never do something like this, but I thought I was dying tonight, like, real death. Then I flew. I think my ability to discern what I should and should not do is broken.

The teapot screams its readiness. He completes his task while I complete mine. I transfer $2,823,419.22, just to be an ass. I hope I'm not committing a federal crime. I think he owes me a goddam explanation of this and so much more.

He arranges our beverages on a table between two leather chairs. I log out and attach my braces so I can join him there. The time it takes me to move ten feet is more than enough for him to nurture a small fire. He takes his time to settle in, as do I. My head is going to explode.

He blows on his tea. "You have questions."

"Many."

He sips.

Maddening as this is, I don't want to derail this long overdue explanation, now that he's finally ready. She'd screamed *I love you*. My eyes fill with tears. My skin tingles. How did he punch power into me? I know that's what he did. I feel it. How? Whose bank account was that? Who—why terrify me? Did they arrange that musical because of what I emailed Mai Kearns? Of course. Why didn't they—

"You're wondering how I met Vin Vanbly."

"No. Not at all. How did—"

"Where else would you meet a man like Vin?" The Butterfly King stares into orange flames. "In jail, of course. He was my cellmate."

EIGHT

THE WORLD IS too bright. Midtown is too bright. I'm tempted to stare right at the emerging sun. Instead, I glance at my empty plate. I don't remember the crusts. What time was breakfast, 4:30 a.m.?

We started out by the fire, then a few hours later he planted himself in front of the beer-bottle wall. Then window seats, facing Chelsea until breakfast. I stood at his side while he cooked our omelets with goat cheese. Four cups of coffee. I'm still exhausted. Lack of sleep, obviously, but more from the onslaught of storytelling, dragging me through New York. The sewers. The library. Waldorf Astoria and Vin's street pummeling. The long nights keeping vigil in the hospital.

He moved us all over the space throughout the night. Was there a deeper meaning to where and when, or was that one way to keep me awake? Every move, every gesture is layered. Considered. There must be a meaning to our every move. I am drunk, I think. On everything.

Rance says, "Vin honored his New York banishment. He stayed away two years. Actually, he stayed away a year longer."

"Why?"

"Because I broke his heart." He speaks with the same evenness he described his jailbreak. "I know this, because he broke mine."

We watch the sunrise.

It burns.

"More orange juice?"

"No."

"Hand me your plate."

The first words spoken in half an hour? Longer? I'm not afraid of silence with him. He is a man who gets silent. It's not an invitation for me to speak, it's silence. I *know* him. I listened to his raw heart all night. I don't know how often he shares his King Weekend with others, but this did not sound rehearsed. He got tense several times, and then he stopped speaking. He cried, describing Vin's limp hand, the long night praying for an awakening. The last twenty-four hours might be the most intimate relationship I've ever experienced, outside Margaret. Including Eric.

The sun bathes Midtown. I've never seen anything like this. This version of New York. This night in New York.

He returns, facing the city. "Twenty plus years since my King Weekend, and I remember everything. Vin's love is wildfire, a power touched once, maybe twice in your lifetime, if lucky. I do not wish for another King Weekend. But there are days when I miss the love we shared. Rarely have I been loved so desperately."

I perceive this new silence as an opening for questions.

"Would you have quit your King Weekend if you had known you were on it?"

"Absolutely. Within two hours. Maybe I wouldn't last twenty minutes, depending on how presumptuous and irritating he chose to be. After my kinging, I witnessed my shortcomings with a disquieting clarity. To this day, it grieves me Vin recognized the heart of a quitter. For a full year, I struggled with shame, mistrusting I was strong enough to remain a Found King. If Vin knew I couldn't surrender willingly, what right had I to be here?"

"Here?"

"Right here. This man." He gets quiet. Sips coffee. "Make no mistake. I love myself for what I endured. I am gentle with my heart and my choices. Still, Vin knew me better than I knew myself. I carry this burden of self-knowledge as best I am able. It humbles me with every remembrance. It reminds me to love those who quit in life."

I assumed strong men recognized their strength at all times. If I am honest, I resent Rance ruining my perfect image of him, strong. Confident. But isn't that what he fought for? The power to define himself beyond what others see? He stares at his city, the sun confirming today's authority. Even muffled by this distance, the day has begun its incessant honking, screeching. New York is gorgeous. How did I not understand this?

He says, "The temptation to quit will be strong."

"Did you ever forgive Vin?"

"Years later, a man I mentored decided to discard his life, his marriage, his two daughters. He fell victim to disappointment. He felt he didn't deserve their love, and he also felt he deserved better. To save him, I stripped his defenses. I wanted him to choose his future, knowing himself fully." He takes another sip. "He chose his wife. He's a better father now, too. He also finally pursues his lifelong dream. However, he ended our friendship the day he chose them. He hates me. I had five dozen cupcakes delivered to Vin the day after my mentee refused me, thanking him for his willingness to lose me in order to better love me."

"What about Vin's words outside the Met?"

Rance says, "I haven't seen Zacchaeus."

"Yeah. What did that mean?"

"Never found out."

"That's not satisfying."

"Some things remain mysteries."

Can I ask this? I have to. I must. "I don't mean to insult you, because I believe everything you told me is true. But you can understand how it's also hard to accept magic powers and ancient prophecy. Randomly blurting out Biblical names. You're smart as fuck. Sophisticated. Independently wealthy, I guess, though I still have no answer about that bank account thing and I'm waiting to be arrested by the FBI or something."

He chuckles.

"Yeah, I'm not...not exactly kidding. This has been a terrifying experience. I think."

"I apologize. I did not mean to laugh at your experience."

"Thank you. So, do you actually believe in this Lost and Founds thing about kings and an ancient tribe?"

"I do. This is not Vin's invention. He's not the only guide. A Found Queen in San Diego invented her own path. She learned the story as a child. Her technique is full immersion, like Vin's, but takes six months. She's in her seventies and each queening takes a lot from her. She hasn't done one in two years. Maybe three. She and Vin aren't the only two finders. The Lost and Founds has always lurked at the edges of humanity. Our numbers are growing."

This can't possibly be true.

"Daniel, the Great Remembering is upon us."

"Yeah, Mai mentioned that. What exactly happens during a Great Remembering?"

"When it begins, we shall see."

"When is that, exactly?"

"Pieces are moving into place. Kearns reaching out was significant. The psychic who scared Vin revealed a king with the initials DC was key to the Great Remembering. Everyone expects the first meeting between Mai Kearns and DC to reveal more about the Great Remembering."

"And?"

"They have not met."

"Why not?"

"They must meet organically, when life draws them together."

"Why?"

He stares at Midtown. "We submit to the unknowing directions."

"That's nuts. You know DC. You now know of Mai Kearns. Why not put them into a room together?"

"That's not how this works."

"Okay, well, that's just fucked up."

"Says the man who spent a month searching for an urban butterfly. The Lost and Founds' origins date back to humanity's origins. A riddle to be solved by humanity over many generations. It has been retold in many cultures, though sometimes only the echo of an echo survives. The love must flow organically, so pieces unlock of their own volition. If Vin outlined what he understands, organizing his knowledge into spreadsheets, new realities would never come to pass. Communication works differently with Found Ones. You kneel before your hated enemy, and a knife he swore to use against you now heals you. Ex-lovers who treat each other with respect open themselves and each other to greater love. After months of being annoyed by a flamboyant little twink, I told him my truth, that I was jealous of his vibrancy, and I wept for my own hardness. He cried with me. We remain close to this day. This is how our mosaic gets assembled. With love. Mai Kearns and DC will meet when it's time."

"Either one of them could be hit by a bus in the meantime."

"Yes."

"Why risk? Fuck organic. Fuck waiting. Get some answers."

"You believe love is passive, a fragile insect with shimmery wings, which if you're lucky, alights upon your sensitive skin. If this is how you conceive love, you misunderstand a Found King's love."

"Well, I guess I misunderstand. Because that made no sense."

Rance says, "Look at the stained glass."

I crane my neck, but I can't turn around enough in my chair. I can't even see the table.

"Come, let's go look."

Another goddamn move.

As we approach the window, he says, "Each bottle was cut by a man in recovery. Polished by a man in recovery. Welded together by men in recovery. Study them."

The sunlight hits it forcefully, pushing green, brown, clear and blue light into confusing blurs, soft yet unstoppable. Infused orange twists around green. The pattern emerges, but like the pulse last night, it's beyond comprehension. Through a few clear bottoms, direct sunlight touches the table in long tube rays. I could watch this for hours. The angles refract—it's more than it seems, but I can't tell what I'm seeing.

"Many come to witness this marvel, the light it bears. See the votive candles? Folks offer prayer to the light and prayers for the men who built it. They pray for strength in their own lives. The window has meaning because of those men, their promise. Is this stained glass magic? Or is the magic in those who repeat the story, honor the men? Do people create magic or does magic exist, waiting for an appreciative eye?"

The fuzziness of light is hypnotic. I don't think I understand a word he said.

"Why only men?"

Rance says, "The women wanted to create something different. They built a museum. Daniel, there are other prophecies in play. We believe a special king brings DC and Mai Kearns together. He may have been kinged as early as 1994 or as late as 2004. Probably not after 2005."

"Because of what happened to Vin?"

"What do you know?" His tone is sharp.

"Nothing. Only that King Weekends ended in 2005. Is Vin dead? I feel like someone would have told me that, if the guy I am questing after is dead. Is he dead?"

He studies me. "Don't worry about Vin. He's not part of this equation."

"What the fuck does that mean? Everyone says *he's the one*. Vin can make you a Found King. Is he in a coma?"

"No."

"Is he dead?"

"No." He pauses. "The King Weekends were difficult on him. Legs, we don't have much time. Let Vin Vanbly's business be his business. Log into the same bank account."

"Look. I'm not out of line asking questions about the big boss. I deserve an answer. Will I meet Vin? Also, I've experienced your great kindness and generosity to me, all night. I feel like I know you. In my heart. Obviously you're calling me *Legs* for a reason. Would you at least tell me why?"

He turns the computer to face me, presenting the bank's login. "In that nickname, I honor your strength. Why would you not wish to be honored?"

"Maybe you think you're flattering me or helping me grow, but it's not cool. It's pretty offensive, honestly. I don't like people thinking they can make me feel better if they show me tough love."

"I have no interest in making you feel better about yourself. That's your job. Not mine. My job is to recognize power when I see it. Call it out. Would you have me ignore yours?"

I scrutinize him in beer-bottle light. I hate him—this powerful man I greedily love—for trying to make me feel better about my shitty legs. He tilts his head, as if I've said something odd. I wouldn't be brimming with tears if I weren't so fucking exhausted. I can't even remember everything that happened to me since last night. She screamed *I love you*. He shoved me. I was so scared.

He sits. "Please. Log in."

Anything to get out of this moment.

My tears sizzle. I inherited my father's rage, smoldering and licking the edges of everything I do and feel. Sit here. Type this. You may ask no questions—okay, now ask *one* question. Shut up and listen. Why do they treat me this way? Why do I allow it?

To my surprise, I am greeted by the roly-poly zeroes, the same ones bouncing across the screen last night. They returned. The balance is $11 million dollars.

Rance says, "We honor the King of Bargains and his son, King Jamie the Dancer, by maintaining the balance, Aric's legacy to Vin. Any Found Ones named on this account—which means all of us—may withdraw money as needed. Someone, or multiple kings, will restore the balance within hours."

"Who did this since last night? Whose money?"

He leaves the table. "I don't know."

"That's a lot of money to replace overnight."

"Yes."

"How will you pay them back?"

"I won't. It doesn't matter. Money doesn't concern Found Ones. However, if someone withdraws more than $3 million, obviously they are in crisis. The phone calls begin, visits. It's not about money, but a king who might need help. Which is why I had you transfer a number under the threshold. Tea?"

He leaves.

Money always matters. It matters a great deal. What if my money runs out? Could I drag myself to a job every day? No. I'm not strong enough for that. All I have is my money.

When he speaks, it's into a cell phone. "Call five."

Uh oh. Now what?

"Send them up."

"Who's coming?"

"Legs, sit at that end. You're the guest of honor."

I have no more strength to argue or demand explanations, I just do what he wants. I hope that's a good enough defense if he just speed-dialed the FBI. But I don't think that. Do I? No. We cried together. I lower myself into the indicated chair. Wearing a bathrobe now, he sits at the head, like we're in a bad movie about rich divorce. Even as he sips, his gaze never leaves me.

The elevator *bings*.

A rumbling, a pack. Voices. I hear them long before I see anyone, voices arguing, laughing, shouting, sparring, loud men, turning the corner, ten or fifteen black men, pouring into the space, white men, too, two at least—oh! They're all over me, yelling, clapping me on the back, one man grabbing my hands and pumping violently, laughing and talking into my face, but I can't hear a single word for all the noise, everyone talking at once.

Someone shouts, "Legs!"

Other men laugh and shout back.

I am the star, everyone clamoring to touch me, say words at me they know I can't hear. For a second I catch the Butterfly King's regard, his hands folded under his chin, eyes fixated on me.

The elevator chimes, and another group comes around the corner.

Same as the first group, men clasp my shoulders, talking at me, and I catch the word "subway." A man sticks a finger in my ear, teasingly, and I bat it away, and other men laugh. Are these the bat men from last night?

The elevator *bings*. More arrivals.

One man leans close. "Hey man, where's the Chrysler Building?"

He's gone immediately, replaced by other talkers, other hands. Someone asked me directions to the Chrysler Building two weeks ago.

"Legs, you got no idea—"

"You had me running—"

The chaos grows, no end in sight as the laughing and talking gets louder, freer. One lighter-skinned man throws himself on the table, defeated. Everyone jeers while he pretends to be dead, until someone sticks a finger in his ear and he leaps up, laughing and chasing. A bony finger touches my ear, and I jerk away, finding myself laughing. This hilarious, loud insanity.

You're not supposed to touch an abuse victim like me, everyone knows that. I hate being touched. But this. This is weirdly okay. Never had friends tease me, not playfully, not like I'm one of the guys. Laugh at me? Yes. Humiliate me? Absolutely. But I'm never in on the joke. I am the joke. I am a minority right now, one of few white men present, though I see two Asians, neither of whom was Hausfrau. They are both laughing, smiling at me. How am I not the butt? Or maybe I am. But this feels different, so different. A man sits next to me and rests his arm on mine—how does that not drive me insane? I can't! Is this belonging? Is this what it feels like to belong?

"If I may."

Rance's voice slices the din.

Noise dies, but not the jubilant spirit. Men nod my way, grinning. One guy, sitting halfway down, gives me two thumbs-up. He bursts out laughing, so I laugh, too, though I don't know why. He's just so damn pleased, I ride his joy. The man next to him watches me in silence and a certain seriousness. I am shocked to recognize him. Thick eyebrows. Serious expression. He watched me with that same expression on the subway. What the hell is happening?

The Butterfly King holds an orange. All hands and arms disappear, giving him room on the table to roll it, like a bowling ball. Slowly, it approaches.

I stop it with my fingertips. Look up.

"I ask you to oblige me, Legs. Please. Peel that orange."

Men snicker. I see smiling faces, whispering, but nobody clarifies my assignment. He says, "If you please."

Reluctantly, I dig my fingers in, feeling that familiar citrus sting. Nobody speaks, making me even more nervous. Why does this feel stranger than logging into a stranger's bank account? I look for confirmation I'm doing this right. Rance is blank. Is this related to last night's oranges?

When finished, orange and peel are side by side. I tried to get off as many white stringy things as possible.

The Butterfly King asks, "Was that difficult?"

Men guffaw, then hide it.

"No."

I'm being set up.

"Could you peel my orange for me?" A man says, rolling his orange toward me. "Me next."

Eight, nine, *fifteen*, an uncountable number of oranges flood in my direction with jeering requests. Where were they hiding these? I join the laughter at this latest absurdity: me, the orange goalie, arms extended, stopping them from leaping over the table. One or two escape and are caught by sure hands. I can't stop laughing. What the hell?

"Legs."

When Rance speaks, silence reigns almost instantly. He leans forward. Every gesture creates an impact, as if he mastered nonverbals and added a few of his own. The man next to me rests a hand on my shoulder, as if we are buddies. It's unnerving.

He says, "How many older black women, do you suppose, ask white men on the subway to peel their orange?"

I peeled an orange for that lady on the subway.

Rance says, "Her name is Ms. Taylor. Her assignment was to start a conversation. She volunteered because she thought you might be lonely. Two things Ms. Taylor likes to do. Visit and cook."

I stare at the army of oranges. "You sent her?"

Rance says, "I sent dozens. Every man in this room spent time with you."

Over the growing ruckus, I hear phrases I recognize.

"Does this train stop in Times Square?"

"Change for a twenty?"

Rance says, "When you arrived, I assigned five men to follow you. Legs, you wore them the fuck out."

"Hells, yeah!"

The man who threw himself on the table, exhausted, does so again. Everyone laughs. He was one of the original five. A hand on my neck gives me a friendly squeeze.

"You forced us to create a surveillance system," the Butterfly King says and inclines his head. "Show him the clipboard."

It appears midway down the long table, handed man to man in my direction. A bunch of pages.

"Because so many people were needed, we had to double-up shifts, and create backup schedules. That's the check-in roster. We had trained the original five, but because of who you are, we were forced to create a twenty-four hour schedule and offer weekly trainings for new watchers."

It's handed to me. There are more than ten pages. Handwritten names, row after row. Times and locations, a section for notes. What I had for lunch. Someone named Max wrote that I seemed sad.

He says, "Nobody can believe your stamina, your determination. You hunted for butterflies before dawn and took cabs to the boroughs late the same night. You were killing us. And we are legion."

The men laugh and shout at me, and my head explodes. I was never alone.

Rance quiets them. "I did not choose your nickname. The community did. They began calling you this because you are an unstoppable force in a city of unstoppable people. You have no idea the respect you command. For weeks, people stopped me for the latest news. Where was Legs today? What did Legs see? Did he take the subway again? How late was Legs in the Bronx?"

One of the white guys says, "Bitch, you supposed to sleep at night."

Everyone laughs.

I wipe a sleeve across my face. Fuck it. I'm crying.

"You'll see Ms. Taylor's signature on page two. After you peeled her orange, she delivered homemade meals to me, twice a week, to pass along. She couldn't imagine you eating restaurant food for as long as you have, so she brought pot roast and glazed carrots, slathered in her homemade onion jam. Ham with scalloped potatoes. Chicken salad with big chunks of celery you could pick out, because growing up, her only sister didn't like celery, and she wanted to be accommodating in case you didn't either. Pork chops and—wasn't it pork chops the other night, Jarrod?"

The men turn toward Jarrod, a man with a light moustache, several grabbing his neck affectionately, tugging him close and shoving him away as he cheerfully swears it's no one's business.

Rance says, "Jarrod ate your dinners. Obviously, we couldn't give them to you. He volunteered. Ms. Taylor a good cook?"

"The best. I got no regrets. None."

His friends laugh, and I laugh too, thinking of him eating all those meals. I love this.

"With gratitude for your dinners, Jarrod will chauffer you for the remainder of your trip."

His friends shove him again, but he cries out, "No regrets."

My gut reaction is hurt, this hurts, because right away, I see in his expression this is not a punishment. It's not a *punishment* to be stuck with me. Why does that hurt so badly?

"Ms. Taylor would like you to join her tonight for dinner. Jarrod will accompany you and explain how he ate all her delicacies. She will not be pleased. Could be interesting."

"No regrets! But send help."

The laughing begins anew.

She made me dinners. She worried about me. I'm so fucking exhausted, yet so alive. So powerful and humbled at the same time. I was furious they didn't give me a sign, but I never looked behind me. I was trailing butterflies, every day.

"You are one stubborn son of a bitch, Legs. So many opportunities to find us. I own three Butterfly Florists. Men on the subway. Ms. Taylor. Hell, you even visited our Little League team in Brooklyn, the Butterfly Boys. If you'd talked to anyone that day, they could have told you there's a two-year waiting list to join our team. Young boys learn how to grow themselves into men they can live with. But you never talked, never engaged in any meaningful conversation. Had to do it all on your own, didn't you? Any man in this room know what it's like to make life harder for yourself? Insist on going alone?"

I hear it before seeing it, the closed fist each man thumps against his chest. I meet their gazes. Nobody's laughing now. I place trembling fingers over my eyes. All of me is dying and living, curling up into a small scared thing and simultaneously expanding, running, racing around New York City, chased by butterfly men. These sheets of paper are now sacred. I already know I will read each name, over and over. I will memorize each name. I already know.

When I emerge from behind my hands, they are watching me. I wipe my face. "I'm sorry."

"You really don't understand power, do you, Legs? You still believe crying is for the weak." Rance studies me. "Gentlemen, morning report."

Pansies secured. Daffodils from Pier Four. They speak in florist language, business code, deliveries, schedules, delivery van repair, and who covers what shifts.

"Who needs flowers today?"

Two different men list family names.

The Chrysler Building man says, "Anniversary of Mr. and Mrs. Catelli's daughter's death. Three years."

The Butterfly King tips his hand. "Bring me the card before you go."

Jarrod says, "Flowers tonight might help Ms. Taylor forgive me."

Men chuckle.

Rance looks at me. "I think Daniel ought to buy her flowers. She prefers pink roses. Speaking of which, two men break down Daniel's suite. He may want to sleep this afternoon. Scent is a powerful thing, Legs. Fucks up your sleep."

He used the flowers to ensure I'd arrive exhausted.

Rance says, "Who's light today—you two? Okay, you men go. Reuse whatever you can."

Numbers and quantities fly through the air, last-minute decisions for weddings and other coverage, trading recommendations on who should deliver to whom. They check in on loners. Families in crisis. They are currently brokering a reconciliation between a middle-aged brother and sister. Deliveries are a cover for their true agenda, which seems to be creating stronger community.

One or two of them nod when I catch their eyes.

The Butterfly King stands. "Abbreviated meeting. I've got to finish business here."

Chairs scrape, men stand, the conversation swells, less jocular, more shop talk than play.

Rance says, "Gentlemen. Say goodbye."

Immediately, they drop, all of them, landing on one knee, heads bowed. Like last night.

"Legs."

I raise my gaze.

Rance spreads his arms, indicating I should do likewise. "Show them respect. Let their blessing inside."

I mimic him, uncomfortable with this expansiveness. I'm dizzy, drunk. Their power, the gift of their combined power. I am lightheaded with orange mist and fuzzy light streaming through beer bottles. I feel unhinged from time and physical space, like nothing is real, nothing could possibly be real.

"Butterflies," says their king, "fly away. Fly away."

He hangs his robe and returns naked, carrying two items: folded white cloth and a rectangle the size of a check. Is it a check? He sits close, the stained glass behind him. Light flows over and around him, dressing him, making him part of the green-and-blue composition. Something's weird in the sunlight. I don't know. I don't care anymore, I'm so drunk on love.

He slides the white fabric to me. "A souvenir."

As I unfold it, I spit all over the polished table. *I (heart) New York* T-shirt. New York City, where I starred in a musical, while I thought I would die against a chain-link fence. Street crossing terror, every day. Ms. Taylor's pork chops. My hands are shaking. I will wear this. Because I fucking love this goddamn mess of a city.

He positions the second item before me. I was right. Bank check. It's worn from folding and unfolding. One million dollars, made out to Terrance Altham. A sticky note covers the signature.

"Is this the one from Vin?"

"Yes."

"You never cashed this?"

"No."

"It's a million dollars."

"Yes."

"You said you and your parents were barely scraping by, so much debt after your brother's death."

"Yes."

"But you didn't cash a million dollar check?"

"I didn't need Vin's money. I needed someone to believe in me, so I would believe it. Once kinged, money came easily. I kept the check for its sentimental value. Under the sticky note is Vin Vanbly's real, legal name."

Was that an invitation? I should grab it before he changes his mind.

"Your choice, Daniel, is to lift it and see Vin's true name or continue questing. Choose."

No-brainer. "I want to continue questing."

My breath catches. He just admitted the Found Ones are kinging me. I will admit it, too. I want them to king me, to love me, broken and useless thing that I am. I'm not useless! Goddamn it, I'm not. I need a minute behind my hands. *Pull your fucking shit together, man.* When I compose myself, the check is no longer on the table.

"Legs, in the middle of the night, you asked me what happened to Lost Kings. I do not know. In Mexico City you will find a king named John Robertson. Ask him. Jarred has a sealed envelope with John's contact information."

"What's John's king name?"

Rance frowns. "Organically, Legs. Knowing a man's king name means nothing unless you discern the power behind the name. You cannot discern the power blurting it out. If I did not share his king name, trust I did so for a reason. It all happens organically, or it never happens."

"Asking—"

"Exactly. Asking. Demanding answers instead of waiting to be invited. It's not a race. You're questing too quickly, too much hurry. King Weekend stories aren't meant to be gulped in rapid succession. You can, of course. That's a different thrill. Different experience. But do you know which you are? If not, you will lose your quest by trying to win."

"I'll do better."

Rance says, "Yes. You will. I'll help you. I command you to do nothing related to John or any kings for a full month. Don't open the envelope. No internet research on Perry or Mai or anyone related to The Lost and Founds. This includes researching the history of The Lost and Founds. Don't research Vin. Nothing. There are no clever loopholes here. Just my command."

No!

"I'm sorry. I'll slow down. But let me search."

"One full month."

"How about only—"

"One full month."

I don't know why I'm so terrified by this. Keep your voice calm. "To get a cheaper flight—"

"One full month."

"I've never been to Mexico."

"One full month."

Damn it, now I'm Hausfrau guy.

Rance collapses his fingers into a temple before his face. I am unable to break eye contact, overwhelmed by him, by hazy blues and greens, dotted with brown, diffused light bathing his nakedness.

"You will return to Ohio. You will digest your New York experience. Reflect on my King Weekend. We're monitoring your internet searches through an unconventional method, so don't try it. After one *full* month, if desired, continue questing and plan a trip to Mexico." His voice is brisk. "Do you have a passport?"

"Yes."

I never tell anyone that! Do not freak about them monitoring my internet searches. Stay calm. Maybe suggest a different compromise.

"Legs, do you know *why* I feel confident you will wait the full month?"

Before I can answer, Rance leaps up, knocking his chair over. I gasp at his full height. Behind him glows refractions of amber and orange, purple and blue, colors shifting in sunlight, wings contoured around his naked body.

He spreads his arms wide and shouts, "*Because nobody fucks with the Butterfly King.*"

I can wait a month.

NINE

THE AIRPORT CAB ride bewilders my New York eyes. Where the fuck is everybody? There are only eighty or ninety cars driving the highways. I can't process the lack of... everything. Wide-open space in every direction makes me feel wobbly inside, unsafe. The cab's speed feels reckless, and I fight panic. I've been in fast cars. New York is full of fast cars, but no open roads. This feels dangerous. I did not expect such a physical shock.

"You said you had three errands downtown. Where to first?"

"Oshman Deli, over on Seventh."

My driver flicks his acknowledgement.

I should go straight home and unpack. I can just order food online. But I want to be downtown. I need to see my city. The downtown skyscrapers have so much space between them, I'm almost offended. Look at all that air! It's like seeing a half-packed subway car. Crowd together, buildings. Be efficient. Why isn't all this open space relaxing me? I was so eager to escape New York.

Where are all the people?

A sunny day, blue skies. Wide, downtown sidewalks, shops, pretty fountains. Lots of green trees and colorful blooms. Where are the thousands, the never-ending ocean, each bobbing head a new wave to be navigated? New York crowds appear and disappear, phantoms in my periphery. What is this—thirty? Forty people wandering out here? I've been assaulted by thousands upon thousands for the past month, pushing, pounding, demanding, angling, swearing as they stumble around me. Where is everybody? This is freaking me out.

On the plus side, I can't believe I ever felt intimidated walking down Fourth Street with this much goddamn space. This is me *strolling*, during which, I look up. Ha. I'm looking up! The cabbie thinks I'm insane, out for a stroll while he drives around the block with my luggage and purchases. I had to walk. So much sky, stretching blue for miles in every direction, all that untapped real estate. Why have I never noticed the richness of the sky?

Eric, check it out. I'm looking up.

Once the cab turns onto my street, I feel renewed panic. There's literally nobody on the sidewalks at this moment. Nobody. I've lived here for the past ten years and never questioned the open spaces. I didn't realize how that much time in claustrophobic New York would impact me—the people, the cars, the constant noise. My neighborhood feels abandoned. I almost want to scream, so someone looks out their damn window. How did New York get so far under my skin? Next time, I'll—Ha. Not even home from the airport, and I'm planning the next trip. This is crazy.

Here we are.

I'm home.

Whoa—the yard is ripped to hell, a landscaping frenzy. I'm surprised the cheap-ass landlord would pay for this much improvement. Probably going to sell the building. Giant dirt piles spilling onto the sidewalk and shovel handles I must step over. I could stumble. Compared to New York? This is nothing. I can't even work up an irritation. I want to laugh so hard, so ridiculously hard. Could a shovel bother me after what I went through? This lightheartedness, where is this coming from?

"If you're willing, I'd like help with my bags. I live on the second floor."

The cab driver grouses, a constipated expression. What can he do, say no to the crippled guy? I don't even mind his attitude. When he meets me at the trunk, I hand him the tip. It's big.

"Thank you," he says with surprise.

"No, thank you. I couldn't manage this without you."

He trudges ahead, balancing my bags.

A month ago, I would have felt guilty about asking, guilty for his obvious frustration when I asked. But fuck him, in the kindest way possible. This man's scowl is nothing compared to a horde of irritated New Yorkers. I grin. New York, it turns out, is the best fucking therapy I've ever done.

After putting away my purchases, I call her. I can unpack later. She picks up on the second ring.

"Hello, ma'am, it's Daniel. I did a few errands before coming home from the airport, so I just walked in the door. ... No, not at all. It's nice you wanted me to call. Did you decide to visit your sister tomorrow?"

Ms. Taylor begins what I assume will be a lengthy explanation.

I can't stop grinning.

The temptation is stronger than I anticipated.

But I can't.

Rance said they track my search history, but that was a bluff. Definitely. They can't hack my computer web searches. Can they? I can't even google whether that's feasible. I haven't downloaded anything that could be considered spyware. Would they go that far? Doesn't matter. To become a Found King, I can't cheat. I can't. What the fuck am I going to do for the next month? I have to finish reading these goddamn books I keep buying. Goddamn books.

I remember Jarrod pointing at tourists crossing against the green. Since I was closer, he said, "Yell at them, will ya?" I screamed out my passenger window, "Watch the goddamn traffic lights!" Jarrod smirked. "Mr. New York."

I didn't realize I'd spend this month shining floodlights on every minute spent there. Jarrod pointing out landmarks from his upbringing. Me, sweating on the subway, complaining to myself, growling at other people. Now I study the clipboard list of names every day, trying to remember faces based on the comments they made. Who looked at me and smiled. Can I email Jarrod? Rance didn't expressly forbid contact. He's like Ms. Taylor, a friend beyond the kings. But is he? I'm not sure. If Jarrod emails first, I'll reply. That's cool. I better not initiate contact this first month. Follow the rules, the spirit of the rules.

They're kinging me.
They're *kinging* me.

From my window, I see the Mexican landscapers digging and hauling dirt. The whole crew is here today. Where do they go for days at a time—shorter jobs? They haven't been here in three days. They're yelling in Spanish, ripping out the chain-link. No fenced yard for the next week, if they stick to the updated schedule. Who knows when they'll actually finish, they're gone so often. That older man seems so disconnected from the others, I question whether he's following the plan. Why do they leave him here working alone for days at a time? Now that I'm avoiding the internet, the backyard is my favorite YouTube channel. This is so much harder than I thought. I want to learn about the Butterfly Boys. Three flower shops! Now that I know who and what to google, I can't. I don't even dare google Ms. Taylor, because that might be considered cheating. I'm assuming she has no online presence. She doesn't own a computer.

I will learn to use my wok. Read a ton of books or throw them away. For real. My hallway closet is stuffed with hobbies that never stuck: watercolor painting, chess, and consoles from my gamer phase. I think there's a goddamn hook rug in there somewhere. I'll clean my storage unit in the basement. After three weeks hustling around New York, this inactivity in my apartment is killing me. I need to get moving. Should go for a walk. I'm not someone who goes for walks. Well, I wasn't.

Only twenty-three more days until I can buy a ticket to Mexico.

Twenty-three days.

There!

I see enough backyard from my living room window to spy an aluminum ladder flat against the ground, the older Mexican guy sprawled next to it. That was a big fucking crash. Holy fucking shit was that loud! He's not moving. And he's alone today.

"Hey! HEY."

He's still not moving. Shit.

I gotta move fast. I march down the hallway as if fighting New York crowds. Back stairs are nothing compared to slippery subway steps, so I descend with reckless speed. Is he dead? Should I have called 911 first? I didn't hear him scream. It's a stepladder, not a roof ladder. He'll be okay. Jesus, why did I insist on a second-floor apartment?

Fucking hurry.

I told myself I could handle a second-floor apartment. Was that me being stubborn, insisting I could handle it? Rance was right. I make life harder for myself. Stop thinking about myself! Focus on the dead landscaper. *He's not dead.* What if he's bleeding? Thank god, I have my phone in my pocket. Can't call 911 until I know what's wrong. Final few stairs. Maybe he's okay.

Throw open the back door, push myself to the stoop.

Oh thank god.

He's alive. He's sitting up, rubbing his arm, checking for broken bones. When he notices me, he glances toward the building.

"Are you okay? I heard you fall."

"No hablo inglés."

I take deep breaths. He's okay. Not as old as I thought. Fifties? Not sixties.

"Are you... are you hurt? *Hurt?*"

He points at the ladder, toward the middle, which I take to mean he wasn't standing on top. "*Me preocupa que yo esté sangrando. ¿Hay sangre atrás en mi cabeza?*"

"No hablo español."

He seems disappointed. "*Maldito.*"

He lurches up, and after confirming his balance, turns around. Points to the back of his head. I think he wants me to check for blood. Can't see any. It would be hard to see blood against hair this dark, but there's enough gray at least red would show. Looks okay. He faces me and I notice his rich brown skin bears the sun's wear and tear. Watching me shake my head "no" repeatedly, he seems relieved.

"No blood."

I'm not sure he understands, so I mime blood and then shake my head hard from side to side. What exactly is my responsibility here? Who do I call? The landlord? How do I reach his crew? I want to offer him my cell, but I'd have to sit to free it from my pocket. He touches the back of his head gingerly.

"Do you want... agua? Agua?" Hollow offer. How the hell would I carry water down a flight of stairs?

"Agua," he says, pointing to a cooler.

He touches his side, probing carefully. Maybe he broke a rib. I don't know. This is weird. Do I leave him? He seems sheepish now, nodding.

"*Una mujer se acercó a la ventana para asegurarse que yo estaba bien. Pero no salió afuera como lo hiciste tú. Muchísimas gracias.*"

I understood *gracias*. "De nada."

In response to his hopeful eyebrows, I say, "No, that's it. No hablo español. Sorry."

He points to the cooler next to the new privacy fence. On his way to it, he limps. Not a heavy limp, not from today's accident, I don't think. I'll stay with him a few minutes. Make sure he doesn't pass out. A few feet away, we pass a smashed planter, ceramic shards. Ah. That's what brought me to the window.

He offers me water. His hands communicate he wants me to sit.

"*Insisto que te sientes y te relajes.*"

I hate this. Like I'm fucking tired all the time. C'mon. He means no offense. Respect his kindness. On a New York sign-in sheet, one person wrote, *Offered Daniel a seat. Declined.* I probably said "No" with ice-cold politeness to a butterfly trying to love me. Could this Mexican gardener be my one true king? I have to think of people differently.

I sit.

He relaxes.

I drink.

He explains the landscaping to me, mostly in Spanish, occasionally miming the plant shapes soon to be here. He knows a collection of English words. He walks to a big hole and says, "Tree."

Yup. I figured that out. Big hole.

He makes violence with his hands.

I don't want to play this air Pictionary. Okay. He's drawing the tree with little finger bursts.

"Autumn? Red trees in autumn?"

"Sí. Autumn. *Otoño.*"

I'll stay twenty minutes. Make sure he doesn't have a concussion.

I find a smallish, terracotta planter outside my front door with a red geranium. A folded slip of lined paper under the bottom has a single word.

Gracias.

She screams, *I love you*!

I bolt to sitting, jerking myself from sleep. My chest heaves. I'm awake. Normally, I scream myself awake after an abuse nightmare. Dad was in ecstasy when I screamed. I didn't scream, not this dream. Before I could, she did. She screamed, "I love you." The fire escape woman wasn't physically in my nightmare—I don't remember any visuals. Just her words.

Breathe.

Take deep breaths.

Fourth time this has happened. *Fourth*. I look around to steady myself. Plaid drapes. Rubber flooring. Last night's milk glass, Jefferson's biography, my cell phone. It's 6:30 a.m. Clothes where I left them, crumpled in the open drawer. I'm okay. I've got to keep looking around. Ground me.

It's over.

I can breathe again.

Nightmares are nothing new, but now she screams. Her pitch, the sharpness, slashes through, ripping open an escape hatch. She frees me before I start to scream.

I don't understand. Did they plan this? Are they rewiring my goddamn nightmares? When she screams, I wake. I'm free. Is this possible? This was the fourth goddam time! This can't be random. Oh god. I'm finally admitting it. It sounds batshit crazy to consider they could penetrate my personal nightmares. But it's happening. The Found Kings are reshaping my nightmares. I bawl into my hands, sobbing uncontrollably.

There is a place for me beyond nightmares.

I can't discuss this development with Ms. Taylor.

Maybe I could, though. Rance said I was free to pursue a friendship with her. Anyway, she prefers to do most of the talking. She asks about my life, mostly what I cook. Recipe details. She wants to know about Columbus. Living outside New York City, I'm like a Martian to her. I don't think we're reveal-your-nightmares buddies, maybe not ever. I don't mind. She never asks about my legs. I don't think she's particularly waiting for me to raise the topic. She's got plenty to discuss. Newspapers. Neighbors. Her sister. She was mad at Obama last time we spoke, though that will pass in a day. She loves him. She loves Michelle more. My first friend is a talker.

Not counting Rance, Jarrod, or any other New Yorkers, my second friend doesn't speak English. Well, *friend* until the landscaping finishes. I guess we won't keep in touch, considering we can't communicate. I'm embarrassed to remember contemplating sucking Horatio's dick for a hot ten minutes before we became friends. Why did I think that? Bored and horny, I guess. Handsome for a guy in his fifties. Good build. Maybe even muscular. Hard to tell under that beige jumpsuit he wears every day. Could be a good porno. The Mexican landscaper and the lonely apartment dweller.

Sexual designs faded when I saw him chewed out by the foreman, Young Buck. That guy, I'd suck off in a New York minute. Sculpted, hairless, muscles hard and rippling. I ignored Young Buck while he dressed down Horatio. I pretended to be fascinated by something on my phone. I couldn't discreetly slip away from the backyard bench; my clumsy draggings always attract attention. Ten minutes after, when Young Buck asked in an irritated way if Horatio was creeping me out, I was surprised by his hostility. He explained Horatio was the owner's brother, and they couldn't get rid of him. Young Buck said, "Let me know if he's a problem." I wish I had barked, "How the fuck could I? You're never here." Horatio does the day-to-day work. He might move slower, but he's attentive to small details and takes minimal breaks. Plus, his half hour nap over lunch. Why is Young Buck an ass to the one guy working consistently? I assume Horatio gets assigned low-priority jobs.

Seemed tacky to think of sucking his cock after witnessing that scolding. Two days later, Horatio pointed at my legs and drew a question mark in the air. I shook my head and said, "No. Por favor." He agreed. We navigated those waters better than I do with people who speak English.

Why do I have to keep retelling everyone? I spoke at a graduate level psychology class a few years ago because Margaret assured me it would be healing. *Which hurt worse, the cuttings or burns? Could you describe the pain on a scale from one to ten? What behavioral triggers did you notice before each event?* It was not healing.

We are all fucked up. Just because I wear my fucked-uppedness externally doesn't mean I owe the world an explanation. Still, I was surprised I did not mind Horatio's curiosity the other day. I have a new respect for curiosity. Doesn't matter. I could tell him the whole story, and he'd never understand a word.

Wait, wait, wait. He'd never understand a single word.

Think this through.

Could I tell him the latest revelation? I haven't told anyone about the nightmares, how she screams. Who would I tell? Nobody. And now, this latest discovery. Could I *tell* Horatio?

I can't tell Margaret without revealing, well, everything. I'm not ready to explain New York City, not the truth. Though, she sees a change in me. We've discussed my confidence.

Horatio told me a story the other day, lasted three or four minutes, and I understood nothing. I think he wanted to hear himself speak. I get that. After days of speaking to no one but UPS and food delivery people, you need to hear your own voice. Make sure you're still alive.

Think this through.

Don't rush into anything.

But this isn't random. They know about thirty-two.

Am I doing this? Today? I have to decide.

They're close to finished. The landlord and Young Buck walked the property yesterday, admiring the fence's stain, the rock formation with corkscrew vines cascading, a gurgling spring of green. Horatio will move on. Probably early next week, if the crew assists. Flower boxes remain empty. Impatiens need planting. Sod's finished, and the watering system is hooked up. Horatio showed me. I have to decide. Do I tell him? I've been considering this for two days. Running out of time.

Horatio pokes his head around the side of the building and gives me a nod. "*Cinco minutos.*"

"No worries. Take your time."

I reposition myself on the bench. I am definitely hanging out back here even after he's gone. It's lovely. I watch the underside of his boots, his ass in the air, as he finishes planting his current tray. I still don't know why he limps, but if I want him to not ask about my legs, hardly seems fair I should ask about his.

The designer did a good job, this combination of bushes and trees. A lovely sitting area near a brick grilling area, and a few tables in case you wanted to entertain. It's very welcoming. This backyard is no longer a thing to be navigated, but a destination. Raised vegetable beds for residents who like gardening. Everyone likes it, just fine. We discuss it. But nobody knows what's happening with the building sale.

He sits with a slight grimace, which I assume means back problems. He signaled *bad back* last week. In silence, we watch Ohio's version of spring.

Can I do this?

No. Too weird.

Horatio points at a bird, leaping from a twig. "*Tordo.*"

I'll look it up later.

I point at the impatiens. "Algeria."

He says, "Impatiens."

Like every bench break, this one ends with words traded, but no conversation having taken place. I thought about pushing for helpful Spanish words for my upcoming trip, but this is Horatio's downtime. Besides, what word could prepare me for what's ahead? Could anything have prepared me for New York? How do you prepare for your kinging? Is Vin going to king me?

Horatio points again. "Tordo."

I repeat it. Strap on my canes. I try to give him a few break minutes alone.

I blew it. Fucked up an opportunity—an extremely safe opportunity—to share my heart. It's not about whether he understands. It's about whether I demonstrate courage. Today, I did not. So, am I worthy of their kingship, whatever that means? How have I proven myself, besides surviving childhood? Tomorrow. I'll be a better king tomorrow.

So many regrets.

Staring at the ceiling waiting for the sun to come up. I betrayed you, Frank. I'm not worthy of kingship. Not ever. How could I think I ever would be? New York forced me to look up, focus on people. How they move. The dangers. I know I fixate too much on the horrors. I mean, I've got plenty of horror for fixation, but perhaps I see no future for myself because I refuse to stop staring at my past.

A month in New York made me philosophical.

They're kinging me.

Why?

They know about Frank. They know I'm a monster. How can they justify this?

I have to tell Horatio. Today. On morning break.

It's 4:30 a.m.

I hate dawn but I hate the night worse.

I'm sorry, Frank.

Today is like yesterday, gray clouds not blanketing the sky but enough to battle the blue. Blue is losing. It's chillier today, which is fine. Whatever. Fear is making me colder than the actual weather.

Young Buck and his crew remain absent. Horatio plants impatiens. The flatbed of his truck has several more trays, pinks and whites. In July, they'll cover everything.

"Hi, Daniel."

I didn't hear the back door open. "Hey, Janelle. Any new sale gossip?"

She smiles. "No more updates. Jeff was going to call their offices. I'll let you know if I hear anything."

"Thanks."

"Sure."

Jesus, I didn't even think about people from the building coming through the yard as I'm telling this story. If I—no. I have to.

When Horatio returns to the truck, I see a flicker of mild surprise. I'm here earlier than usual. He sits and exchanges the pleasantries we know.

I spy a flitting bird and point. "Thrush."

He says, "Thrush."

"Yes. Tordo is thrush."

Horatio says, "Thank you, Daniel."

We lapse into familiar silence.

I'm not ready to speak, but the end of Horatio's time is near, and my throat is thick with panic.

Now or never.

Now or never.

"I want to tell you."

I want to vomit. Am I really doing this? I refuse to meet his eyes, so I stare at the new maple.

"My father was a doctor. While I was growing up, he tortured me. Always in the garage. He knew exactly where to make cuts. He knew where to inflict burns without them showing. He saved breaks for special occasions, a few years apart, so as not to draw suspicion."

Outside of therapy and the disastrous psych class, I've never discussed this. I can't believe the abuse is only the prelude to what happened in New York. 7-16-32. They're kinging me.

"When I was sixteen, he lost control. He backed over my legs with a station wagon. Twice. His story was Mom did it by accident, but the police figured it out immediately. For years, I assumed I would die in that garage. I accepted it as a fact. I decided my revenge would be to leave behind proof of my murder. I smeared drops of my blood over everything. The handles of rakes and yard tools. The underside of his workbench. So much blood under that bench. The electrical cord of every power tool. Not enough for him to see or clean. I had watched cop shows. I knew they had special lights to spot it. After the station wagon, I told the police about my blood. They found more than a hundred samples, dating years back. Dad went to prison. Don't know what happened to Mom. I'll never see either one of those monsters again."

My voice shakes. Horatio remains quiet. He knows this is hard for me, even if he doesn't understand the words.

"I needed money for surgeries and to live on my own. Found a lawyer. We sued dad's insurance company for malpractice because dad was my personal physician, which made him professionally responsible for my well-being, regardless of his status as world's worst father. I sued for $25 million. My lawyer promised we'd never win that much, but he insisted we demand big."

Keep it together.

"Whenever we appeared in court, my lawyer wanted me to play the victim, demanding I look as weak as possible. I was in a wheelchair at the time, which helped. He hired a nurse to push me. I hated that. He often scolded me because my angry demeanor wasn't increasing sympathy with the jurors. He'd yell, 'Do you *want* to win this case? Do you?' I hated him. You know what I wanted? To run. I'd already seen enough specialists to know I'd never run, let alone walk. I mean, I get by. But I'll never walk without canes."

Don't look at him. Don't make eye contact.

"The lawyers battled daily over the definition of abuse and what should be allowed as evidence. My father had already been convicted, but the money awarded me from the civil case depended on quantity and severity of abuse. Was dragging me to the garage by my arm abuse? No, because it didn't leave a mark. But this arm grabbing, six months later, *was* abuse, because he ripped my shirt. Or did he? Was the shirt already ripped? Could the ripped shirt be presented as evidence? No? Their experts reviewed the x-rays of my broken arms, arguing I may have done it to myself, trying to escape. They conceded abuse on many occasions, but my mental state made me accident-prone, so maybe these permanent scars resulted from my own clumsiness. I had to listen to their lawyer team argue I *fucking wanted it*, deep down. After each day in court, my lawyer berated me. He had sunk a lot of time into my case and worried it wouldn't pay off. He wanted a makeup artist to make me paler. More sallow. I refused."

Gray clouds are now losing to the crisp blue sky. Sunlight reflects against upstairs windows and sprinkling the impatiens in trays, ready for planting. The day is turning beautiful. I take more breaths. I've only told Margaret about this next part. When she returns to it, I get agitated. I can't discuss it for more than a few short minutes.

What would you risk to find a lost king?

"On July sixteenth, 1994, my father threatened me with his gun. He made me choose who got shot, me or my dog, Frank. About two months earlier, he made me put my mouth around the barrel and sing 'The Star Spangled Banner.' He said he'd blow my head off if I screwed up the words. On the sixteenth, he promised one of us would die. He made me choose. I chose Frank."

I hate myself. I fucking hate myself.

"Their lawyers argued I wasn't abused in that incident, only the dog. My lawyer screamed it was the most insane form of emotional abuse. For an hour they argued semantics, trying to prove the dog's owner was technically my father, and therefore his property to kill. My lawyer argued the dog was a gift, thus mine. They argued the dollar amount on emotional damages. The judge kept yelling at them to quit associating dollar amounts. This was the thirty-second incident called into question."

Do this. Tell this.

"I flipped out. I started screaming, 'Does it matter? Thirty-one or thirty-two, does it fucking matter?' I started bawling. I screamed, 'We concede. We concede! Stop talking about it.' I collapsed on the table. I couldn't stop weeping. I felt so humiliated."

Frank, I'm so sorry!

Don't start crying. Don't start. I'll never stop.

Horatio puts his hand on my shoulder. It calms me.

"The judge ordered a recess. Jurors were escorted out. Every day, I tried to prove I was strong, not some weakling who deserved it. I never showed weakness. That day, I lost it. I had betrayed my only childhood friend a second time. My choice killed him. Years later, I denied the incident was even important. Frank was my only friend."

Listening to the words leave me, I find myself surprisingly lighter. The worst is over. Why was that so hard to speak? I think about Frank daily. Relive that day. Relive the court day. On my darkest days, I feel Frank's breath, his excited panting. I know he didn't get a full life, and it was my fault.

"My lawyer praised me for my masterful performance. He was giddy. He promised my breakdown was even better, more heartbreaking, given my chilly courtroom presence. While he danced around me, spouting excited settlement figures, I cried harder.

"They settled for $20 million in addition to all court costs and lawyer fees. I won the money by betraying my only friend. Again. The lawsuit money is poison. I hate it, but I kept it."

I stare at the maple tree until I can speak.

"Since returning home, I've been reliving every minute of my month in New York. That padlock combination was 7-16-32. On July sixteenth, the lawyers argued over the thirty-second instance of abuse, which I conceded was not abuse. I think—"

Don't lose it. Don't lose it.

"I think the Found Kings were communicating they believe my version. The thirty-second incident mattered. They read the court transcripts. They're telling me they believe in me. They think Frank mattered."

Keep it together.

I focus on a tordo in the tree. The sunlight grows stronger. The coldness in my lower back, the adrenaline leaving me. Eventually, Horatio stands and looks me in the eye, confirming it's okay to leave.

"*Te compadezco que algo te causa tanto dolor.*" His tone is sorrowful.

I wait a few minutes and then drag myself upstairs.

Although it's only 11:00 a.m., I crawl into bed.

I'm sorry, Frank. I'm so sorry.

When I come home from shopping, I'm horrified to see the flowerboxes in front stuffed full of pink geraniums. Everything planted, watered and green. No way Horatio finished on his own.

Shit, they finished!

I race around the side. Everything's picked up! Nothing left to be planted! Shit. Fuck. I lost my chance to say goodbye. I went shopping this morning to avoid him, to avoid facing what I shared yesterday. I didn't think they'd finish today. He's gone. My friend is gone.

The name of the landscaping company was By Design. I could hunt him down... but why? For what purpose? Even if I found the crew, what would I say? Thanks for listening? Thanks for sharing cookies on a bench with me? Would I trust Young Buck to translate my words? He hates Horatio. Fuck it, it's too late. My friend is gone.

I never said goodbye.

A night of contemplation didn't give me any resolution. Do I track him down? Why? I will shake this morning fog with caffeine from the coffeehouse. Prior to New York, I would never walk there. It's seven blocks. Too far. But now? I walk anywhere. Through my building's glass front door, I see blue skies. This sucks. What exactly would I say beyond *goodbye*? Let's keep in touch? How?

Outside, a woman walks her dog. The empty streets seem normal again. Blue sky looks normal again. New York is over. The month of waiting is almost over.

On the front cement stoop, I spot a terra cotta planter with a single pink geranium, not here yesterday. Tucked under the bottom is a scrap of lined paper. On the paper is written one of the few Spanish words I knew before I met Horatio.

Amigos.

TEN

HOW MUCH LONGER can I nurse this Sam Adams? I should buy a third. Nah. They could announce the plane's departure at any moment. When they said we'd leave "within the hour," they technically didn't lie, because they never clarified which hour. It's been three.

It's hard to catch the bartender's eye.

I imagine John Robertson's been told I'm coming, but nobody said when I would show. If he were Mexican, his name would be Juan. Google Maps' street view reveals a completely ordinary building next to a 7-Eleven. The faded pink exterior suggests nothing exotic, just gritty, crumbling cement. If not for a blurry red sign with fading letters, I would assume it's a residence. The Found Ones are sending me to a Mexican bar. They cannot blame me for googling this. I did as commanded, waited a full month, plus an extra two days.

The bartender flicks me a nod.

Why not? "Yeah. Another one of these."

He fills someone's wine glass, and another, then throws together another three or four drinks. He's fast. So many of us, drinking impatiently. Maybe plane delays make for a good tip day, but is it worth all the impatient people?

If this guy isn't Mexican, why Mexico? Why send me to a bar? My new mantra: 7-16-32. We believe you. Do I also believe in me? I'm trying. I'm trying to look up, Eric.

When the bartender delivers, I toast Eric.

Drinking alone at an airport bar seems the perfect place to reminisce about the only man I dated. I demanded he owed me another chance. I even said, "I'm damaged goods." Eric said, "Aren't we all?" He said it wasn't the responsibility of the three-week boyfriend to fix me. That was my job, and in thirty years, if I hadn't given it much thought, why should he assume that burden? Touché but *ow*.

What I hate remembering is how I played the one miserable card in my possession, the "I'm weak" card. Eric refused it. He treated me as an equal. Maybe others tried? Maybe I ignored their attempts. I don't know. Since New York, I find myself revisiting past opportunities, wondering if I was so busy looking down, I let something important slip.

Though we haven't talked in years, I feel an urge to call him, pretending I'm now whimsical and free-spirited. I could explain my grand Mexican adventure, chasing a fairy tale after spending a month in New York. I know it's a bad idea. We didn't date long enough to fall in love or become significant to each other. The only reason Eric means so much to me is because I've never dated anyone else.

Announcement.

That's our flight. Same thing they said earlier, mechanical problems.... Well, shit. Flight canceled. They'd be delighted to fly us to Mexico tomorrow.

Damn.

A collective groan rises from the gate area, echoed by the bar crowd. An instant mob swarms the counter, demanding hotel vouchers and speedy rescheduling. I hear yelling. I could never demand my rightful place in a mob. I'd never make it to the counter, even standing three feet away. There are many races in life I will never win.

My fellow drinkers crowd the bar, eager for the young bartender's attention. The handsome man I've observed along the bar's curve grimaces. Even with today's disappointment on his face, he's still got a sexy businessman vibe. Forties? Sharp tie. Suit might be expensive. I don't know about such things. Like the others, the businessman motions for his bill, not as quickly as a woman, smeared with aggressive blue eyeshadow, snapping her fingers, miming writing.

"Hey," she says. "Cash out."

Jesus, he gets it. Everybody wants their bill.

Into her cell, she says, "Well, how many extra miles for this catastrophe? I expect to be compensated."

Everyone within a ten-foot radius hears her sharpness. I'm not happy with the airline either, but damn, lighten up. I've waited a month to continue my quest, and I'm keeping my shit together, lady.

The businessman shoots me amused chagrin, dipping his head toward her in a split-second "Can you imagine?" look. I chuckle. Shake my head. I like that he noticed me.

She disappears into the angry throng.

The businessman passes me, saying, "Cheers."

Cheers.

I guess I'm spending the night in Phoenix.

Definitely a step down from the Belleclaire. That was a gorgeous hotel. This place is pleasant, exactly what you'd expect in an overnight stay paid for by the airline. Pleasantness. The lobby attempts sophistication on a limited budget. The faux-wooden floor is durable enough to absorb the scuffs of a thousand travelers. I shouldn't complain. It's not slippery, my rubber-tipped canes grabbing traction easily. I don't have to stare down with every step. That's something. The bar area looks... pleasant.

Funny how my brain has already rewritten New York. I crawled into the Belleclaire's king bed night after night, hating that I was the celebrity cripple in the penthouse. I regularly woke in the middle of the night, terrified by a chorus of honking and screaming ambulances. Did I ever sleep well there? Not until the last two nights. Most mornings, I woke desperate, knowing I'd repeat fruitless searches all over again. Until one day it wasn't fruitless.

I have to laugh at my idiot self. The Belleclaire was lovely! New York was amazing! I feel glowing affection for each of those wasted days. Butterflies chased me every single day, even when I could do nothing but look down. I was never alone. I've rewritten New York better than Shakespeare could have.

As expected, plenty of bar stools are available. Ten people in the bar? A dozen? I prefer stools—easier to climb than chairs.

Can I do that with my whole life? Can I rewrite a life I hate, like replacing miserable New York in favor of amazing New York? Is it possible? I'll never *fondly* recall my childhood. But what if... what if one day I wasn't obsessed with my past? What if I were so ridiculously happy with my present tense, I could unhate? Is that like unkneeling?

This place is similar to the airport bar. Both offer bland décor, inviting you to stay for a drink but not too long. Low-hanging amber lights attempt to convey a cozy, intimate environment, but they're so bright, the effect is squandered. I recognize three drinkers from the airport. We must be the hardcore crowd. I'm not here for the drinks. I came for company. Maybe I'll talk to someone tonight. Me, out in public looking for conversation! I'll never understand how New York City rewrote me so thoroughly.

Don't lie. You know how. They knelt on one knee, clutching the bats and oranges while I gasped for breath in a throne of arms.

Lisa the bartender hails me with a pleasant, three-star greeting. I wonder if she's really a Lisa or if this is a Debbie-not-Debbie situation. Probably a Lisa.

"Pinot noir, please."

She says, "We offer several—"

"Anything. Pick one that people like."

I hope I wasn't snappish. I gotta shake this off. I'm still irked, thinking about the rebooking agent. She offered me an earlier flight tomorrow if I was willing to accept coach. I said, "I only fly first class." My response was too vehement. I'd sounded like some rich bitch. I should have explained I can't drag my legs back to coach. The aisles are too narrow. On the other hand, I shouldn't have to explain my damaged legs. I spend my whole life wondering how much to explain and to whom. I have to let go.

"Oi, mate, you missed your friend."

I lean forward to spy the sexy businessman from the airport bar, the man who said "Cheers." I didn't recognize him without his suit. He's my age or older, copper-colored hair closely cut, longer in front. His ears stick out, which I didn't notice earlier. I like his ears. They're cute. Was he talking to me? The other nearby guy is absorbed in his Sudoku. Businessman is looking at me. He meant me.

"What friend?"

He snaps his fingers and scribbles furiously in the air with an imaginary pen. "She left a while ago, yeah? Complained our Lisa watered down her drink."

"We do not water drinks," Lisa says with an edge of defiance.

"No, no, lovely. She'd lost the plot. Total knob. Knobette." The Brit raises his glass. "Cheers to awful customers."

Lisa is too professional to encourage this Brit's toast, but she pours him a refill, her subtle expression of approval. This makes me chuckle. It seems the airport lady leaves an impression on everyone. More importantly, he's talking to me. What do I do? I want to prolong his observation into a conversation. Having a friendship with Ms. Taylor has emboldened me. "I suspect she's rarely wrong, wherever she goes."

He chuckles. "Some people never are."

"I'm surprised she didn't demand her way onto a flight out tonight."

He says, "Nobody controls airline mechanics, mate. Not even the airlines."

"She can't snap her fingers at them?"

"Power has limits."

The Brit crosses behind the Sudoku player to sit at an empty stool two down from me. Now what? I've never had a bar conversation. What if he's a total prick? What if he asks about my legs? Calm down. It's a bar conversation. I can fake a cell phone call.

He asks, "Mexico City?"

"Allegedly."

"We'll make it. Bloody well better."

"British?"

"English. Great Britain describes the entire islands. English describes people from England."

"Sorry. American ignorance."

"No," he says and exhales. "I didn't mean to be so crisp. Long day. Apologies."

"No need, but accepted."

He looks weary, but then again, I'm sure I do, too.

"To surviving a long day."

Our glasses clink.

He says, "My name is Alistair."

"I'm Eric."

Fuck! *Why did I fucking lie?*

"Business or pleasure, Eric?"

I feel myself blushing. "Pardon?"

Alistair says, "Mexico City for work or pleasure?"

"Pleasure, I guess."

"Most people go to Cancun."

"I know someone in Mexico City."

I lied about my name, and I'm sure it's obvious. I bet I'm still blushing. Why the fuck did I say Eric's name?

"How about you, Alistair? Work or pleasure?"

"Work. But if I do it right, pleasure. Pharmaceutical sales in emerging markets. Spent the last two hours rescheduling every one of tomorrow's seven appointments. Bloody mess."

We get quiet. Neither of us are verbose, I guess.

"Where are you staying? What hotel?"

He throws me a sharp glance. Too personal? I almost want to explain I don't care where he's staying. Just making conversation. I'm not good at this.

"Private resort. Stayed there before. It's nice."

I murmur appreciation for nice resorts, something empty. We sit in silence for a few more sips.

I have to explain myself. "I asked because I have no idea what to expect with my hotel. I've never been to Mexico City. Or anywhere in Mexico."

"Your friend didn't advise you?"

I know I'm still blushing. "Surprise visit. Can you recommend restaurants?"

"Several. Blinding good restaurants, freshest fish and vegetables you'll ever find."

As he elaborates, I ponder the pointed look. Why did he react that way? Gay resort? Is that why he didn't want to share? I'm getting a vibe, something almost flirty but not quite. Probably not. He probably wants to ask me how I was crippled and figures he needs to establish rapport first. People think it's less rude if you've been chatting aimlessly for ten minutes. No wonder I avoid bar conversations. Any conversations. But what if he's gay? What if we have something else in common beyond the flight?

Take the risk. 7-16-32.

"If my hotel doesn't work out, would you recommend your resort?"

"It's not for everyone," he says slowly. "Primarily gay clientele."

He says the second half with ease, as if he's decided to be honest. He may not be ashamed, but that doesn't mean he wants to have the Big Gay Conversation with a stranger. I can relate to avoiding certain topics.

"Even better. Since I'm gay."

He looks pleased.

The barrier broken, we converse in earnest. He elaborates on discreet gay-friendly restaurants he thinks I may enjoy.

"Oh, and don't walk back to your hotel late at night. Your legs will make you a target, to some at least. That's the only worry."

I bristle at the mention, but that's it. He switches topics. He advocates interesting spots outside the city: a hot springs, a farm, and bluffs or something. He mentioned my legs as if their brokenness is merely a fact, which it is. I'm not sure how I feel about this. He asks about my international travels, and it's embarrassing to say I have none. I explain I have a passport, just not cause to use it. I skirt explanation as to why. Fleeing the country is an escape I hope to never need. Dad is in prison, but he could be paroled. Even in a hotel bar, with a sexy pharmaceuticals guy, all stories lead to my childhood. No wonder I spend so much time looking down.

Before I leave the restroom, I test myself. Did two glasses of wine impede my abilities? No. I feel good. Can't slip or stumble. Could never get buzzed enough for that to happen. All clear. I feel drunk, though not on red wine. The sheer delight in connecting. Neither one of us are chatty, which means lots of silent periods, though once we began discussing travel, he opened up. Why do I not attempt this—talk to new people and listen? Okay, yes, I've heard more about big pharma than I can absorb, but who cares? This feels like inebriation, making another new friend. Doesn't matter that it's temporary. This one speaks English, so hey, I'm getting better at this.

Hair looks okay. Smile—teeth check. Good.

Go back out there and flirt.

When I reach my seat, I'm pleased he gives me time to adjust myself, settle my canes.

"Good piss?"

"Yes. Very refreshing."

We both chuckle. I like his directness, but I don't know how to play along.

He says, "Would you like to have a drink in my room?"

Yes! "I'm sorry. I can't."

He apologizes profusely, and then I apologize.

Then silence.

"Too forward."

"No, no...."

"My cockup. I often mistake friendliness for attraction."

"You didn't fuck up. I'm...." How do I explain? This time do not lie. "I'm not experienced meeting men, Alistair. I don't know how to... do this."

He smiles sideways. "I believe there are photographs on the internet. Videos, perhaps."

I laugh. "I'm not a virgin, you tosser. Did I use that right?"

"Pretty well, yes."

"I don't. This—I don't know this part. Do we kiss? Do we cuddle afterward? After ten minutes of cuddling, do you awkwardly suggest it's getting late so I know to leave? Do I acknowledge you tomorrow when we're boarding the same flight or would you rather forget it?"

While these thoughts bother me, I hope he sees the real issue—my legs. I don't know how to navigate my own legs during sex.

"Yes to kissing, yes to cuddling. I do have an early flight, but you're welcome to sleep over."

"It's more complicated than that."

"Are you married?"

"No. Single."

Even though I find him sexy, I don't want him seeing burn marks. Also, I fucking lied about my name, like a psycho.

"Cheers. I will respect your decision, yet may I ask, what is complicated?"

I find myself framing words I do not wish to speak. I hate this. I don't want to hear his answer. "Is this about my legs?"

"How?"

"Are you attracted to me *because* of my legs?"

Alistair frowns. "I haven't seen your legs."

"Some men are into disabilities. No judgment, but I have a right to know."

"Ah. No, Eric. Not your legs."

"The last couple guys who hit on me did so because my legs are fucked up. They find it hot to kiss and worship them. It's creepy."

He swallows the rest of his drink. "Are you a top or bottom?"

"I prefer top."

"I prefer bottom," he says, grinning while staring forward. "So, it won't be your legs I'm after."

I chuckle when he chuckles.

Alistair says, "I don't approach men in bars in general. Though from what you've revealed, I suspect more than you. Let's stay. Drink another drink. Flirt. Talk about things that matter, like HIV status and condoms, where we like to be kissed, comfortable positions for fucking"—he leans closer—"and whether you like your come gobbled...."

Oh god, I really do.

"If we're compatible, Bob's your uncle."

7-16-32. I'm risking this.

I lift my finger. "Lisa? Two more bloody drinks."

Alistair laughs. "Well done."

Alistair faces me and unbuttons his shirt, the only light coming from the bathroom. My heart pounds. I have too many scars, burn marks, angry memories relived when I get touched. I dread the exact moment when my battered legs are revealed. There's no mood killer like a horrified, "Holy Jesus!" I prefer sex with the lights out. Still problematic, but only fingers see in the dark.

Our first night together, Eric insisted my overhead light remain on while he inspected my naked legs, like conducting an autopsy. I hated him while he did that. I realized I had misjudged him; he was into disabled kink, after all. When he finished, he said, "There. Now I've seen your legs. You never have to worry about me seeing them accidentally, because I just studied them. Honestly, I don't mind fucking in the dark. But a candle or two might be nice as mood lighting. Also, mirrors are fun. I like to watch myself suck cock." For the first time ever during sex, I laughed. Eric did that for me.

He says, "Eric."

My face—I know I look guilty. Why did I lie?

"Let's get off your bloody pants."

7-16-32! 7-16-32!

He massages the lump of my cock through my jeans. "Does this feel all right?"

He grins. He knows the answer is yes. Shitty as I feel about lying, my cock rises. I think he asked because he maybe wants me to talk dirty to him. Say something dirty.

"Yes." Okay. That wasn't my best.

He leans in. I love kissing him.

He speaks in a rusty voice. "Fancy my cock massage?"

"Yes. Real good." I have to get better at dirty talk.

He changes angles, zips his thumbnail under my balls, which might be a little rough naked, but on jeans feels like the right amount of rough.

A sound escapes me.

Our kisses taste like hard liquor and the mint he popped a moment ago. I like the hard liquor taste better, somehow more authentic.

He unzips me. "Splendid cock."

I laugh.

He chuckles dirty.

Guys always say they like my cock. It's the easiest landmark in the neighborhood to compliment. Each one of my meager list of sex partners has said it. *Nice cock.* It's the equivalent of saying, "What twisted legs? I hadn't noticed because I like your cock so much."

I start getting soft.

Why does self-esteem shit pop out during my one—oh. Oh! My softening cock is enveloped. His mouth, the suction, the heat, oh god, *oh god*, all the way to the base, his lower lip on my sack, and god, it's *still in his throat.* His sucking becomes wetter, and I collapse on my back, driving up my hips, thrusting deeper into his throat. The surprise gags him. I love when a guy gags, suggesting it's my power married to his hunger which drives us.

Oh god.

I forgot sex can be good.

He's better than previous sex partners, more skilled in his throat strokes, pulling back to nibble the head of my cock and then catch the spittle that drips down my shaft. I love how his fingertips massage my scrotum, like he's a massage therapist and those balls had a hard day. That feels amazing.

"You failed to mention your cock gets huge, Eric."

"Is that a problem?"

"Never. Bit of a size queen. I did not know I would be so amply rewarded. When I pull off your jeans, should I be cautious of your legs? Are they tender?"

Fuck. Fuck! *I hate this moment.* "No. It won't hurt."

Whoa—that's it. They're off.

I didn't have time to get soft.

Instantly, he drops his whole throat on my cock.

Oh god, oh god, oh god!

I don't know how long it lasts, the rocking, the motion of his lips touching my balls, like pushups to the head, and yeah, it's a fat head. Maybe I do have a great dick after all. God, I love getting sucked. I need a boyfriend who loves sucking dick. He backs away and kicks off his underwear, presenting me with his own perfect dick.

"Gentleman's sausage?"

"Do English people really say that?"

"Only when trying to charm an American." With one hand, he guides me.

Sucking cock feels like Christmas, a holiday I love, yet painfully infrequent. Actually, sucking dick is more like leap year day. He strokes my wet cock while simultaneously pushing into my throat. I'm probably not going to last long. I hope there will be a second round. I'm already more sexually at ease with Alistair than Eric. I've never felt this relaxed about sex.

Is this because of who Alistair is or has something in me shifted? Maybe I'm ready to have great sex, broken legs and all. If a guy is cool with my legs and wants to fuck, why would I get anxious? Fuck thinking about this! I've got a dick in my mouth. I luxuriate in the humid scent, the earthiness, the humming moans I hear when I suck him good. I am a starving man at a cocksucking buffet, and I intend to gorge myself.

Wait until I get into his ass.

The second time I fuck him, I feel powerful, frogging him. I love this grunting, lovemaking fuck, which despite the latex, feels raw, wolfish, it teases out this dominant quality in me, dominant in a protective way. I want to pleasure this man. I want to bring him pleasure. I squeeze tighter, this willing prisoner in my arms, pushing my cock deeper. I savor the wet sloshing, dirty and delicious sex and sticky pleasure.

"Listen to the sound." That's the dirtiest thing I've ever said tonight, and it feels raunchy.

He grunts. "You're fucking *big*."

I pull out—almost out—in long, slow strokes, eliciting groans, an Englishman's groans, and I wonder if the English are more tolerant of people with disabilities. I may have to move to London. Alistair hasn't demanded answers about my legs. He just wants sex. I am inexhaustible this way, my best position. My arms are solid muscle, strengthened by weight lifting and dragging myself everywhere. Holding myself up, push-up style, for the past twenty minutes, and my arms aren't even tired. I can make this one last.

Let's do this.

Let's fuck.

He says, "I can't... can't take much more."

"Want me to pull out? Jack off?" It's my turn to tease. I'm not surprised he's exhausted. The first fuck didn't last long, twenty minutes or so, but this one.... "Want me to come?"

He moans softly, pushes back, raising his ass to indicate his desire.

Good.

My balls are boiling, and thinking of how good this will feel, cumming in a man's ass. I love the tension, my cock pounding him, his ass fighting me, accepting me, every inch, every inch of me feeling welcome. More than welcome. Wanted. I feel wanted. I relish it.

He gasps. "Oh god!"

Getting closer. I love this, I love this, I love this, I love this, I love me. Wait, *me*?

I scream.

I buck into him.

He yells.

Everything pours out of me, my balls spurting hard, kicking juice through me, into the condom, as deep as I can push it.

He screams.

Aftershocks are maddening, my balls, my face, my arms, the sweat, his twitching, an orchestra of sensations, an orchestra collapsed after the last note. The trumpets *splaaaaat*, and someone accidentally kicks the bass drum, knocking over the cymbals. Oh god, this feels surreal, him, his squeezing, my cock still fucking, like the orchestra's conductor who doesn't know when it's time to get off the stage. Stop. I have to stop fucking him.

How did I feel so much energy thirty seconds ago?

Right now, nothing but weakness. Depleted. I love it. That condom must be sloppy with my seed, gobs of it. My softening dick sneaks out, such a transformation from its bold slams during the last, what, hour? Two short breaks, maybe more than an hour. Alistair can take a pounding, that's for sure. I slide to the side, reluctantly. My heart pounds a standing ovation. Wow. I love good sex.

I roll the condom off my dick. I was right. Big load. What do I do with this? Can't easily get to the bathroom. I'll pinch it closed so nothing drips out. Hold it, I guess.

I'm still gasping.

I'm not the only one.

He turns with a bashful grin. "I'm completely knackered."

I need to remember every second with Alistair. Maybe we can see each other when he's back from Mexico. I know this is a one-night stand, and I can't get weird, but I've never fucked like this, so intimate, loving, and also so goddamn raunchy. Maybe this is normal but not for me. Not this good.

"That was brilliant."

Say something sexy. "I loved being inside you."

Slow kissing affirms neither one of us feels regret. My poor limp cock refuses to play. Okay, pal. Three orgasms is enough for today. We had great sex! Hallelujah for canceled flights.

I love his green eyes, green like a forest fern and browns like tiny twigs, flecks of gold skimming the surface. Remember these eyes.

Softly, he says, "Eric."

I wince.

"What's wrong?" He raises himself on one elbow.

Why did I lie? After hours of breathtaking intimacy, the beauty we created is undone by my lie, my selfish, stupid lie for no fucking reason whatsoever. Why the fuck did I lie? Because even if New York changed me, I still don't want to be me.

Say the words quickly. "I have to confess something."

"Hold up, mate. As your picking-up-strangers-in-a-bar mentor, I must inform you, those are the last words any man wants to hear right after sex." He smiles in a dreamy way.

I'm going to destroy that smile. He'll hate me. Why didn't I admit it before we slept together? Damn it, I'm a weird, shitty person.

"Alistair, I don't know how to explain or justify this. I lied. My real name isn't Eric. I got flustered in the hotel bar. My name is Daniel."

He looks visibly relieved. "We're using real names? Oh good."

What?

"My real name is John. John Robertson."

Wait.

Wait.

I don't know why it takes me so long to make the connection. "Are you—am I supposed to meet you in Mexico?"

"Yes."

This is John Robertson? This guy? He's—he's... He smiles and lifts my hand to kiss the underside, right under my thumb. What the fucking hell? *He lied to me?* My brain explodes in thirty directions—questions, more questions springing from parent questions, offshoots demanding explanation.

"You're John Robertson?"

"Alistair is an alias I use when I travel on sensitive business."

"You're King John?"

"I am. Are you hungry?"

John Robertson seduced me! He just kissed the underside of my thumb.

He says, "Probably too late for room service but not pizza delivery. Somewhere nearby delivers, surely."

I had sex with a king? Was sex his assignment? Why did they insist on Mexico? What—why didn't he tell me his name? Despite the multitude, one question slips out first.

"What's your king name?"

Alistair—John says, "That is a very, very good question."

Did his voice just change?

ELEVEN

I smirk, surveying our damage in morning light. We wrecked this room the way lovers do. The top sheet is crawling across the floor as if trying to escape. Even two corners of the fitted sheet are undone. The blanket remains over the headboard, where we stuffed it last night to muffle my slamming him from behind. Pizza box, contents devoured. On the breakfast cart, corners of French toast, assorted egg scrambles, mostly eaten, well, as much as we could. With no hesitation, he'd ordered three breakfasts and extra bacon. I'm not sure why this impressed me. John's appetite for living is insatiable. *King* John. Even in the room's sitting area, where we drank hot tea an hour ago, there are spilled sugar packets and tea bags in soggy collapse. Our clothes are scattered. I've never participated in ruining a hotel room.

I should feel exhausted, but mostly I feel blurry satisfaction. I picked up Alistair in a hotel bar for sex and spent the whole night awake with John, discussing Burning Man. The Snake men and the search for Michelle. Vin's gold coins. Dancing with fire. La Contessa. The kiss which woke Vin Vanbly, a kiss John could never explain.

From the shower, I hear singing.

I should dress.

For the first time ever, I'm not scrambling to put on pants. Even with Eric, I still was self-conscious after sex. Today I don't fucking care. That's remarkable. John loved me last night, and I loved him. I can admit that. He's a part of me now.

Is it possible to love someone this deeply, recently met? Or is this infatuation? I have so little experience. This feels like love, the depth of it. Eric was a great boyfriend and an incredible presence, but that wasn't love. John literally changed my life. I am a better man for hearing his story, for lying naked in bed, eating pizza. Even if he emerges and screams at me to *get out*, he can't undo my immense gratitude and joy. That sex was mind-bending. The hours afterward, sexy King Weekend intimacy as he unburdened his heart.

Was it *king sex*? Is this how Vin Vanbly felt all those years fucking on King Weekends? A bliss I've never experienced physically. Infatuation would be wanting more sex, and, yes, I do. I want to drink in last night, over and over. I want to bless him for a joyful, intimate experience without awkwardness or shame. I want to communicate how much it meant for him not hurrying to be finished with me. But I want to call him next week to hear about his day. What he made for dinner. This feeling…. I also want to fuck his brains out.

Shower's off. He's still singing.

I save my pants for last, because now this has become a test to dress at a normal rate. Will I try to hide my pants drama from him? The twisted contortions I go through to coax jeans over my shattered legs? Specially tailored for easier dressing, yes, but it's still not pretty to watch.

Hell, I fucked the dude twice last night. I would have fucked him raw—to complement the intensity—but he insisted on condoms, and I respected his decision. Tops rarely get it, especially when the bottom is undetectable, like John. If sex this good is possible—if I can feel so loved and loving through physical intimacy—well, hell, I want more sex. Is this another outcome from New York? From therapy? From him being a king? I'm curious, oh so curious, and I don't require an answer. I love basking. If I plan on being more sexually active, I should consider taking PrEP.

John explained some men find kingship in how they handle their HIV diagnosis. For others, the stigma is close to unbearable. Paths to kingship vary. He told me to look around. See the possibilities. I'm looking around, John. I'm seeing possibilities. My eyes well up. I'm becoming a king.

It's unbelievable to consider John once thought himself nothing—worse than nothing, because his ordinary self wasn't enough. The man I met, or rather, the *men* I met—Alistair and John both—bubbled with quiet confidence, like too much soda in a full glass of ice. How could a man so fizzy with life ever doubt himself?

The bathroom door opens. John is naked, drying his hair. "Hi, cutie."

I want to say something playful in return, something sexy, but I don't know how. I've never had anyone call me *cutie*, not casually, and mean it. The best I can do is beam, grinning my pleasure. Have I ever been this happy?

Calm down.

This was a beautiful one-night stand. Maybe more, but don't get ahead of yourself. This man owes you nothing. Well, maybe one thing. The next step on my quest.

I don't want to stop hearing about his King Weekend. *Start over, John.* Let me analyze nuances, moments when I recognized myself in your experience. Aren't I my own version of Alistair most days, terrified of the ordinary dullness of Daniel?

"While you showered, I thought of another question. You said you and Michelle escaped Burning Man. How?"

"Michelle slept through our escape. Guards inspected the vehicle, waking her to ensure she was okay. She demanded ice and a soft drink, and when they couldn't deliver, she turned her back, asleep in five seconds. Honestly, it was the best thing she could have done. If I had instructed her to do that, she wouldn't have."

I laugh. I feel like I know her. "I assume you two are still in touch."

"Daily. She's the worst," he says, drying his cock and balls. "As much a pain in my side as the day we met. I swear, she courts legal trouble for the sole purpose of pushing my buttons."

That's not what I was hoping to hear. "I'm sorry. Also, I saw what you did there with *courts* legal trouble."

He grins sexy at me. "Lawyer puns. Yes, Michelle is terrible. Then again, this is her first business, so she's bound to make mistakes."

"Oh. What business?"

"She designs clothes for gender fluid people. She wants to incorporate other designers' styles, adding her unique spin, which I keep reminding her you simply can't do. She claims lawsuits are the best way to 'get a meeting.' She thinks getting sued is a networking strategy. She's nutters."

I laugh without reservation. Beautiful, beautiful Michelle.

John joins me, sitting on the bed. "She had some not-great years. She is proud of her work in recovery, and she goes regularly to meetings. She leads them. Years ago, I was desperate for her to attend college. She insisted it was 'not her path.' She wanted to develop her fashion line immediately. Couldn't wait. Now that she's getting offers to appear in magazines, she wants to go to college. That woman is maddening."

"Difficult client."

"Too difficult. I fired her as a client seven years ago. No way would I take that level of shit from anyone other than family so I adopted her. On paper, she's my daughter, but my parents and siblings now consider her our youngest sister. Like any bratty baby sister, she's the absolute worst. You should hear my mom and Michelle fight over football. They're both sports nuts. Dad, our older sister, and I leave the room."

He shivers, as if shaking off her mojo, then smiles and takes my hand. "I had fun last night and all morning, talking with you."

"Me too. May I ask something else? Did you see Vin at the next Burning Man?"

John's smile vanishes. "No."

"Oh."

"He was banned for life."

I don't know why this shocks me the way it does.

He says, "Though legally, he was not culpable for any wrongdoing, Burning Man never rescinded their ban. He never returned. Of course, that hardly mattered after 2005."

What the fuck happened in 2005?

John grimaces. "Whoops. I forgot I didn't need to say that."

"Say what?"

John says, "Here's the thing about my King Weekend. Vin probably shouldn't have attempted to king me. I was more than he could handle. He felt an attraction for me, had kinged men at Burning Man, so it seemed like a good gamble. But I had too much baggage. I pushed too hard. There are times when Vin simply has to say *no*."

"But it worked."

"Yes. I remembered my kingship. I will always love Vin for taking a ridiculous chance, but he skirted dangerously close to failure. He sacrificed. Until years later, I had no idea how much each kinging took out of him."

A pang of jealousy races through me. I want Vin Vanbly to love me, to believe I'm worth that kind of risk. It's hard to admit you might be nothing, your life a waste. Or to admit you want things you might never have. I want to run. I want to be in love. I want to get kinged by Vin Vanbly. Hell, I'd be thrilled with any two of those three.

John rises and heads to the closet. "Daniel, would you accompany me to the lobby? I've got to use their business lounge to rebook my flight. I asked Michelle to do it, but I doubt she did."

I'm not sure what part of that surprises me more. "You're not going to Mexico?"

"I guess not. Not since I met you here. I have a class action lawsuit in Mexico City, but testimony doesn't begin until next week. As long as we're in Phoenix, Michelle and I can meet with one of the designers she's pissed off. See if we can't settle things amicably. Fly home tonight."

"Michelle is here?"

John laughs. "Who do you think got grabby about her drink bill at the airport bar? I needed her to make a minor scene—her specialty—so I'd have a reason to initiate conversation with you."

"I can't believe I met Michelle. That absolutely tickles me."

"You did. Didn't require much acting on her part either." John removes a crisp shirt from its hanger.

I met Michelle! I don't even remember her face.

He says, "I wasn't exaggerating about Vin. That night in the desert changed him. After that he kinged only men who hovered right on the precipice of crossing over. He altered the weekend itself, spending only thirty hours instead of forty, hoping to minimize what he felt was his damaging impact on their lives. The light side of Vin grew brighter, and the dark side of him got darker. He felt he was being ripped in half."

"Is that why he stopped in 2005?"

"Vin began to doubt himself. He started involving other kings in a kind of screening process, meeting with questing candidates to validate whether the man had strong possibility."

Is that me? A man with strong possibility? My heart beats faster.

"When did the other kings begin participating in Vin's kinging?"

"Never. They just evaluate candidates. Vin didn't want to involve other kings directly, because he understood the consequences. He was unwilling to share that burden with men he still loves with all his love. Daniel, anyone can cross into the kingdom without ever having heard the tale of The Lost and Founds. True, few do. It's hard to thread that needle. Most people never get the luxury of a guide, let alone one from ancient prophecy. The Ghost Who Walks Among Us is an anomaly. When I shadowed him at Burning Man, I had no idea. I was lucky."

The mention of prophecy shocks me, but his words disturb me on a deeper level. He's lucky. I'm not. I have always worn *unlucky* around my neck, like Olympic bronze. Silver goes to kids with cancer, and the gold to anyone under thirteen who wins an early death. Having your dad run over your legs intentionally—twice—at least earns a spot on the winners' podium. There has to be *lucky* and *unlucky* or nothing makes sense. I'm not lucky.

"How do I look?"

John stands before me in charcoal-gray slacks and a mint-blue shirt, perfectly pressed. Shimmering. Shiny black shoes, and his hair fluff-dried and just... charming. I don't see how anyone could find him ordinary. There's a beautiful *everyman* quality beaming from him, brighter with each passing minute. He's like peanut butter. Everyone loves seeing peanut butter in the kitchen cabinet.

"Smashing." I immediately redden. "I wasn't making fun. It slipped out. I was thinking about Alistair."

John reaches for me.

After small adjustments, I stand. Cross to him. I can't hold hands in any traditional sense, but he doesn't seem to notice, wrapping his hand around my forearm. I like him feeling the strength in my arm. No one has ever tried to hold my arm this way, but it feels wonderful.

He says, "After my King Weekend, I could never pretend to be Alistair. These days, he feels like a distant cousin, a man whose life I once lived. I can't allow myself to forget that being Alistair allowed me to feel superior to others. They were idiots for not seeing through my deception. I will not allow myself to forget the ugliness Alistair represents, even though I miss him. Through you, I got to visit him again last night."

He's looking at me, expecting something. What?

"Daniel, truth can be beautiful or ugly. That's the biggest, fattest question mark. Through which door will you drag your truth?"

He pauses, and I don't know what to say. I'm nervous.

He says, "Got everything? Wallet, phone, keys?"

Why am I nervous?

Something is not right. That thing in the room about truth? In the elevator, he again mentioned how *selective* Vin is these days. What did that mean? My heart sank as we descended. Something is not right.

The elevator doors open.

The lobby is packed with people, most everyone buzzing around the breakfast buffet on the far side. My heart beats faster. He wanted me in front of all these people when we said our goodbyes. We didn't kiss before we left the room. Why? He didn't ask to see me again—and I didn't either. Why not?

Something's up.

I try to make my voice sound normal. "What are we doing, John? What's happening?"

With his hand, he indicates a slightly less populated section, near the drop-in couches. A half-dozen people chatter there, protective of their luggage. There's nowhere to sit, not together, no privacy, so when we reach that area, we both lean against the back of a couch.

"Daniel, here's how questing works. First we do a phone interview. Yours was with Kearns. Then an on-site visit. You did yours in New York. Vin was on the phone, and he followed you in New York."

"I thought he was in a coma."

"What? Why?"

"Everyone's been saying things like, 'In the year 2005, *everything changed*,' cue the ominous music. He's okay?"

"Oh, that. Smoke and mirrors. Sorry. If this was going to happen, we wanted you obsessed by how he changed in 2005. He's fine. Still lives in St. Paul."

If this was going to happen?

No, no, no.

They're already kinging me. I'm in the middle of it. They—they have to. Rance said—

"During your on-site, you passed him sitting on a street corner, sitting on a bucket playing a guitar. You didn't notice him. No big deal. It's not always about giving money to the homeless, though you didn't win any extra points with Perry."

Don't panic. Keep my voice calm. "John, I couldn't stop for every homeless person. The people behind me would have knocked me over, the way I move."

"I know. We get it. That wasn't crucial in the final decision, just an observation."

What final decision?

"Vin felt it took you too long to find the Butterfly King. Rance argued it took as long as it was meant to take, given nobody had ever attempted what you did. You impressed Rance. All of New York clamored on your behalf. Despite what I said about the homeless thing, Perry was always in your corner. You're from Ohio, like his dad. It was Perry who originally forwarded your apology email to DC. DC suggested if you took the bait and found another king, then it was time to loop in Vin. Let Vin decide whether to king you."

"I don't understand."

John, don't be saying what I think you're saying. Don't do this.

"Ultimately, it was Vin's decision. He didn't see himself being able to pull it off. I told you, he's very selective these days. He's worried about fucking it up."

I know what he's going to say. "Pull what off, exactly?"

"Vin's not going to king you. He told me to give you his regrets. Perry, Mai, and everyone you met in New York argued on your behalf, so Vin asked me to provide another opinion. My job was to meet you and chat. I didn't know you were going to be handsome and lovely. I didn't know I would be so attracted to you. Our connection was very real, even if it was Eric and Alistair."

"What opinion did you give Vin?" My voice is sharp.

John is penitent. I see sorrow in his eyes, but it's too late. I hate him.

"When you went to the bathroom last night in the hotel bar, I gave Vin my thumbs-up, but it didn't change his resolve. I'm sorry."

"Why did he ask you for your opinion if he wasn't going to listen?"

"I don't know."

"He was in the hotel?"

"He was on our cancelled flight. He was in the hotel bar last night, too."

Vin Vanbly followed me. Watched me. Decided not to king me. He thinks me unworthy. I allow myself to sink against the couch. My hands tremble. I'll fall. I'll goddamn fall over.

They aren't kinging me.

"Hang on." He reaches into his pocket and then reads his phone. "Text from Michelle."

My brain reels. A feeling is growing in me, something very familiar, very dark. My hands are shaking harder, betraying how deeply this hurts. They aren't kinging me. Vin Vanbly decided *no*. Because I didn't give money to every homeless person? I took too long to find Rance?

What happens to Lost Kings? Nothing. They get dumped in a pleasant hotel.

He slips the phone into his jacket's breast pocket. "Surprise, surprise. She rebooked our flights after all. She's in our limo. Ah, there."

From our vantage point, we see straight through the lobby's floor-to-ceiling windows. A white stretch limo awaits him. The passenger window lowers halfway. Michelle is inside? I can't believe this. They aren't kinging me.

"Daniel, I'd love a second date, if you're interested. We both have money. We could travel, meet somewhere, and continue to learn about each other. Spend a week together."

What? Is he insane?

"You want us to date? After telling me Vin Vanbly rejected me? Seconds after telling me I'm not king material?"

Hold it together. Hold it together in front of this asshole.

"Don't look at it like that. It's not that you're *not* king material. Every man is. Just not one of Vin's kings. There are many ways for a man to achieve his kingship. I hinted at that last night and this morning. Yes, it's hard but possible. I can't say much about it, or I'll accidentally provide false clues that could derail you."

My heart is pounding. My arms are shaking.

John pulls out his phone again. "Sorry. Michelle keeps texting me to hurry. I have to go. I understand this is a lot to absorb. I'll email you, and if you want, we can talk about another date. Please consider it. I really like you."

Was this pity sex? Horror and rage flame through me, scorching every glorious memory. *Pity sex.* I was discarded by Vin Vanbly, the one man—according to these goddamn stories—the one person you could trust to find the best in you. To help you. And his emissary offered his ass as the consolation prize.

Please, Vin. Please help me!

"Goodbye, Daniel. I loved meeting you."

He leans in. I jerk my head back. Does he honestly believe I'd kiss him? John looks sorrowful. I see the startling depths I witnessed last night while he rode my cock. I felt dazzled to feel such love. He's got stars hidden in his eyes. All of it burns away. It was fucking pity sex! Rage and horror curl into a fist.

He says, "I'm truly sorry. Don't forget, every man is the one true king. There are other ways to enter the kingdom."

If I speak, I'll scream, *I hate you.*

He pulls out his phone, texting already—unbelievable—and strolls away. I can't believe this. I cannot fucking believe—razor-sharp pain stabs its way up my legs, the jagged tips traveling higher, puncturing my stomach, slashing the air from my lungs.

Perry wanted to king me.

Mai wanted to king me.

I can't breathe.

Rance and all of fucking New York vouched for me.

As much as I hate him right now, John wanted to king me.

But Vin Vanbly doesn't want a crippled king. You can watch from the sidelines, but you can't play. I picture one of those videos where liquid iron is poured into factory molds. I am that molten liquid. A scorching pricks my skin and makes me sweat angry droplets right out of my scalp. I raise my hands to witness them vibrating at a speed I could never make happen consciously.

This is rage? *This* is how fury feels?

All those years I cried angry tears—wondering how a father could abuse his son—and it felt nothing like this. Hell, that was mild irritation compared to this can't-breathe feeling. Is this how my father felt before he beat the shit out of me? Before he forced pliers into my mouth, threatening to yank out every goddamn tooth? After years of wasted therapy with Margaret trying to not become him, it's finally time to accept I am my father's son.

I am his rage. His raw, pink hatred.

I hate you, Vin Vanbly. *I hate your fucking guts.*

Like dad, I'm no quitter. I'm not ending my quest. He's a garage mechanic. John let slip he still lives in St. Paul. I found a fucking butterfly in New York City. I can find this asshole garage mechanic in a much smaller city.

My skin feels itchy and wet, like it's boiling off my flesh. Hate burns through me, a volcano finally releasing its slow-pouring death, rage-tears streaming down my face, obliterating every thought, every shred of decency I thought was at my core.

I have a role to play in The Lost and Founds.

I'm the villain.

I'll have to get a gun, of course. Practice firing. On the plus side, I've got my answer. I know what happens to Lost Kings. They murder. I'm going to St. Paul, Minnesota. When I find him, I'll kill him.

I'm the guy who kills Vin Vanbly.

TWELVE

I T'S HIM.
I found him.

He's right there in coveralls. Working in Vincent's Garage. The name on the lapel reads *Vin*. Saw it clear as day through my binoculars. Don't react. Don't let Jian see me react through the rearview mirror. Give no reaction. He's staring out the windshield anyway.

My heart is pounding, but calm down.

Calm down.

On my first day in St. Paul, Minnesota, I found Vin Vanbly.

Got him.

Two hours since I confirmed him in Vincent's Garage, and I'm still reacting as if it were only thirty seconds ago. It's insane I feel this—I can't even name it. What is this feeling? It's like all the feelings. Sloppy ball feelings. I had hoped the mechanics might get lunch at the bar across the street. It looks like it would serve greasy burgers, shitty fries. I had hoped to see Vin cross the street. He wouldn't see through the car's tinted glass. He has no reason to suspect I hunted him down after rejecting me. But it's almost 2:00 p.m., way past lunch. I can't believe it was so easy to find him. First google search—*garage, St. Paul*, and *Vin*. It's definitely Vin Vanbly. He came outside three times. Well, not at all during the last hour, but I saw that name badge three times. I didn't think he'd be so chubby.

I want a drink. Strong drink. I've waited long enough.

Time to begin phase two: asking questions. Someone in this bar must know something. I can't approach until I know more. I have to be smart. Discreet. Maybe they don't know anything. Maybe this is crazy. Paranoid. This kinging thing warped my brain. Things are happening inside me. Unpredictable things.

I'm becoming... unstable. I'm remembering things. Things I do not like. Twice in Columbus, I lurched, caught up in a spontaneous memory about Dad. The only reason I was even out wandering the streets is because New York addicted me to walking. Dad used to call to me from the garage, giving me time to hide. No. No more remembering.

I hate this.

I've rehearsed what to say to Jian. Act casual. "I'm going inside the bar for a while."

"Okay, Mr. Daniels."

He's exactly what I needed in a driver. Of course, I knew that at the Wisconsin rest stop. I told him, "Don't come in." From the restaurant, I watched to make sure he didn't go anywhere or do anything. He waited a full three hours until I returned. Never asked a single question. After that, I knew I could spy on Vin without having to explain myself.

"If you need me, text. Don't come in."

"Yes, Mr. Daniels."

I'll never stop him from calling me that. Makes me feel, I don't know, like his overlord. I dislike it. So what? He's polite. Careful driver. On the plus side, I've successfully trained him to not open doors for me. Those were awkward arguments, curbing his good intentions. Natural instinct to help the cripple.

I glance at Vincent's garage. Nobody is outside. Good. Once my car door is shut, I focus on the ground in front of me—no uneven spots. Just get to the front door without being seen. Roomier sidewalks in St. Paul. Very livable. This rundown, blue-collar neighborhood reminds me of mine back home. Everything around here needs a new coat of paint. Or a new roof.

Garlic houses. A girl from grade school called houses like these garlic houses. Lisa? Was that her name? Why would I recall her now? I'll bet she didn't intend an ethnic slur, but the people she learned it from surely meant one. Was that because the houses look poor? Run down? God, we were eight? Nine, maybe. Home was immaculate. White furniture, gleaming floors. I associated that spotless perfection with Dad's rage. To me, a garlic house sounded pretty damn good.

Focus on the door twenty feet away.

I haven't thought of that grade-school girl in twenty years. I think her name was Lisa. Who cares! Quit remembering shit like this. I can't control what's surfacing. Glaciers inside me are thawing, splitting and chunking into the ocean, deafening in their destruction of my calm. This garlic house memory wasn't bad, but the next one could be. Focus. Don't lose your footing over a stupid, goddamn memory. Two days ago, I remembered how he would take notes when I howled in agony. The way his pen scratched on paper. Stop. I cannot. Handle. This. Shit.

Door.

Grabbing the handle for balance, I steal one more glance at Vincent's Garage, cranberry block letters outlined in faded navy blue. Three bays, all closed. Nobody's outside. Good. I'll never get close to him unless by surprise. I have a few ideas that may accomplish that. Door is heavy. I brace myself and swing open. *Oof.* Very heavy. I shove in a cane, forcing it to remain open until I twist myself inside. I explored a lot of office buildings in New York. Every time I dragged myself inside was a public announcement: *the cripple's here.*

Super dark in here except for that far corner. Can't walk until eyes adjust.

Vin was way chubbier than I expected. Like, fat. And that ponytail, half gray and half blond? Not working for you, bud. Grizzled mutton chops. I expected... more. I don't know. What did I expect? That Vin Vanbly would glow with light, and I'd recognize his aura? Did I expect grooming? He's just this overweight slob who doesn't wash his long hair. It's all so disappointing.

So why are my hands shaking?

Eyes still adjusting. Sitting in the middle of the long L-shaped bar, another guy my age, no, definitely older, head forward so all I see is scraggly tangles, tattoo sleeves down both arms. Lady on her cell in a booth against the far wall. Arguing, sounds like. She looks like a cheap receptionist. I hear the crack of a pool shot. No carpet folds or uneven surfaces. I can manage this easily. It's dim, so keep looking down.

You spend all your time looking down.

Fuck that.

Fuck you, Eric.

I believed in myself. I looked up, and got dumped by the first potential boyfriend since you dumped me, and in the same sentence discovered I'm not king material. Double dumped. Some lives, you look fucking down. And fuck you, Vin Vanbly. Fuck you for crushing the hope I might one day look up.

This bar stool is perfect, far enough from Greasy Hair I don't have to initiate conversation. Still, I may want to ask him questions. It's mostly the bartender I should grill. He must know things. He's busy with a woman at the far end. Gives me a few moments to get situated.

I can't believe I found Vin Vanbly in less than a day. Everybody kept saying The VV keep a low profile. Perry warned me they protected Vin from seekers like me. Right there, name on his coveralls. Took me almost four weeks to find Rance.

I remember my joy in staring at that shining plaque. I had achieved something impossible. Of course, that moment is ruined, knowing even then Vin had already decided I wasn't good enough. Rance said it wasn't a race. Maybe he—stop. I can't live like this. Rehashing who said what and when. But why invent a customized musical with oranges and baseball bats? Her screams transformed my nightmares. Online that's called *psychic surgery.* You don't—you can't undertake a thing like that lightly. *That's* how they treat a questing candidate?

I shouldn't have assumed they committed. Duh. When you're pursuing a King Weekend, and Vin Vanbly never contacts you to schedule one, what kind of idiot assumes he's already being kinged? Why blame him? He never promised me anything.

It's me. I'm deluded and gullible as fuck. I'm also driving myself nuts. No, I *am* nuts, dwelling on this rejection for three weeks. Who rents a car and driver to stalk someone they never met? I could be arrested. Jian could be arrested. No. He doesn't know anything. He expresses zero interest, and I tell him nothing. He's fine. But am I dragging him into something I have a responsibility to share? What's going to happen when—Mom used to sing to me, before—

Goddamn it, no.

Where the fuck is the bartender? I want a drink. This—I need to plan my next move. I'm not ready. I didn't think I'd find him the first day. Is this why Vin decided I'm not king material—I'm not a good planner? John said it's about Vin's confidence, but fuck that. Fuck John so much. We were so amazing together. We had king sex! I hate him with all my Lost King heart.

Find Vin. Demand answers.

I need that fucking drink.

Without turning, the bartender gives me a "just a second" finger.

Whatever.

I want a beer. No. I want *shots*.

I have to figure this out. What exactly is my game plan?

Greasy Hair's hand trembles, raising his drink. He's wasted in the middle of the afternoon. On a Thursday. Maybe I won't talk to him. But if he spends a lot of time in this bar, who knows? Past experience says avoid drunk people at all costs. Jesus, bartender, what the hell are you doing down there? What if I have to share something about myself to get them to open up? No. Nothing. For the thousandth time, I don't tip my hand under any circumstances.

Last time I was in a bar—well, I guess it was a Columbus gay bar two weeks after New York. I still can't believe I visited a gay bar after years of boycotting. Visited several in New York. I have a nickname in that city. How weird is that? I have Ms. Taylor in my life. Can I still be friends with Rance after Vin ended my questing? My heart hurts. I'm so tired of recycling these thoughts. Fuck it. I can be goddamn friends with anyone I want.

Vin Vanbly can deny me a King Weekend, but he can't undo butterflies chasing me through New York. He can't take away the roster people or Ms. Taylor. As much as I despise Vin, as cruel as John's abandonment, through their shitty king club I met her. I have a friend now. More than one, if I count Jarrod. We've shared a few emails since the month ban was lifted. I would never have met Horatio except for my New York friendships.

What the fuck do I have to do for a drink? Okay, finally, he's coming. Korean guy. Thirties. Strong square jaw. He doesn't look friendly. Not Korean after all. He's Chinese.

"What's up."

"Shot, please."

"Of what?"

"Vodka."

"You don't sound sure."

"You know what? I'd rather have whiskey. Yeah."

He smirks. "Top shelf, I assume?"

"Sure."

I pretend not to notice his snark. Yes, I'm a fraud. If you confuse vodka and whiskey, you're not a sophisticated drinker. What a dick. He pours for me and leaves, back to the woman at the far end. Greasy Hair indicates he's ready for another, and he gets ignored. Bartender's got a 'tude.

A toast to Ms. Taylor. Thinking of her as my friend pulled me out of my darkest thoughts. I imagined her face hearing the news I murdered someone, and realized I couldn't go through with it.

Holy shit that burns. Fucking *burns*. Oh man, don't cough. Do not cough. Do not make a fucking idiot of yourself——I bark out some hard coughs. That shot was strong.

Fuck do I care what that bartender thinks of me? Why am I smiling? Because that shot made me instantly drunk? Maybe. Or maybe I genuinely don't care what he thinks. I'll never be over this king bullshit unless I get answers. Why didn't I pass Vin's king test? Was it my legs? He has to explain.

The bartender returns. "Another?"

"Sure."

I should wait a minute before drinking this. I can't get drunk. I can't. I have to be able to navigate this shitty bar without falling over. Bartender doesn't look at me as he sets it down. He's already walking away.

Ask now.

"Hey, is the garage across the street any good?"

"Dunno."

He's still walking away.

"You don't take your car there?"

Light pierces the bar, which means someone opened the door. I glance briefly to see an older man wearing a cowboy hat. Do people wear cowboy hats here? Is that a thing?

The bartender doesn't turn around. "Why do you care? You can't drive."

Asshole! "I have a driver. He drives my car. That cool with you?"

Greasy Hair says, "I worked there."

"Shut it, Thomas." The bartender fires a finger in his direction. "Not today."

My heart beats faster. Dad would sharpen the screwdrivers in front of me, make me watch. He'd screw them in until my skin tore. Goddamn it, *I can't keep remembering this shit*! My hands are shaking again. I don't want to remember the pantry closet smell. He pretended not to know where I was to give me false hope.

I eventually learned he treasured the moment he discovered my hiding spot. *Stop thinking about this shit.* The kings weakened me. This goddamn questing made me weaker than I've ever been. They're forcing memories out. I cannot get drunk when I am this physically close to finding Vin Vanbly. Keep it fucking together. I can't take a sip yet. My throat still burns. I bet Greasy Thomas barely notices the kick.

Keep it together.

"I used to work there." Greasy Thomas's voice is hoarse. "He fucked me over."

Who? Who fucked him over?

Thomas taps the bar. "I'm taking a shit. Pour me another. Do it, Greg."

Bartender Greg never leaves his conversation at the far end.

Thomas says, "Greeeegy."

The man in the cowboy hat says, "Yo. Can I get a beer?"

Greg returns, visibly annoyed. "What kind?"

"What's on tap?"

"C'mon, man. You've ordered beer before. Look at the toppers."

Wow, Greg is a dick.

"Goose Island."

As Greg pours it, he casts a sour expression in Thomas's wake. Thomas is already careening under pool-table light. I bet Greg hates this job. I wonder if he owns this shitty bar. Maybe a relative owns it. He can't be the owner, not with that fuck-you attitude.

He delivers the cowboy's beer. "Way to pull off a hat."

The cowboy says, "Fuck you."

The bartender faces me. "When this dirt bag gets back from his dump, don't rile him up. Don't buy him drinks. He'll insist, but don't do it. You'll leave in an hour, and I'm stuck with that asshole until closing. Be cool."

I nod in surprise.

"You want another shot?"

"Still got the last one."

"Tab or cash?"

"Tab. You need my card?"

He turns away. "Later. Pretty sure I can tackle you before you make it to the door."

Asshole!

My anger fades. How often did I hear comments like that in New York? Jesus, I don't recognize this part of me, this *letting go*. I'm exhausted by how I view the world now, seeing Lost Kings and Lost Queens. If every man is the one true king, Greg the Asshole Bartender is my one true king. I'm so confused how I feel toward every single person. Three pages of names, New Yorkers I assumed were everyday assholes, donated their free time to follow me. They believed in me. The men of New York honored me with their choreography. The pulse. If this douche bag is a king, maybe I am one, too, with or without the help of these VV guys. Maybe I could be kinder to Greg, who works a shift where he will make almost no tips. I have to tip him big. Honor him. Maybe somewhere out there, a Lost King will be kinder to me.

No. Stop thinking this way.

Perry infected me, that's what's wrong. I can't stand this, *forgiving* people. Could I ever forgive John's pity sex? Fuck that. Some things are not forgivable. Was crushing my legs not enough of a life lesson that people are horrible? I had to have my heart crushed, too? What else must I lose to learn this basic life lesson? People suck. But Ms. Taylor made meals for me—twice a week—because she worried about me. She didn't even know me. Rance. Rance was beautiful to me. Once there was a tribe—no! The story is bullshit, but at least, maybe, I can toast the possibility of Found Kings and Queens.

To possibilities.

Christ, this is why I do not drink whiskey. Still burning my throat. *Gak.* I may cough again. How can I not forgive Greg when he reminds me of a New Yorker? Rance shoved me without physical contact. I remember how those seconds felt, airborne, mystified. I fell up into a throne of arms. I fell up. Isn't that proof of something?

Ha. I am drunk.

No, I'm not. But I don't think I am. This constant disorientation is how I live now, confused, hurting, furious, *so* furious, exhausted by fury. Pondering forgiveness and curiosity, wondering if I was not strong enough to be welcomed. Yes, I want to be happier. Yes, I want friends in my life, but I will never forgive Vin. Never. Any softening toward him is just guilt over the gun permit I started filling out online. Doesn't matter I never finished it. For almost twenty-four hours, I wanted his death. Planned for it. I feel terrible—no, fuck that.

Fuck feeling terrible!

Fuck guilt!

That man elicited my most feared truth—I am every atom my father's son when it comes to rage and hate. Which means for the rest of my life, I will drag Dad with me, every goddamn step. I can never forget that—how I became him in a three star hotel lobby. Vin Vanbly ruined my life.

Suck down the rest.

Jesus, what is wrong with me? This is—I never do this. Three months ago, I would never fucking do this. It's 2:00 p.m.! No more drinking. I can't fall over in a shithole bar. Be New York strong.

Eventually, I'll have to confess everything to Margaret. Can't keep canceling appointments. What do I say? *What's new, you ask, Margaret? Well, I felt sad last Tuesday. Also, I applied for a gun permit so I could kill a man I never met. Do you think that's worth discussing?* It's not great mental health to stop telling your therapist important things. She's too important in my life to treat her this way. This is not good. It's the kings, they're making me—no. I am making my life crazy. I take responsibility. But c'mon. They did New Age surgery to my brain. Rance used that pulse to physically lift me from the ground. How can I not hold them responsible?

I can't handle running logic circles anymore.

Greasy Thomas emerges from the bright lights from the pool table corner like a returnee from the afterlife. I wonder if he washed his hands. Probably not. He said, *"He fucked me over."* What if Thomas was a questing candidate like me? Anger scorches through me, all of me. Or is that the whiskey? What do I want from Vin? Second chance? Punch him in the face? No. Maybe. If I did that, I'd fall over. Vin Vanbly is a fucking asshole, and I want another goddamn drink.

"*Hey.* Another drink, please."

Greg responds but takes his time.

I think he's deliberately going slower.

"Thank you. Sorry about my tone."

He walks away.

I dedicate the first half of this shot to Ms. Taylor's pot roast, and specifically, her amazing glazed carrots. Who knew carrots could taste that way? I'm definitely getting used to this, because that half-shot went down smoother. What the fuck. Chug it. To Lost Kings everywhere, and the people who fucked us over.

Greasy Thomas raises his glass. "Greg, I'm using up one of my benders."

"No you're not."

"I have two left."

"Don't care. The month isn't even half over."

Why is Greg shooting me dirty looks? I didn't do anything.

Thomas says, "*Greggy.*"

There's surprising sharpness to Thomas's tone.

The woman on her cell phone approaches, clinking the remaining ice in her glass. Greg takes it without comment. The hard crack of pool balls suggests a new game. Light breaks behind me. More people entering. I hear a man and woman's conversation.

Thomas says, "He fired me. No reason."

"Thomas." Greg's word is a warning.

"It wasn't my fault, Greggy. I did what he wanted."

"Give it a rest."

"Greggy." The same sharp tone.

Greg relents and snatches Thomas's empty glass. I'm surprised. If this guy is already blotto, why serve him more?

Thomas says, "He called me the Quiet Strength. That was my king name."

Greg says, "Nobody called you that."

I can't breathe.

I'm not sober enough for this. Oh, shit. I am definitely drunk.

Thomas says, "He gave us all special names as a warning. Keep your mouth shut. We knew the score. I played along."

Greg glares at me. "What did I ask you?"

"You just poured him another drink. I didn't do a goddamn thing."

Wow, I am fucking furious, right away.

Greg scowls.

Lost King or not, fuck Greg. I don't have to do what he wants. And I'm totally drunk. "Hey Greg, pour a second drink for this guy. They fired him, and it wasn't even his fault."

"Hell yeah, Greggy. Cripple's buying me a drink."

Greg pours again without comment. I'm letting that cripple comment slide. Can't deal with that right now.

Thomas raises the glass in salute. "Up yours."

I nod.

He says, "I get three benders a month. Per impetuity. It's a monthly credit of four hundred a month, per impetuity. Which works out to about three benders, and if I spread them out, a couple drinks other days. All free."

I can't think of the right word.

He leans closer. Drunks always want to discuss my legs or touch them. Why did I pound those shots? I can't defend myself while drunk. This is a fucking disaster. Am I going to blame someone else for this, too?

Thomas licks his lips. "Per impetuity means for life."

"Why were you fired?"

Goddamn it, he's sliding his stool closer. This is not good.

Thomas says, "Bullshit about missing shifts. Other mechanics missed shifts. We aren't the most reliable, ex-cons. I got singled out because I knew."

"Knew what?"

Dad created hiding spots for me, to thrill me into thinking I'd discovered someplace new. Quit remembering!

"Knew what, Thomas?"

Thomas raises his glass, deliberately sloshing in appreciation. "The scam."

"What scam?"

"It's pretty, isn't it?" He swallows the rest. "Clear. Perfection. I don't like the flavored ones. They make one in caramel. I don't like it."

"What scam?"

"The owner had very expensive tastes. Gay homosexual hustlers, coke. He drove an RX 330, which he said was a gift. Probably was."

"I don't know what that is."

"Lexus. Top of the line. We stripped it for parts when he was broke again. Champagne tastes on a gay homosexual blue-collar budget." He guffaws.

He's talking about Vin. Don't feel drunk. Don't listen for Dad's shoes.

Thomas circles the rim with his finger. "He was an okay boss. He knew cars. He was good at fixing them. He could cook books well enough to stay afloat. But he was an asshole, and I'm not saying that just because he was a gay homosexual. He could make you feel like shit in two sentences, and the first sentence was uplifting. I didn't come up with that, by the way. My ex-wife used to say that, and I'm repeating it. He'd be gone from the garage for a month or two at a time, working the scam. The garage was better when he was gone."

Wait. Slow down.

Thomas says, "I never said a thing. Never talked. Still, he fired my ass."

"What's the scam?"

Thomas rambles, a related complaint. How did I not see this coming? This king business is a goddamn scam. Of course it is. *I can't fucking believe this.* I need to concentrate. Why am I drunk? I never get drunk!

"—would have. He called me the *quiet strength*. It worked. I never told. Queen Andrea, the Secret Keeper. She was his accountant. Not too subtle, right? He made us all distrust her, made us think she knew things about each of us. It was bullshit, but he'd hint around the edges. He could make you hate your best friend."

He tinks the glass with his fingernail.

"The tapping means you buy me another drink. I started using my fingernail to make noise because you weren't noticing me tapping. Are you a mental cripple, too, or just the legs? What happened to those fuckers? They're angled wrong."

"None of your fucking business. Tell me about the scam, and I'll maybe buy you a drink."

"No, drink comes first. Lubrication. Greeeeeeeeeggy. Greggy!"

Don't react. He's telling you things you need to know.

"Hey, cripple. If you're not a 'tard, buy me a fucking drink. Let's be gentlemen about this."

Maybe they were never going to *ask* for money. Maybe they're going to steal it. I have to check in with my bank. Oh fucking shit. Like, right now. I can't! I can't call my bank lady while I'm drunk. I don't think I'm slurring my words, but I'm not right in the head.

"Cripple guy. I'm still tapping."

"Greg!" My gruffness surprises me. "C'mon."

I can't call the bank—I have to learn the scam. They can't take my money! Calm down. My bank passwords are triple protected. They are required to call me for verbal confirmation.

Thomas is gleeful. "That's it, Greggy. This is bender two. Pour it, baby."

Greg stares sourly at me. "Did we not talk about this?"

Thomas says, "The trick to selecting a bender night is to do it when someone else will buy a few drinks. Supplement the free booze. When you are per impetuity, you make it last. It's every alcoholic's dream. Sorry for what I said earlier, calling you a cripple. Handi-*able*. Back in prison, I knew a guy who was handi-abled. He was cool. Of course, he wasn't always crippled. During his first year, he got a hardcore beat down for disrespecting blacks. Never walked again. I'm Thomas."

The cowboy says, "Another Goose Island."

While Greg serves him, I'm surprised by a sharp crack from the pool corner. That sound is getting under my skin. Once I figured out Dad liked the game of my hiding, I couldn't decide whether to deny him and wait in the garage or let him fulfill his desire to hunt me, maybe satiating a hunger that would lessen his rage—no. I'm not thinking through strategies. Been through that with Margaret. Who I am currently disrespecting in the highest order. I need her help, but how could I call her now after how I've treated her?

"What's your name? Don't make me call you *cripple*."

"Daniel."

Why did I just share my fucking name? What happened to my *no information shared* plan?

"Thanks for the drink, Daniel. Were you always handi-able?"

"I bought your drink. Tell me about the scam."

"All business." He exhales heavily. "I was trying to be friendly, asking you how your legs got to be all fucked up."

"Just tell me the scam."

"Okay. Don't get testy. I was just curious. What happened?"

"Fuck that. Tell me about the scam."

Thomas pouts but takes another swig. "Vin would tell them fairy tale stories, and fuck them, and they would give him money. Or cars. He'd find a mark, and together they would binge on gay coke for a full weekend. Vin would bring them around and say, 'This guy's on his king weekend.' We were all expected to get down on one knee. Say our king names aloud, if he wanted. It was a show. He and his butt buddy were always messed up on gay coke. That's what the party guys called meth."

Get through this. Get through this insanity. "Who would he scam?"

"Gay homosexual rich guys. Older straight guy, once, a black man whose son had just died, father-figure thing. I don't think they had gay homosexual sex. If a guy was rich and sad, that's all Vin needed." He gulps the rest of his drink.

Dad would click the ratchet wrench while he counted down from ten. Forgot how that sounded.

Thomas says, "I was loyal. He shouldn't have fired me. Don't matter if I say anything now that he's dead."

I'm definitely going to vomit. "How? When?"

He leers. "One of his rich marks must have paid for a hit. A car fell on him in his own shop. Get real. An experienced mechanic? They said the lift was old. Broke. That's bullshit. Straight up murder. Or he got sloppy doing gay coke. But probably murder."

What the hell is happening? What about chubby Vin in overalls? I can't inhale these surprises fast enough. It was stupid as fuck to get drunk so quickly. Jesus Christ, I gotta get out of here. I have to call my bank. The cowboy tosses bills and leaves. Thomas taps the side of his glass again. My bank would have called if someone got to the third protocol. He arranged those boards as a hiding spot. He liked to find me.

Goddamn it.

"I'm tapping the glass again, Daniel."

I'm fucking pissed. "No. Tell me something goddamn useful."

"Okay. Jesus, don't get so down on me. I know I'm a drunk, but I need a drink. Greggy. Greeeeeeeeeggy!"

Greg returns but won't look at me. "Thanks, asshole."

I can't even answer. I watch him slosh vodka.

Thomas wipes up the spill on his fingers and puts them in his mouth. He nods. Raises his glass. "He called the scam The Lost and Founds."

This is not happening.

Thomas drags greasy strands behind one ear. "Every person was the one true king. Meant you had to do whatever Vin or his helpers told you. For mechanics, you ignored the gay coke hidden in cars."

I can't believe this. I cannot fucking believe this.

"The quiet strength." He taps the side of his glass. "Fired me anyway."

His glass is empty.

Thomas will be back soon.

Sober up.

Review what I learned.

The Lost and Founds is a huge fucking money scam. Vin's buddies got a cut. Vin insisted they call themselves The VV. Vin died in 2005. His friends scattered, went underground. Another fact: I'm a fucking moron idiot. But New York was not a scam. He pushed me *up.* The power of their blessing was not a scam. Is Vin manipulating Rance? Or is Rance—no. I know his heart. Vin's dead—Thomas hinted at proof. John told me Vin decided not to king me but Vin Vanbly is a corpse. Someone's lying. Of course, it's John. Fucking *asshole.* I can't think this through. It's like trying to figure out Dad. Impossible hours trying to anticipate and outthink him. I have to change my bank passwords. I should have done this while he was in the bathroom. Julia. Yeah, Julia something. I have to check on my accounts.

I'm going to vomit.

Okay, good. He's coming back. Let's...let's get answers.

"How are you sure Vin Vanbly is dead?"

Thomas throws me a smile I do not like. "You asked the right guy." After he adjust himself on the stool, he produces a folded paper from an inside jacket pocket. He passes the newspaper clipping to me. It's a police blotter from 2011. Cemetery destruction, grave dug—oh god—...*bearing the surname Vanbly.*

Don't freak out. "This isn't proof. His first name—"

"I dug him up." Thomas's hair hangs over his eyes, and he speaks in a low voice. "That was me."

Whatever prejudice I had about ex-cons doubles down, listening to his hoarse, hissing laughter, watching his tangled hair jerk when his body jerks. I have to leave town. I'll call the bank while Jian packs for us. Coming here was a huge mistake. No tears. Keep it together. This guy is drunk and dangerous. I'm in fucking danger.

"Why?"

He taps his glass.

My voice is hoarse when I call Greg's name. I remember how all those oranges rolled toward me on the table, and I felt loved. *That was not a lie.* Ms. Taylor is real, too.

Greg no longer fights it, but if he could get away with spitting in our drinks, he would. Wait, why two? He thuds it in front of me.

"On the house. For being so awesome and helping me out."

Damn, quite the snarl. Fuck you, too, Greg.

"I used to be good at drawing." Thomas takes a long sip. "I had a job at the garage. Drew in my free time. I was married. Her name was Fredi. We had a kid. Thank you, Greggy."

"Fuck you, pathetic drunk."

"I am what I am."

My hands tremble. Breathe. Just fucking breathe. Thomas's hands shake, too. He wears his misery as I wear mine. He is a person, not a vending machine for information. Vin ruined his life. His vodka is gone, already. Jesus, he drinks a lot.

"Tell me about the cemetery. Please."

"You're an asshole," Thomas says. "You think because you've got fucked-up legs, the whole world should bend over for you. That's bullshit. I've got problems, too. Fredi and I were in love. Well, not in the last years, but we were at one point."

"I meant no disrespect. I'm trying to keep my shit together, so would you please, just please tell me why you did...that?"

Thomas glances toward Greg, who is back with his friends. "Five years after he was dead, The VV started working the scam again. Found a new sucker. Promised him an audience with Vin Vanbly."

I'm the rich sucker.

"They told him Vin was still alive, he faked his own death in 2005 due to his enemies and shit. That was in case the mark ever did web research and found the death certificate. There's not much else about Vin online. The VV made sure of that. They always made a big deal about 2005 in case the mark hired a detective."

He glances around. "They would promise some chump Vin was considering him for a King Weekend. That was the new twist on the scam, promising a King Weekend with Vin. But they weren't as good at it without him. They must have made mistakes because a mark got suspicious. Really fucking rich guy. Found me here, drinking with friends. I told him not to fall for it because Vin was dead. He and his detective already found the death certificate but this mark wanted iron-clad proof, like, no-argument proof." Thomas leans in. "He wanted a DNA test. Offered big cash for me to bring him Vin's finger. Fredi said she'd leave me if I took that job. But we needed the money because she was blowing it all on gay coke."

Definitely going to be sick.

"She found out I did it. Took off with our kid. I'm an alcoholic, ex-con. No duh she got custody, even though she was fucked up on gay coke."

I can't listen to this insanity, I can't believe I was fucking stupid enough to fall for this. It was only a matter of time before someone discovered my wealth. I confessed it, right in an email. What the fuck was I thinking?

"... rich enough he could buy this bar. Promised me a bar tab impetuity. Smart for both of us. I'd blow through any money he gave me. He knew I'd demand more. As long as the booze flows decent, I can't threaten him. I'm chained to this bar like a dog. I can't even demand more booze, because I tried that once, and he knocked my impetuity down from five hundred to four hundred per month."

He leans in. "It felt so good to break his finger, I kept going and broke seven."

He's proud of that?

"Vin shouldn't have fired me for no reason."

Thomas shoves his glass so hard, it skids down the bar right past me.

I can't catch it.

"Buy me a fucking drink, cripple."

Time slows as the glass slides straight over the edge, gliding in the air, and my legs jerk instinctively to rise up, as if there were time to snatch it. It smashes against the floor. Greg turns slowly, no longer masking his fury.

I have to get out of here. I have to go.

Thomas says, "Cripple broke it. Get us another round, Greggy."

Greg says, "Thomas, you complete fuckhead. You're gonna fucking sweep that shit up. God, you're an asshole."

"It slipped."

Greg disappears, yelling as he picks up broken glass. "I'd fucking force you to do this if I didn't think you'd smash everything back here, you piece of human garbage."

I grab my canes.

"It was an accident."

Greg rises. "Not so fast, slick. Gimme your card."

Thomas says, "Charge him for another two drinks."

Greg says, "Fuck you, Thomas."

"Bender *two*, Greggy. I won't slip no more glasses."

"Fuck you. This is a new low, breaking shit."

When Greg grabs my card, my hand is visibly shaking.

While swiping it, he says, "As predicted, I'm stuck with this drunk on what could have been a relaxing night. Thanks for that. You know whatever Thomas tells you is a lie, right? Anything you want to hear, as long as you're buying. You get that, right?"

Thomas says, "Plenty of people can verify."

"Name one."

"Fredi."

"Who nobody ever met, your coke whore."

"Don't talk shit about her."

"You call her a gay coke whore all the time. You just did to Mr. Crutches, here."

"Once and that was by accident. She's a gay coker. Same as Vin was."

Greg barks. "She's fucking imaginary."

"She's real. We have a kid."

"Again, never seen."

"Who brings kids to a bar? Duh."

I have to fucking leave. I can't take any more.

Thomas crosses his arms on the bar. "I haven't seen my boy in a few years, so, I can't blame you for not believing me on that one. It's okay, Greggy. The gay homosexual hustler—Fitch. He's still in town. Vin hired him all the time. He can verify."

Greg says, "Do you even realize how you're a cliché of a cliché? Fill-in-the-blank ruined my life. Broke up my marriage. I'd be a good daddy if only *blank* hadn't happened. The only person who ruined your life was you. And you're ruining it right now, not in the past. And you're ruining mine."

"It's true," Thomas says with the same hoarse vulnerability I heard when I first entered.

Over his shoulder, Greg says, "Your card was declined. Big shock there. Gonna make a run for the door?"

The hair on my neck bristles. They got my money.

"Hang on." Greg says glumly. "Went through."

Oh my god, oh my god, oh my god. I have to call my bank.

Greg swaggers, taking his time. "You racked up quite a bar tab. Might want to think about a hefty tip."

Everything moves in slow motion while my brain streaks from one panic after another. *They're going to take my money.* This is worse than I ever thought possible. He flops the sales slip in front of me with a pen. My card clatters to the bar. There's nowhere to hide. He'll find me. They'll take everything because I'm weak.

Greg says, "Don't rule out a solid fifty bucks. Considering I have to spend the next twenty minutes making sure there are no shards of glass in every cabinet. Think of that as a starting tip and then be generous."

Thomas says, "Vin called Fitch the Finder of Beauty, I think to get a cheaper rate. Fitch went online I heard."

"Nobody fucking cares, Thomas."

"I'm not a liar. I'm a drunk. Tell the cripple about my monthly credit."

I have to think about how to sign my name, I'm so goddamn confused. I have to call Ms. Taylor. I have to warn her. Wait...wait. Ask about the bar credit.

"Greg, a hundred bucks if you're honest. Is the monthly bar tab real?"

Thomas says, "I don't think Greggy would serve me if he didn't have to. Three benders and a few low buzzes per month."

Greg's not denying the monthly credit. He won't look at either of us. Shit. Everything Thomas said is true.

I fumble to standing.

"Thanks, handi-able."

Be careful, be careful.

Greg says loudly, "Quit reaching for the bottle, man. I'm standing right here."

"Did Daniel pay for another drink?"

"I'm not cleaning up your vomit. If I get you a drink, you have to go sit by the bathroom."

Thomas groans. "It's too bright."

The VV is stealing my money.

I throw up before reaching the door.

THIRTEEN

WHERE ARE YOU, Julia Lundstrom?

I left her a message two hours ago. They said she'd call back. They keep telling me I'm a priority client, so where is she? Two-and-a-half hours. They assured me there was no suspicious activity, but I want to speak with her. She knows my situation.

Am I doing this? Meeting Fitch?

Five minutes.

I couldn't sit around waiting. Fitch wasn't hard to find. Spread cheeks, puckered hole, representing Minnesota's finest escorts. Couple of the same standard reviews you read on every escort's page. Friendly. Hung. Felt comfortable around him. Based on the private photos he unlocked for me, he's not bad looking. Nothing's going to happen physically, so why am I nervous? I'm nervous because they're scamming me. I'm being fucking scammed. Thomas's face saying the word seven, that ghoulish relish. Fuck, what am I doing here? Why did I come? Why am I at this shithole motel?

Julia hasn't called in the last two minutes. Ms. Taylor's not picking up. I have an appointment. I'm gonna do this, I guess.

The enormous sign with a burned out letter promises *YE we have cancies*. Of course you do. Thick weeds make the parking lot surface almost as much green as black. Brick exterior looks sturdy, I guess, if you're searching for compliments. Red awnings burnt into pink. Broken soda machine near the front office. We drove through a middle-class neighborhood to get here, just a block over. Car dealership across the street, and down there, a Walgreens. How can this shitty motel exist here? They must get out-of-towners who skipped internet research. Married nooners. Escorts like Fitch.

"I'm going inside."

Jian says, "Are you sure?"

"I won't be long."

"Should I text you after a certain time?"

The hesitancy in his voice, the closest he's come to questioning me. He's making me think twice. No. I have to do this. Make my voice sound normal. Relaxed.

"Less than an hour. Probably half an hour. I'll text if I need anything."

"Yes, Mr. Daniels."

He has a right to be freaked out. I vomited on my shoes and he had to clean them off before I could get in the car. My tip better be double what is normal.

Leaning my first cane out the car door, I don't feel wobbly. I'm calmer. I extricate myself with care. Jian looks away.

It's only 6:00 p.m. Sun's so high, feels like mid-afternoon.

Navigating the parking lot is easy, even with crevices and weeds. After New York, everything is manageable. Where is Ms. Taylor? She can't be getting groceries this long. She didn't have plans to visit her sister. Two hours. This is not a big deal. It never dawned on me she may not have voicemail. I guess she always answers right away. Could the VV be using her to get to me? Is she in danger?

Room 118 in grey letters. This is it.

I knock.

The door opens.

The surprise on his face is evident, and while he makes a quick study of me, I do the same. He's hot, well, maybe once. He didn't age well. Dark circles under his eyes. Pale skin. He looks exhausted after a whole bunch of days being exhausted. He scans the parking lot.

"I'm Daniel, obviously. Hello."

He continues to block the door. I can't have him slam the door on me. I have to get inside.

He says, "You didn't mention your legs."

"Is that a problem?"

"I charge extra for weird stuff."

Do not react. "And why would you assume I'm into *weird stuff*?"

Fucking asshole.

He says, "Chill. I do watersports and bondage. I meant, like, leg sex stuff."

"I should have revealed my hideous deformity over the phone." Stop. I need his cooperation. "I should have said something. Sorry. I am not into weird sex stuff. May I come in? Getting tired of standing here."

My tone is not friendly. Stupid, stupid, stupid.

He moves aside.

Nobody comments on my smile. My hair. The mole on my neck. My clothes. Hell, my biceps got fatter since New York. Notice that? Nope. I'm nothing but my legs. They called me *Legs* in New York.

Don't cry.

The room has a distinct smell, yet nothing I can identify. Ammonia? No. The edge of the bed is the easiest place to sit, but I don't want to give him access to the door. He could leave after I pay him. I need answers.

"You have the money? I get paid up front."

"Could you drag that desk chair right here? So I can sit and take out the cash?"

"Sit on the bed."

"I'd prefer to chat for a few minutes. Get to know you. I'm new to this. I'd feel more comfortable this way."

He jerks the chair into place, communicating his displeasure. He drops on the bed corner, a leg on either side. He wears a plain gray T-shirt and old sweats. It's disappointing to see him dressed like laundry day. What do I care? We're not having sex. He tries to appear relaxed. He can't look me in the eye for more than three or four seconds, stealing glances at my legs, trying to determine where the angles go wrong.

Oh, yeah. He's definitely high. Well, shit. Not good. Very not good. Thomas didn't get aggressive, but I got lucky. Fucked-up people want to talk about my legs. See how fast I can move. Touch me. I have to be careful with this guy.

Fitch says, "How's the weather?"

Mom cooked cabbage once. The whole house—"Sunny. How's life as an escort?"

I have to check my attitude, but how can I when I'm assaulted by smells and sounds every few seconds? One time she cooked cabbage. How is that worth remembering right now?

He says, "I hate to be rude about money. Best to get business settled so we can enjoy ourselves."

This affable, gym buddy shtick is not working. You're a decade beyond Abercrombie, bud.

"Sure."

"Thanks. Normally I have guys leave it on the dresser, but since you can't get up without taking ten minutes—"

I can't believe this.

"—just throw it on the floor. Out of the way."

I toss the bills.

He stoops, but before touching it, straightens. "You're not a cop, right?"

"No."

"Are you a law enforcement agent from any level of government?"

"No."

"Cool. Thanks. You understand."

I think it's a myth cops have to answer that honestly. He scoops up the money and walks to a dresser missing two knobs. He's counting subtly, but when you're clinging to youth, and you've got a big drug problem, I would imagine every dollar matters. I feel sad. Yeah, he's rude but his life isn't perfect either. So many Lost Kings.

He flashes me that jock grin, meant to seduce. "Thank you."

Gross.

I hear that word regularly—*gross*. People spontaneously utter it when they see me. I make deliberate eye contact to let them know I heard. Yet I had no problem thinking gross about him. Thomas was right about me.

"Should I call you something other than Fitch?"

"Fitch is fine. You know I'm a total bottom, right?"

"Yeah, your profile said so."

"When guys see my big dick, they want me to fuck. I don't top. You can suck it. Sometimes it gets hard. No guarantees."

He stands up and yanks down his sweats. He nudges himself closer. His shirt flies over his head.

"Wait."

His body surprises me, more buff than I expected. Definition. And a big dick. Mine is bigger.

"Fitch, I need to talk."

He sighs, sitting.

"I have to know someone a little. Sorry."

"We only have an hour unless you want to extend. Just to be up front."

"I get it."

"It's a big dick," Fitch says. "If you want to touch it while we're talking, I can drag your chair closer to the bed. You don't have to move."

"Thanks. No."

"Are you nervous about your legs?"

"No. Could you please pull up your sweats?"

He does this without complaint.

"Thank you. I'm nervous, Fitch, because I don't want to have sex. Just talk."

"Serious?"

"Yeah."

"Dirty talk?"

"No."

His gaze jerks around the room. "I keep the money. There's no discount for not having sex."

"That's fine."

"Talk about what?"

Here goes. "Vin Vanbly."

For a second, his gaze sharpens. "Which agency?"

"I don't understand."

He got—he got gorgeous for a second, his icy green eyes clear and—what just happened?

"You fucking people. Fuck you. I don't even care what agency. You're all assholes."

"I don't understand what you're asking me."

"What I don't understand is why you people can't let this go. He was a low level drug dealer at best."

"Okay. You knew him."

"Don't be a dick." He leans back on his elbows. "This is not my first or even fifth time with you assholes. Are you FBI? DEA? You guys always begin solemnly confirming everything I say, like you respect me. Establishing a bond so I'll open up and tell you the secret of his scam. I tell every agent the same thing, whether they take the good cop or bad cop route. I don't know shit. I never did. I'm not talking about that fat turd. I'm keeping the money. Get the fuck out. Now."

"No." My voice is small.

I'm hiding behind the ironing board. He found me here before, but what can I do? Jesus, *focus*. I will not be intimidated. No more hiding.

"I'm fucking staying."

Fitch says, "Great. Stay. If you're not going to fuck me, and we're not going to talk about that asshole, what now? Maybe the front desk has board games."

"I paid you."

"For sex. Not talking."

"I paid for your time."

"Great. You can watch me nap."

He slides back on the bed.

"Fitch, please. Please. Just tell me about the scam. I'm not trying to intimidate you. I'm nobody intimidating. Look at me."

He glowers. Flops on the bed.

Will he reveal more if he thinks I'm with the FBI? Or is that a disadvantage? I feel like my honesty a second ago softened him.

"Once a FBI agent sucked me off." He lies on his back and speaks to the ceiling. "He paid for my time, like you. I refused to tell him anything. Only because there's *nothing* to tell. After thirty minutes of quiet time, he wanted my dick down his throat. You can suck me off. I may get hard thinking of you stupid agents paying to suck my cock and then putting in an expense report for it."

Arms behind his head, plump with muscle, hairy pits exquisitely curved. No. Now he appears to be a drug addict, hollow, darting eyes; sagging lumps not muscle. Eyes are playing tricks. My brain is spinning out of control. Truth. Tell him the truth.

"Here's the deal. My name really is Daniel. I'm not with any government agency."

"I've had agents say that, too."

"Well, I'm not."

His life is hard. Maybe I can trust him for a second. Tell the man the truth.

"Fitch, I—I'm afraid. I'm afraid and I'm goddamn sick and tired of being afraid. Someone is trying this Lost and Founds scam on me. I need help figuring this out."

Jesus, this is a disaster! Quit talking!

"It truly sucks to feel this intense fear, right when I'm learning maybe—maybe my life could suck less. I just started making friends."

What is fucking wrong with me?

"That's super sad." Fitch stares at me, his drug-haze penetrated briefly. "If I believed you. I once had an FBI agent say he was CIA, promising me national security was at stake. Some other dick pretended to be FBI and later confessed he was state trooper. You fuckers say anything to get a new lead. There are no fucking leads. He was a client. If I knew I'd be haunted by you guys for a decade after he was dead, I'd never have let him come in my ass. Not worth this harassment."

Forgive him.

"I'm sorry for this guy dragging on you, but I'm not writing a book about this subject because I find it amusing. Some very real people are trying to rope me into a Lost and Founds scam. I'm in trouble. I was told you could at least tell me about the scam. I'm not asking for anything you have been holding back. I just—I don't even know what's going on. Please."

He studies me and then flops back down.

"I don't know anything. That's what I keep telling you people. Or, whoever you are."

Why would I think to forgive him? Quit telling the escort your goddamn feelings. I take some deep breaths.

"If I can have a minute to breathe, okay? I'm pretty freaked out."

"It's your hour."

I found the blog about Perry by accident, following links. That was completely random. Is it possible they hijacked my browser so whatever web address I typed launched that blog? If not, how did they lure me in? I can't process this.

He turns over. The sleekness of his panther body—gone again. "If you're not an agent, you must be rich."

"I am."

He flips and faces me, sitting up. "Okay, prove you're not an agent. Go get money. Two grand. I'll tell you every single thing I know about Vin Vanbly. Here's a preview. I wasn't lying when I said I know nothing. I have zero information on the scam. None. For two grand, I'll tell you sex stuff. Drug stuff. I'll answer every dumb question. You people think it's significant when *I* misremember something. It's not. I don't even remember what he looked like anymore. People forget, which is normal when they aren't involved in a thing. He was nothing to me."

I never tell anyone I'm rich. I never talk about the money. *Forgive yourself.* I do not have time for this New Age bullshit.

"Hey." He snaps his fingers. "You look as fucked as I am."

"I am fucked. Not by drugs like you. I'm afraid. And right now, I'm terrified you won't help me because I don't know what's happening."

Fitch has the decency to look away. Why can't I stop myself?

He says, "If you're a new agent trying to make a name on this cold case, no agency will reimburse two grand, not when I'm aggressively promising zero new information. If you really are rich, who cares about the money, right?"

"I'll pay you."

I'm not afraid of what I shared with him. He's a Lost King like me. I could make this a great day for him, financially at least.

Fitch says, "How long to get the money?"

"I'm not leaving the room."

He sits up. "You agents are cocksuckers. I fucking knew it. After I blew my load down that FBI asshole's throat, he said, 'You owe me a new lead.' Still had my come on his lips."

"I'm not leaving because I have the money with me." My voice is shaking.

Even though Vin Vanbly was a con artist, aren't we all trying to get found? Isn't the story true because it's true? Ms. Taylor is a queen in my life. Jesus, calm down. I count out more money than he demanded. I find no resistance to paying. He could have responded with cruelty to my breaking voice. He didn't.

"Here's three thousand dollars, Fitch. I didn't lie about being rich. It seems The VV has revived Vin's scam. I think."

He counts bills and considers me. "I never met one of their marks."

The look on his face, like something got answered. Don't get pissed right now.

"Whatever you know, however slight, may help."

He says, "Bad news for you. I will tell you everything I remember about that turd. I'll repeat it, so you get to hear it twice. And there will still be time left on your hour. Don't wait until the last five minutes if you want to suck my cock because it takes me longer than that to get hard. Okay. Which do you want to know first, drugs or sex stuff?"

Don't confront him about that look on his face a moment ago.

Don't do it.

"I saw your expression a second ago. You think I fell for this scam because of my legs."

Damn it.

He laughs. "Wow, big stretch. But yeah, a solid connect, slugger. I did think that. At first. But I decided I was wrong. It's not your legs making you a victim. It's your face. From the minute you walked in—well, not *walked*—you looked like someone who needed a fix. You are grim, man. Your face betrays you. So, yeah, you seem like the kind of guy who could be scammed."

"Bullshit."

"Fuck you. I read people, same as you. I have to. The sooner I get some impotent fuck to spurt a load, the sooner I'm free. I know what men need. I have to."

We glare in unfriendly silence.

"How often do agents come around?"

Fitch says, "Once a year. More than that in the first couple of years. It's always some greenie trying to break a cold case to make his name. Money and drugs were lost. Never found."

"How did it disappear?"

"This is where you get what you paid for. I don't know. I don't know anything about his garage, the mechanics, the scam. He paid for sex. I gave him sex. He paid a lot of money to eat my ass. He liked to talk. Big talker. Stories of kings with crazy names and fairy tale shit."

His eyes are so green, brilliant green.

"We partied. I made sure he paid upfront every goddamn time. We were not pals. He did a lot of drugs and liked pretending to be rich."

"What can you tell me about his king stories?"

Fitch says, "Nothing. I never listened. I never cared. He was high. I was stoned."

"Did he ever reveal any king names?"

He draws his knees to his chest. "You all ask the exact same questions."

"I'm not an agent."

"Or you work for a government agency with a lush expense account."

"I'm not from any agency. I swear."

"Honestly, I don't care. I'm keeping it."

"What agencies come around?"

"FBI. DEA a few times, sniffing out drugs. Rangers? Is that a thing? Private investigator once, checking out a lead from his home state. He was a good guy, sorta. He was disappointed I refused to give him any gossip. I tell everyone the same thing. I never listened to Vin's bullshit, and I don't know anything about the drugs or how the scam operated. They always say, 'Just talk about him. Maybe memories will come back to you,' like nobody ever suggested that."

This was a waste of time.

"You can't trick secrets from me or get me to reveal his favorite color was blue—I don't remember because I never cared. I didn't listen."

"Do you know any of his friends, this group calling themselves The VV?"

"Nope."

"I was told they revived the scam after his death."

"Okay."

"You don't know?"

"An agent told me that two years ago. The one who sucked my cock. He could have been lying. Don't know. Don't care."

"Anything you heard secondhand from agents is worth repeating. I literally know nothing and these VV people are scamming me."

"I've told you everything."

The room still smells stale. You can't not notice it, a combination of no fresh air and sour cleaning supplies. This was a waste of time. "Is it possible Vin faked his own death?"

"Sure. Why not? I only knew he was dead when an agent—legit FBI, I think—showed me autopsy photos. Vin would go through long periods of laying low, so I didn't even notice his absence. Looked like him in the photos, from what I remembered. A lady agent later told me someone dug up Vin's corpse. I do not understand the obsession with this guy. He was a low level criminal, the kind to be caught in his grandma's basement, you know? Nothing special. Nothing to warrant this kind of attention, a decade later."

"Did someone really dig him up?"

"Go to the bar across the street from the garage Vin once owned. Vincent's Garage. Sign's still up. You'll find a drunk who makes money telling people how he dug up Vin's corpse."

"Thomas."

"You know what's irritating? I recognized his name when you said it. Never met him, but you people keep asking me questions about him, so now, I know it again. Me, Thomas the drunk, and his meth whore, ex-wife, Fredi. She used to party with Vin. Had a queen name, too. She's probably still alive, unless she overdosed, which is likely. I only used tina for fun. She was hardcore. Go see her. Be sure to negotiate on price, because for forty bucks and a needle, she'll give you the 'I don't know shit' speech, too. I can tell you sex and drug stuff. That's it."

"How do I find her?"

"Gimme your phone. I'll type in her address. I wouldn't be surprised if she's not living there, though. I haven't seen her in years."

He leaps from the bed with surprising alacrity, and I remember he's high. I feel queasy handing him my phone. Why did I surrender it? I have no self-control right now and I don't understand why. I'm in a room with a druggie and I just handed him my fucking phone. This is what insanity is like. I'm not even keeping myself safe anymore.

He hands it back. "Few years ago, I drove to her crazy stoned, like, out of my mind. I spent the entire drive obsessively drilling the house numbers and street name, because I was paranoid I'd forget. Turns out I had written it on a piece of paper tucked into my jeans, but I didn't remember that. She's in your Contacts under *F* for Fredi."

There's her name. She lives in St. Paul.

"If you two aren't friends, why did you go to her house?"

"To compare stories. We both hustle. We wanted to trade names over who threatened solicitation charges, who said national security was at stake. We laughed about that. They think they can break us, but there's nothing to break. She doesn't know shit either."

I should leave. Ms. Taylor might have called back. Julia for sure.

"Vin paid extra to bareback, in case you're interested in sex stuff." Fitch's eyes dart around the room. "These days, thanks to PrEP, nobody pays. Financially, that was a huge loss. Guys would pay a lot, especially if I resisted. Complained it was too *risky*, then showed off my ass. It's not bad, right?"

He turns and pulls down his sweats.

"Yeah. Pretty great."

"Thanks. Vin paid extra for raw."

Fitch sits. His beauty saddens me. Regardless of our own tragedies, we all share one. We grow old. We die. No one escapes that cruel father. I hope three grand buys him a couple days free of escorting. Or, more likely, I paid for the overdose that kills him.

Oh shit.

"Please don't—this is not my business—please don't overdose on drugs with that money. Please. I just realized how much money I gave you, and now I'm worried."

His eyes narrow. "If I stick three dozen needles in my veins and become the poster boy for Never Try This, fuck you. That's my decision. Second, I'm not going to buy drugs." He relaxes. "I need a new car for outcalls. You're off the hook."

His face flickers, and the workhorse becomes a chestnut stallion, a beauty rarely witnessed. Yet, head cocked, the drug addict is back. Am I still drunk? Or is this stress? My brain is going to explode.

Fitch says, "More standard answers. I don't know where Vin's money went. I don't know how the drugs worked with the garage, which cars had them. He was average in bed, but he paid a lot. Gross body hair. No idea who his dealer was, which was odd, because we knew people in common. He only drank gin. Pretended he was this globe-trotting sophisticate. Bareback. I mentioned that, right? That about covers it."

I still don't know what to say.

"From the cocksucking agent, I heard this VV group would promise an audience with Vin. Big fucking honor. Tell the mark Vin wanted to meet somewhere in the middle of the night, then ditch him. By that time, they had his money. Sorry. I promised you I didn't know anything and now I'm keeping that promise. You were not deceived in any way by me."

My brain is broken. I cannot fucking handle this shit.

"Oh, yeah. He always wanted me to shout *King Vin* while he came. Over and over. *King Vin! King Vin!* Drug-wise, I don't know much about his party. I brought weed a couple times and he never reciprocated, so I stopped. We both partied on our own."

How could I have been so amazingly deceived? Because I was desperate to believe. Because I'm weak.

Staring beyond me, he says, "We're done. Unless you want me to repeat what I just told you, which I will. But no interruptions, okay?"

"Once was enough. Are you sure there's nothing else?"

"Jesus, I just said that. Go see Fredi. She could use the laugh."

"Earlier, you said you knew what I needed. What is that?"

His eyes are puffy again. "Why?"

"Just tell me."

Despite his scowl, I feel we share the same sadness.

He says, "Same as every man. Release."

Jian's still in the car. I see his profile.

Don't care if Fitch sees me from the window. One missed call. Julia. After hellos, Julia apologizes profusely. I try not to be a dick, but I want her to stop talking. When it's my turn, I keep my voice even while assuring her that her colleagues explained everything, I needed to speak with *her*.

"I should have been available. I'm sorry."

She's going to run through the story again. I can't ask her questions until she unburdens herself and I make her feel better.

"—new client and a difficult closing. I'm so sorry."

"You're fine, Julia. Really."

"I let you down."

I'm an asshole. "I appreciate your calling me back after hours. A conversation with you will make me feel better, so thank you. This is a crazy day for me. I may get a call from a friend in New York and if she calls, I have to take it."

"No problem."

"If we get interrupted, I promise you to call right back once she and I finish. You're confirming, short version, everything is okay?"

"I personally reviewed every report before calling you. Based on our conversations, Mr. Connors, I know what to look for. As they mentioned earlier, the only suspicious activity was a random phishing attempt."

"Yeah, they said that earlier."

"It's very common."

She explains its name, how it works, why it would not work in this situation. She does not speak down to me, but more like if we share a professional curiosity in how this technology works. I love that about her. I am comforted. I am calmer.

Fitch unnerved me.

This is the release I needed. He could see it.

"And you checked prison connections?"

"I did. I have the protocols we wrote up together right in front of me. Should we review them?"

This is good. This is good. She is speaking my language. This helps. Maybe this will be okay.

"I love the way you explain things, so thank you."

"Oh, it's no problem."

"You're making me feel weird when you keep calling me Mr. Connors."

She laughs. "Okay. Daniel. I'll get better. And please don't hold it against the bank. If my letting you down means you want a different consultant, I have no problem stepping aside. You're a great customer. I actually like talking to you, and I would want what's best for you, even if that means you want to work with someone else."

I feel every inch the rich asshole I am.

"We're fine. This phone call was exactly what I needed."

"Oh, good. If the threat persists beyond ten days, we'll pull together a new threat assessment team to review protocols like we did three years ago."

"Thank you, my queen."

Oh shit.

"Sorry. Slip of the tongue. I was looking at playing cards, deck of them. And, the queen of diamonds just. Well, I had turned it over. I meant to say, thank you, Julia."

What the hell was that?

She laughs. "I do that too, especially when I'm talking to my mom. I zone out and say the name of whatever I'm staring at."

I want to die. "The mind plays tricks."

"One more thing. Just for kicks, let's look at the phishing report. Hang on."

I listen to her keys clattering.

These guys—they're deep in my head. Paranoid about money. I vomited in a bar. Called Julia a queen. Thomas's hands never stopped shaking. Is that what happens to Lost Kings? Never-ending trembling and one of your best life memories becomes breaking the fingers on your dead boss?

"I'm back."

I know I just jumped a little.

"I want to review it with you on the phone, just for peace of mind."

"Great. Thank you."

They performed psychic surgery on me. To get my money? That's not true. I can't tell what's real. Dad would wear his polished black shoes. He wanted me to hear his approach from wherever I hid.

Julia says, "Found it. Yeah, easily defeated. If your password isn't the word password, you're not even—thirty-seven thousand people's accounts received that same type of attack." She pauses. "In the last hour. Sorry. Thirty-seven thousand in the last hour. I got distracted."

Julia's calm unnerves me.

"Only about 10 to 15 percent of phishing attempts originate within the United States. I would expect any of a dozen countries as the originating IP address, but your phishing attempt came from St. Paul, Minnesota. Interesting, but it changes nothing. I looked up my own account last year, and over a thousand phishing attempts. I had no idea. One day there were two-hundred and thirty attempts and I couldn't recall what happened that day to get that kind of cluster, but the next day there were none. And the normal attempts for the seven months. No reason."

She says more. I try to listen. She promises to call if there is any account activity. When the conversation ends, I text Jian, twenty feet away.

I need help getting to the car.

FOURTEEN

FITCH GAVE ME the wrong address. I don't know why I'm surprised. Why would I think he told me the truth? Maybe he typed wrong. The tree-lined street boasts houses in the half-million dollar range. Maybe not that much, but nice fucking houses, detailed with care, Victorians with tricolored spindles wrapped around deep wooden porches. This street, this house, cannot be the home of a junkie who sells herself for forty dollars and a needle.

Two stories, brick base and avocado stucco. Thick chocolate beams match the dark brick, accentuating the warmth and sturdiness. I'm not sure what style of house you'd call this, but I recognize money. Wide fireplace, it seems. Thick lawn between homes on either side, a contest of happy greens. Enclosed sun porch in front, a ceiling fan running laps around a light fixture with delicate crystal flutes.

Halfway house? No. Not possible. This place is money.

A kid appears in the screened porch, watching my car. He pushes the front door open with great concentration, and after letting it slam, plops on the top step. Four? Young. Elbows on his knees, heels of his hands supporting his chin. Dark, curly hair. Bi-racial.

This can't be Fredi's house. The lawn is freshly shorn, and shy yellow flowers curl up the front step's iron railing. Fire-red geraniums with hot pink blooms rising from the center, like a vulnerable heart. Under the picture window, orange blossoms trailing over the sides of a window box, contrasting the avocado. Why would Fitch send me here? He was *high*, that's why. That's all the explanation needed. He was high. He probably invented an address. Just typed out anything to be rid of me.

I wish the kid would go inside. I know he can't see through the tinted windows, but I don't like his staring. It makes me feel like a stalker, Jian and I just sitting here. I have to figure out my next move. Can't go back to the hotel. I made us check out. The phishing attempt. It's them. We have to leave town. Poor Jian. He's bewildered.

Recalling the bellhop's kiss at the Belleclaire, I now feel shame. I was so happy to believe their king stories, I didn't notice they were scamming me.

I'm calling Ms. Taylor again.

Pick up. Pick up the phone. Please. Come home. Nothing. Maybe if I let it ring long enough, someone will answer it. Maybe I should let it ring for an hour. She has that neighbor she doesn't like. I don't know. She would have told me if she were visiting her sister. She would have mentioned it. Answer, answer, answer. I'll let it ring a few more times. Three more times. Three... two... one. Okay, three more times. Final three. Three... two... one... fuck. Could they have involved her against her will? Is she being held, I don't know, prisoner? That's insane. I've only been trying to reach her for less than eight hours. Calm the fuck down. Okay, three more rings. Three...two...two and a half... Fine. I'll hang up. I'll check email again. Maybe Jarrod responded in the last five minutes. Maybe my notifications are turned off, somehow.

Jian clears his throat. "Mr. Daniels?"

I glance up. Oh, Jesus. That kid stands right next to the car. He's... he's talking.

I power down the window.

He scratches his arm. "Are you Daniel?"

I—

"My mom is waiting for you. She told me to bring you back."

Who the fuck is this? "You know my name."

"You have to come around back."

Jian says, "Do you know this child, Mr. Daniels?"

If I answer with the truth, he won't stay. Jesus, he's already confused. Don't lie to him and make it worse.

"Kind of."

I was older than this kid, but not by much, when Dad called me into the garage. My hands are shaking.

The kid says, "Are you Daniel? If you're not, you have to tell me. I'm not supposed to talk to strangers."

"Yes, I'm Daniel."

Jian says, "You definitely know him?"

I scan the house for an adult face, someone to ease this bewilderment. Nobody. The ceiling fan still makes its lazy rotations.

"Where's your mom?"

He points. "She's in back. We have to go back."

Jian says, "Mr. Daniels."

His tone is neither questioning nor demanding, but it's a confrontation nevertheless. No explanation as to why we checked out. No explanation right now as to why this child knows my name. What can I say? How would I explain?

"This will only be a few minutes."

My phone *dings* a notification. New email—from Jarrod. *She's busy and will call you back.* Oh thank god. What the fuck, Jarrod?

"Kid, give me two minutes."

Once the back window powers up, I reply, asking for details. Maybe I can catch him before he signs off email. She's okay. That's the main thing.

Last time I saw dad, he—no.

"Jian, I know I've been odd. You deserve an explanation. Right now, however, I have another odd request. Could you follow me at a short distance, close enough to keep me in view but far enough **SO** it's not obvious?"

I see his eyes widen in the rear view mirror.

"I know. I know. I shouldn't ask this of you. I'm just—I need help." I hate asking for help. "This is totally weird, I get it."

"Mr. Daniels, should you be here?"

The kid knocks on the car window. His voice is muffled, but I can distinguish the word "C'mon."

"Something strange is definitely happening. You are owed an explanation and you will get one. It's nothing illegal, I promise you. I was told to find this kid but I didn't think he'd be so young, which is why I'm surprised. I have to talk to his mom in the backyard. I guess. I'd feel better if you kept an eye on me."

Am I putting Jian in danger? Maybe. No. No danger.

Am I putting myself in danger?

The boy knocks on the car window again. "Hurry. I'm hungry." He darts away, running down the cement sidewalk between the two homes.

"You're getting a huge tip when I get home, regardless of your answer now. I already decided double to whatever is normal in this type of driver situation."

"I don't know what's happening, Mr. Daniels."

"I know. When I interviewed you, I told you I would not explain much. That was a condition. You do not have to follow me. I asked too much. Sorry. You don't have to follow me."

"I worry for you, Mr. Daniels. You do not look good."

"This has been a hard day. Please don't worry."

Jian acknowledges he heard me but does not change position.

The kid runs back to the car. "Hurry, Daniel. We're getting mac and cheese."

Open the car door.

This is stupid.

Stupid.

I fucking hate this feeling, knotted inside. Moments like this, I hate my legs worse. I can't make a speedy exit. I drag myself through the routine, one cane, one leg. Then the other cane... it always takes so fucking long.

They're scamming me, I get that. But involving a kid is horrible. He was too young to sit alone on the front steps. Who does that? Why is this young kid doing their bidding? Granted, the neighborhood looks safe enough. He looks normal.

He races away, yelling, "We're coming, we're coming!"

I follow.

Jesus, I thought today was reconnaissance. Here I am, almost 8:00 at night, headed into a stranger's backyard because a kid knew my goddamn name. He runs toward me, stomping his feet, talking nonstop, though his voice doesn't carry. I can't hear a word.

When he reaches me, breathless, he says, "What's wrong with your legs?"

I say, "They don't work."

"Oh."

It never bothers me when kids stare. They have no context. Why does it bother me when adults do? They have no context either. Because adults are supposed to know better. How? How would they know better? I'm nothing traditional. Nobody ever says, "Oh, sure. I had a buddy whose father ran him over." I have to be more patient.

He says, "How do you run when you play?"

"I can't play."

You just never play.

I hate these new whisperings.

"I'm a good runner. Watch."

He sprints away.

I smell the rotting garbage under the kitchen cupboard. Goddamn it, I almost just keeled over, remembering that stink. I only hid there a few times because the garbage smell made him angrier. He did not like the garage fouled unless it was with my blood. Jesus. I am fucking unstable. This is bad.

"Hey, kid. Quit running."

"Don't call me *kid*. I'm Vin."

I twist to stop myself from falling. I am so goddamn tired of people fucking with me. "What's your last name?"

"Mergnet—Mergnets—it's hard to say."

He takes off into the backyard. Without turning around, he yells, "Watch me run!"

I'm pretty sure I would have thrown up if he said Vanbly. I don't know what to believe. Mai Kearns lied? I visited his website. I mean, true, I never actually set foot on his farm. I guess it could be fake. But those were respected newspapers who wrote about him. You can't fake archives.

Everything looks suburban. No cigarette stubs or needles or—I don't know what I expect to see. There are greens poking out of garden plots along the side of the house. I recognize tomato plants. Fat peas dangle from a wooden trellis, assembled with twigs and twine. The trellis pattern is almost obscured by vines, but something about it is familiar. Trick of the imagination. I'm obsessed with patterns mimicking that pulse. Earlier, I hallucinated with Fitch. Something is wrong with my head. I have to find out what they did to me. Vin stops at a wooden arch. To enter the backyard, you cross under hundreds of purple flowers. Fucking hundreds. Overpowering and yet, individually, so tiny. It confuses my vision, so many... I feel dizzy.

"Go through here." He disappears through the arbor.

Could his name really be *Vin*?

I stop moving forward, angle my canes so I can look behind me. Jian stands on the front lawn, almost between the two houses, too far away for us to speak. Phone is in his hand. I nod my thanks. What am I doing? What the fuck am I doing?

I face forward, surprised again at the overwhelming purple. Irrationally, I feel nothing bad can happen once I enter, because this homeowner loves flowers. What logic is that? Bad people can love flowers as much as good ones. I use my right cane to push the gate open, attempting to breathe purple as I pass. Are these morning glories? No, they're smaller than that. Not sure why I'm so obsessed with them. It's most likely a coping mechanism to avoid the terror I feel.

This yard feels like a Buddhist temple, though I can't say that from personal experience. It's just the immediate impact. I feel calmer. Safer. There's a wooded center, a grove. Obviously, these three neighbors share this space, this small glen. Birch trees, ornamental grasses, colors poking from odd angles, and I see a landscaped path through the center.

Vin races to the far end, the side nearest us. Okay, I guess I go there. The name isn't a coincidence. My god, I am in over my head. As I draw closer, I see it's as much garden as grove. Surprisingly dense. Deep inside is a bridge, bright red, and, yeah, I hear water trickling. It's pretty. Orange and yellow petals spill into the grass. Something is right.

"Come here," Vin says, pointing. "You gotta begin here."

"Where's your mom? You said I had to meet your mom."

"She's at the center."

"Of what?"

"Da gardens. C'mon."

"Can't your mom come here?"

"She said you have to go to her."

I can't see anyone. "Where is she?"

Vin ignores me, attempting to climb a board, a swing, hung from two sturdy ropes. The board keeps eluding him, but eventually he succeeds by straddling it like a horse, hanging on tightly while it rocks. The expression on his face says he is surprised by his success.

"Look what I did."

"I see."

"I can't always do it."

I adjust my canes so I can turn, and *yes*, there's Jian, watching me from the side of the house. I jerk my head toward the entrance. He nods. He understands I'm going in. More than double the normal amount.

They won't murder me in front of this cute kid. Jian won't have to call 911. Jesus, what am I saying? The fact that I'm having these thoughts is the problem, not the probability of them coming true. I take a few crooked steps toward the brick path, ignoring the woolly logic allowing me to move forward. They can't kill me.

Sure they can. People are murdered for less.

The path is wide enough for two, which means my canes won't crush the flower beds on either side. I'm shocked, the way colors shock you. Vulnerable yellows buds, so tiny, creep to the brick's edge, touching it, waiting for someone to notice them. Little lambs. Blood red blooms over there, snaked through by vines. White impatiens ahead on the left. There. A black woman sits on a bench.

Vin didn't lie.

I know he's not Vin Vanbly, but thinking those words makes me feel exhausted, sad for being tricked. She's just sitting. Dad liked to trick me, promising—no. Dad doesn't come in here. This space is different. A blanket of tiny white flowers, shaped almost like a pillow. I want to nap. To wake feeling refreshed. Keep walking. The path is clean and surprisingly even.

Go deeper.

Looking down feels like the best option, a pleasure for once, not just a necessity. I approach a koi pond, lily pads bumping each other lazily. Small arranged stones— an old symbol that used to mean something. I can't think what.

I hear rustling behind me. "Move. Please."

Vin grasps my right cane and lifts himself over. He has no concept of how rude that was. Yet he's not scared, like the bellhop. I prefer kids. Although her back is to me, I'm close enough she can hear me. No one else is around.

"Excuse me," I say louder than normal. "Your son—"

She says, "Walk the path."

"I don't—"

"Walk the path, *please.*"

Unbelievable. Does she not understand what I'm going through? Fuck her. Fuck this stupid path, this fucking scam, these lies. Walk the path, *please.* Fuck her. Can't turn around and talk to me? Would it be so awful to continue, watching peach-colored koi ripple through water? Cross the red bridge? Take a moment to get calm. Think about what you want to ask. Go forward.

Following the circuitous route feels like a board game, me constantly turning and twisting, coming upon little vistas and curiosities making me wonder why those flowers are here, that big rock is there. It's hard to feel threatened at a wishing well surrounded by a community of geraniums—pink and white—all crowded around to see how the wishes turn out. I draw closer and see a small stack of pennies and a gold-plated message carved into a metal square.

Name your fears and cast them out.

Fuck that. Fucking con artists. Fucking asshole lying cons. Fuck you, Mom. Why the fuck didn't she ever do a goddamn thing? Yes, she was damaged by that psycho. I was her kid.

No.

Do not go there.

Can't even see Vin. Where did he go?

I come upon a patch of marigolds, and behind them taller, the feathery grasses I saw earlier. The impression is elders protecting children who think they're older than they are. You're supposed to protect your children.

Ahead, a sturdy stone bench looks inviting, and I could use a sit, emotionally if not physically. What are these things that look like miniature cabbages and carrots? Rabbits must love this place. Maybe planted specifically for them, a little buffet in this—I'm calm again. How?

The path turns, revealing her, waiting on another stone bench, wider than the last. Three people could fit there. She's not on her phone. She's not reading a book. She's just... waiting. Hang on. Don't feel soft toward her. She's part of the scam. Earlier today, they tried to fucking hack my account!

She's in her thirties, but beyond that, I have no idea. I can never tell anyone's age. Lavender dress, folded over her knees. Thick necklace, dark purple beads, rounded like Jordan almonds. The bench is positioned under a birch tree, the branches threaten to touch her but never do. I can see the back of the avocado-and-brick house.

She is no meth user.

"I'm Fredi. Sit with me."

Vin kicks a ball through the backyard. When he sees me, he yells, "Can we go now?"

She raises her voice. "Not yet, baby."

To me, she says, "Sit."

I feel inelegant in her silence, lowering myself, wrestling my canes, struggling to do what everyone else accomplishes without thought. I bump her twice, murmuring apologies. Why am I apologizing to the people scamming me? Rage races through me. When I look around, the rage fades.

She faces me. High, round face, light purple eyeshadow, very little lipstick. Her expression is serious. Did she get clean, and Fitch not know about it?

"I have questions—"

Fredi interrupts. "Vin wants to meet you tonight. At midnight."

I look at her son.

"Not mine. Big Vin. Vin Vanbly."

"He's dead."

"He's alive. There's a café in South Minneapolis on the corner of Nicollet and 43rd Street called Anodyne."

"I was told he was dead." My voice is shaking.

What is happening?

Fredi says, "Anodyne hosts jazz night on Thursdays. Vin will be there. He wants you to show up precisely at midnight. Come through the front door. If you're not seated at his table by 12:03, he will leave. Do not show up early."

"Hang on."

"Daniel, not before midnight and not five minutes after. You have a three-minute window. Do you understand?"

"Not in the slightest."

"You have a three-minute window."

"Two different people told me Vin was dead. There was a newspaper article."

"You were deceived."

"I was also told you're a meth whore. That a lie as well?" How is the surprise in her eyes genuine? "A drunk in a bar said that."

She glares. "Really."

"Thomas. He called you a gay coke whore. Said you got custody of your son in the divorce."

"Little Vin," she sings his name. "Get your jacket from the back porch. We're stopping at a divorce lawyer's before we get your mac and cheese. Daddy's in a shitload again." She snaps open a purse and takes out her smartphone. "He should not have said that."

Vin jogs closer, clutching his ball, watching us curiously, like we are the zoo.

"Go inside and get your things. We're leaving."

"Mac and cheese time?"

"Yes, baby."

He runs away.

"You're still married?"

"We'll see."

She texts furiously, conveying a lot of sentiment. I can't read the words, but I see a few all-capped ones.

"People are lying to me." The words sound as pitiful as I feel. "Can you please tell me what's happening?"

She throws the phone into the purse. "What were his exact words?"

"Just what I said. An escort also said you were a meth whore. He gave me this address."

She grimaces. "If they both said it, this came from Big Vin. Oh, he is dead. Telling a grown woman to rub liver on her hands. Making a man call his wife a *meth whore* in a public bar, where people can overhear. Daniel, you had better show up between midnight and three minutes after, because it's your last chance to see Vin Vanbly breathing. Put the ball down, baby. Get your jacket."

Vin yells a question, but I can't hear it.

She stands.

"Wait. You have to explain this."

Her phone *bings*. She pulls it from her purse and reads a reply. "Thomas says he was forced to say it. Said Vin came into the bar, listened to every word."

"Vin Vanbly?"

Fredi says, "In a cowboy hat."

I'm going to pass out.

"He won't be wearing a cowboy hat at Anodyne tonight. You won't recognize him. Remember. Three-minute window."

"Please don't leave. I am begging you. None of this makes any sense."

"Go inside. You'll know which table."

"Fitch said a late-night audience with Vin was part of the scam. You're scamming me."

"Look into my eyes."

"Mom, you said we were going!"

Without breaking eye contact, she says, "You have your jacket?"

"No."

"Go get it."

She takes both my hands in hers. My instinct is to jerk free. She holds them with intention, not trapping me exactly, but communicating strength. She will relinquish them if I insist. I see the truth of her, richer than I first imagined. Not because I thought less of her—well, I did when I thought she was a junkie. I did not understand how much she would reveal, soft petals unfolding, the exquisite truth of her. Thorns don't prick if you caress them.

What the fuck does that even mean?

She says, "Show up at Anodyne between midnight and three minutes past."

"Why?" I squeak out the word.

"Look at me. Take a moment. Do you believe I'm involved in a scam?"

"No."

"Addicted to drugs?"

"I don't think so, no."

Please don't hurt my heart.

She says, "They're kinging you, Daniel."

I burst into heaving sobs.

When I can breathe again, Jian stands at my side, eyes downcast, hands folded in front. He brushes the dirt off my cell phone, which has fallen out of my pocket. He hands it to me in silence.

Fredi and her son are gone.

FIFTEEN

Look at how normal everything is. A normal coffeehouse. A woman and her daughter, maybe. They look alike. Iced coffees. Normal chatting. Guy reading a book. He's drinking herbal tea, I think. Well, it's a teacup. Sidewalk people walking by the hedges bordering this small yard. I like it here, two-story Victorian home-cum-coffee shop on this busy street. Dark interior, quiet music, and real couches in every room. This wraparound porch is better for me right now. I need air. Crisp June air. Weird there's still sunlight in the sky this late. I'm less than a mile from the Anodyne coffeehouse, which means if I decide to go, I'm not far.

Will I go?

I should definitely not go.

I cried only once since Jian helped me to the car. Even now, trying to guess who is lying, I could bring myself to bawling in seconds. Jerking off to porn, I've edged my cock for hours. This feels like edging my... my what? I don't understand. Pull it together. Calm down. Fredi's eyes showed kindness. Firmness. I don't believe she was lying.

Of course she was lying, you fucking idiot.

What kind of asshole—who knows he's being scammed—still falls for it after they break it down for him? If Vin coordinated my kinging, John followed Vin's orders. They're both assholes. Get a fucking grip. What kinging?

There is no kinging!

Obviously.

Fitch was wrecked. If he's not drugged out, that was an Oscar-level performance. His were druggie eyes, dull and constantly scanning the room. Except for odd flashes of something more. None of it even matters. They can put a crown on my head. They can give me a cute name. What they can't erase is the sewage in me, oozing into chunky rage when I vowed to kill Vin. John said, "We're not kinging you," and I became the man I hate most in the world. A king name won't erase that. I'll never forget how I felt. What they evoked.

I hate them.

The craziest part? When this insanity ends, and I'm back in Columbus—destitute most likely—I'll still be me. Lost Kings don't matter. Found Kings don't matter. You're always just you. No magic transformation of these shitty legs. No miracles. Sitting here, calmer, I can finally admit what I secretly hoped for. They could heal me. Make me walk. Run.

Fuck whatever manipulations they're doing—they're amateurs. Real crazy is hoping someone can physically transform my broken legs. Make me a real boy again. I wasn't even conscious of that hope until I wept in the garden. Listen to me! *Wept in the garden*, like I'm fucking Eve from the Bible. I guess that would make Vin Vanbly the serpent. I took a chomp because I'm such a goddamn easy mark.

None of it matters.

I've got to calm down.

I should have ordered a lemon bar, except I'd vomit if I ate it. Take a sip. Breathe. In roughly twelve hours, I will stand on Ms. Taylor's building stoop and confirm she's okay. That's the only thing that matters. Obviously, Jarrod didn't understand my level of worry, or he would have replied to my emails. Or phone calls. Or snaps. I do not get Snapchat. What's the point of those videos?

Where is she? Why is she not responding?

Am I going to meet dead-or-not-dead Vin Vanbly? I don't know. I don't know! Can't fly out until the redeye, so why not? No. Fuck no. Ten minutes ago, I confirmed with Julia there's been no new account activity. If my money is protected, what do I have to lose?

I feel like I'm back in court, staring at my angry reflection in the polished table. Lawyers rage inside me. Go? No. Stay away from con artists who announce, we're fucking with you. Yes, but your Honor, I've confirmed the money is safe? Where's the risk?

Maybe it's not about the money. They could be setting me up to get murdered and somehow get the money from one of the charities—no. That's not even... I don't know. Either I'm being kinged and they're fucking with me, or it's a scam and they're *fucking* with me. I'm not going.

Caffeine helps. My hands aren't shaking. That's good. Can't have my hands jitterbugging while I strut to meet the man I wanted to murder. If I go. If he's there—I should have finished the gun permit. No. Not funny. I can never make light of that. Because of this quest, I became my father. I hate Vin Vanbly. Always will.

Can today still be the same fucking day I found chubby Vin at Vincent's garage? I was so pleased with myself. If he wasn't Vin, why was he wearing a *Vin* nametag? If Fredi wasn't lying, that could have been him. Or, not.

In Columbus, it would be dark. I can't believe I'm obsessing over the sky when my life is a gasoline-filled swimming pool.

The porch boards creak as two gay guys stroll to a table farther away. I assume they're gay. The bearded guy is cute. Yelp says it's the best gay coffeehouse in Minneapolis. Just twenty feet away, people are jogging, eating ice cream, dog-walking, one dude carrying his leashed cat against his chest. Feels like a weekend. It's all so normal as my life spirals into the shitter.

A muscle guy pulls a gray dog in a wagon. They're coming into the yard. Thick biceps. Italian. Don't stare. Maybe the New York muscle guys who scorned me did it because I gawked. Nobody likes to be ogled, I know that. I forgive you, New York muscle—no! Fuck them. They aren't kings—there are no kings.

Poor Jian.

Had to be upsetting to find me sobbing. That was a variation of my worst fear. At least he saw Fredi and her son, verifying I'm not entirely crazy. I wish he had followed them. No. It was good he stayed. I needed help. He thinks I'm nuts. I hope he's had luck finding a great hotel. How much do I tip for being an emotional wreck and putting him in danger?

If Fredi told the truth—stop.

Stop.

I need a five minute break from this!

That dog is pretty old if he needs to be pulled in a wagon. His daddy is a gym queen, bulging arms. I dislike him. While he fiddles with the wagon, the dog abandons him, slowly climbing the front steps. I wish I could pull off a tank top. Last time I tried, I heard a guy mutter to his pal, "Upside of crippled. Killer arms." He thought I wouldn't hear him.

No, no, *stay away, dog.*

No!

Here he is, all muzzle and slobbery. His eyes stare me down. He won't leave, and his Italian daddy won't get over here. Get off your fucking phone, man. Get your dog. Get down, you fucking—I hate this.

"I'm sorry," Italian guy says. He skips up the stairs and tugs the dog by the collar. "Pilgrim. Don't be rude."

The dog resists. Big dog, pushing against me. I forgot the rasp of being licked. I never pulled the trigger, but I did. I killed Frank. Don't cry. Do not cry. I'm overreacting to everything. Where am I at midnight? I can't go. That dog is going to fucking knock over my coffee.

He says, "I'm sorry about that. He's a retired police dog, so he's very friendly to people. He helped solve crimes. When his human partner retired, she moved to Florida to live with her sister, so we adopted him. My partner named him Pilgrim, for the sole reason of walking into the house and saying, 'Howdy, Pilgrim,' every single time. Also, he names our dogs after restaurants we love. Have you been to Pilgrimage Café on 38th? So good. So yummy."

"No."

"You should try it."

Go away. Just fucking go away.

He says, "Can I ask a favor? I know it's imposing, but obviously, Pilgrim likes you. Can he stay with you while I grab a coffee? Two quick minutes. I'll order and come right back."

Say no. Say *no*!

"Please? I worry about him."

"Okay, but hurry."

"Will do."

Goddamn it, why did I say that? Be a *king*, Daniel. It's not a big deal. There are no kings! It's a fucking scam and they are so confident in my stupidity, they explained it to me. I don't hang out with dogs. I can't.

"Pilgrim, be good, okay?"

After another admonishment, he disappears inside, then pokes his head through the door crack to catch Pilgrim staring after him. "I'm serious. Be your best for, what's your name?"

Goddamn it, I don't want to trade names. "Daniel."

"Be your best for Daniel. I'm Mark."

The door closes.

Mark opens the screen door a crack. "Be right back."

The dog woofs.

Why did I say *yes*? Because he's hot? Fuck that. People probably do stuff for this idiot all the time because he belongs on the cover of Men's Fitness. Fuck him. Fucking gay elite. When I approach a stranger, they think want spare change. When he approaches, people say, "How *can I help*?" And *be a king*? Where the fuck did that come from?

Pilgrim does not care about Lost Dogs or Found Dogs. He nudges higher, intentions clear. No way, dog. I'm not getting my face slobbered. But is this so terrible, interacting with a dog? Interacting with the world? Yes. Yes, it's all terrible. I am no friend to dogkind. If you knew what a monster I was. Please don't put your head in my lap. Okay. There it is. His head is in my lap. Front paws on my legs, leaning up. No, dog. We can't touch heads.

We almost touch heads.

I can't. I can't believe I'm even near a dog. This isn't me. I want to be who I was before the blog post. I was miserable, but at least I wasn't scammed out of millions. Losing my mind. Sobbing in gardens. That was a fucking stranger's house! Get down, Pilgrim. We can't be friends. It's been more than two minutes. Where is this asshole for his dog? My face is gonna get licked any second now.

When it's finally him, I want to complain but why? It's over. He's going away. Why do I even care? I'm free until midnight.

I'm definitely going.

He carries a pea-green soup mug, same as mine, white foam spilling over. "Thanks. That took a long time. Sorry. They don't like it when I bring him inside. They have health codes. But I can't leave him alone. Someone might steal him."

Why would anyone steal an old dog?

"Do you mind if I sit?"

Yes, goddamn it. "I kinda do."

Mark says, "Just a few minutes, I promise. Quick break on a long walk. I won't even drink half of this."

"Hey, man. I'm going through something right now. I need to be alone. I can't do chitchat while I'm working things out."

"Absolutely." He sits and stares into traffic.

"Could you sit somewhere else?"

Mark says, "I'm in the same boat. I'm wrestling with whether to tell my husband something. Hey, we could help each other out. We could play a game called Big Secret. We tell each other the thing we're struggling with and get advice from a stranger. It's a good game to get perspective. People are playing on Facebook. Strangers play with strangers. The only rule is you have to be respectful."

"Not interested."

"I'll go first. My husband and I had mind-blowing sex but it was also super kinky. Should I tell him I liked it? If I do, he'll make it happen again. I'm honestly not sure if it was once-in-a-lifetime weird sex or something worth repeating. If I express even the slightest interest, he'll arrange a second time as a surprise. I'm not sure I want that. It was pretty weird."

Why is this happening?

He says, "What do you think? Should I discuss it with my husband even though I'm not sure what I want?"

"You can't expect me to answer that."

He nods. "Too much information. Sorry. Big Secret cuts through the bullshit of small talk and goes right to something that matters. You don't have to play."

After setting down his cup, he massages his dog with both hands. "Seriously, two minutes and we'll leave. I tell Pilgrim big secrets all the time, but he never shares his. Do you, buddy?"

This dog is creating panic in me. I can't be around him. I can't lose it right now. Do something. Anything.

"Tell me more about your husband."

Mark says, "That's not how Big Secret works. You give advice with almost no information, because you want that person's initial opinion."

"You could at least tell me what kind of sex, so I'd know if it were dangerous or not. Diapers or bondage? Fisting, or I dunno, wasps?"

Quit discussing this! Get him to fucking leave.

He raises his mug. "Interesting you would say wasps. Okay, a few details. Last year on his birthday, we visited a foreclosed house, boarded and everything. When he lived there as a kid, he was terrorized by rats in the basement. We broke in, went to the basement, and had crazy sex."

"In the rat basement."

"Yes."

"Were there rats still living there?"

"Some."

"That sounds disgusting. And filthy."

"Right. Although, I don't actually know how many rats were down there. I don't think many."

"But you're not sure."

"It was dark."

"You guys didn't bring flashlights?"

"Not exactly."

"You two just decided to break into his childhood home for basement sex? You didn't bring flashlights?"

"There was a dim source of light. In the glow, it didn't seem like a ton of rats."

"And you're interested in doing this again."

He laughs. "Don't judge me. Also, I didn't say I liked it, I said there are things I don't understand about that night, and I want to get another opinion."

"I think I have a right to tell you, as a stranger, I am judging the shit out of you right now. Sex in a rat-infested basement."

He says, "We wore hip waders, the kind you use for fishing. Neither of us got bit, though one ran over my husband's foot. He didn't care. I screamed. Thing is, I'm not sure what turned me on. The location? The rats? The fact that my husband was thrilled to make a happy memory where he was once so miserable? There could be a thrill factor as well. We got caught by the police."

"No."

He nods. "Super embarrassing. We had finished—barely—when cops clomped down the basement stairs, responding to a 911 call. They heard us fucking. We were loud. Maybe getting caught turned me on? I don't know. I hope it wasn't the rubber waders."

"You're not sure why you were aroused."

"There was a lot going on at the time."

"Were you arrested?"

"Almost. We got out of it. They confiscated the light source and made us put our fingerprints on it. Took photos of both our IDs. They said they'd run our finger prints and as long as we didn't show up with outstanding warrants, they'd file a report saying they never encountered anyone. They figured out we weren't career criminals when they saw we had three dogs waiting in the SUV. Oh my god."

He bolts upright, and Pilgrim jerks his head in response. "I told you so many details! That's not how Big Secret works. Forget everything I said. My question is, do I discuss it with him when I'm unsure? Do I risk him planning a surprise repeat?"

"This is way beyond any of my sexual experience. I'd say most anyone's sexual experience. Pass."

Mark says, "I'll tell one of my closer friends eventually, but I thought I'd get an outside perspective. Talking helped. Thank you. First time I've discussed it."

He takes another deep sip.

"Tell him." I'm surprised to hear my conviction.

"Yeah?"

"Yeah. Don't hold back. To be honest, I also think that's terrible advice, but that's what I'm saying in this moment. The two of you should figure out what made it hot."

He considers this. "Okay. Thanks. Please don't tell anyone my big secret."

"Easy promise. I will never be tempted to repeat this story. Trust me."

We both chuckle. How is he so comfortable about his weirdness?

"Why would you tell me this?"

"Pilgrim is an excellent judge of character."

Do not cry. Do not fucking cry.

After a short silence, I feel lighter. Better. Something distracted me from my midnight debate.

"Here's an idea. Fuck your husband in an abandoned building, no rats. Another time have sex where you're likely to get caught."

He nods. "Isolate the sexual variables. See? That's why Big Secret works. I hadn't thought of that." Mark leans across the table. "Your turn."

"I can't."

This stranger did the impossible, freed me from obsessing for two minutes. That's worth something. Maybe I could tell him.

He says, "It doesn't have to be sex stuff. But it could be."

How did I get into this conversation? "Okay. It's not about sex. I need to make a life-changing decision by midnight."

Mark raises his eyebrows. "You may have to say more."

"Let's try it your way first. If you had to make a life-changing decision, how would you approach it?"

Mark scratches behind Pilgrim's ears, and looks around. We watch the mother and daughter leave. More people with ice cream pass on the street.

"Do it."

"Yeah?"

"Yeah. Go for it. If it's plastic surgery, I have a different answer. If it's something fun, like flying to Italy, I say do it. Why midnight? What happens if you don't decide?"

"I leave town without answers, which is unsatisfying but less risk."

"It's risky?"

"No. Not exactly"

Mark looks alarmed. "People don't say *it's not risky* unless there's an actual possibility of danger."

"No danger. I misspoke. I'm meeting someone in a public setting at midnight. I don't trust this person. I'm nervous."

"I totally change my answer. Don't do this. Do you need police involved?"

Goddamn it. Goddamn this fucking stranger.

"Daniel, don't get mad. Your eyes say you're mad. I'm saying what any reasonable person would—if you intend to hurt yourself or others, do not do this. If you tell me enough details I stop worrying, I promise, *promise* to honor your big secret. I don't want you hurt. I think that's fair."

Fucking—I didn't want this goddamn conversation. But someone is worried about me and my reaction was to get instantly enraged. Everything is so fucking extreme, right now, every damn thing. Less than two hours ago, I wept in a stranger's backyard. I need to calm down.

Breathe.

"I'm meeting someone from online at a coffee house tonight. Midnight. Nobody is going to get hurt. In fact, my driver will wait outside, ready to dial 911."

"That doesn't sound good."

"We scouted the location, big floor-to-ceiling windows. I'm in zero danger. I'm just nervous."

He visibly relaxes. "You won't leave with this person?"

"Under no circumstances. Only talking."

"I don't know any coffeehouses open that late."

"Jazz night or something. It's on their website."

"Oh, Anodyne. I forgot. I went twice, but that was, like, two years ago. It's fun. I switch back to my original opinion. I think you should go. But if you're meeting strangers, and it makes you nervous, take insurance. Me. Well, me and Pilgrim both. We'll get a table. Anodyne is very dog-friendly. I can keep an eye on you. That way, you'll know someone in the room."

I love this!

"I can't ask that."

He says, "We don't mind. My husband is working long hours lately, and I just drank a ton of caffeine. Pilgrim, why didn't you stop me?" He rubs their heads together. "You're supposed to stop me, officer."

"You're really kind to offer. But, no."

Mark says, "You are definitely a native. I grew up in New Jersey. I didn't know this Minnesota thing where you say *no* the first two times and then the third time, you say *yes*. If I want something, I say 'Can I have that? Now?' First time. I'm not shy."

Rance told me to quit making life so hard for myself.

"I'm from Ohio, so I'll skip right to *yes*. To be honest, I'd love knowing someone else in the room."

"Good. Pilgrim, you wanna have a late night? Bark once for yes. Okay, buddy. Bark later. That's smart. Save it for private barking. We'll walk home. I'll shower. We'll get a table around 11:00."

"I can't believe you're willing to do this."

"I like jazz. It'll be a nice night out."

How did I go from zero friends to so many?

It's because they're kinging you.

No, they're not. It's a scam.

Mark continues a conversation directed at Pilgrim, describing details of the place, the pig's ear he can expect as reward.

It's terrifying to live like this, open to new people. He might ask questions about my legs. I don't want to talk to the gym god about my legs. Maybe he hasn't noticed. Of course he noticed. He just hasn't asked. Not yet. I wait for them to bring it up. This is why I hate meeting new people.

"Okay, Daniel. What else do I need to know? Who are you meeting?"

"I'd prefer not to share more details. Could we talk about something else?"

He leans in closer. "If you want to talk about something else, you know that light source I mentioned a few minutes ago? The one the police confiscated?"

I nod.

"It was a snow globe with sentimental value. My husband wants it back."

"You said the police have it."

"My husband used the internet to find out where they store evidence. It's in a warehouse. He wants us to steal it." Mark glances furtively at nearby tables and lowers his voice. "I might be having danger sex sooner than I thought."

SIXTEEN

WITH THE WINDOW down, I hear music wafting through the giant glass panes, the tables crowded with late-night lovers of jazz trios: a heavy female vocalist, a slovenly guitarist, and an old hipster who thumps a bass in a knit cap pulled down low.

11:55 p.m.

What if I go in, and he's not there? I leave angry, and Jian takes me to the airport. How many times do I go over this? Mark's inside. Verified it as Jian drove slowly around the corner. If Vin Vanbly is there, I get answers. Assuming he's not dead. Assuming this isn't a huge financial scam. Thomas's newspaper clipping showed only a last name, so it could have been anyone named Vanbly. I should call Julia again. No. I called her forty minutes ago. No new account activity. My money is fine.

"Jian, I know this has been a crazy day. Thank you for everything."

"They're coming."

"I'm sorry?"

"I said, you're welcome."

My hair prickles. "That's not what you said."

Jian looks confused. "Mr. Daniels, you said *thank you*, and I said *you're welcome*."

I heard him wrong. I'm hallucinating. That was an auditory hallucination. Earlier, visual. This is not good.

He says, "Mr. Daniels. you look very tired."

He already believes I'm a nut job. I keep asking too much.

"I'm fine. I'm sorry. Just exhausted. It's been a long day and you have been more professional and amazing than I could have hoped for, so thank you. Thank you for staying with me. We go from here straight to the airport and then you're free to stay here for a few days and I'll pay for vacation, or you can drive home. Soon as you drop me off. If I raise my hand, please come in. Okay?"

"Mr. Daniels, please."

I don't have the energy to argue, not even with someone on my side. I know my voice will sound weary. I can't help it. "I have to do this."

I can't even exit after this humiliating honesty, nothing easier or harder than every time I take five minutes to drag myself from a car. I'm meeting a magic man—a stranger—I wanted to murder. Who might already be dead, and that's not the worst case scenario, because, I'm definitely being scammed. Despite the significance of this meeting, I will show up damp under my pits because of my shitty life and these shitty, fucking legs. I'm so tired of hating myself. I wish I could stop dragging that around, too. I should have been able to run.

I slam the back door. After I rap it, he powers down the front window. I have one last thing to say.

"Jian, I know I'm repeating myself. Any suspicious cars—"

"Are you leaning against the car?"

I'm surprised by his tone. "No."

Jian says, "Take two steps back."

"Why?"

"Back up two steps."

I do as he asks. "What's wrong?"

Jian says, "They're coming."

As the car screeches away, air rushes past me, cold. That's the exact squealing tires sound you hear on television. It's... where the fuck is he going? My luggage. My toothbrush. My laptop. He's been with my laptop all evening.

He said, *they're coming*.

The sedan swerves hard, disappearing around the corner.

My pocket buzzes. How many rings before I have to answer it? I dread seeing her name. Who else would it be? I stare where the tail lights were last. What makes me think they'll return?

I should answer the phone. It keeps buzzing.

They warned me they were going to steal from me, and then, they did. I drank coffee while it happened. Probably. If I don't answer soon, voicemail.

Looking at the phone, I hate I was right. "Hello, Julia."

"Daniel, hello. We agreed I'd call once alerted to any activity."

I can't breathe.

She says, "Did you change your online password three minutes ago?"

I am destitute and crippled. I'm an idiot and also, I am worthless. Everything is a dark hallway, everything going black, but I manage to make my mouth say the word, "No." Those two small letters, so quiet, when everything in the universe screams into infinite bewilderment and horror. I flash through all the hiding spots where he found me. The pleasure he took in breaking my arm. He recorded the sound of the break so he could listen to it later. I could never stop him because—I am nothing. I have always been nothing.

There are no kings.

Julia says, "We have a problem."

SEVENTEEN

I'T'S MIDNIGHT.

I'd hang up, call back, text her—anything—but every second counts. I need her to explain once more. She said the password change originated on my end, which means they aren't liable. I can't even panic properly, because a recorded voice cheerfully promises the lowest overdraft fees for new checking accounts. Who the fuck still has a checking account? Quit talking! Where is Julia? Why am I on *goddamn hold*? Someone talk to me. They got everything. Jian was with my laptop unsupervised for hours. I don't need Julia to confirm it.

I can't breathe. I can't stand. My arms are quaking. I keep looking at the end of the block, where Jian disappeared, not sure what I expect to see. I jerk my gaze to the coffeehouse. Which one is Vin? Two black men sitting against the wall are playing chess. Why during jazz? Oh god, who fucking cares! Let them play chess! You're destitute. Homeless soon, without money. I hate the lawsuit money and I'm fucked if I don't have it. *What do I do?* Get a job? I can't do anything useful.

Vin Vanbly could be one of the chess players. No, he's white. Or is he? Yes. Rance confirmed it. But could Rance have lied? Yes. *I don't know.* I can't think. Another black man, this guy on a first date, third date maybe, almost touching the back of her hand, not ready to commit to anything in public. She is smiling. She's pretty. I want to scream at them, scream the horror of my fucked up life. Their body language says not a first date. Third date? Why am I still on hold? *My head's exploding.* Goddamn this sales loop repeating again. Goddamn this. Quit fucking looking where the car disappeared. Jian's gone. With your laptop.

How could he be in on this? I interviewed him in Ohio. Did The VV approach him after I hired him—bribed him? He's been telling them my every move. Their plan worked. I'm ruined.

A large woman with a platinum white bob throws her head back in peals of laughter, nothing I can hear, but wow, to have such a great life, a life where you throw your head back in joyful laughter while you're listening to jazz, loving your goddamn life. Fifty feet away, I'm dying, crumbling into self-hatred at what a waste of a person I am. No wonder he beat the shit out of me. Everyone recognizes a faggot loser.

Jian, I trusted you!

No. I'm not a faggot loser. I know that.

I'm still crying. I've been crying for the last five minutes.

Pull it together. It's 12:01. Go inside.

Chunky young hipster, white guy, thick black beard, holding hands with a woman—no. He's too young to be Vin. Fuck him. Fuck Vin Vanbly and his goddamn lies. If he's in there, shouldn't he check his watch? Glance outside to see if I'm here? He is a bear. That must mean he has facial hair. That guy? Someone else? Oh god, I haven't even thought of Ms. Taylor. Could they have taken her? Please, *please* let her not be harmed. Please let her not be harmed because of me. I can't even face that thought. One of the chess guys has a beard. Is he Vin? Would Vin play chess? Is chess a clue? *There are no clues! You're penniless, fag*—No. I've done my therapy, but this is pushing every button, even ones I thought were healed, this— thirty more seconds. Thirty seconds. Where the fuck is Julia? She has to return.

Woman with a sparkly sweater and a butternut-colored blouse. Could Vin Vanbly be a woman? No. Of course he's a man—or is he? What am I thinking? But if Vin Vanbly is the urban legend used to prey on—group of five, three women and two men. Either of them? Third-date man, make your move already. He's falling in love. They will remember this date for all the best reasons while I am outside, destroyed.

It's goddamn fucking 12:02.

Mark glances my way.

I nod.

He can't see my tears. He doesn't know what's wrong. He gives nothing away, just goes back to listening and casually stroking Pilgrim's head.

I deserve this. They warned me I would be scammed. What can I accomplish on hold? Nothing. I lost everything. I should hang up and come in. After vowing to never trust someone in a way to make myself vulnerable, I proved I am weak. People can see I'm weak. Every time I leave the house. And for that reason, I am now destitute.

I hang up.

It's over. I lost.

Mark will help me. Get to Mark.

Three cement stairs. Each one seems important, these enormous seconds before it is confirmed. I am an urban legend of stupidity. I can live without the money, somehow. How will I live with the shame that being hobbled for life was *not enough* of a life lesson? I fell for it again, the very next opportunity I opened my heart.

I open the door.

Pilgrim faces Mark, wagging his tail. Mark talks earnestly to the dog's snout, probably explaining the concept of jazz. Frank died because I chose him. A strange relief floods me. I can stop fighting the horror I am, because tonight proved it's all true. Dad sensed I was weak and easy to abuse. VV figured the same.

All these people sitting near the door, and not one offers to help. Normally, I'd hate them for offering. Tonight I'm discovering how weak I truly am. They took everything. I have to get a cab to the airport before my credit cards are cancelled.

Jian! I trusted you!

Made it inside.

I don't want people helping me, except when I do. Don't look at my legs, except when you imagine how strong I must be to survive. No, don't think that either. Don't put me on a goddamn pedestal I could never climb off. What do I want? What do I goddamn want?

Help me, Mark.

When he looks at me with mild alarm, I cry.

Pilgrim tugs free and heads toward me, navigating tables pushed together. I hate his kindness. If only I could make you understand, I am no friend to woofers. Stay away. At the same time, I'm joyful for this small blessing, to be welcomed with love, befriended—this is what insanity feels like: weary, bleary, shaking. Horrified he's so close, wanting his forgiveness, which I could never have. He's here.

Howdy, Pilgrim.

I reach for him, fingers quivering. I want to feel the softness of him, but I can't extend my fingers far. In this moment, I am drunker than in the bar several weeks ago, where Thomas—or was that today? Jian betrayed me. Like John. Like Vin. Like my father, a man whose only role is to protect you. Pilgrim nudges closer, letting me touch his head. So soft.

No!

What happened?

Pilgrim collapsed.

Immediately, people jump in front of me, blocking my view. A woman cries out, drawing attention.

I barely touched him!

The music stops as the ripple spreads. Crowding around. The chess players, the third-date couple. Everyone's staring. The bass player comes out from behind his instrument.

"I didn't see it!"

"What happened?"

More crowd in. I can only see Pilgrim's black and gray legs.

"He's dead." Third-date man says with surprise, and the word circulates through the crowd.

No, no, no, no, no, no, no—

The singer touches her forehead and says, "No."

I've done it again. I kill dogs.

I am a horror.

As I fall, I fully grasp how deeply I hate myself. I should have begged Dad to kill me. I should have died for you. Forgive me, Frank. I hate myself to death.

The sword passes through me.

Oblivion.

Breathe.

I'm alive.

I'm crying but slowing down. Breathing. Nothing remains but the shape I wept out. Sensations crawl over me, four dozen centipedes skittering up my spine, tickling over my skull. My worst nightmare. I fell, weeping before strangers. Someone is tweeting this. I'm being filmed on four different smartphones. A blog tomorrow will read, "Last night, I saw this crippled guy lose his shit...."

Something isn't—I'm not on the floor.

Why didn't I hit the floor?

I feel big arms around me, holding me. Behind me. I fell onto a person? I lie on my back, resting against his stomach. The bass player in the knit cap. His muscular arms. He's sniffling. He was crying with me?

This isn't possible.

Tordo?

"Mi amigo," he whispers. "You found me."

I have no time to register this shock, because my face is tongued by a thick cow who wandered into my hysterics.

Horatio says, "Ease off, Pilgrim."

Mark says, "He's sad he made Daniel cry. He's kissing away the tears."

"Back him off. He's eating Daniel's face."

"Those are kisses. Right, Daniel?"

If I open my mouth, we'll be Frenching. What just happened? I didn't kill Pilgrim? No one's talking. Silence.

"Mark."

"Okay, okay."

A sword passed through me. What the fuck was that? I saw it.

I didn't kill the dog!

Mark pulls the cow away so I open my eyes, the absurdity of this moment fighting for comprehension in my brain. I'm lying on the floor, sort of, in the arms of Horatio, who speaks English. Pilgrim stands a foot away, not dead, eager to return to interspecies make-out, and everywhere around me—an entire jazz audience watches in complete, absorbed silence.

"Mark. It's time."

"I know. I need to say goodbye."

7-16-32. Something is happening.

Horatio lifts me as I struggle to sit. His name isn't Horatio.

"Mark, please don't go."

His face falls. "I have to. It's the right thing. But I don't want to."

"Please." I try to keep my voice even. "Help me face this."

"I will, from down the street. Pilgrim and I will send good thoughts and king energy. I can't be here for this next part."

Mortification seeps in. How do I get out of here? I don't dare look away from Mark, but why is nobody whispering? No telltale clicks from cell phones snapping photos.

Pilgrim tugs latitude from Mark and leans forward to lick my face. I turn away and, surprising myself, cough a muffled laugh. Electricity sizzles through every cell—*I'm going to be fine.*

"Goodbye, Daniel. For now."

"Mark." My throat hurts.

Pilgrim chooses his steps carefully, like he did making his way to me moments ago. Love floods me, shocking me like ice water, filling—something empty. As people watch Pilgrim's retreat, I glance around. The chess players are both in their forties, I'm guessing. Hipster Beard, his big paw on his girlfriend's, watches Mark leave, but her gaze shifts to me. She has Egyptian hair, straight and black. I look down. I'm not ready. People make room, adjusting their chairs, still in goddamn silence.

He didn't *pretend* to garden for a month; he planted flowers every day. He laid sod. He dug holes. He worked ten-hour days. That wasn't an act—or rather, it was an act. For me. The door jingles. *Don't leave!* Pilgrim looks back, at me, at something.

Ms. Taylor is okay.

They didn't take my money.

I want to be angry, or maybe I am. I don't know. Every emotion flashes and disappears, lightning on humid summer nights. Anger rages hot, but so does liberation from anger, and this overwhelming—I'm not ready to say it's *love*—but why am I fighting it? It crackles, blinding the night. I wipe away tears, wanting this part over. I need a moment to... adjust... to a new reality.

Into my ear he says, "I should explain a few things."

I bark like a dog.

"Later, though. We have unfinished business right now. Look around. You know who I am. You know why you're here. So when I say, 'Look around,' I hope you're hearing a polite command, not an invitation. Look. Around."

Okay. I can face this. I remember explaining to Frank about being brave. Oh, goddamn that hurts.

Hipster Beard's girlfriend with Egyptian hair watches me. She is kind. He looks down, mirroring my awkwardness. My humiliation. Do I feel humiliated or am I telling myself I feel it? The loud group of five—loud no more. Attentive. The twos and threes at the smaller tables watch me. One woman adjusts her arm. Third-date couple watch me. I'm ruining their date, but surprisingly, that's not the expression either wears. He is worried. Her eyes are red. She's been crying.

He says, "Everyone is here by private invitation. I face-to-face interviewed every person in this room. Twice. Once accepted, each person read a report I wrote, summarizing your life. Your childhood abuse. The station wagon. When necessary, I elaborated with details from the court transcripts. Everyone knows how Frank died and how your father made you choose. The lawsuit and the thirty-second incident."

How fucking dare—

"Everyone in this room survived childhood abuse. Some, physical. Others, sexual. Some, emotional and mental. Some, all the above."

The third-date man rolls up his left sleeve. Burn marks up and down his arm. Why are there so many of us?

"Look around."

I wipe my eyes.

Hipster Beard's eyes fill with sorrow, his and mine. He wasn't looking away with awkwardness. He understands weeping. The loud group of five, do they even know each other? Both chess players? The vocalist wipes her eyes enough to keep her gaze soft and steady. The guitarist, who I dismissed as slovenly. The laughing lady with the platinum bob. And Vin Vanbly.

Mark wasn't abused.

Vin says, "Tonight you have a once-in-a-lifetime opportunity."

I'm on my King Weekend. Right now.

"Everyone came to witness. They came to be part of your healing and maybe bring extra blessing to their own sorrows. None of us deserved what happened. We were children."

Although two or three heads drop, most remain steady. A few nod. Before I touched Pilgrim's head, before I went down, they *knew* how Frank died. Platinum bob lady—she's not laughing now. At this moment, her life is not glamorous. The man at her table, big Adam's apple, watches me as I study him. He interviewed to be here. For me.

Vin says, "Daniel, I know this is a lot to absorb. Listen to my voice. You have an opportunity to talk about Frank. How you met. What you loved about him. Describe his appearance. This might be your only chance to talk about your childhood friend without discussing how the relationship ended. You will stop the story before your father made you choose. There will be no follow-up questions."

I might vomit.

I'm horrified. But. I can't deny the thrill of... something. Could I talk about Frank, knowing I don't have to explain the last time I looked into his eyes?

Vin says, "Take a breath, Daniel. We've all had an intense time tonight. Lean forward, and I'll turn around so my back is to yours. It'll be more comfortable. If you choose to speak, great. If you choose silence, we all sit in silence and ponder how much you must have loved Frank. Whether you talk or not, this time is devoted to honoring Frank."

No one speaks during our awkward maneuvers. Vin positions himself at my back. They came here for me. I can't talk about Frank. No more crying, not in front of them. They know way too much about me.

Silence.

I no longer fear eye contact. Obviously, those two are not on a third date. He wanted me to witness. Maybe he has body issues, too. Do the chess players even know each other? Guy in yellow shirt, long hair: abused. Egyptian hair woman: abused.

Time passes.

There's little movement—scratching a neck, crossing arms, but they are surprisingly still, as if they were coached sudden gestures would frighten me. Like a deer. This is insane.

I laugh.

Nobody grins or smiles in response. One woman drops her head.

Doesn't anyone else think this is absurd? They don't even know me. They don't—they do know me.

No.

Don't say anything!

Don't do this.

Don't do this.

I love you, Frank.

"I was nine when Dad got Frank from the pound. He was a mutt." I can't stop the words. "Dad broke my arm the previous week. He had never gone so far, and I think it surprised him. Took almost four months before he physically hurt me again. The dog was part apology, part bribe. When a kid breaks his arm, people ask questions, like, 'Did it hurt? You said you fell out of a tree, is that right?' The dog was a misdirect, so I'd have something else to talk about. I guess you guys already know my father was a world-class surgeon, used to making careful plans and perfect execution. He was not prepared for such damage to me, noticeable to others."

No, no, no, no, no, no, no.

I look down. I don't want to talk about Frank. What good comes of this? Nothing. I've recycled these thoughts a thousand times, reliving, replaying. What good is living this out loud? In therapy, I've discussed the impact. I've never talked about—I'm done. I'm not saying anymore.

We are silent, all of us.

My throat tightens.

A car drives by. I watch through the coffeehouse windows until all I see are two red taillights. I wonder where they're going this late. Probably home. A few minutes ago, I was financially ruined by Horatio. Then I killed a dog. Then it all got better.

Do this.

"I tried not to be friends with him. I knew it wouldn't end well. After a week of me calling it Dog, Dad demanded a better name, so I thought of a bully at school. He'd pushed me down several times when I was already sore. I thought if I named the dog after the bully, it would help me not love him. The bully's name was Frank."

My voice cracked.

I'm sorry I named you after a kid I hated. I'm so sorry.

"I'm sorry, I can't do this."

Nobody speaks.

Crying jag prevented.

I don't *have* to do this. I don't have to at all.

In fact, I feel no pressure. They already know how he died. I feel a strange... elation? It's mixed with horror, so I'm not sure *elation* is the right word, but there's a thrill of freedom. I don't have to explain or justify. They know the details of my life, and they lived the details of theirs. This isn't fun for them. They didn't come tonight for *fun*. They honor me with their silence, the way I must honor him.

I must honor Frank.

"I tried not to love Frank. He followed me everywhere, through every room. Every boy's dream, right? I hated when he licked my hand. I hated when he sat because I sat. I used to sit real still for long periods of time so he'd get bored and wander away, but he never did. He'd move closer so my leg touched his. Sometimes he'd put his jaw on my knee. Dad made me walk him, of course, while he and mom strolled behind. Norman Rockwell. He had an obsession with us imitating those families in the paintings. At night, he'd go apeshit in the garage, making me scream.

"Frank had a mostly white face with brown tufts of hair under his eye. One day I realized it looked like someone punched him and gave him, well, a brown eye. Bruised but healing. I hated the idea of someone hurting him, so I petted him. That was wrong. Once I started...."

I love you.

"He trembled and cried. Only then did I understand how desperately he wanted me to like him, to be kind to him. I knew how miserable that felt, because I wanted someone to be kind to me. To like me."

Stop talking!

"I didn't know the word *leverage*, but I knew loving Frank made me weak. Weakness was a concept I understood well."

Why stop now?

"The next time Frank licked my face, I didn't stop him. I couldn't. I began to watch his food being poured, making sure Dad didn't hide broken glass, like he sometimes did to Mom or me. He rarely did that. Glass could shred us internally, which would draw attention. But once, I reached into a bag of chips and after a stabbing pain, jerked out my bloody hand. I thought he'd never stop laughing. Every night, I watched Frank get fed so I could prevent any broken glass from getting devoured. That's how Dad knew I cared.

"When I was at school, I worried about Frank, which made days more bearable, because I could focus on something other than the terror of school. I would run home. In fact—"

This catches me by surprise, the strength of this memory.

Vin says, "Take a few deep breaths. It's okay."

I'm sitting on the floor surrounded by careful listeners. I never sit on the floor. Vin Vanbly sits at my back. I feel him pulsing a message into me somehow. *It's okay. You're okay. It's okay. You're okay. It's okay.*

I'm okay.

Something is right. Many things are right.

I'm being kinged.

"Running home from school is one of my only memories of running. Racing, out of breath. I forgot about that. When you're a kid, you never think, 'Savor this experience.' I didn't know I wouldn't run in life."

Take a breath.

"When I'd get home, Frank was always crazed to see me, running the length of the yard. Safe. Happy. Every day before dad came home, I got to love him. Hug him. Play fetch and be happy with him. I don't know if Mom told Dad we played fetch. She would have, if he asked. I tried to stay out of her sight and just love on that dog. I even grew to love his name. I felt kinder toward the school bully because *my* Frank was such a better Frank than he was."

I never stopped loving you. It just hurt too much.

"Before dad got home, I would take Frank to my room. Sitting on my bed, I would explain how I had to pretend indifference for a few hours. I couldn't show him the love I felt because it would get us both in trouble. I liked to pretend Frank understood. But each evening, after I banished him, I listened to him whimper on the other side of my door. I'd lie on the floor and whisper, 'Go away. You have to go away.' Frank wasn't a good actor. Not like me."

If I could have one more day. Just one chance to see my best friend.

"At bedtime, Dad insisted Frank sleep in my room. I acted like I hated it. Those nights when I felt relatively sure he wouldn't return—usually the night after the night of a long session in the garage—I would make a fort out of my sheets and blanket, big enough for the two of us. I pretended we were camping on a mountainside far away, nothing but green trees and blue streams and wild horses in a meadow below, because I loved horses. We camped and told stories. Sometimes he barked because I got him so excited, recounting one of our mountain adventures."

That's it. That's all. Vin said don't explain how it ended.

"I'm done."

I talked about Frank.

Breathe.

I can't believe I spoke about Frank to a room full of strangers. But they are not strangers.

Minutes pass.

Vin says, "Frank."

"Frank," says the third-date man.

"Frank," says his companion, the woman in midnight blue.

"Frank," says Hipster Beard.

What happened to Hipster Beard? Who hurt him?

"Frank."

"*Frank.*"

"Frank."

All corners popcorn the name, bouncing it around. It's like Frank is racing around the coffeehouse with quiet glee. Their voices are not chipper. They know how it ended, but they're not judging me. I don't know how to describe this amazement, this... I don't know what it is exactly, the overwhelming relief of it all.

I drop my head and let the tears come.

I don't sob like before. I don't have enough inside me for that. I just cry. Something flows from me, a feeling I haven't experienced in a long time. I cry because it hurts to love Frank, but it's better than hating to remember him. I take shallow breaths, a lot of them, eventually returning to myself with longer ones, as Margaret taught me to do.

He says, "Take some deeper breaths."

"Okay."

A minute later, Vin speaks quietly. "How are you doing?"

"I'm okay. Tired."

I don't dare tell the truth—I feel alive.

"Folks," Vin says.

I feel him lean up. "It's time to bless Daniel. One sentence. A few words. Just like we discussed. If you're not feeling present, stay back. Talk to a counselor. Counselors, would you identify yourselves again?"

Four different hands rise: yellow shirt man, both chess players, and a woman in the corner with two others at her table. She's wearing a paisley scarf around her neck. I didn't see her.

"Daniel, usually with a blessing like this, I tell people to put a hand on your back, shoulders, arms, maybe head—if that works for you. Any non-intimate body part. Of course, with someone who was abused, all these hands coming out of nowhere can be terrifying. If you think it might trigger you, let me know. But if you think you can let love in, this blessing could change your life. Totally your call. No shame. Also, no abdomen or chest touching, nothing below the waist. In this case, with you sitting on the floor, I'd normally tell people they could touch your legs—normally that's a safe place—but this is a choice you have to make. Do you want people blessing your legs from the knees down? Fingertip touches only. No thighs or overly-intimate. Your call."

Why am I not more horrified by this idea?

He says, "This is a life moment demanding you be ruthlessly honest with yourself. Can you handle this blessing?"

"Yes." The word slides out of me easily. "People can touch my legs."

Nobody, nobody ever touches—

I owe them.

No, I don't. But I want to give something back, be as open and vulnerable as they are... if I can. I can endure this.

I regret my approval as they rise from their chairs, zombie-like and I am weak. I'm so weak right now! Hands reaching out—fingers near my shoulder. Oh god! They're going to touch my legs! The searing pain—*the crunch*—

"You are courageous," the jazz singer says into my ear, her voice breaking over *courageous*.

Third-date woman says, "Blessings on surviving."

"You're strong."

"You love so beautifully."

The horror of hearing this shocks me more than all the hands. I'm not—my love is weak!

"You loved Frank."

Not enough!

A woman I haven't noticed until now, middle-aged, thick in the middle, wearing a long peach skirt, bends to one knee. She grazes my knee with her fingertips and whispers. What did she say? I couldn't hear. She withdraws, lost in the throng of those crowding around me. What happened to her as a child?

"You have courage."

"I admire you."

I can't hear everyone!

"Your heart is so full of love. I want more of that for me."

Who is this guy, whispering over my foot?

"I will never forget this night."

"You are a beautiful person."

I'm not beautiful! Can't you see? They can't. They're busy assaulting me with gentleness.

"Frank was lucky to have you."

I got him killed!

"He knew how much you loved him."

I've done therapy. I've said words similar to these and sometimes believed them to varying degrees. *I am worth it. I am courageous.* I've never bombarded myself with those words, attacked myself with love. They *believe* what they're saying. How can they, when none of it is true? I wasn't enough.

I loved Frank. That one is true.

"I wish we'd been friends as children."

Nobody wants my friendship. I make people uncomfortable. Except Ms. Taylor. And Rance. And Jarrod. And this room full of strangers.

"Bless you, love. Bless your love for Frank."

"You inspire me to open my heart more."

"Frank was loved."

You're killing me!

"Your courage."

"Now I love Frank, too."

I'll never know their stories. Maybe we will talk later. I don't know. I don't know what I'm thinking, what's happening. I am so dazed, made dull with love and loving.

I am loved and loving.

"You inspire me."

"I bless your resilience."

I am empty. I am light.

Eventually it ends, though the quiet reverence remains. Under Vin's direction, those nearest raise me to standing. I rise with such grace, so many hands righting me, holding me, easing my transition to the canes, the experience is *delightful*. That was exquisite, especially since we were all once so weak. Look at all these strong and kind people.

In New York, I fell.

Tonight I was raised.

We are escorted to the door. No words, no whispering, just attentiveness. Vin passes into the night, holding the door for me. I turn without grace. I have to thank them. I open my mouth but nothing emerges. The best I can manage is a nod. I will never have words to explain this night. Third-date man with burn scars. Platinum-bob lady cried. I need a roster. One of the chess players is huddled with a young Hispanic woman, talking quietly. How can I memorize their faces if they look down?

Vin says, "Daniel, we have to go."

Night air fills my lungs as I move through the open door, exiled from the most love I've ever experienced. Vin Vanbly stands before me, zipping up a brown leather jacket. Two people assist me down the first step. He's the bass player in his knit cap, the old hipster. They assist me down the second step. He is Horatio. Hands right me after the third. Cowboy in the bar, though I don't remember his face. We stand on even ground, and my helpers return inside. The woman in the peach skirt, whose words I will never know, raises her fingers to me through the glass. Who are you?

The night is brisk, waking me. June scenting air, lilting and delicate. The last time I stood here, I was destitute. I'm so fucking tired. I smell lilac, I think. Purple ones.

Coffeehouse people, I love you.

Vin says, "Are you hungry? I could go for waffles. Banana chocolate chip, I'm thinking."

Do I want *waffles*?

Once I start laughing, I can't stop.

EIGHTEEN

I N THE CAR, I steal glances.

"You can look."

It's still confusing, merging the two. I'm thrilled to see Horatio. I do not like Vin Vanbly. I don't like what he did. Before I get too outraged, wasn't every King Weekend tale a cautionary tale? Perry abandoned. Mai's failures magnified through a treasure hunt. Did I think it would be easy? He married my nightmare fear of breaking down in public to the most tender, honoring love I ever experienced. I don't know how to feel. He ghosted me. *Ghosted*... that's the right word. I don't know what that means. No, tell no lies from this place of damage and light, cursed awareness to air behold—

What?

The fuck is that? Why is there a shitty poem in my head? No, it's something else, just out of reach, and if I try to recall it, it spins into numbers. I'd cry more, but I'm too damn tired. I'm confused. I can't let myself forget about the rage he exposed in me. He turned me into my father. What I went through today. He ghosted me hard. I don't know how to think. I hate him, right?

Face the air.

Not many cars cruise through sleepy Minneapolis this late, a city I will now always associate with fresh air, assaulting me hard through my open window. I need this air, gulping every molecule into me. I don't know how much adventure I have left. Why were those words snaking through my head, and why were they twisting in light, like backyard sparklers? I can't even remember them now. It's a blur. My eyes hurt.

Horatio's hair is still black, but shorn close to the skull. No thick luster.

"I assume you dyed your hair. Mai and Perry both told me you were blond."

"Two shades of black. Additional three shades of gray for my sexy side burns. Those were a bitch but we needed subtlety."

"Your skin was darker."

"I tanned extensively every day. We hired a Hollywood makeup artist. She managed my daily appearance. No prosthetics or cosmetics could be used, of course, because the plan was for you and I to become bench friends. Close up, you'd see makeup. We spent a lot of time on my arms, applying her custom browning lotion. Like she was basting a turkey, she'd pop me into the tanning bed for a while, slather me up, and grill me more. We dyed my chest hair. Look."

He unbuttons his top one.

Sure enough. Right under the neckline.

"Why? You never removed your coveralls."

"If a wasp got in, and I freaked out, I might have to strip. I like to think I could endure a wasp sting, but I've never been stung. You'd be surprised how many random variables can fuck up a kinging. Those first few years, I had some real nail biters. Rance set me on a better path. She injected collagen into my face to reshape it in subtle ways. At night, she would tug it to make it sag farther. Downtime was brutal."

I spit on the dashboard. I can't believe I'm laughing with Horatio.

"You look younger now than in Columbus. God, it's so weird that you...I can't even process this, to be honest."

"Sure. It's a lot. By the way, you're the new owner. Paperwork got signed today."

We pass under a streetlight. Right there—at odd seconds, I see my backyard friend.

He says, "Still with me? I said, you own it."

"Own what?"

"Your apartment building. You're the new owner."

Seems I should be more surprised than I am. "I don't understand."

"I needed to landscape the property so we could meet. Your building wasn't even on the market but I made a ridiculous offer. The owners would be stupid to walk away. I had conditions. A team of my choosing had to be permitted to landscape the yard before the close date. Even if I backed out of buying the building, they'd keep the $200,000 down payment and $20,000 in free landscaping."

Can I really be surprised by this?

Vin says, "Your building has some serious plumbing problems, you know."

"You were behind this. Nobody understood what the fuck was happening with the sale."

"I believe it."

"The updates were vague and contradictory."

"Agreed."

"Or used legalese that made no sense."

"Thank you."

"A lawyer lives in our building. He said it was like a legal riddle."

"I'll take that as a compliment."

"Definitely not intended as one, but I guess you did this deliberately."

"Correct."

"You annoyed and worried everyone in the building, not just me. People were worried about eviction."

Vin says, "What's the lawyer's name?"

"Jeff."

"Had you ever talked to Jeff prior to the building's sale?"

"I recognized him from the lobby, but no."

"Meet other tenants?"

Ellen. Nicole. Andy and Janelle down the hall. Oh. Vin Vanbly forced us to talk to each other.

"They hate you. The people in the building."

He says, "I'm not surprised. Hey, it's your property but I have a suggestion. Cut them a serious break on rent and they'll forgive. At least for the next year, while we figure out this plumbing situation. Tell them it's compensation for the stress of the sale."

"Every time I hate you, I remember you're Horatio. But you're not Horatio. I have to stop thinking of you that way."

"True. But we can visit him sometimes. Talk about our month together with few words. Do you remember the word I taught you for thrush?"

"What if I don't want to own a building?"

"Sign it over to Jeff and the others. Or there are kings who flip properties. Donate it. Sell it. Don't decide tonight. This space you're in right now is not a great place for making life decisions."

I own the apartment building. Huh.

"What if I'd spoken Spanish?"

"You don't. We tested you in New York."

"You're kidding."

"Rance had his crew. I had mine."

"This hurts my brain."

"I had to learn your habits. You eat pastas for lunch, never for dinner. Sodas only in the afternoon. One coffee in the morning. You own quite a few red shirts, you favor the right side of the street for no reason I can comprehend, and you have a slight preference for Asian men."

Eric was Japanese.

"You didn't cruise every Asian guy, of course. And the men you did, you were discreet. I happened to be studying your face through binoculars, so I caught a few of your double-takes."

"Are you responsible for the muscle guys who talked shit to me?"

"No. I don't know whom you're referencing. I only followed you for a week. I know it seems I have no personal boundaries, and yes, I assaulted your privacy. I can only say there is a line, different for me than you, different for me than most people. I must never cross it. It's a silver thread, blindingly thin. I have studied it my entire life. Men casually scorning you crosses my line. It dishonors you for no reason."

I haven't even begun to absorb what happened to me in the last... I don't know. Weeks of my life have passed in a matter of hours. He terrified me into believing all my money was stolen. How do I fucking feel about that? I don't remember when I last ate.

"You okay, Daniel?"

"What if I had taken an online course and could recognize bullshit Spanish?"

"*Te hubiese deslumbrado con mis maravillosas habilidades lingüísticas, hablando en un amplio ámbito de temas relacionados a plantas y pájaros. Y comida. Yo nunca me canso de hablar sobre comida en ningún idioma. Quisiera tus mejores gofres de arándano, por favor. ¿Cuán espeso es tu almíbar?*"

"Okay. You speak Spanish. What was that?"

"Mostly about waffles. Mark and I lived in Honduras for a year. We still prefer to argue in Spanish. Sounds prettier, and because we have less sophisticated vocabularies, when we get angry and can't think clearly, we blurt out things like, 'I hurt. You hurt me.' Really cuts to the heart of things."

Why has it taken so long for me to make the connection? Mark's rat sex was with Horatio. God, I hope he doesn't notice me cringe. I can't believe I know a weird sex secret about Vin Vanbly.

He says, "We created a teeny mess which required us to sneak out of the country. I had to become Horatio for two months before our escape. No professional makeup artist. Just friends and a healer who rubbed herbs on my skin to alter my appearance."

"No."

"Yeah. She was good. Funny thing is, a few years earlier Fitch warned me not to go. One of the last things he said to me on his King Weekend. I didn't listen. Things worked out okay, but it was a scary time. On the plus side, Mark and I got a godson out of it."

"What happened?"

"Story for another day. Point is, I was Horatio before I met you. In fact, whenever you left the building, I could relax my guard and reminisce. I miss Horatio. He was a good man."

"Was Mark on the landscaping crew? I know he wasn't the young guy who yelled at you."

"No, that was our godson. Mark was not a landscaper. However, he was in Columbus. Every night he and the dogs kept me company while I tanned. They liked licking the sauce off my arms. Vernie would get pissed and slather me up."

"Did I meet Vernie?"

"Not yet. She has done some bad-ass film work."

"I bet Mark had an easier time pretending to be Honduran. Easier than you."

"Mark insisted on being an Italian porn star, stage name *Marco Po*. South America treats porn stars like celebrities. He was all frosted tips, sparkling briefs. I could not talk him out of it, so the plan became he hired Horatio as his body guard after a club altercation. You know what? Let's not discuss this. We have enough topics. Open the glove box."

I laugh. "I'm afraid."

"No backtalk, mister. You're on your King Weekend. Open it."

I don't know why things are so goddamn funny right now.

Standard envelope. It's full of cash.

"The three grand you gave Kevin, plus his hourly rate. Take it now if you like, or leave it in the car and we'll stow it with your luggage. Which, by the way, is now at my house in St. Paul."

"Of course it is."

"Mark and I hope you'll stay with us a few days or a week. We have planned a few parties celebrating you, and you'll probably want to rest between. We can find you a good hotel if our home is hard to navigate. Actually, you've already been to my home. You met Fredi in my garden."

I don't know how to be surprised anymore.

He says, "I'm a landscape architect now. It's satisfying to see someone burst into tears and not realize why, when all they did was walk through a city park honoring grandmothers. Honestly, I'm bragging. Doesn't work with most people. Sensitive ones, those closer to the kingdom, they feel it. My company—"

"By Design. I almost called them to find you."

"I had planned for that possibility."

"I feel I have to say the obvious—you understood every word."

"Let's not talk about that in the car. Let's save that for a bigger conversation titled The Deception of Daniel Connors."

"I could use a few more answers."

"How about this? Let's not talk about Horatio until we're inside. A few other questions might be okay."

I feel grateful, which is strange. Why feel gratitude for his answering questions to which I deserve answers? I should be more demanding. Will answers stop my brain and heart from back flips? I lost my shit back there tonight. Completely, utterly. I haven't even given it much thought. I'm not ready. Ask more questions.

"Jian works for you?"

Vin says, "Jian and I met many years ago on the Golden Gate Bridge. He and his husband were on their honeymoon. I had the pleasure of reconnecting with them through Perry. He runs an international business. He flew in from China to be interviewed for the role of your driver. Calling you *Mr. Daniels* was his idea. He felt it made every exchange more awkward and tense, him being over obsequious. Now, that's a great word. Obsequious. Say it with me."

"How is that possible? I selected him from three candidates recommended by the owner. I interviewed each one. Even I didn't know who I'd pick."

"All three candidates were my people."

"How is it you own an upscale driver service in Columbus?"

"I do not."

"What if I'd rented a car in Minneapolis?"

"Even better."

"How did you know which Columbus company I selected?"

"Your search history. Rance told you we were monitoring it."

"That's completely fucked up, by the way."

"It is."

"What if I'd rented from a national chain?"

"You didn't."

"But I could have."

"If you did, I would have enacted Plan B. There's always a Plan B. And Plan C. Once you asked for recommendations from Aspen Car Services, I created an opportunity to chat up the owner, Naomi Parks. She and I played Big Secret. Naomi had a problem I was uniquely qualified to fix. Once she trusted I meant you no harm—that my intention was to honor you—she agreed to help. Granted, I didn't supply her every detail. If she knew we were going to pretend to scam you, I'm sure she would have hesitated. She's a good person. I promised her selfies of you and me together in the next few days, both of us giving the thumbs-up. Also, I would appreciate it if you called Ms. Parks when you're back in Columbus. Let her verify you're okay. Will you do that?"

"Yes."

Vin offers no additional explanation, and I guess I don't need one.

He says, "I don't leave much to chance on a King Weekend."

"Obviously, Fitch isn't an escort."

"Correct. Fitch—Kevin—is running for mayor of St. Paul next year. He would very much appreciate you not blogging about how he was involved. Conversely, you have full permission to blog about every detail. He will publicly confirm whatever truth you write about him. Kevin and I discussed this. To participate in your kinging, he had to accept you potentially sharing every detail. We will not deny you your reality. However, he *requests*—if it's not a big deal to you—not to name him specifically. Ultimately, the decision is yours."

In this moment, Fitch has made me sadder than in the motel. He sacrificed his future to be part of my King Weekend. He sacrificed more for me than anyone I've ever known.

"I vow I will never reveal his name."

Vin says, "Don't decide right now. This a big night. Anything you say tonight isn't binding."

"I don't need time. My answer will never change. I vow."

I vow, King Fitch, to honor your sacrifice. I sputter a laugh, remembering how he'd dropped his sweatpants, this future mayor. How did he make those flashes of gorgeousness? Despite everything Vin has done, it is Kevin who loved me best. I don't understand it, this place beyond words. Something is not crooked inside me. Kevin's sacrifice righted something.

I vow, Kevin. I vow.

"Daniel? You okay?"

"Kevin's eyes were glassy. I didn't imagine that. I know what to look for because drunk and high people like to harass me. How did he do that?"

"Contacts. Eye drops. Same makeup artist. Vernie knows her shit."

"How does he do that thing where he appears stunning, and then goes back to looking wrecked?"

Vin laughs. "He looked wrecked, huh? He's going to enjoy hearing that. New topic. The woman who called you before midnight is our friend Lauren. She's a voice mimic. Rance flew to Columbus to open a new account with Julia's bank. Lauren accompanied him to study Julia's exact tone and inflections. Rance returned to Columbus today to close the sale of your apartment building and insisted Julia attend the all-day closing. We had to make sure she wasn't available for your phone calls."

My god.

"How could you have planned the closing for today? You didn't know when I'd reach Minneapolis. Or even that I'd come for you."

"I was pretty confident you'd come within a month."

"How?"

"Perhaps we haven't been properly introduced. Hello, I'm Vin Vanbly. I'm a tad manipulative."

I can't stand this insanity. I need more air.

He says, "One of my exotic clauses in the apartment building contract was the less-than-twenty-four-hours-notice closing date. I knew as soon as you arrived, you'd discover Vincent's Garage right away and our endgame would go into effect that same day. By the time Jian crossed into Minnesota, everyone was on high alert. The minute you walked into the bar, we updated Anodyne's website with the jazz night information. Booked a room at the motel so you could meet Fitch. Notified the coffee house crowd that tonight was the night. When you left Columbus, Rance flew in for the closing."

"Hang on. I talked to four different people at my bank. And when she called back, Julia had very specific account information."

"Yeah, that was the real Julia. You only talked to Lauren at night."

"Were you guys behind the fake phishing attempt?"

"She told you about that, huh? Good. That was Mark's handiwork. He used to be a hacker. We weren't sure she'd even report that to you, honestly. All afternoon, Rance had been praising her thoroughness in communication, her attentiveness to details. We had hoped some of that praise might make her little a extra attentive when reporting in with you. Mark will be pleased to know his contribution found your ears."

"I don't understand. Who called me at midnight?"

"That was Lauren. Remember the day I got us fresh churros from my pickup? I stole your phone. Cloned it. Returned it."

"I thought I dropped it."

"Helpful Horatio found it for you."

"Unbelievable."

"I looked at nothing on your phone, I promise. Thin line. The only change was to reprogram Julia's number to dial Lauren."

"You—you're terrifying."

"Did you actually listen to any of the kings' stories? Anyway, Jian handed you our clone after Fredi left the garden. He stole your real phone while assisting you back to the car. For about two minutes, you had two cell phones in your pockets. Every time you checked in with Julia after that, you were calling Lauren. After Jian drove off with the fake update, Lauren called."

I have no idea what to say. What to think of this.

"Your phone is in the glove box."

There it is. Comparing the two side by side, I see they found the same blue case, and made a scratch along the back to match mine.

"Recognize this?" In a familiar tone, Vin strongly urges me to open a new checking account—lowest overdraft fees in town. "Come inside!"

"Holy shit. That asshole was you."

"I was trying to get you to *come inside*. That recording repeated those words over and over and over."

Why would he go so far for me?

"One more thing about Jian. I'm authorized to tell you this—need to tell you this. Jian was abused as a child. All three of your potential drivers were abused as kids. Again, it's that thin line. I would not permit you to weep in front of someone who did not understand a similar anguish. His abuse was not the same as yours. No one will ever understand what you went through. I know I put you through hell, Daniel. I also made sure you were never there alone."

The night races through us, vanishing under the streetlight behind us.

"Why threaten my money?"

"Short version, you told me to. After being warned not to ask Kearns any questions, you did. You asked if we would drain your bank accounts. That was the reveal I needed. Your money was your glue. Tonight, I needed you unglued. He's a talented pooch, but with all tonight's excitement, Pilgrim might have barked. Jerked his leg. I needed you distraught with immense fear and loss for you to believe—for precious seconds—you killed him. You needed to lose everything for tonight to work."

"A dog was strategic to my kinging." I need to say those words aloud. "You trained a dog."

"Actually, playing dead is only one of his many abilities. Vernie dyed huge parts of him gray to make him appear older. He doesn't need to be pulled in a wagon. You needed to believe he was frail and old."

Cry or laugh? I have no fucking idea.

"It was always about Frank." Vin's voice softens. "On the phone, when Mai told you how one of the bubbas had to put down his dog, you took a sharp breath."

"I don't know why I'm just now connecting these dots, but obviously you were listening that day. Of course you were. You just admitted you heard my bank question."

Vin says, "In that moment, I didn't realize why that sharp breath was important. Not until we looked into your court transcripts."

"I never heard you on the phone."

"We were on mute."

He must see my expression, because he answers immediately.

"Yeah, *we*. Me and my court. Everyone agreed if I came out of retirement and tried a kinging, this time it would be with a king's court. Four men guiding me, acting as both my moral compass and advisors. I made all final decisions related to your King Weekend. Their job was to help me find the best way to love you."

We are silent for another block.

"How did you get access to my court transcripts? They aren't public record."

"Could we save this for inside? Face to face might be better for some explanations."

"How far to the restaurant?"

Vin says, "We've been circling it for the last ten minutes. If we're ready to go inside, I'll turn around. We're only two blocks away."

"Every man I met on this quest told me about your incredible deceptions, and I still fell for it."

"Let's hold off on that big conversation until I get some hash browns and eggs."

"What about waffles?"

"Those, too. I haven't eaten in three days. I've been anxious. Haven't kinged a man in many years. Hang on. Yesterday, Mark made me a steak sandwich with roasted garlic. Half-omelet this morning. Whatever. I'm still ravenous. Aren't you?"

Vin chatters about favorite dishes, interrupting himself to ask questions about foods I like. I participate as much as I can. Flashes surprise me, visuals overwhelming my sight. The way her hand reached out, touching my leg. She'd said, "Brave." Who was she? One young guy had said, "You are stronger than me." Am I strong? They'd touched my legs! How did I allow that? I would never—

"...have a salad, of course, but you've had a long day. I think you need a full entrée."

What had third-date man said? Details are fading.

Vin says, "Don't worry about that. You may remember a few people and their exact words. Most of it, you'll remember in fragments. It's okay. Let it become part of you."

Holy shit. "How do you know what I'm thinking?"

"I'm a landscaper. I study the terrain. I know which thoughts in old Daniel are gnarled trees to remove. I know where to plant cheery little impatiens all around your perimeter. Hey, here's a fun fact. I designed your apartment building's landscaping around your personality."

He can read minds.

"I can't read minds. I make good guesses. I'm wrong often enough to humble me, which is why I now have a court of advisors. At the same time, for tonight to succeed, I spent a lot of time anticipating your experience. Also, you're frowning and working your lips. I get it. Your life was changed tonight. You want to memorize and then *memorialize* every second. Every spoken word. You won't. You can't. That's not how the experience changes you."

"How does it change me?"

"Don't need to worry about that. It's already happening. You're beginning."

"What the fuck does that mean?"

He points. "Across the street. There."

The restaurant is an upscale diner, a stand-alone building with a long stretch of front windows so foot traffic can observe happy eaters. Olive-green awnings hang perfectly still, asleep like everything else. The convenience store across the street is closed, as is other nearby businesses. Two cars are in the small parking lot. A man sits inside at the bar. Twenty-four-hour restaurant? Looking down the street—either way—I see only one moving car.

Vin is silent until the car is parked. "I'm friends with the owner. She's only open for us. Before we eat, you need to have a conversation. With John."

Fuck no.

He shuts off the engine, and it feels like my heart stopping.

"John has words he needs to say. I told him he could have ten minutes of your time. This isn't an in-depth conversation to resolve everything. He wants to apologize. He needs to apologize. Tonight. Can you deal with that?"

I stare straight ahead, not understanding the dark shapes outlined. Houses. Trees. It's too dark. I don't want this. On the plus side, I'm not exhausted anymore. My heart is pounding.

He says, "When I say, *'I'm asking you to listen,'* I mean it the same way I told you to look around the coffeehouse. This is your King Weekend. You do what I tell you to do."

My head snaps his way. "I liked you better when you didn't speak English."

"Look at me, Daniel. I gave you that command to get you angry and out of your head. Look at my face. See the softness I feel in this moment. You don't have to do anything you don't want to do. Here's the thing. If you don't talk to him right now, you might permanently lose the possibility for healing between you two."

"Hang on, Vin. Give me a minute."

I take a breath.

Then another.

I don't want to say more to regret. I am pissed at the ease with which he pushes buttons in me. Why do I fight to protect myself when there is no defense? Surrender to grace. *What grace?* That is not a thought I would think. Where are these goddamn words coming from?

"I apologize for what I said about not speaking English. I didn't mean it."

"I know. Good breath. Take another."

"I'll be more careful with my words."

"I know."

"I'm not this rude."

"Except when you are."

Goddamn it. "Hey. You push me."

Vin says, "I do. Yes."

"I'm trying to roll with everything happening tonight."

"You're doing great. I'm impressed."

"You're asking me to see a man who broke my heart. I'm exhausted. Emotionally stripped raw. I've been crying for weeks, it feels like. I'm—I don't know how I feel about you, about what you did, about tonight, about anything. I can't think of a worse time to see John."

"You're probably right."

"After the best, most connected sexual experience in my life, he dumped me."

"Yes."

"One of the worst heartbreaks I have ever felt."

"I'm not surprised."

"Why did he do that?"

Vin stares out the windshield. "In my opinion, he should not have seduced you."

Fight the fucking anger rising! "Hey Vin Vanbly, every fucking King Weekend I heard about was a giant fuckfest, so I'm not sure you're best qualified to represent sexual restraint."

"Probably not. Then again, I knew I could never date a man I kinged. I always walked away. John likes you. He wants to date."

This is—this is impossible to think through.

Vin says, "Can I have a moment to bitch about relying on others during a kinging? It's hard enough navigating a man into the kingdom when you control every variable. Involving others is a nightmare. First, John seduces you because it 'felt right.' I warned him of consequences. He felt the Found Ones were nudging him, and his heart was guiding him. But I knew a reckoning would come. And then, Fredi. Everyone wants to play. Nobody wants to take orders."

I am stubborn. I know it. I'm still not sure what my answer will be. I need another few seconds to consider. "What did Fredi do?"

Vin tenses. "When you and Jian pulled up in front of my house, she was supposed to rub raw liver on her hands, so that when she sat with you in the garden, some got worked into your hands. Not gobs, but enough smell to make sure Pilgrim came directly to you. We didn't know where that would be exactly, but I worried it would be somewhere crowded, like a coffeehouse. Sure enough, *coffeehouse.* I was right. Nobody listens."

"She refused?"

"She decided it was tacky. She announces this right as Little Vin plops down on the front steps. I argued with her. She just absolutely refused. You'd think we were ordering a pizza, not crossing someone into the kingdom."

"If I'm not ready for John?"

"I don't know. Nobody's following orders this weekend, so I guess we'll punt. I'll rent a clown or something. You like clowns?"

"Not particularly."

"Well then, talk to John."

I want to argue. I remember how he strolled through the crowded lobby, texting as he strolled away. I hated him. Still, tonight I survived falling and weeping in public. How could a ten-minute conversation be worse?

Vin says, "You're ready for this. I know you are."

"Yeah. I am."

"Good. Let's go."

I can survive ten minutes of excruciating conversation. John destroyed me. Did he? Am I destroyed?

As I extricate myself from his car, dread creeps in, but so does something else, something foreign, another confusing, unnamed something. An untwisting. An unclenching. Maybe I am more ready for this than I thought. Do I feel *strong*? No. Not strength, exactly. I am curious to see how I will handle this. Thank you, Mai Kearns.

Vin leans against the trunk, waiting for me, while I move one leg, then the other. I don't feel rushed. I don't care how long I take either, which is entirely new. What if I weren't focused on my legs every second, every goddamn single moment? What if I was polite, and moved at my best speed, but didn't feel guilty if people waited for me? These are not new ideas. I've tried fooling myself into believing them for years. Maybe now I believe. I am someone who takes longer. That's how it is with me. It's a fact, and I don't have to feel shitty about that.

When I join Vin, he nods. We cross the dark parking lot.

He says, "I recommend the scallops in red curry. Spice level is hot but not scalding. You know what? Never mind. Your choice."

A chuckle ripples through me. He really is hungry if he's ordering for me.

Every indication suggests a closed restaurant: the low lighting, the empty tables. As we pass the front windows, I see John sitting at the bar. Soft overhead light glows on his reddish-brown hair, and I remember the attraction I felt toward Alistair. I've dreamed of eviscerating him with words, but what do I really want? I'm not sure who to be furious with—Vin, John, Alistair, or Horatio. Do I even feel fury?

I flash to seeing hands on me, on my legs. Their whispered blessings. *You are strong.* I also remember my rage, the way my scalp sweated when I decided to murder Vin Vanbly.

Vin reaches for the door's handle and tugs it open.

John turns.

Shit. Shit. What do I say? What do I want?

Vin says, "I'll be at our table, around the corner, over there. When you're done."

I nod.

John stands. Wipes his hands on his jeans. "I won't speak for long. Vin told you I want to apologize?"

"Yes."

"I want to be precise in what I'm apologizing for. It's not for sleeping with you. I do not regret our lovemaking. That was incredible. I also realize I may have permanently damaged the chance of anything romantic ever developing."

I feel I should say something. "I thought Found Kings never made mistakes."

"We do."

He maintains eye contact. It's curious to witness regret without shame. It makes him look more vulnerable.

"Hopefully, less colossal fuckups when it comes to relationships and people, but yes, mistakes. My role was always to inform you Vin had rejected you. I was to give you the speech in a Mexican bar, where you were alone in a foreign country. Vin wanted you isolated and vulnerable when he freed your rage."

How would that have felt? The day was always going to be horrible, no matter where it happened.

"You might have hated me under any circumstances. The plane delay gave me the idea to become Alistair at the airport bar. I did not count on being so attracted to you. While we had drinks in the hotel, and you used the bathroom, Vin tried to talk me out of it. He promised the crucible of your kinging would blast any romantic connection in unpredictable directions. I heard what he said, but being with you felt necessary and right. I felt the kings were urging me, my heart was urging me. But the next morning, walking to the limo, I finally understood Vin's warning. With every step I felt your hatred explode exponentially—and completely justifiably. If I'd turned around and said, 'Daniel, it's all a setup, but my feelings are real,' maybe you would have forgiven me, but probably not. The scarring was deep and immediate. In addition, anything I might have said at that moment would destroy your one shot getting kinged. Even if you had miraculously forgiven me and we fell in love, one day you would comprehend what I had stolen with my selfish desire to have you love me, and you would have hated me even more. Opportunities to reclaim your kingship are less common than I implied. In those seconds I departed, I began to comprehend the damage I had done, but my only option was to keep walking."

John looks ill.

He says, "Give me a minute."

Silence.

I shift my weight.

He clears his throat. "I called Vin from the limo. I told him someone needed to watch me until I was in no danger of calling or texting you. I spent the next two days with others—until all of us felt confident I could be trusted to stay away from you. Vin's manipulations on my own King Weekend fooled me—he made it look easy. Even knowing he loved me deeply, I still didn't understand how hard it is to walk away from that kind of love. I underestimated the consequences on us."

He straightens. "At that hotel bar, I made a decision. I'm not sorry I slept with you. You're an amazing lover. I just wish I hadn't done it during your kinging. For that, I'm sorry. Now I must live with the outcome, however you feel about me. Thank you for listening."

He's not the one.

"I don't know what to say."

John says, "Whatever you feel, whatever you decide, is fine. I needed to explain that I understood how much I damaged you. Another day I will listen to you describe that morning explained from your perspective. I owe you that. Well, if you wish. Again, thank you for listening. Enjoy dinner. This place has great salads."

I nod, which is all I have in me. My arms tremble.

John leaves, passing through the heavy door. I survived the conversation. I watch his retreat in the dark mirror behind the bar. *Goodbye, John. I will definitely spend time thinking about you. About us.* If I ever get some alone time. Or sleep. Sleep would be so nice right now. Adrenaline is still pounding. How am I still conscious after what I've been through?

Can't think about that.

Time for dinner with Vin Vanbly.

NINETEEN

As I REACH the main dining area, Vin waves me over, as if that were remotely necessary. We are alone.

"I already ordered spicy Rangoons."

"How?"

He nods at a door against a back wall. Kitchen access.

As I unstrap my canes, he describes the restaurant's porous waffles and blueberry syrup thickly absorbed. He watches me without watching, like when a server brings menus, and you observe but you're not invested. After everything I've been through, it strikes me funny. For him, this moment is nothing new. He watched me daily in my backyard. He studied me through binoculars in New York. He doesn't care about my legs. He's not kinging me because of my goddamn legs. I don't know why this surprises me. My ability to react to surprises—to anything—is broken. He's not kinging me because he feels sorry for me.

"Coleen is coming back for our drink orders and to see if you want an additional appetizer. I'm happy to split the Rangoons, but you might want something on your own. Whatever you want. Dinner's on me."

Dinner? After everything he has done for me—*to* me—how he crucified me, liberated me, I don't even know what I'm thinking right now, everything dying inside me and living—I start laughing. *Dinner's on me.* Yes, that's what matters, who pays for our goddamn dinner. I howl, as if this is the best joke I ever heard.

Vin looks at me quizzically, trying to understand what set me off. His face. *His face.* I can't breathe.

When I recover, two people are here. Vin sits opposite and a blond woman stands next to the table. She's grinning. *Oh.* Suddenly, I feel sad. Not once in my entire life have I ever laughed this hard. Not ever.

The woman says, "Oh good. I was worried he'd never stop. What did you do to him?"

Vin says, "Nothing! Maybe. I may have broken him slightly."

She says, "Hey, Laughy. Can you hear us?"

Vin's grin, like someone anticipating the punchline, the empty restaurant, John careful not to apologize for sleeping with me but *when* he slept with me. *Laughy.* Like anyone would mistake *me* for a man who laughs a lot. But it happens again, laughter overtakes me, racing in front, daring me to catch up, to run, to run, to run!

I run.

She's gone when I sit up.

Vin is smiling, wiping away his own tears. "It's funny to watch someone laugh hard. You have a great laugh, Daniel."

I want to reply, but my throat tightens. No one has ever said that. Things are going to be different in my life. I will laugh more. Music spills into the dining area, and sure enough, when I glance over, she's pushing the door open with her backside.

Vin says, "Rangoons. We can eat."

Laughter rises, as if *I* was the one fixated on food. No, stop. Don't laugh. I need to rest.

The woman from earlier delivers a steaming blue platter. She's older than Vin. Maybe the same age range, hard to tell. Her strawberry-blond hair falls in two long parentheses over the sides of her face, knotted into a ponytail behind.

She tips the plate. "Cream cheese, habanero peppers, scallion, and shrimp in my own breading, fried lightly. They've got some kick. Not Minnesota kick, real kick. The drizzle is a ginger balsamic fusion. Sop it up with the arugula bed, and it's salad. Vin said you might also want another appetizer."

"I haven't looked at your menu."

She smiles. "I figured. I heard you from the kitchen. I'm Coleen Rakolini."

"Daniel Connors. Hi."

"Nice to meet you."

"Thank you for staying open so late."

Vin reaches for the first Rangoon, and she slaps his hand. "The person who knows both parties is supposed to introduce us and spare us social awkwardness."

"You two did okay." He reaches again.

She slaps his hand. "Let Daniel try one first. Daniel, how's your kinging?"

"Honestly? Insanity, following an afternoon and evening of total chaos and terror. How's your night?"

"Less dramatic. If you want something not on the menu, ask. Maybe I'll have it or can whip something up."

Vin drops his Rangoon. "Ow. Hot."

Coleen says, "The universe is punishing you."

"I don't believe in a punishing universe."

"Well, then it's me punishing you. Daniel, if you like curry, consider the scallops. Distract your tired brain by warming your belly."

Vin says, "I made that recommendation in the parking lot."

I nod. "Sounds good. I'll have that."

"Wine? Beer? Soft drinks? I have—"

"Water would be great. Thank you. A lot of water. I think I'm dehydrated."

"Not surprised." To Vin, she says, "You're having a ginger salmon filet on a bed of squid ink pasta drizzled in dill sauce. Testing an item for the next menu."

He nods. "Thank you. Sounds delicious."

She says, "All six dimensions for feedback."

"Got it."

"Daniel, anything else? Hot towel? Advil? Vin can be a bit much."

The understatement makes me laugh, the laughter I thought was contained. I can't stop it!

Vin shakes, laughing at my laughing.

I'm so fucking tired. How does a person deal with this much... everything? Vin's laughter dies, too, and he blots his eyes with the cloth napkin. When we breathe normally, he picks up a second Rangoon and toasts me.

"Welcome back. Try one."

"Okay."

"Unless you don't like cream cheese or shrimp. You're not obligated. It's spicy."

"No, no. I'll obey."

He grins. "Obeying is good."

Wow. "Hey, these are amazing."

"I know."

"No, like *really* amazing."

"I think so, too."

We chew in silent appreciation.

Vin Vanbly never stopped kinging me. Never *intended* to stop. Why is it easier to forgive Vin than John? Maybe because I never thought I'd see Horatio again, let alone enjoy a conversation. Maybe because I'm so goddamn relieved I didn't follow through with murdering him.

"This is not how I thought our first meeting would go."

Vin says, "I'll bet. We discovered your application for a gun permit."

His directness surprises me.

"Daniel, I need to discuss two things about your father. One you probably already know, the second involves the gun permit."

"No. Not now."

The strength of my resistance unnerves me. After everything I experienced tonight, I refuse to talk about him. I won't ruin tonight, bringing him into this. I can't.

"I get it. You're exhausted. But I'd like us to enjoy dinner without this conversation dangling, so I'm obligated to pursue it. When Mai spoke about the necessity for total surrender on a King Weekend—and you flew to New York to find the next king—you agreed to the terms. You know that, right?"

Anger rising. Nobody talks to me about my father, except Margaret. I picture myself falling in the coffeehouse—my worst nightmare came true—except it might have been the most amazing moment in my life. Can I fall further? Can I let myself be knocked to the ground again?

He says, "*Por favore*, amigo."

"Cheap shot, Horatio. Just give me a minute."

"Of course. The first thing, you probably—"

Damn it. "How is that giving me a minute?"

"The first thing you already know, having been in therapy."

"Did you talk to Margaret? *Goddamn* it." They fucking talked to my therapist?

"No. Another thin line I would not cross. We followed you and discovered you visited a therapist. That's it. No contact."

My rage falls.

"Given what we did to you tonight, and how your life circumstances changed in the past hour or two, I'm hoping you might be able to hear these words from a new place. I'm sure you and she discussed how there was never any choice between you and Frank, right? Frank was always doomed. Forcing you into a choice was just another layer of your father's psychological abuse."

You're wrong, Margaret.

"Your father ran over your legs at sixteen. He killed Frank when you were eleven. It took him five years to escalate to killing you. When you were eleven, he wasn't ready."

I am terrified to hear these words. Margaret had addressed this, and I'd screamed at her for ten minutes because I couldn't—I can't let go of this responsibility. It's disloyal to Frank.

"Your face muscles are getting tense. You're angry, aren't you?"

"I am."

"Your love for Frank is fused to guilt. Well, it was. Not anymore, not after tonight. You were afraid if you stopped feeling guilty, his death was fine. No big deal. If you don't hate yourself for Frank's death, his death wasn't tragic."

"Fuck you."

"Fuck me because I'm wrong? Or fuck me because I'm right?"

Tears form. "I don't know."

"You do know. I'm not wrong."

What if my choice didn't matter? I want to scream until I can't hear my voice. I chose. The least I can do is take responsibility.

"Tonight you loved Frank without guilt. How did it feel to love Frank again?"

I can't speak. He knows. He sees me quivering.

Vin says, "I experienced something similar when I was a kid. His name was Christian. I convinced him to hide in the basement of our foster home. There were rats down there. A lot of rats."

Do not react.

"Christian couldn't handle it. He freaked and ran upstairs—to them. The upstairs men. They were rapists. I always hid from them in that basement. I should have known he couldn't handle the swarming rats. None of the kids could. Just me. In fact, I had given up trying to convince others to hide down there with me. During my own King Weekend, I remembered a detail I hadn't thought of in more than twenty years. Thirty, maybe. That night, as I was trying to protect Christian, one of the men yelled, 'Don't let them get to the basement.'

"Daniel, that man manipulated me. Planted the idea. Of course, I ran straight for the basement, dragging Christian with me. The men knew Christian wouldn't be able to handle it. They played me. These days, if I see an adult manipulate a child, I never think, *that kid is an idiot.* Do you? Ever?"

"No."

"I was manipulated into thinking it was my idea. My choice." Vin reflects my grief. "You didn't kill Frank. Your father manipulated you into believing you chose."

I put my face in my shaking hands. I can't take much more of this.

"I would add one last thought to this topic. Daniel, listen carefully, because I want to rip off a Band-Aid. Here we go. If you continue to believe you're responsible for Frank's death, you're doing exactly what your father wanted, decades later. He's still got you."

Asshole!

"Your expression—your rage—leads me to the second conversation."

I hate Vin Vanbly, first class fucking asshole, strolling through the toxicity in my brain. But is he right? I don't know. *I don't know.* It's not his words or tone that's so aggravating, but that he understands the terrain better than me.

He bites another Rangoon. "You should eat another before they get cold. Second topic. Where's your gun?"

To give myself something to do, I take another. I haven't processed the first revelation. Margaret tried to get me to see this in therapy, and I fought her. Too upset to talk it through. Comes up every now and then, but I never let her discuss it. Vin's strolling through my twisted brain like he doesn't even mind the exercise.

"Where's your gun?"

"I don't understand your question. I'm having a hard time listening."

"I'll bet. You never finished the application for a gun permit. I'm asking metaphorically, where's your gun? Why didn't you kill me?"

"I'm a coward."

"Is that it? Rance ordered you to go through the chain-link fence. Instead, you turned around to help a middle-aged Korean woman you thought was being attacked. Given your inability to fight, some might call that stupid. Or extremely courageous."

"It was all fake. There was no danger."

"You didn't know that. Cowardice is off the table. Let's go back to my question. Where's the gun?"

"Fuck you, Mr. Thin Line. Do you understand what you did? You made me feel the raging hatred *he* felt. All that toxicity he passed through genes. You turned me into my father. I don't care how great your fucking kinging is—you can never undo that."

"Good. I worked hard to drive you there."

"Well, fuck you." *I hate this guy.*

Vin says, "Here's my theory. It's about love. Deep down you secretly believed if you ever unleashed your most creative, most wildly-loving self—allowing yourself to be consumed by life's passion—you'd also unleash your father's capacity for hatred. Let out the light, let out the dark."

"Therapy bullshit."

"Maybe. And I could be wrong. Still, I decided the key to your passionate, loving self was to prove you're not your father. To accomplish this, I forced you into an explosive hatred you've never experienced—or maybe you learned to suppress. Set aside your immediate frustrations with me and answer honestly, if not aloud. Have you ever experienced greater hatred than when John walked away?"

"No."

"On a scale of one to ten?"

"Four hundred. I wanted you dead. I wanted to be the one who killed you."

"Right. You went home and filled out an online gun permit."

I hate him, fucking chewing right now, savoring food while discussing the worst day of my adult life.

"This isn't amusing to me. I was committed to your death. I mentally blew your head off thousands of times in those first days."

"Thank you. I hope you're not just saying that."

"Fuck you."

"Look at my face, Daniel. Look. Do you think I'm unaware of the darkest manipulations I worked on you? Am I laughing right now? Answer my question. Why didn't you get a gun?"

My head is spinning. Where is he going? What does he want me to say?

"Still want to hurt me? Here's my arm. Stab me with your fork."

Coleen emerges, holding drinks.

"Rip off my skin with your teeth. Go ahead. Feel that rage. Do it."

She watches our intensity with no expression, then leaves our drinks and retreats.

Vin says, "I unlocked the full force of your father's insane rage, yet you didn't kill me. Even now, you refuse to physically hurt me, knowing I deliberately drove you into that emotional brick wall at one hundred miles per hour."

What is he saying? Why am I spinning, spinning, spinning?

"I knew you wouldn't kill me, Daniel. I risked my very life on it, and I happen to fucking love my life. Why? Because the love inside you was so much bigger than you understand. As Horatio, I witnessed your kindness every day for a month. The treats you brought me. The friendly way you listened, though you could not understand my words. When I pretended to fall off that ladder, another tenant, first floor, opened her window and looked out, but didn't come outside. You raced down the stairs.

"When your father felt that murder rage, he abused you. He chose death. I forced your darkest passion, just as strong as his. But you abandoned the gun permit. You didn't act on your murder impulse. You chose life. Hate me if you want, but now you're free to unlock your life's passion, because your heart finally has conclusive proof you'll never *ever* become him."

My sobbing begins the minute he finishes speaking.

I wipe an arm across my face. "I just remembered something I didn't ever want to remember."

"Tell me."

"Is that a command?"

He says, "If you need it to be."

I still don't like him.

Vin says, "I know. I can be annoying. You'll get used to me eventually. I'd really like to know what you remembered. Please."

Do this. Fall further.

"My dad liked sports. Baseball. He loved to see teams lose. He loved players and fans who cried during post-game interviews. Obviously, he was drawn to the

Chicago Cubs. When I was—I don't know—nine? Eight? He was watching the Cubs. I was in physical agony over what he'd done to me the day before. Trying to sit upright and not move, both to minimize the pain and not draw attention."

I've never volunteered this much about my father, not ever.

"Cubs were losing. Latest player struck out. Staring at the screen, he said, 'They cannot win.' He wasn't talking to me. But his easy confidence, his knowing this to be a fact—it's the moment I realized he would kill me. He would never let me win. Not ever. I was his personal Chicago Cub."

"That's horrific."

"I know. I didn't even remember it until now." My hand rests against my forehead. "Please quit making me cry."

After a moment or two of silence, Coleen backs out of the swinging kitchen door. As she approaches, the aromas precede her. My stomach twists with a sensation I had forgotten. Hunger. A few moments of setting down hot plates and food small-talk is perfect. Coleen presents the cobalt plate before me, plump buttery scallops floating in a sea of red curry, potato wedges clumped like salty islands. Fuck hunger. I'm starving.

Vin says, "You're gonna love that."

I just volunteered an abuse story about my father. That's not me—that's never me. I barely talk to Margaret about him some weeks. I thought that rage in the hotel lobby was proof my destiny was fulfilled. What if Vin's right? What if the proof is in the action? *I'll never become him.* Is it possible to trust that? Could the Cubs win the World Series?

Vin picks up his fork and mutters happy words.

Coleen says, "Hon, I'll bring you more water. What about a ginger ale? Something fizzy to give you a little boost?"

"Yes please."

"Vin—"

"Coleen, don't say anything. Don't tell me what flavors to look for. If you want my feedback, say nothing."

"I won't."

"You were about to."

She says, "You don't know me."

Vin says her name, a soft rebuke. She leaves. Right before she swings into the kitchen, she says, "You were right. Tell me if there's too much clove."

She disappears.

Vin says, "I need about five minutes to savor a few bites. You okay with silence?"

"I'd love silence right now."

The curry is hot and, yes, comforting. So smooth. These scallops are as buttery as they look. Coleen was right. I needed this. God, I needed this.

Vin chews carefully, intent on his meal. He raises his eyes, and without words, asks how I'm enjoying mine. With exaggerated slowness, I toast him with my fork, acknowledging his recommendation. He closes his eyes. I close mine. This is good. I need the silence. I can finally breathe for a moment. Eat. Not laugh or cry. In this silence, Horatio lives. Our friendship was silence. Hello, friend. I'm so damn exhausted. And hungry. I am so goddamn hungry. How did I not know that? What has he done to me?

What has he done to me?

With his eyes closed, chewing gently, he says, "How's dinner?"

"Unbelievable. One of the best meals I've ever eaten. I had to put my fork down twice to savor."

"Coleen's good."

"No, this exquisite."

He offers me a bite, and I decline. I'm sure it's amazing, but I don't want to interrupt this taste in my mouth. "Hey, what happened to ordering waffles and eggs?"

He smiles. "She had other plans for me. Beyond my control."

"During our silence, I thought of something to ask."

Vin says, "Shoot."

"What if I feel that murder rage again?"

"I doubt you'll ever hate that way twice."

"But it's in me."

"Daniel, I worked five angles to emotionally escalate you to that rage. It's a volatile, intricate emotion, not easily achieved. Your real question is, what if passing one test is not enough proof you're not your father."

"Maybe." My voice is small.

"Well, rest assured, knowing you were tested a second time in the car, moments ago. Completely unplanned. Kevin's choice to participate in your King Weekend meant he willingly handed you power to destroy a decade's worth of public service and relationship building. You can still take that all away—as I mentioned earlier, no decisions made tonight are binding. You're in altered space. But let's review your immediate reaction. Within literal minutes of learning how deeply and unjustly you were manipulated—deceived on an unforgivable scale by all of us, including Kevin—what was your first reaction to his situation? Very first words? *I vow.* First words out of your mouth."

My throat is tightening. I put down my fork.

"Didn't your father hold power over other lives? I'm not talking about as a surgeon. I'm talking about you and your mother."

I can't look up.

"Did he use that power to destroy?"

I can't open my mouth.

"The word you're seeking is *yes*. However, your immediate response to having this same power over another person's life was to vow protection. Does that sound like your dad? How many more tests before you accept it?"

Accept it, like I'd refuse an escape from a lifelong curse. I'd love to *accept it*. He doesn't understand. It's more complicated.

Or is it?

Accept it.

That guy tonight said, *you are courageous.*

I'm not!

I need a break before my head implodes. "Everyone said you were a mechanic."

"Yes. Change the topic by all means. Good strategy. But never forget you were tested twice. Both tests were extreme. Twice you proved you'll never become him."

I'm going to scream. Or pass out.

"Take a breath, my friend. That's right. Deep breath. Yes, I was a mechanic. I quit. My turn to change the topic. I'd like to talk to you about Thomas."

I can't take much more.

"Thomas begged to participate. Pleaded. Everyone thinks a kinging is going to be such a grand adventure, such larks. I warned him, if I designed a role for him, he couldn't back out, and he probably wouldn't enjoy what I assigned. He agreed, and I was right. He hated his role. He hated calling you a cripple. A 'tard. If you're upset with Thomas, you're upset with me. I scripted his lines and told him specific insults to work into conversation. We rehearsed together until he said could speak with the tone I approved."

"How is that different from the muscle guys in New York?"

"Only my people were in the bar. Only they heard, if they heard anything. I designed that experience to expose specific vulnerabilities."

"What about Greg?"

"King friend. He had scripted lines, too."

"Had the bar people read your report on me?"

"No. Only the people in the coffeehouse saw that."

"And you just happened to have all your people in the bar that afternoon?"

"Jian texted us you were headed to the garage, so we got my people in the bar first. He also drove a longer route to give us a few extra minutes. I'm friends with the owner. After you came inside, he waited outside and asked any real customers to come back later."

"You were there in a cowboy hat?"

"Yup. Making sure Thomas and Greg didn't need help. Are you sure you don't want to try this? The dill sauce is incredible."

"No."

Vin says, "I can see by your clenched jaw, you're upset."

"I am." *They blessed my legs.* Why did I let people touch my legs? "Too much has happened. I'm not even sure why I'm angry. These feelings... I feel...."

What do I feel? Rage? Blessed?

"A kinging ain't pretty, Daniel. It's wrestling demons into the mud and losing. Kings rise after men fall. Thomas has been sober for fifteen years. To participate, he had to revisit an old version of himself, a man he loathes. He sat on a bar stool, doing shots of water, risking his own sobriety to participate. In case you thought he was having a good time, he wasn't. That trembling in his hands was real."

Another layer of confusing hurt. Forgive him? I can't process this. I don't know how else to respond, other than to ask more questions. "How could you be sure I'd go into the bar?"

"It was one of three possibilities. We prepped other locations where a similar scene would have taken place. One scene for that bar, one at your hotel—although I wanted to avoid that, as it was too similar to John's encounter—and one at a funeral home, but you didn't go for that clue. Ever since you arrived, Thomas and Greg have been in a van, four blocks away from you at all times, ready for action."

"I'm at a complete loss to understand this. Any of this."

He studies me in a way I don't comprehend, like he's looking for something. "Your father stuck a metaphorical sword in your chest. Your whole life, it's been quivering, jutting two feet in front of you. Anyone can flick it, making your life hell. All they have to do is call you a cripple or ask what happened to your legs. The trick is, you can't pull that sword out. The only way to free you was to push the sword through."

"That's bullshit."

"Is it? When you collapsed on the coffeehouse floor, did you finally accept—for a split second—everything your father said was true?"

"It's not true. I never deserved—"

"Of course not. I've witnessed your power. The love you have inside you. Listen to what I'm asking. In those seconds, did you accept everything he said as *true*?"

I consider his words. "Less than one second."

"Yes. And in that magic half-second—that quarter-second—you surrendered to the sword, and it passed through. It can never stab you the way it used to. That part of your life is over. Did you deserve what he did?"

"No."

"Does any child? The people in the coffeehouse deserve what happened to them?"

"Of course not."

"How about a child who cries a lot? Or a gay kid?"

He knows my answer.

"What about kids who don't share toys?"

"No one."

I speak with a quiet strength, and... I don't know if I can think this—*can I think this?*—an acceptance. I don't have to convince myself anymore. I believe it. I goddamn believe it. I never deserved this.

The sword passed through me.

Vin leans forward. "What happened just now? Your eyes got laser focused."

"Nothing." I put trembling fingers to my forehead. I can't take much more.

"C'mon. Trust me on this. I study micro-expressions, and I've been watching your face. What happened? What did you just remember?"

"I didn't remember anything."

He says, "Did you see one this weekend? A sword?"

"I don't know. Maybe."

"Describe it. Please."

"I'm not sure—I don't believe in this."

"So don't believe in this. That's fine. Just tell me what you saw."

"Long blade. Heavy. Medieval thickness, I guess. Not fancy, but three fat rubies in its handle. Big ones. A gold-and-red braided cord wrapped around the handle, like ceremonial. I'm babbling."

When I meet his eyes, Vin's expression is wary. "You saw the Crimson Blade."

"I don't know what I saw."

"In all my kingings, only two others witnessed it on their weekend."

I can't think anymore. *I can't think!*

He says, "Men who saw the Crimson Blade—"

"Stop. Please." My whole body is shaking. "I need a break. From talking. From revelations, from analyzing how I felt and how I feel at this exact moment. I'm... trying my best. I'm grateful and exhausted and angry, or maybe not angry—I don't even know. Could we please talk about something else? Maybe you talk but not about me? Or we go back to silence?"

He studies me.

A moment later, he says, "Sure."

Relief surges. "If that wasn't the right thing to ask, I'll do what you want. I'll do my best to submit. But I'm struggling. My brain is broken. My heart feels broken. I keep forgetting to breathe. Was your kinging hard? Did you feel like smashed dinner plates but also happy birds flying everywhere? I'm talking weird."

He stirs his remaining noodles. "You're making perfect sense. To answer your question, despite being one of the few people intimately acquainted with kingings, no, I was not prepared for being so completely destroyed."

"Tell me? Please? I need to not talk for a while."

He takes another mouthful of noodles. Chews slowly. These meager seconds of his silent deliberation are like fresh Minneapolis night air. I gulp it down.

He says, "My kinging began on St. Patrick's Day. Actually—backing up—I had an incredibly stressful two weeks leading up to St. Patrick's Day. I had finally agreed to let my older brother, Malcolm, tell Mark my history. The story was long overdue, but I couldn't speak it. Since Malcolm was coming to Minneapolis for a retired policeman conference the same weekend as my birthday, we agreed Malcolm would tell Mark. His conference was a lie. Malcolm was coming for my kinging. I suspected nothing."

"Why couldn't you just tell Mark?"

"I was convinced my story would destroy our relationship. So, for two weeks, I lived in panic. Didn't sleep. Felt like shit. Then, for a few hours on St. Patrick's Day, we sat in an overcrowded bar, and I endured Malcolm recounting my former life. I thought I would die."

"On your birthday."

"I always hated my birthday. This made it worse. On the way home, Mark and I had a big fight. But Mark didn't hate me. I was in shock the relationship wasn't over. Like you said, broken dishes and happy birds. I felt goofy. When we got home, I chased him into the house, right into a massive surprise party. I always hated surprises, so I freaked out. Complete meltdown, bawling on the floor. Couldn't stop."

His eyes fill with tears, and reflexively, mine do, too.

"Like me an hour ago."

"Exactly. I sobbed in my adopted father's arms for like, I don't know, a long time, telling him I was sorry and how much I loved him. Then, people kept handing me beers, and I guzzled them down, hugging everybody." He pauses. "I was so happy. I accepted how much I was loved. What I didn't know was that they had handed me alcohol-free beer in the wrong bottles. I did four Jell-O shots that were just green Jell-O. All night, friends kept isolating me to share why they loved me. I felt drunker. I kept drinking. I didn't understand they were preparing me. My real nightmare hadn't even begun."

He takes another bite, chewing and gazing around the silent restaurant. The music from the kitchen stopped a while ago. The moment leads to several moments, both of us nibbling and looking down. He nods at my plate. "You doing okay?"

"It's like I never ate scallops before. Nourishing is too limiting. If I concentrate, I can taste individual spices, or the whole. I have choice over which flavor dominates. How is that?"

"Food might taste different for a while. Your taste buds are changing."

"No. No more revelations. Please."

"Right. Back to my kinging. All evening, Mark was at my side, holding my hand, spitting beer out his nose when we laughed. At midnight, the doorbell rang. Malcolm told me I had to answer the front door myself. The party got quiet, and I threw it open. I hate surprises, but that night, I was excited. For the first time in my life, I welcomed a surprise." He raises his fork. "May I?"

"Sure."

He drags a potato through the curry. "I had realized my king name, both mine and Mark's, at the beginning of the party. I thought that meant it was over." He chuckles. "On any of my King Weekends, whenever a guy figured out his king name, the weekend wasn't *over*. Hell, it was usually only in the first third or middle. Duh."

"Who was at the door?"

"Everyone. Every man I had kinged, minus the ones in the house. Minus the men who chose not to stay in touch for various reasons, like Kearns. I saw them all in a single glance, scattered around the front lawn, all wearing charcoal-gray trench coats. Every fucking man. All of them had never—as far as I knew—been together at once. They carried torches and pitchforks. Literal torches, thick wooden branches wrapped with kerosene rags. Big flames."

"Jesus."

"I always thought I was a monster, and hours after my story was revealed, a mob came for me. On my birthday. To top it off, I was drunk, or so I thought. While I tried to absorb this king horde in my front yard, I was blindfolded. My hands were bound. They lifted me, carried me from the party, the ones in the yard helping to bear my weight."

"That sounds terrifying."

"For a control freak, my worst nightmare. I fought. I cried. After a few minutes, I experienced this kind of, well, death. Went limp. Life was over. After that it slowly dawned. I felt loved. I was safe. I thought I was completely drunk, so everything was fuzzy and slow-moving."

"Rough thing to do to an abused kid."

"Absolutely. But they weren't acting spontaneously. For years, they met at Burning Man to discuss how to king me. Loss of control was a carefully-integrated strategy. That did not change how horrible it was. I always tried to anticipate my kings' reactions. I could have never predicted that feeling. At last, I understood my arrogance.

"The kings had arrived in the week prior to my birthday, working logistics, finalizing contingency plans. They had hired a local self-defense expert, someone experienced in working with abused children. He taught them blindfolding, binding, and safe holds. They trained for days."

"Still, brutal."

"Yes. You should never fuck with an abused kid like that."

We make eye contact, and I know he's apologizing for everything he did to me.

Vin says, "That night, they forced me to either trust their love or die. They eased me into a van, where I was cradled in loving arms. I bawled. Then, exhausted and drunk, I got quiet. They vocalized a song, a song without words. *The* song."

My plate is empty. I don't remember finishing.

"After we arrived at the destination, they walked me blindfolded over snow and crunchy grass. When I stumbled, they kept me upright. I was never in danger. It was tender. I hated the experience, too. They removed my blindfold and we stood in a cemetery, right at the gravesite of Melvin Vanbly. My birth date. It's traumatizing to see your own headstone."

I never thought to google *Melvin.*

"I wanted to piss myself. Collapse. Yet every man I had ever loved—minus a notable few—stood with me. Mark. Malcolm. Perry. Darwin. Ryan. My father. He was ninety-three and needed as much walking assistance as I did, but he insisted on being there. We stood around my grave, middle of the night, nothing but flickering torchlight. The tombstone wasn't new. It had weathered. They had been planning this for years.

"Rance spoke, and to get through the experience, I focused on the orange cuffs of his king shirt under his trench coat. He announced Melvin had to live again. We had to dig him up. Two shovels were produced. He explained how taking turns, two kings would dig until the coffin was exhumed. They promised there really was a coffin, it was really six feet under. They would only dig while I told stories about Melvin's life. If I stopped talking, they stopped digging."

"Thomas showed me a newspaper article."

"Yeah." A smile crosses his face. "My kinging made the Pioneer Press police blotter, which is kinda cool."

If I'd had to stand in a cemetery discussing my childhood, could I? Would I go that far to obtain this kingship, whatever it is? I don't know. Maybe. How far did I go tonight?

"They explained I was not drunk, so I had no excuses. Completely sober, I had to confess every hated flaw, describe every Melvin weakness in great detail to men I loved and idealized. Many of them knew one Melvin story—a detail here and there—so I could not lie. I talked. Every man took turns digging. Even my father lifted a few shovels of dirt. It was hard for him, but he loved me that much."

I see his grief.

"Mark held my hand. He cried when I cried. This was much worse than the early part of the evening, when Malcolm told my story. This time, I had to reveal it all myself. Thank god it happened. Thank god it could never happen again."

A flood of happiness gushes through me. Terrible burdens have been lifted tonight, and I can't understand what I feel, because I've never *not* felt heavy. I talked about Frank with love, surrounded by people who didn't judge me. All because I fell.

Vin pushes away his plate. "You'd be surprised how long it takes to dig a grave. In movies, it's a short video montage and then done. Digging semi-frozen March dirt takes a long fucking time. They had rented a machine to warm the earth but still, long time. I had to tell every single Melvin story I could remember.

"I had run out by three o'clock in the morning, but they weren't done digging. They insisted I keep talking. I forced myself to tell the story of the first kinging, the one story I never wanted told. Just before dawn, I finished it, hating myself. Obviously, I've never been physically dead, but I felt... I felt unalive. Even with Mark at my side—especially with Mark there—I wanted to die. Every king knew the worst of me. I assumed they all hated me as much as I hated myself."

"The first kinging in history?"

"No. That was eons ago. *My* first kinging."

"I assume you won't tell that story tonight either."

"It's a long story. Better for another time. That night, by the time I finished, the coffin had been exposed, a real wooden coffin."

"Oh god."

"Right? Handmade. Rough. Unpolished. This fit my idea of an anonymous death, the kind of coffin a child in foster care might get. The kings had constructed it years ago, at DC's suggestion. DC also ordered the tombstone. He decided it would be necessary for my kinging. Right before dawn, they ordered me into the open grave. I was glad to escape their faces, so I jumped in. They threw down ropes for me to secure around handles. I was instructed to lie on top. Mark climbed down and lay on top of me, also crying, and the men grabbed the ropes. Pulled us up."

Vin's face is sorrowful.

"The ropes cracked as they strained. The sound was how I felt. When Mark and I were raised from the earth, I saw they had stripped off their trench coats, every king shirt exposed, all those sparkling colors in dawn's cold light. Even Ryan the Protector, whose left arm was deformed since birth, had rope wrapped around his right forearm and bicep, straining from exertion. Nothing will ever compare to that moment, reaching the light, being surrounded by men who heard my worst and still loved me. I was handed a crowbar and told to pry open the coffin. Inside was my king shirt. Mark's, too. We were both kinged that weekend."

"What was Mark's worst nightmare?"

"Watching me suffer. Being powerless to help."

Mom—no. I can't tackle another issue tonight.

Vin says, "When Mark was a teenager, his older sister died. They were very close, and he was powerless to stop it. That night, he watched a version of that happen again. Older and wiser, he could still do nothing. He surrendered."

He smiles. "Mine is a tuxedo shirt. I would never have picked white for my king shirt, something so gloriously pure. It didn't quite fit because I'd lost a little weight, gained a little muscle. But it's perfect. I love it. Every time I wear a tuxedo, I wear my king shirt. The buttons are real diamonds. The good ones, not blood diamonds."

"What about Mark's king shirt?"

He smiles. "You'll see it later."

Oh, right. Parties. How can I talk to people in my state of mind?

"If you spent the night digging up a grave, why didn't the cops come?"

"I still don't know. I was told DC handled everything, but I suspect Malcolm influenced that. DC told Malcolm and Mark it was finally time to king me. DC planned a double kinging, me and Mark both, which, trust me, is exceptionally difficult. I've only done that once." Vin looks at me expectantly.

I wait for him, but he's clearly waiting for me.

He says, "So, who is he?"

"Who's who?"

"DC. Who is he? Which king?"

"I don't understand."

Vin says, "I assume you've met him."

"Me?"

"Yeah. They said you'd know first."

"I don't know anything. I don't even know what DC stands for."

Vin frowns. "They said he would step out on your King Weekend. You're the first one to know his true identity. Whenever I ask, they stick out their tongues." He leans back and spreads his arms across the booth. "You sure you don't know?"

"I have no idea. Nobody told me."

"Huh. You know, for a few years, I thought DC was your pal, Ms. Taylor. Her middle name is Caroline. I thought maybe DC was Dame Caroline. Plus, the one time I met her, she did not like me, not one bit. Since there's a prophecy that DC will kill me, I thought, why not? Nothing more than glancing suspicion, really. She doesn't care about the kingings."

"Murdering people doesn't sound like Ms. Taylor."

"That too. I knew DC was supposed to be a king—someone I kinged or will king—but I had run out of potential suspects. For a little while, I wondered if it was you, given your initials."

"You don't seem terribly threatened by the prospect of your murder."

He leans back. "I've had a good life. I surrender to the unknowing directions."

I'm not going to ask what that means.

He says, "You seriously have no clue who DC is?"

"None."

"What have they told you about him?"

"Not much. Perry's email said DC makes suggestions the kings sometimes follow, but he doesn't lead The VV. Also, DC protects you from internet people."

His eyebrows arch. "What people?"

"I don't know. People. Men who refused your invitation but are now looking for you. People seeking truth about The VV."

It's funny to see Horatio's face—Vin's—twist. Someone else gets to be surprised. He says, "Huh."

"The exact wording in Perry's email was, 'The VV protects Vin in his current state.' I thought that meant you were in a coma. What exactly is that state?"

"Happy." The warmth starts as a smile but spreads into his relaxed arms and uncurls his fingertips. "I'm happy."

His words strike me in a profound way, like a light falling into a dark basement. What if it's possible for me to be happy? What if I let light into the dark?

"You men demolished dinner."

Vin says, "Yikes, Colonel Sneaky."

"I tread lightly." She pours me water. "Vin, more wine?"

"No, I'm good."

"The salmon?"

"Amazing. I can discuss it tomorrow, all six metrics. Not tonight. Tonight is about Daniel."

"Fair enough. Daniel, need more food? Soda?"

"No, I'm stuffed. One of the best meals I've ever eaten. I'm not kidding."

"Good. I could tell you needed it." She moves to Vin's side of the booth, and he scoots aside to accommodate her. "How soon?"

Vin says, "Soon. They're finishing."

She nods. "I'm ready."

"Who's coming in to help?"

Coleen says, "Jason. Jeanne, too."

As they discuss small details, it's obvious the coffeehouse people are coming. This night was grueling for them. They need her sustenance. This restaurant will be packed.

"Col, three gingerbread cookies. Frosted ones. To go." To me, he adds, "They have raisins."

She says, "They're always frosted."

"Yeah."

"So, why ask for *frosted ones*?"

"I'm subliminally encouraging you to select the ones with the most frosting."

"Subliminality is not your strong suit."

Vin says, "Good word for not really a word."

"Any of these for Daniel?"

He says, "Make it four cookies."

"Any for Mark?"

"Five."

She laughs. "A man your age is going to eat *three* heavily-frosted cookies in the middle of the night? After that dinner? And spicy Rangoons?"

"Fine. Four."

She turns to me. "You're welcome to more than one cookie, by the way. Piggy, here, plans to eat three."

Vin says, "Okay. Three total. One for me, one for Daniel, and one for Mark. I have to save room anyway. Daniel, you won't believe the cake. Eight tiers, four of which are connected by candy bridges, orange gumdrop slices as paving stones. Two tiers are dedicated to you in New York. One tier is us in your backyard. I landscaped the frosting myself. Fredi lets me help sometimes."

He baked me a cake. And terrorized my life.

Coleen says, "Vin tells me we have a mutual friend. Mai Kearns."

"I only know him by phone."

She says, "Mai used to eat at the diner where I worked. He put me in touch with Vin when I told him I wanted to relocate here."

"You moved here from DeKalb?"

"I moved to Bali for three years and Mexico for two years. Then Portugal. Then Minneapolis."

"Wow. Adventurous."

"I always wanted to live in other countries. Over the years and mountains of bills, I had forgotten. Mai got me talking about it. He funded my first year abroad."

Vin says, "Now you live the exotic life of a Minneapolitan."

She says, "Quiet, or two cookies, neither one for you. Daniel, a pleasure."

Coleen extricates herself. She fed me when I was broken and exhausted. I feel desolate she's leaving.

"Coleen, your food was....You don't know what this means, to eat so well, I...."

My throat tightens. She loved me with food.

"I have an idea," Coleen says. "Vin makes me cry, too. I told him I wanted to be part of this. I'm honored to serve you, King Daniel." Her declaration is heartfelt and quiet. Without fanfare, she leaves.

Why am I crying over her departure? I need some fucking sleep.

Vin says, "While she's getting our cookies, do you need a bathroom break? We have to get going."

"Please say we are going somewhere with beds."

He laughs. "Apparently my hipster look is really working for you. That or scallops make you horny."

"To sleep. Jesus. Just sleep. You know what you put me through?"

Vin says, "No time for napping. Neighborhood stroll. Walk off dinner. We still haven't talked about my deception as Horatio."

"Are you serious?"

"This neighborhood is safe. Oh, please. Don't look at me like that. You can handle a long walk. You're a New Yorker."

I laugh! No one invites me on walks. Never. Where is this laughter coming from? I love it.

"Enough with the evil eye. I'll go on your damn walk. Horatio."

"Bueno. Because I have a story to tell you." Vin leans forward. "Once there was a tribe, where each man was the one true king. Each woman, the one true queen."

Everything's going to be different.

TWENTY

M Y CHEST IS sparkling with sequins. My upper arms are sparkling cherry red. Every breath, my shirt shimmers, alive. I hated my king shirt when he first revealed it, reminding me of all the blood I hid in the garage, but almost immediately, I reversed myself. I orchestrated my escape with blood, secreted throughout the garage. Once the police found it, there was never a question of my returning. I'm alive today because of the color red. I chose life. I love this shirt.

Vin says, "This is where we say goodbye. For now, at least."

What?

Vin nods at the paved path leading into the dark, up a hill. Looks steep. He can't be serious. We walked for over two hours. My arms—I'm so fucking tired. He can't leave me now, when I am at my weakest.

"Whenever I king a man in the Twin Cities, he goes up that hill to greet the dawn. Alone."

"I don't know if I can."

He says, "You can."

I feel the heat which comes right before tears.

We are silent while he waits for me to leave. I can't go until I say it aloud.

"Vin. Horatio. I can't frame my feelings around what you—tomorrow, I will find a way to express myself. I loved the story of my king name. Loved it. I love my new—I am hesitant to say *life*, but life. Memories. Whatever. But I will hate myself if I don't tell you the truth." Say it fast. Get it over with. "I'm still a Lost King."

"*Tu fin de semana del rey no ha terminado.*" Vin juts his chin toward the dark path. "Go. Your King Weekend isn't over."

There's no light. He wants me to trudge up a dark hill.

Softly, he says, "It's time to greet the dawn."

Alone.

Once again, I'm alone.

I was tricked into believing I killed a dog tonight, which unlocked how I believe the worst of me—the not-worth-loving part of me—and after collapsing into the arms of my favorite landscaper, I was loved through my self-hatred by a coffeehouse full of jazz lovers. People who understood. I saw the Crimson Blade, whatever the fuck that means.

I stop.

I'm climbing an unfamiliar hill in pitch black, my legs fatigued beyond physical understanding, body numb, emotions shattered into splinters. Climbing an unfamiliar hill in darkness is high on my Things To Avoid In Life, and I feel nothing but love. Tears swim in my lower lids, waiting for permission to jump. *I love you, Frank*, the only true and beloved friend of my childhood. I still love you, buddy. I always will. You didn't deserve what happened to you. I forgot how much I loved you. I only remembered the horror.

My arms tremble.

Focus on getting the next cane forward. One at a time.

I smile.

Although no one can see it, it's a big fat smile. For Frank. For me. A room full of people loved Frank tonight. I'm on a fucking *King Weekend*. I believed in them. I chose them. They chose me. Well, DC chose me. Move that next cane forward, don't focus on the trembling. God, I love smiling. I love these unfamiliar muscles creased in a grin. I am weak. I am broken. Who the fuck isn't? Who fucking cares if I'm still a Lost King? Who fucking cares?

Walk up your dark hill? No problem. Alone? Arms sore? Drunk on exhaustion? Sure. I laugh out loud, the sound shocking me. How did I not recognize he did it *again*? Vin wanted me exhausted for this final hill, thus, the two-hour walk. I laugh. That motherfucker. He wanted me to use my strength—my kingship—to ascend.

How do I know that? Don't care.

Renewed energy flows through me, followed immediately by confused shame—you can't laugh like this, alone, close to falling over. Manipulated beyond understanding. Laughing means ignoring life's constant beatdowns, and I know firsthand—fuck it! Fuck that thought. I can laugh when I goddamn want. This realization makes me hurt. Why do I never choose laughter? If people make fun of me, I could choose laughter. Fuck 'em. I could laugh instead of grinding my teeth. It's gonna happen, so why not laugh?

Move the next cane forward. Plant it on the tilted path. Lean into this. I'm still me. I'll probably always worry about falling. Even now, I cringe as each cane lands.

Remembering my fall earlier tonight makes me want to sing! In New York I was pushed into the air and fell into a throne of arms. Tonight, I was loved and blessed after I fell. Maybe falling ain't so fucking bad. So, *yes*, I will climb. I will ascend. I will climb ten fucking miles for these crazy motherfuckers, because a king named DC read Perry's email and said, "Let's do it."

I'm not a terrible person.

I've been making that argument for years, that's not new. I only believed it, like, 95 percent, which is the equivalent of 0 percent, because if you don't believe in your innate goodness 100 percent, it's no faith at all. That psycho didn't go after me because he smelled weakness. Or because I was gay. He was a nut job.

They didn't care about my legs when they decided to king me.

Well, not kinged, exactly. King or no king, I now have friends. Careful—the path gets steeper here. I can do this. I feel this is near the top, though I have no proof. Arms are shaking, but what do I care? I might fall! Good. Fall over! I know how to get my ass up.

Push. Push.

As the path levels off, trees are easier to identify as I enter what must be a clearing. It's not sunlight, but it's a few degrees lighter than total darkness.

I didn't get kinged. I'm okay with that. I'll take the life of a Lost King under these conditions. This is the life I've been waiting for. I love thinking these dramatic thoughts, because the last twenty-four hours have been the most dramatic in my life, and considering what I endured all those years, that's saying something. I never imagined feeling intensity—allowing myself to *feel* intensity—without it being associated with the worst kind of panic. Dread.

That's it.

Arrived at the top.

That wasn't so goddamn bad. God, I like laughing. I need to start laughing my ass off. That shape must be the bench, a large tree next to it, the bench facing—I drag myself closer—facing east. Of course. Vin wouldn't let it face any other direction. Ha. Behind the bench, the path continues up. Fifty feet behind me, a thick stone tower is impressive in the lessening dark, a castle tower, squatting sturdily, probably sandstone. The top is the shape of a witch's hat, outlined against the sky. Cool.

I manage to seat myself, extracting my canes. I've always hated my canes. Maybe I could try liking them instead, for helping me get around. In this magic spot, anything seems possible.

This is all very cool.

Ha! None of this is *cool*. It's terrifying. Exhilarating. Murderous rage, howling laughing jags, inexplicable memories bursting free. Vin said there's a huge party this afternoon, evolving and morphing into other parties over three days. All the kings want to meet me. Is that possible?

My smile fades.

Vin will warn them I am a Lost King. He has to. Maybe they won't want to see me if I didn't cross over. I don't think it works like that. Vin didn't seem surprised when I said I was still a Lost King. Maybe they won't care.

To my left, Saint Paul. Minneapolis to my right, presumably. Too many trees shade the downtown area, but as the light grows stronger, that distant shape could be a downtown skyscraper. This commanding view makes me want to fly, skimming the tree-lined cities below. I would love to fly. That must be the highway. Not many headlights this early.

Even though I'm not facing it, I feel the dark tower behind me. There should be a platoon of greasy orcs back there, a chorus of hissing as they continue to travel the path up, up, up! This place is spooky in a thrilling way.

The sky lightens by degrees.

I am here to greet the dawn.

I laugh.

Everything is hilarious right now. I don't mind being alone. I fucking danced my way up that hill. Faced with that worst-case scenario, I danced. I'm gonna be okay. This makes me cry, because I'm so goddamn relieved. I'm still toying with those words to extract the full meaning, what my future holds, but I am starting to get it. I'll be okay. The sword passed through me.

I sob while the leaves become visible, not black shapes but living things again—touched by a color that soon will be green—and I cry because it must suck to be a tree and have people carve in you. I remember when dad carved into my arms with a utility knife, then stitched it up. He was escalating.

I'm gonna be okay. I wipe my face.

Better than okay.

I don't have to become a Found One to say *yes* to my life, to say *yes* to laughter. In this moment, I say *yes* to being a Lost King, with all my faults and fuckups. I am pretty glorious. I understand that now. I've been focusing all my energy on what I didn't have. No more. I say *yes* to this version of being a Lost King. I'm going to be beautiful. Starting right now, I am beautiful. I am fucked up and beautiful.

There.

The sun.

A sliver of light, not yet on stage but in the wings, waiting for its entrance seconds from now. Here comes the dawn. So many things are goddamn funny. I love these nut jobs. Why do they think sunrise is so special? It's magnificent, sure. Symbolic return of light. All those days of sunlight, and I never noticed, so busy looking down. This is your life, Daniel. It's time to look up. Wasted opportunities to show mercy to myself, stop blaming myself. He was a monster. I know that! Every day, I contemplate how much of a monster he was, and you know what? I'm going to start giving myself days off. I don't know if I can, but I'm going to try. I'm going to love myself into taking vacations from monster-analysis, and I'll do it by making my current life irresistible. I'm weary from hating. Hating myself for something that wasn't my fault. I didn't fail him. I was a kid.

He failed me.

A groan emerges, a secret chamber within me creaks open, an escape hatch into light, an escape inside me all along, but I couldn't figure how out to access it. The fire escape woman screams *I love you*, and I wake from my nightmares. I can escape my wide-awake nightmare, too. I don't have to hate myself. The light can come in. I choose to be a Lost King who fucking loves his life.

Light pours over the horizon.

I let the deep groan emerge from my full sternum, my chest, my throat, using my power to make this sound, so it's no longer a hesitating creak but the sound a man makes, a man not afraid of power. Is this bliss or sorrow? The sound matches my feelings, wooden, creaking, cleaving my soul in half, loving myself through the misery I endured, what Frank endured, and at the same time, plowing a trench so sorrow quits bleeding into joy.

Wait.

I'm not making that sound.

Oh shit, the sun!

I squeeze my eyes together and jerk my head away. Damn it, why did I do that? The sound comes from behind me. I blink. I can't see anything except two purple suns. That sound is music. It's a musical note. It's from... a cello.

"Amazing, isn't it."

Above?

I search the tree branches, but I still can't see anything. There's a cello behind me, whispering another low note, groaning into a wooden something, a tree, because with music, it's sketching the tree of life.

The voice above me says, "I never tire of hearing Perry play."

I made love to that voice. "Hello, John."

"Good morning, Daniel."

John shifts, and the branches move. I see movement, not shapes. Eyes are still fucked. He was up there all this time?

The cello shifts, like a heavy breeze, still quiet but in a slightly different direction. The music still outlines the tree and its sacred leaves, but... it changes. The first groaning note signaled the *awakening*. What awakening? What leaves? Where are these ideas coming from?

He says, "What did you decide for breakfast?"

You loved me, John, and you goddamn meant it. You're central to the wildest, worst day of my adult life. It was one of your worst days, too. We share that now. Is that enough to move beyond it?

"Scallops and curry."

"Good choice."

Forgive John, the cello says. *Forgive and love.* I don't understand this. I've never heard music this way. It's speaking with almost-words. My eyesight returns. There's John, like a panther.

I turn my torso, best I can. It's Perry. I recognize him from the photos. He sits behind a glossy caramel cello, not far from the tower. As he pulls his bow across the strings, sunlight flickers across his golden shirt. He wasn't sitting there when I arrived. I saw the shape of the tower, so I would have seen him.

Colors return, lush green in trees and grass bathed in morning sun—movement. People. They come down the path from above. There's Rance, so imposing, stepping down the hill with great tenderness, for she leans against him—*Ms. Taylor*. I cry out. Behind them, Jarrod wears a cunning smile, as if he devoured another pot roast intended for me. Next to him, Fitch. My God. He looks nothing like the drug-addled escort I—God, he's... he's... I understand now. I understand. He's the Finder of Beauty. Staring at him hurts my eyes. Tears fall. My king, oh my king! You sacrificed for me. And what the fuck is Ms. Taylor doing here? She never leaves New York. Never.

From the path I took, Vin reaches the clearing in his tuxedo shirt unbuttoned at the top, diamond buttons refracting rainbows, flitting in and out of existence all over him and Mark. Mark in black silk holding Vin's hand. Pilgrim bumps Mark's leg, sniffing the ground. Fredi carries Little Vin, his mouth yawning wide, fast asleep. Jian nods and mouths the words *Mr. Daniels*, making me cough, because that happens sometimes when you cry harder.

Mark says, "Don't mind us."

I laugh.

Jarrod unfolds a chair for Ms. Taylor, and as they're seating her, I allow myself to feel how shocked I am. Ms. Taylor gives me an eyeful. She is not okay with this bullshit. She would never use the word *bullshit*, but that's exactly what she means.

I laugh.

Thank you, first friend. I can't face her and them, their love pouring into me. I turn and look into the growing sun, another fat inch higher into today. *Ow.* I did it again—stared right at the sun.

Mark's voice is near when he says, "May I sit?"

"Please."

He says, "Good morning, John."

"Good morning. I'm climbing higher so I'm not eavesdropping. Call if you need me."

Mark says, "Be careful up there."

As I press my fingers against my eyelids, Perry's quiet notes evolve, swaggering into newfound strength that doesn't quite fit. But it will. This is the adjustment period. The strength will fit me. I am confident I understand what he intends. *Forgive yourself for growing new strength.* It's right in the music.

Mark says, "According to Vin, kings have to greet the dawn alone. Always *alone*. Why, I said? We should all be here. This way, we can all greet the dawn alone but together."

"You're changing the king story."

He says, "Oh, please. It's not like Vin wrote it. He repeated what he heard. I mean, sure, kings are probably supposed to greet the dawn alone. He's usually right. Maybe there are exceptions. Like you." He snuggles in next to me. "It's pretty, isn't it?"

"Mark, I'm still a Lost King."

"Yeah, Vin told me." He laughs. "Damn it, I looked right at the sun."

I glance at the sun. *Ow.*

I laugh!

Or maybe I am still crying. I've never wept from joy. Even sun blindness can't ruin this moment. Maybe that's the secret to kinging, to just believing yourself a Found King. Found Queen. Who cares if you're not? What if I choose to live like a Found King, until one day it finally feels authentic and true? Mark doesn't care I'm a Lost King. Why should I?

What happens to Lost Kings? *Something fabulous.*

I feel his approach a second before Vin leans between us. "Mark's not bothering you, is he? He's not talking too much?"

Mark says, "Unbelievable. You lied to him for a month in another language. You made him believe he was robbed and then you made him fall. Then you walked him into exhaustion and you still ask if *I'm* annoying him."

"Just let me know if Mark's bothering you."

He takes a step back.

Mark says, "I shouldn't scold Vin for lying, because I lied, too. I'm sorry I pretended not to know who you were at the coffeehouse. Vin gets real grumpy if you don't follow his orders."

I don't know how to stop laughing!

Vin leans in. "Horatio was more theater than outright lying."

Mark says, "Give us a moment, *Horatio.*"

"No hablo inglés."

I love my new friends. "Mark, can you deliver a message to someone?"

"Sure."

"Would you tell DC this is the best thing to ever happen to me? I can never—" My voice stops. I owe my new life to a man I've never met, whose initials I share.

Before Mark can respond, Vin turns around. "Okay. C'mon, guys. You promised he would reveal himself this weekend. Here we are. 'Fess up."

Perry stops playing. "His King Weekend isn't over."

Vin says, "Quit dicking me around. Who's DC?"

Fredi says, "Language."

Ms. Taylor clears her throat, and although she doesn't look directly at him, her message is clear. Yeah, she really doesn't like Vin. Over the quiet bickering, movement on the path catches my eye. A newcomer comes from Rance's direction, carrying two bottles of champagne. John Deere cap. That's Mai fucking Kearns. He grins and tips his head in my direction. *Holy fucking shit.* That gray in his hair is so fucking sexy.

Vin says, "You guys promised."

Mai pants like a dog, his tongue flat and waggling. Is he panting because he's— no. They all are. Tongues hanging out.

"See?" Vin turns to me. "Every time I ask about DC, they stick out their tongues."

He's wrong. They're not *sticking* out their tongues. They're wagging them. Perry growls. Rance rubs a paw behind his ear. Only one man doesn't, and I know why. Because *he's* DC.

"It's you. You're the king they call DC."

Mark nods. He turns to face the crowd. "You win, Vin Vanbly. I'm exposed. Since you have to know every damn secret, it's me."

John barks.

Vin says, "Me what?"

Fredi says, "No barking. I have an impressionable child."

Mai says, "How impressionable is your kid while he's snoring? Although those snores sound fake."

Mark says, "I'm DC. Are you happy now? Mr. I Have To Know Everything?"

Vin says, "Guys, seriously. Who is it?"

Rance says, "Did you really never figure this out?"

Vin says, "It can't be Mark."

Mark leans closer to me. "Because of my king name, the King of Lost Dogs, the guys started calling me the Dog Catcher."

Vin says, "Someone just tell me."

"Keep your voice down, bubba." Mai draws him away from us. "City people are sleeping."

Mark is DC. I don't know exactly what to say. "You arranged my King Weekend."

Mark nods solemnly. "Well, we all did. I told everyone I thought we should do it."

"Why?"

Vin raises his hands. "Stop. Hang on. The prophecy says DC is going to kill me."

John says, "He's married to you, so we know he has motive."

Fredi says, "Mark, let me know if you need a weapon. I'll poison some frosting, and you can put it in the employee fridge labeled *Do Not Eat*."

Mark says, "I'm not going to kill you, you big baby."

Vin says, "The psychic—"

Rance says, "She said DC would *destroy* you. *Unmake* you. She never used the word *kill*."

Mark says, "Babe, why do we take our shoes off by the back door? No, don't interrupt. Just answer. Why remove our shoes?"

"I don't understand."

"Just answer. Why do we remove our shoes and wipe our feet on the mat, even on nice days?"

Vin looks around warily. "For the dogs. Set a good example."

"Good. And how much red meat do we eat?"

"Celebration steaks. Not much else."

"Why not?"

"Red meat isn't great for you."

"Before me, how often did you eat red meat?"

"Four times a week. Give or take."

"And why do we keep our shirts one finger-length apart in the closet?"

"You have to see the colors in the morning to decide what to wear."

"Why do we exercise every day? Why do we make the bed most mornings? Why do we compost? Who reorganized the garage? Why do we color-code your business expenses?"

Vin looks bewildered.

Rance says, "Vin, he unmade every aspect of your former life, including your status as a Lost King, just like the psychic promised. It was Mark who decided it was time to king you. He outlined how he thought it should happen. We added details. Changed a few things."

Fredi says, "I picked the font for your grave stone. You have no idea how satisfying that was."

Vin says, "Why would you buy my headstone?"

Mark says, "I don't think you realize how much frozen pizza and fast food hamburgers you ate when we first met. Figured it was a good investment. Besides, I got tired of waiting for you to king me. I found this amazing shirt. Daniel, touch this fabric. Sexy, right? See the almost shimmering pattern? It's amazing. When I found it, I knew right away this was mine. Even though it was 20 percent off, I had to save up."

"How is this possible?" Vin turns away from us.

Mark says, "Anyway, I knew I could never wear my king shirt without Vin getting one, too, because, you know, he'd complain. 'I want a king shirt. Where's my king shirt?' That kind of thing. He likes to complain."

While Vin argues details with Kearns and Rance, Perry plays and the music lights Kevin from the inside. How is he so... different? I notice two people who are not here. "Where's Thomas and Greg?"

Mark softens his gaze. "Thomas thought his being here could ruin your experience, so he decided to stay away. Greg wouldn't come without Thomas. They're together right now. I convinced Thomas to come to your party later today. He's worried about attending, given things he said. It would mean a lot if you took him aside. Just talk."

Perry begins a new song.

I hear a cork *pop*.

I forgive you, Thomas. With love in your heart, you typified the worst of the world. I forgive you, new friend. When I see you, I will weep in your strong arms, because you loved me enough to let me despise you, and using that same love, kept your distance. My heart is on fire. Morning colors are so vivid. The deep cobalt sky, still losing night, the sun taking over, making it day. The red. Everything is so red.

"Champagne?"

Mai Kearns offers a crystal flute. Even his voice is sexy. I don't want champagne, but I reach for it on the slim chance our fingers touch. They don't.

"Thank you."

He grins at me, muscular chest visible under his sparkling flannel. I love the gray in his hair. So fucking distinguished. An evergreen mist breathes around him, like the scent in a forest.

He jerks his head toward my canes. "You walk around on those all the time?"

"Yeah."

"I bet you got strong arms."

"I do."

He grins. "I like strong arms."

Is it possible he is flirting with me?

Mark slides closer. "I think he's flirting with you."

Mai chuckles and offers him champagne, but Mark declines.

Mai says, "You should visit the farm. Bring your shittiest work boots."

I laugh.

He takes a step back, then returns to the others. I can't hear the exact conversation, but Vin is protesting something.

"If you're DC, that means you and Mai Kearns met."

Mark says, "Yesterday, for the first time."

"Wasn't something big supposed to happen? A prophecy about the Great Remembering."

"Yup."

"What happened? Can you tell me?"

Mark looks surprised. "Daniel, *you* happened. You're the first king of the Great Remembering. It begins this morning."

"That's—that's not possible."

Mark nods. "It is. You're the one who starts everything. There are prophecies about you, too."

"That can't be right. I'm not anyone. I don't even know what the Great Remembering means."

He shrugs. "It's already begun. Everybody loved collaborating on your King Weekend, trying to find the best ways to love you. When the next candidate steps out of the shadows, we'll be more ready."

"Mark, it didn't work. I'm still a Lost King."

"I know. But your King Weekend isn't over."

Fireworks keep exploding inside me.

He says, "We learned how unpredictable a kinging can be. We had a path all laid out for you. We assumed, after receiving Perry's email, you'd do more research on him, and discover his charity work. Once you uncovered the Bolinas Project, you'd find kings and queens around the world who aid him. We assumed you'd reach out to one of them, so it was a big surprise when you went after Mai Kearns. We weren't prepared for that. That's when I suggested we involve Vin. I asked Perry to forward your email and explain the circumstances. To entice Vin out of retirement, I told Perry to promise DC would reveal himself."

This isn't possible. I'm nobody.

"Vin instructed Mai to casually say during the phone call, 'Can you believe Perry and the Bolinas Project?' We tried to steer you back on track. Nope. Instead, you flew to New York, and in a city of millions, you found one butterfly. You kept inventing the path to your own kinging, swinging your strong arms until you got your way. Everyone's gossiping about how clever you are. How strong. Mai's nickname for you is 'Ohio Bubba.'"

I'm not sure if I ever stopped crying. I can't feel my face.

"Everyone wants to spend time with you, which is going to be difficult, because Vin told me your king name. Speaking of which, we may as well rip off that Band-Aid as long as everyone is here." He scrambles to his knees, half-turns, and says, "Guys. *Guys*. Daniel wants to tell you his king name."

I laugh and wipe my face. I can't breathe, and yet every draw is icy and sweet. The group gets quieter, though not entirely quiet, because Ms. Taylor has taken to grumbling about the chair.

Rance says, "Yes, ma'am. Someone should have thought of a seat pillow."

Jarrod says, "I'll grab something from the car."

Rance says, "There's a blanket in the trunk."

I can't turn easily, and you know what? I don't want to. I want to face the east. Staring into the sunlight, I strengthen my voice. "I am King Daniel the Dancer."

The cello music stops.

In a low voice, Perry says, "You made him a *dancer*?"

Rance says, "What the fuck?"

Fredi says, "Language."

Mai says, "Your kid has been faking sleep since I got here. I see you smiling, you faker."

Perry says, "Vin, you know how dancers are."

"He'll never have time for New York." Rance sounds genuinely aggrieved.

Vin says, "Guys, I can't help it. He's a dancer."

Mai says, "Wake up, little bubba."

"Dancer suits you," John says.

I look up. "Thank you."

Mai says, "Busted. You're laughing, Little V."

Mai Kearns laughs louder than the rest of them, muffling his mouth with his hand, and it makes my heart skip. I'm gonna visit his farm. He assumes—*assumes*—I'm the kind of man to own shitty work boots, despite my legs. Because he sees me as whole.

Rance says, "We need him in New York."

Ms. Taylor grumbles but I can't hear the words.

Kevin says, "C'mon, guys. He can't walk into the kingdom, not with those damaged legs. He could only dance."

Kevin's not insulting me. He thinks I have dancing legs. Can I love my legs and end my curse? I know the answer. I said *yes* climbing this hill, and I will say *yes* to all the love I deserve. I say *yes*. I am a goddamn dancer.

Mark says, "They're nervous they won't get time with you. The dancer kings can be a little cliquish."

I howl, laughing at the lunacy that I would turn down friendship. Me, who spent the last seven Christmases alone, pretending it was by choice. They want me. Behind me, men are still complaining.

Kevin says, "I heard he was amazing in that New York musical."

"Yeah," Rance says with resignation. "Dancer fits."

I look down. My hands are tingling.

I look at the sun, no longer fighting it. It somehow hurts less, staring directly. "Mark, I have to ask. Why did DC choose me?"

Mark is quiet for a moment, watching the sunrise. Well, daylight. Sunrise is over. Nothing happened to me, other than my hands tingling and my heart filling so full of joy, I could scream.

He says, "I went to your website. You have three different links to no-kill shelters."

We are silent.

Wait. That's it? "Are you saying you liked the links on my blog?"

"Yeah."

The smallness of his declaration confuses me. I am unable to comprehend my life.

"Anyone could have those links on their website. Literally anyone."

"No. Only people with compassion for dogs."

No wonder I didn't get kinged. He didn't gather enough evidence. I gaze at the sun. I don't care if I go blind.

"You picked the wrong person." My words sound petulant. "I don't deserve this."

"Are you sure? If every man is the one true king, how much are you supposed to do? Aren't you already a king?"

"I'd like to believe that. But I'm not."

Mark rests a hand on my shoulder. "Years ago, I thought I would die young. I believed that for many years. I guess because of my sister, who did die young. Maybe it felt disloyal, wanting to live a long life. Maybe some weird fusion of guilt and self-hatred that I couldn't save her. I dunno. Vin taught me I could let go of this idea about my death as a true fact. You can change how you think about yourself, Daniel. You can decide to stop believing. Or maybe start believing."

What if I stop insisting I am a Lost King? What if I let in enough love to grow some uncertainty?

Mark's grip tightens, and I decide, right then, not a single day more. Not one more day will I waste making ironclads about my life. Maybe I am a Found King. Maybe I deserve joy. Yes, actually. I will have Found King joy now, like an all-you-can-choke-down buffet. I want joy. I want love. I deserve love.

Behind me, I hear Vin. "Just tell me the truth. Is Mark really DC?"

Rance says, "How did you not see this coming?"

Vin says, "You guys are fucking with me. Aren't you?"

Mark says, "Be right back."

I laugh.

"Pilgrim, keep Daniel company. Okay, buddy?"

On Mark's request, Pilgrim saunters over, and after sniffing the bench, hops up with ease. He's not as old as he looks. He scoots next to me. I welcome his presence. His love.

The sky colors melt, burn together, red and subtle pinks disappearing into gold and seeping blue, the last shards of silver, pink and purples merging, slurring, singing the song of light, the juxtaposition of joy and sorrow. Can a cello make these complex harmonies, like flower petals and wind merging into light? In this place, I feel the searing white pain—and I'm okay.

What's happening?

The tingling races into both shoulders. I can't see my fingers. I feel like I'm stoned on sunlight, staring right at it. When Mark said, "be right back," I trusted him. I weep with relief to feel this love, to feel *trust*—much harder for me than love—and to know it so thick inside me already.

Vin and Mark are in each other's arms, focused on me.

I am part of this.

Ms. Taylor. The Finder of Beauty.

We are all part of this.

The cello music merges with air, creating ethereal bubbles translucent with letters and symbols and numbers, the song, the glorious song. That's not the cello. It's from the trees, the rocks, the hanging man in the branches above me. Frank. The coffee house people. The champagne bubbles create patterns, messages through numbers.

I stare at the sun.

They warn you in school, but I don't care. The song turns me inside out, and I am full of grief, yes, but I am so, so full of love. So much more love. Impossible tears, a constant lubrication. All this excessive, ridiculous crying was practice, necessary to trans—oh.

Oh.

Why are there numbers embedded in sunlight? Billions of eights. Trillions times trillions of thirteens. It's all Fibonacci. How come I've never heard about this? It's in the *sunlight*, illuminated through my constant tears.

They vibrate.

Twenty-ones and thirty-fives multiplied by infinity. The stars are the key. The golden curve married to Fibonacci opens the eastern gates. What does that even mean? My heart pounds.

The Burning Man stars.

The Song of All Things.

We are all destined for—my god. *I remember.*

O.

I remember.

EPILOGUE

The events of this Epilogue take place in 2018.

THE LUGGAGE SPINS round and round the carousel. I don't even know what I'm looking for. "What color is your bag?"

Daniel says, "Navy blue. It's a duffel bag with wheels. Thanks, Luke."

"Sure."

What a weekend.

I fly to Nashville to see Chad. Two hours after I arrive, we break up. Long distance isn't working. We both knew it. I'm stuck there until Sunday, so we try to get along all day Saturday, being gentle with each other. We ended up snarking, then fighting for hours, then crying, followed by great sex. Laughed over Thai chicken pizza. One more screaming breakdown late Saturday night. I slept in his bed, and he slept on the couch, both of us miserable. Sunday morning breakup sex, and our final goodbyes.

You know your life sucks when you're weeping alone at the Nashville airport bathroom, and a crippled guy feels sorry for you. No, not cool. His name is Daniel. Don't think asshole thoughts about this guy who showed me nothing but kindness.

He waited for me to emerge from the bathroom stall so he could ask if I was okay. Talked to me in the waiting area and made me want to tell him everything. He traded his first-class ticket for coach, dragging himself back to my row. I would have died of humiliation, but not Daniel, apologizing and making jokes to those he inconvenienced. I was humbled by his cheer. His thoughtfulness. I'm tearing up again.

Do I believe his story? Or did he invent it to distract me from my own misery? Does it matter? It worked. There is one question I'd like to ask before he takes off, but will I ask? I am embarrassed I want an answer.

His phone *bleeps*. Text.

Daniel looks up and around. "He's here."

Instinctively, I look around too, for a man I will not recognize. Midway Airport's baggage claim is a giant mess, everyone dragging luggage at cross-angles, timing their intersecting paths so they don't have to slow. Cars outside honk. Overhead announcements about where to find trains and cabs to Chicago. Loud conversations into cell phones.

Daniel didn't even know I was gay. He heard muffled sobbing and was worried. Am I the kind of person who would wait in an airport bathroom to check on a stranger? I don't know. I don't think so. I should ask him quick before his husband arrives.

A hot cowboy swaggers toward us. Holy shit. Sexy, brown corduroy jacket, like Heath Ledger wore in *Brokeback*—is that his husband? It is.

They kiss.

Daniel says, "Luke, this is my husband."

The man extends his arm. "Hey. Mai Kearns."

"Hey." My voice sounds feeble. "Luke Penn."

He is smoking hot, tight body. Salt and pepper hair, trimmed tight. Do not imagine this farmer naked. These two fuck in cornfields when the stalks are high. They fucked in a grain silo once, according to Daniel. But only once because their loud screams echoed.

Mai's eyebrows shift as he stares at me. I know I'm blushing.

He says, "Danny, you fucking did it again. Told some stranger about our sex life."

Daniel says, "Don't be mad. We live on a farm. It's fun to talk to someone new."

Mai says, "We talk to new people all the time. You give daily fucking tours. Paul's got international families staying in his guesthouse year-round. Talk to *them*."

"Don't you think their kids are a little young to hear that kind of talk?"

"Can't you find other topics besides our sex life?"

"Can I help it our sex life is worth talking about?"

Daniel teases his husband while the farmer grumbles in reply. Mai wraps his hand around Daniel's forearm, an affectionate gesture. It's easy to see they missed each other.

Mai says, "What is with you and airport men?"

Daniel says, "The smell of burned pizza makes me chatty."

When Daniel's luggage arrives, I am not needed. Mai tosses it over his shoulder with ease.

Mai says, "Luke, good to meet you. Bingo's going crazy out there, Danny."

"You brought him?"

"Of course. Say your goodbyes. We gotta stop at the grocery on the way home."

Daniel says, "What for?"

Mai says, "Dinner."

"Can't we call Randy or Boog? Someone must be cooking tonight."

"Nah." Mai gazes out the tall windows. "I figured you'd make me dinner. Gnocchi with caramelized onions and bacon. I think you feel like cooking."

Daniel chuckles. "Yeah. That sounds good to me, too."

Mai nods at me. "Luke, nice to meet you."

He strides away.

Daniel says, "I gotta go. I'm in the doghouse for bragging about our sex life."

Ask!

"It was good to meet you, Daniel."

I want to embrace him, tell him what it meant to spend the final hours of my miserable weekend bathed in his light. The gift of his—I don't know. I don't understand my own thoughts right now. I feel dizzy.

Ask him!

He turns.

"Wait. Wait. Is everything you told me real? About the kingings?" That's not my real question.

"Yup."

"There's a secret cabal of gay men—"

"And straight men. And women. And folks in between."

"—and you people go around *kinging*—"

"And queening."

"Okay."

"Also, we do crownings. Some peoples' gender is their own business, or it's flexible, so we call that a crowning."

"How is that different?"

"That's a long answer, and we're out of time, Luke. It was great to meet you. I know you'll survive the breakup with Chad. You're gonna be okay. Better than okay."

I feel strained, desperate. He's been spinning light into me ever since I met him. I'm afraid to ask my question, afraid it betrays I believe him. *Odd, you may think, and wonder how any work got done—*

"Wait, before you go. You and your husband. Is it hard? How do you guys make it work?" That's not the real question either. Why is it so hard to ask?

Daniel says, "We both changed for each other, got more accommodating. It's hard for me, living on a farm, uneven footing everywhere, literal shit all over my canes every single day. I now own four pair. Barn canes, outdoor canes for the fields and yard, and my house pair. Most nights, Mai and I sit in the kitchen, and he cleans my outdoor canes for me while we chat about our day. Oh, my fourth pair are my travel canes, which I'm using now."

"They're stunning."

"Thanks. My friend Boog made these as a Christmas present. You know, Mai changed for me, too. Since I'm already in the doghouse, I may as well tell you. Mai only liked sucking dick when we first met. He was willing to give butt sex another shot when I told him how important it was to me. Now he loves it as much as I do. We both learned to get more accommodating. Speaking of which,"—he leans closer and lowers his voice—"I gotta go carbo load for makeup sex."

He repositions himself on his canes. Turns away.

Last chance! Am I afraid because it feels like asking about my future?

"*Daniel, wait*! You never told me—what happens to Lost Kings?"

It takes him a moment to turn back. "I never found out. If you're interested, you could ask someone else. I hear there's a King Who Loves Turtles."

He turns away and crosses the airport.

In the distance, I hear a voice booming. "Let's go, bubba!"

Daniel shouts a reply.

I see the truth of him, something I couldn't recognize until now, but it's true. With every powerful, faltering step, he dances.

THE END, FOLKS...
OR IS IT? (NO, IT IS.)

I'd love it if you wrote a review. But I'm asking you like White Castle asks for feedback. Did you know that if you write an online review, WC gives you two free sliders on your next visit? Totally worth it. I'm sorry I cannot promise a gooey cheeseburger with succulent grilled onions. Would that I could. I'd get more reviews, undoubtedly. (God, I love sliders.)

So, here's my White Castle deal. Write a review. Doesn't matter if your review is one star or five stars. As long as you write at least one sentence, it counts. And you can copy the exact same review for each site. After your review goes live, email me. pickwickinkpublishing@gmail.com

- Write a review for Amazon, and I will email you a document titled, "Secrets in The Lost and Founds." I offered a version of this for those who wrote a review of *Come Back To Me*. With updates relevant to this book, this document is now roughly twenty-six pages, documenting Easter eggs throughout the series. Clues to Vin's real name, how Mark was foretold in small clues. King names, plotlines. The world religions integrated into each novel.

- Write a review for Goodreads, and I will email you a PDF explaining the archetype dance throughout this book. How a Shadow Magician pierced Daniel with a sword and only the Golden Lover had the power to permit the sword to pass through. If you're into Robert Bly and masculine archetype stuff, you may enjoy this.

- Write a review for some other website (your blog, Barnes & Noble, Amazon in other countries, etc.) and I will email you the first three chapters of my next novel, *Zacchaeus*.

Every review helps. So, thank you again. If you'd like to sign up for my infrequent mailing list, jump on board. I send a newsletter for new books, and maybe two to three others during the year. http://eepurl.com/bYya6v

HOW TO READ
THE LOST AND FOUNDS...

Hi. I'm Edmond Manning, author, and enjoyer of butternut squash soup with green onions sprinkled on top. I designed this series to be read in four different sequences. If you're the kind of reader who likes to reread books, I'd like to present a few options.

#1 – Traditional Sequence: This is the sequence in which the full novels were published. (Heh. I used 'in which.') In my opinion, this is the second best sequence for first-time readers. It's probably how most everyone reads this series, like books in a series are supposed to be read. The normal way. Nothing wrong with that.

1. *King Perry*
2. *King Mai*
3. *The Butterfly King*
4. *King John*
5. *Come Back to Me*
6. *King Daniel*

#2 – Heightened Cliffhanger Sequence: Designed to taunt and delight readers who want a little extra sriracha sauce splashed into their Vin Vanbly. I may be biased, since I wrote all the words, but for first-time readers, this is probably the best way to read the series. Seriously. Higher level of craziness and mystery.

1. *King Perry*
2. In *King Daniel*, read chapters 1-3
3. *King Mai*
4. In *King Daniel*, read chapters 4-7
5. *The Butterfly King*
6. In *King Daniel*, read chapters 8-10
7. *King John*
8. In *King Daniel*, read chapter 11
9. *Come Back to Me*
10. Finish reading *King Daniel*

#3 – **Chronology Sequence:** If you wanted to read "oldest to most recent adventure," you could watch Vin Vanbly grow into his kinging skills. Some inside jokes and plot will be explained prematurely, and that might make it "less fun" when you come upon them later, so I do NOT advocate this for first-time readers. I advocate this sequence for readers returning to the series. Read the Chronology Sequence and you'll see different patterns. (Hint: look at how Vin's language usage evolves....)

1. *The Butterfly King* – takes place in 1993
2. *King Mai* – takes place in 1996
3. *King Perry* - 1999
4. *King John* - 2002
5. *Come Back to Me* - 2005
6. *King Daniel* - 2013

#4 – **HEA Sequence:** SPOILER ALERT. This sequence is close to the Traditional Sequence with one exception: *Come Back To Me* is read first. If you're a first-time reader who really needs to see a Happily Ever After, try this. There are a number of inside jokes, plots, and surprises that will be a little less fun because you didn't read the books in the traditional or heightened cliffhanger sequence—just want you to be fully warned. Also, this is probably the darkest book. But it DOES have the romantic HEA and it's a pretty big happy, which for some folks might make reading the remaining books easier.

1. *Come Back to Me*
2. *King Perry*
3. *King Mai*
4. *The Butterfly King*
5. *King John*
6. *King Daniel*

Acknowledgements

King Daniel represents the end of an era for me.

Thank you to my best pal, Ann Batenburg. You nurtured me from the start. Rhyss DeCassilene became my first editor. A.J. Rose and Kate Aaron loved me through many rough drafts and final edits. Jonathan Penn has always been one of Vin's best buds, and along the way he became my bud, too. LC Chase has created so many great covers for me, including this one. Thank you!

Theo Fenraven edited this work, and I'm grateful. I appreciate the directness of someone who says, "Don't do that." I appreciated Fen's emails to see 'where the fuck are you in finishing this book?' Ashley E., Keith Jarvis, and Kaje Harper found many fixes that would ruin your enjoyment of the story. It's humbling to have your final, FINAL copy editor find 34 errors. (Clarification: those are mistakes I added doing rewrites after Fen's edit. Fen didn't miss them during his pass.) Max Winebenner-Palo and Jeanne Gilbert both did final FINAL final FINAL reviews. Wow. You guys were fantastic.

I am supported by a community of writers. Kaje Harper, Marshall Thornton, Lloyd Meeker, Posy Roberts, J R Jen Barten, Rory Ni Colieain, Brigham Vaughn, Theo Fenraven, Kate Aaron, AJ Rose, Jason Weidermann, Barry Brennessel, Brandon Witt, Angel Martinez, J. Scott Coatsworth, Jonathan Mack, Andrew Holleran, and too many more. I know I already offended someone by omitting their name. I'm sorry. Remember, I'm an idiot.

I have many readers to thank for suggesting to their friends, "Read this series." I thank you. All my love. Tony Ward, I wish you were here for this. I thought we'd cross this finish line together.

I end with a private note to the Bear Walker king, Theo Bishop. Come home, Theo.

ALSO BY EDMOND MANNING

The Lost and Founds:
King Perry (Book 1)
King Mai (Book 2)
The Butterfly King (Book 3)
King John (Book 4)
Come Back To Me (Book 5)
King Daniel (Book 6)

Non-fiction:
I Probably Shouldn't Have Done That

Other works:
Filthy Acquisitions
Hunting Bear (short story in *A Taste of Honey* anthology)

ABOUT THE AUTHOR

EDMOND MANNING has always been fascinated by fiction: how ordinary words could be sculpted into heartfelt emotions, how heartfelt emotions could leave an imprint inside you stronger than the real world. Mr. Manning never felt worthy to seek publication until 2012, when he accidentally stumbled into his own writer's voice that fit perfectly, like his favorite skull-print, fuzzy jammies. He finally realized that he didn't have to write like Charles Dickens or Armistead Maupin, two author heroes, and that perhaps his own fiction was juuuuuuust right, because it was his true voice, so he looked around the scrappy word kingdom he'd created for himself and shouted, "I'M HOME!" He is now a writer.

In addition to fiction, Edmond writes nonfiction on his blog, www. edmondmanning.com.

For more book fun, join his mailing list: http://eepurl.com/bYya6v
Email: pickwickinkpublishing@gmail.com
Facebook: Edmond Manning
Instagram: theedmondman
Twitter: @edmond_manning

CARAMELIZED ONION GNOCCHI

Ingredients:

- 1 tablespoon thyme
- ½ cups olive oil
- 2-1/2 cups peeled and diced onions
- 1 cup red wine
- 2 15-ounce packages of potato gnocchi
- 1 cup grated, aged Asiago cheese (or more if desired)
- 1 package bacon
- Salt and pepper to taste

Steps:

1. Bring a large pot of salted water to boil.
2. Meanwhile, cook the bacon, crumble into smaller pieces. Set aside.
3. In a large skillet, over medium heat, warm the olive oil. Drop in a diced onion. If it sizzles, the oil is warm enough. Add the rest.
4. Cook down the onions, stirring occasionally until they are soft and lightly browned, roughly twenty minutes.
5. Raise the heat to high, add red wine, and cook until the wine is evaporated. Onions are deep burgundy in color. Set aside in the skillet.
6. Add the gnocchi into the boiling water. Won't take too long for these guys to cook. They float when finished.
7. Reheat the onions in the skillet. Stir in gnocchi, thyme, and bacon.
8. When everything is warm, add the cheese.
9. Serve immediately.
10. Rub belly.